ACHTUNG!

ESCAPE STORIES

ESCAPE STORIES

Edited by
Elizabeth Bland

Illustrated by
Malcolm Barter

CONTENTS

First published 1980 by
Octopus Books Limited
59 Grosvenor Street
London W 1

Reprinted 1981

ISBN 0 7064 1174 9

Printed in Czechoslovakia
50398/3

AN OCCURENCE AT OWL CREEK BRIDGE

Ambrose Bierce

A man stood upon a railroad bridge in northern Alabama, looking down into the swift water twenty feet below. The man's hands were behind his back, the wrists bound with a cord. A rope closely encircled his neck. It was attached to a stout cross-timber above his head and the slack fell to the level of his knees. Some loose boards laid upon the sleepers supporting the metals of the railway supplied a footing for him and his executioners—two private soldiers of the Federal army, directed by a sergeant who in civil life may have been a deputy sheriff. At a short remove upon the same temporary platform was an officer in the uniform of his rank, armed. He was a captain. A sentinel at each end of the bridge stood with his rifle in the position known as 'support', that is to say, vertical in front of the left shoulder, the hammer resting on the forearm thrown straight across the chest—a formal and unnatural position, enforcing an erect carriage of the body. It did not appear to be the duty of these two men to know what was occurring at the centre of the bridge; they merely blockaded the two ends of the foot planking that traversed it.

Beyond one of the sentinels nobody was in sight; the railroad ran straight away into a forest for a hundred yards, then, curving, was lost to view. Doubtless there was an outpost farther along. The other bank of the stream was open ground—a gentle acclivity topped with a stockade of vertical tree trunks, loop-holed for rifles, with a single embrasure through which protruded the muzzle of a brass cannon commanding the bridge. Midway of the slope between bridge and fort were the spectators—a single company of infantry in line, at 'parade rest', the butts of the rifles on the ground, the barrels inclining slightly backwards against the right shoulder, the hands crossed upon the stock. A lieutenant stood at the right of the line, the point of his sword upon the ground, his left hand resting upon his right. Excepting the group of four at the centre of the bridge, not a man moved. The company faced the ridge, staring stonily, motionless. The sentinels, facing the banks of the stream, might have been statues to adorn the bridge. The captain stood with folded arms, silent, observing the work of his subordinates, but making no sign. Death is a dignitary who when he comes announced is to be received with formal manifestations of respect, even by those most familiar with him. In the code of military etiquette silence and fixity are forms of deference.

The man who was engaged in being hanged was apparently about thirty-five years of age. He was a civilian, if one might judge from his habit, which was that of a planter. His features were good—a straight nose, firm mouth, broad forehead, from which his long dark hair was combed straight back, falling behind his ears to the collar of his well-fitting frock-coat. He wore a moustache and pointed beard, but no whiskers; his eyes were large and dark grey, and had a kindly expression which one would hardly have expected in one whose neck was in the hemp. Evidently this was no vulgar assassin. The liberal military code makes provision for hanging many kinds of persons, and gentlemen are not excluded.

The preparations being complete, the two private soldiers stepped aside and each drew away the plank upon which he had been standing. The sergeant turned to the captain, saluted and placed himself immediately behind that officer, who in turn moved apart one pace. These movements left the condemned man and the sargeant standing on the two ends of the same plank, which spanned three of the cross-ties of the bridge. The end upon which the civilian stood almost, but not quite, reached a fourth. This plank had been held in place by the weight of the captain; it was now held by that of the sergeant. At a signal from the former the latter would step aside, the plank would tilt and the con-

Evidently this was no vulgar assassin.

demned man go down between two ties. The arrangement commended itself to his judgment as simple and effective. His face had not been covered nor his eyes bandaged. He looked a moment at his 'unsteadfast footing', then let his gaze wander to the swirling water of the stream racing madly beneath his feet. A piece of dancing driftwood caught his attention and his eyes followed it down the current. How slowly it appeared to move! What a sluggish stream!

He closed his eyes in order to fix his last thoughts upon his wife and children. The water, touched to gold by the early sun, the brooding mists under the banks at some distance down the stream, the fort, the soldiers, the piece of drift—all had distracted him. And now he became conscious of a new disturbance. Striking through the thought of his dear ones was a sound which he could neither ignore nor understand, a sharp, distinct, metallic percussion like the stroke of a blacksmith's hammer upon the anvil; it had the same ringing quality. He wondered what it was, and whether immeasurably distant or near by—it seemed both. Its recurrence was regular, but as slow as the tolling of a death knell. He awaited each stroke with impatience and—he knew not why—apprehension. The intervals of silence grew progressively longer; the delays became maddening. With their greater infrequency the sounds increased in strength and sharpness. They hurt his ear like the thrust of a knife; he feared he would shriek. What he heard was the ticking of his watch.

He unclosed his eyes and saw again the water below him. 'If I could free my hands,' he thought, 'I might throw off the noose and spring into the stream. By diving I could evade the bullets and, swimming vigorously, reach the bank, take to the woods and get away home. My home, thank God, is as yet outside their lines; my wife and little ones are still beyond the invader's farthest advance.'

As these thoughts, which have here to be set down in words, were flashed into the doomed man's brain rather than evolved from it the captain nodded to the sargeant. The sargeant stepped aside.

★ ★ ★ ★

Peyton Farquhar was a well-to-do planter, of an old and highly respected Alabama family. Being a slave owner and like other slave owners a politician, he was naturally an original secessionist and ardently devoted to the Southern cause. Circumstances of an imperious nature, which it is unnecessary to relate here, had prevented him from taking service with the gallant army that had fought the disastrous campaigns ending with the fall of Corinth, and he chafed under the inglorious restraint, longing for the release of his energies, the larger life of the soldier, the opportunity for distinction. That opportunity, he felt, would come, as it comes to all in war time. Meanwhile he did what he could. No service was too humble for him to perform in aid of the South, no adventure too perilous for him to undertake if consistent with the character of a civilian who was at heart a soldier, and who in good faith and without too much qualification assented to at least a part of the frankly villainous dictum that all is fair in love and war.

One evening while Farquhar and his wife were sitting on a rustic bench near the entrance to his grounds, a grey-clad soldier rode up to the gate and asked for a drink of water. Mrs Farquhar was only too happy to serve him with her own white hands. While she was fetching the water her husband approached the dusty horseman and inquired eagerly for news from the front.

'The Yanks are repairing the railroads,' said the man, 'and are getting ready for another advance. They have reached the Owl Creek bridge, put it in order and built a stockade on the north bank. The commandant has issued an order, which is posted everywhere, declaring that any civilian caught interfering with the railroad, its bridges, tunnels or trains will be summarily hanged. I saw the order.'

'How far is it to the Owl Creek bridge?' Farquhar asked.

'About thirty miles.'

'Is there no force on this side of the creek?'

'Only a picket post half a mile out, on the railroad, and a single sentinel at this end of the ridge.'

'Suppose a man—a civilian and student of hanging—should elude the picket post and perhaps get the better of the sentinel,' said Farquhar, smiling, 'what could he accomplish?'

The soldier reflected. 'I was there a month ago,' he replied. 'I observed that the flood of last winter had lodged a great quantity of driftwood against the wooden pier at this end of the bridge. It is now dry and would burn like tow.'

The lady had now brought the water, which the soldier drank. He thanked her ceremoniously, bowed to her husband and rode away. An hour later, after nightfall, he repassed the plantation, going northward in the direction from which he had come. He was a Federal scout.

★ ★ ★ ★

As Peyton Farquhar fell straight downward through the bridge he lost consciousness and was as one already dead. From this state he was awakened—ages later, it seemed to him—by the pain of a sharp pressure upon his throat, followed by a sense of suffocation. Keen, poignant agonies seemed to shoot from his neck downward through every fibre of his body and limbs. These pains appeared to flash along well-defined lines of ramification and to beat with an inconceivably rapid periodicity. They seemed like streams of pulsating fire heating him to an intolerable temperature. As to his head, he was conscious of nothing but a feeling of fulness—of congestion. These sensations were unaccompanied by thought. The intellectual part of his nature was already effaced; he had power only to feel, and feeling was torment. He was conscious of motion. Encompassed in a luminous cloud, of which he was now merely the fiery heart, without material substance, he swung through unthinkable arcs of oscillation, like a vast pendulum. Then all at once, with terrible suddenness, the light about him shot upward with the noise of a loud splash; a frightful roaring was in his ears, and all was cold and dark. The power of thought was restored; he knew that the rope had broken and he had fallen into the stream. There was no additional strangulation; the noose about his neck was already suffocating him and kept the water from his lungs. To die of hanging at the bottom of a river!—the idea seemed to him ludicrous. He opened his eyes in the darkness and saw above him a gleam of light, but how distant, how inaccessible! He was still sinking, for the light became fainter and fainter until it was a mere glimmer. Then it began to grow and brighten, and he knew that he was rising toward the surface—knew it with reluctance, for he was now very comfortable. 'To be hanged and drowned,' he thought, 'that is not so bad; but I do not wish to be shot. No; I will not be shot; that is not fair.'

He was not conscious of an effort, but a sharp pain in his wrist apprised him that he was trying to free his hands. He gave the struggle his attention, as an idler might observe the feat of a juggler, without interest in the outcome. What splendid effort!—what magnificent, what superhuman strength! Ah, that was a fine endeavour! Bravo! The cord fell away; his arms parted and floated upward, the hands dimly seen on each side in the growing light. He watched them with a new interest as first one and then the other pounced upon the noose at his neck. They tore it away and thrust it fiercely aside, its undulations resembling those of a water-snake. 'Put it back, put it back!' He thought he shouted these words to his hands, for the undoing of the noose had been succeeded by the direst pain that he had yet experienced. His neck ached horribly; his brain was on fire; his heart, which had been fluttering faintly, gave a great leap, trying to force itself out at his mouth. His whole body was racked and wrenched with an insupportable anguish! But his disobedient hands gave no heed to the command. They beat the water vigorously with quick, downward strokes, forcing him to the surface. He felt his head emerge; his eyes were blinded by the sunlight; his chest expanded convulsively, and with a supreme and crowning agony his lungs engulfed a great draught of air, which instantly he expelled in a shriek!

He was now in full possession of his physical senses. They were, indeed, preternaturally keen and alert. Something in the awful disturbance of his organic system had so exalted and refined them that they made record of things never before perceived. He felt the ripples upon his face and heard their separate sounds as they struck. He looked at the forest on the bank of the stream, saw the individual trees, the leaves and the veining of each leaf—saw the very insects upon them: the locusts, the brilliant-bodied flies, the grey spiders stretching their webs from twig to twig. He noted the prismatic colours in all the dewdrops upon a million blades of grass. The humming of the gnats that danced above the eddies of the stream, the beating of the dragon-flies' wings, the strokes of the water-spiders' legs, like oars which had lifted their boat—all these made audible music. A fish slid along beneath his eyes and he heard the rush of its body parting the water.

He had come to the surface facing down the stream; in a moment the visible world seemed to wheel slowly round, himself the pivotal point, and he saw the bridge, the fort, the soldiers upon the bridge, the captain, the sergeant, the two privates, his executioners. They were in silhouette against the blue sky. They shouted and gesticulated, pointing at him. The captain had drawn his pistol, but did not fire; the others were unarmed. Their movements were grotesque and horrible, their forms gigantic.

Suddenly he heard a sharp report and something struck the water smartly within a few inches of his head, spattering his face with spray. He heard a second report, and saw one of the sentinels with his rifle at his shoulder, a light cloud of blue smoke rising from the muzzle. The man in the water saw the eye of the man on the bridge gazing into his own through the sights of the rifle. He observed that it was a grey eye and remembered having read that grey eyes were keenest, and that all famous marksmen had them. Nevertheless, this one had missed.

A counter-swirl had caught Farquhar and turned him half round; he was again looking into the forest on the bank opposite the fort. The sound of a clear, high voice in a monotonous singsong now rang out behind him and came across the water with a distinctness that pierced and subdued all other sounds, even the beating of the ripples in his ears. Although no soldier, he had frequented camps enough to know the dread significance of that deliberate, drawling, aspirated chant; the lieutenant on shore was taking a part in the morning's work. How coldly and pitilessly—with what an even, calm intonation, presaging, and enforcing tranquillity in the men—with what accurately measured intervals fell those cruel words:

'Attention, company! . . . Shoulder arms! . . . Ready! . . . Aim! . . . Fire!'

Farquhar dived—dived as deeply as he could. The water roared in his ears like the voice of Niagara, yet he heard the dulled thunder of the volley and, rising again toward the surface, met shining bits of metal, singularly flattened, oscillating slowly downward. Some of them touched him on the face and hands, then fell away, continuing their descent. One lodged between his collar and neck; it was uncomfortably warm and he snatched it out.

As he rose to the surface, gasping for breath, he saw that he had been a long time under water; he was perceptibly farther down stream—nearer to safety. The soldiers had almost finished reloading; the metal ramrods flashed all at once in the sunshine as they were drawn from the barrels, turned in the air, and thrust into their sockets. The two sentinels fired again, independently and ineffectually.

The hunted man saw all this over his shoulder; he was now swimming vigorously with the current. His brain was as energetic as his arms and legs; he thought with the rapidity of lightning.

'The officer,' he reasoned, 'will not make that martinet's error a second time. It is easy to dodge a volley as a single shot. He has probably already given the command to fire at will. God help me, I cannot dodge them all!'

An appalling splash within two yards of him was followed by a loud, rushing sound, *diminuendo*, which seemed to travel back through the air to the fort and died in an explosion which stirred the very river to its deeps! A rising sheet of water curved over him, fell down upon him, blinded him, strangled him! The cannon had taken a hand in the game. As he shook his head free from the commotion of the smitten water he heard the deflected shot humming through the air ahead, and in an instant it was cracking and smashing the branches in the forest beyond.

'They will not do that again,' he thought; 'the next time they will use a charge of grape. I must keep my eye upon the gun; the smoke will apprise me—the report arrives too late; it lags behind the missile. That is a good gun.'

Suddenly he felt himself whirled round and round—spinning like a top. The water, the banks, the forests, the now distant bridge, fort and men—all were commingled and blurred. Objects were represented by their colours only; circular horizontal streaks of colour—that was all he saw. He had been caught in a vortex and was being whirled on with a velocity of advance and gyration that made him giddy and sick. In a few moments he was flung upon the gravel at the foot of the left bank of the stream—the southern bank—and behind a projecting point which concealed him from his enemies. The sudden arrest of his motion, the abrasion of one of his hands on the gravel, restored him, and he wept with delight. He dug his fingers into the sand, threw it over himself in handfuls and audibly blessed it. It looked like diamonds, rubies, emeralds; he could think of nothing beautiful which it did not resemble. The trees upon the bank were giant garden plants; he noted a definite order in their arrangement, inhaled the fragrance of their blooms. A strange, roseate light shone through the spaces among their trunks and the wind made in their branches the music of aeolian harps. He had no wish to perfect his escape—was content to remain in that enchanting spot until retaken.

A whiz and rattle of grapeshot among the branches high above his head roused him from his dream. The baffled cannoneer had fired him a random farewell. He sprang to his feet, rushed up the sloping bank, and plunged into the forest.

All that day he travelled, laying his course by the rounding sun. The forest seemed interminable; nowhere did he discover a break in it, not even a woodman's road. He had not known that he lived in so wild a region. There was something uncanny in the revelation.

By nightfall he was fatigued, footsore, famishing. The thought of his wife and children urged him on. At last he found a road which led him in what he knew to be the right direction. It was as wide and straight as a city street, yet it seemed untravelled. No fields bordered it, no dwelling anywhere. Not so much as the barking of a dog suggested human habitation. The black bodies of the trees formed a straight wall on both sides, terminating on the horizon in a point, like a diagram in a lesson in perspective. Overhead, as he looked up through this rift in the wood, shone great golden stars looking unfamiliar and grouped in strange constellations. He was sure they were arranged in some order which had a secret and malign significance. The wood on either side was full of singular noises, among which—once, twice, and again—he distinctly heard whispers in an unknown tongue.

His neck was in pain and lifting his hand to it he found it horribly swollen. He knew that it had a circle of black where the rope had bruised it. His eyes felt congested; he could no longer close them. His tongue was swollen with thirst; he relieved its fever by thrusting it forward from between his teeth into the cold air. How softly the turf had carpeted the untravelled avenue—he could no longer feel the roadway beneath his feet!

Doubtless, despite his suffering, he had fallen asleep while walking, for now he sees another scene—perhaps he has merely recovered from a delirium. He stands at the gate of his own home. All is as he left it, and all bright and beautiful in the morning sunshine. He must have travelled the entire night. As he pushes open the gate and passes up the wide white walk, he sees a flutter of female garments; his wife, looking fresh and cool and sweet, steps down from the veranda to meet him. At the bottom of the steps she stands waiting, with a smile of ineffable joy, an attitude of matchless grace and dignity. Ah, how beautiful she is! He springs forward with extended arms. As he is about to clasp her he feels a stunning blow upon the back of the neck; a blinding white light blazes all about him with a sound like the shock of a cannon—then all is darkness and silence!

Peyton Farquhar was dead; his body, with a broken neck, swung gently from side to side beneath the timbers of the Owl Creek bridge.

FREE MEN

André Devigny

André Devigny, a resistance fighter in the Second World War, has been arrested by the Gestapo and imprisoned in Montluc military prison. He is under sentence of death. In the limited time available to him, he learns how to pick the lock on his handcuffs, then, with the aid of a spoon, he loosens the wooden boards of his cell door.

His plan is to escape through a skylight outside his cell. He weaves lengths of rope out of his bedding and makes a grappling iron out of the metal frame around the light in his cell.

As he is on the point of escape, another prisoner, Gimenez, joins him in the cell. They decide to make the attempt together, and Devigny carefully removes the boards in the cell door. . . .

Gimenez took the boards from me one after the other and stacked them away. In the half-light we could just see the faint, barred outline of the gallery rails; it was too dark to make out the cell doors on the other side. I put out my head and listened. Only the creaking of beds as sleepers turned over, and occasionally a bucket scraping along the floor, broke the silence—that hostile silence against which we had to struggle for what seemed like a century.

For two long minutes I remained motionless. Then I pushed one arm out into the corridor, turned on one side, and crawled forward like a snake. I stood up cautiously. The light was on down below; but, as usual, its feeble rays were swallowed up in the vast gloom of the hall.

Gimenez passed me the light rope, which I at once took over to the latrines. It was followed by the rest of our equipment. I went back to the cell door to help Gimenez. We both stood there for a moment, listening. All was still. Slowly we moved towards our starting-point.

I tied one end of the light rope round my waist—the end, that is, which had no grappling-iron attached to it. Three steps, and we were standing by the metal rod. The rope would pay out as I climbed; I left it coiled loosely on the ground. Gimenez braced himself against the wall and gave me a leg up. I stood on his shoulders, both hands gripping the rod, and tried to reach the edge of the skylight. I pulled myself up slowly, with all the strength I had. But it proved too much of an effort; I had to come down again.

The weeks of confinement I had undergone since my previous successful attempt must have sapped my strength more than I thought. We went back to the latrines to give me a few moments' rest. I inhaled deeply, waiting till I got my breath back before making a second attempt.

I had to get up there, whatever happened.

Jaws clenched, I began to climb. I got my feet from Gimenez's hands to his shoulders, and then to his head. My fingers gripped the metal rod convulsively. Somehow I went on, inch by inch; at last my fingers found the frame of the skylight, and I got my legs over the horizontal rod, which shook in its rings as my weight hung from it. I got round the ratchet supporting the skylight without touching it. I was sweating and panting like a man struggling out of a quicksand, or a shipwrecked sailor clinging desperately to a reef. Eyes dilated, every muscle cracking, I gradually worked my way through the opening. Then I stopped for a minute to get my strength back. I had managed to preserve absolute silence from start to finish.

A few lights twinkled in the distance. The fresh night air cooled my damp face. It was very still. Slowly my breathing became normal again. Carefully I put out one hand onto the gritty surface of the flat roof, taking care to avoid touching the fragile glass in the skylight itself; this done, I hauled myself up a little farther and got my other hand into a similar position. With a final effort I completed the operation, and found myself standing upright on the roof, dazed by the clear splendour of the night sky. The silence drummed in my ears.

For a moment I remained motionless. Then I knelt down and slowly pulled up the rope. The shoes were dangling in their bundle at the end of it. I let it down again and brought up our coats. The third time I salvaged the big rope; it was a difficult job to squeeze it through the narrow opening.

Go slowly, I thought. Don't hurry. You've got plenty of time.

I unhooked the parcel and put it aside. Then I paid out the rope once more. We had agreed that Gimenez should tie it round his waist so that I could take up the slack and make his ascent easier. I waited a little, and then felt a gentle tug. I pulled steadily, hand over hand, taking care not to let the rope bear heavily on the metal edge of the skylight. We could not risk any noise. I heard the rods creaking under his weight; then, a moment later, two hands came up and got a grip on the sill. Slowly Gimenez's face and shoulders appeared.

I bent down and whispered: 'Don't hurry. Take a rest.'

He breathed in the fresh air, gulping and panting.

My mouth still close to his ear, I said: 'Be careful how you pull yourself up. Don't put your hands on the glass.'

He seemed as exhausted as I was.

I untied the rope from my waist, and he followed suit. I coiled it up carefully, took a piece of string out of my pocket, and ran a bowline round the middle of the coil.

There we both stood, side by side, in absolute silence. Gradually my breathing slowed down to its normal rate, and I began to recover my strength. It was hard to get used to this immense, seemingly limitless space all around me. The glass penthouse (of which the skylight formed a part) stood out from the roof and vanished in darkness only a few feet away. I made out one or two small chimney-cowls here and there. The courtyard and the perimeter were hidden from us by the parapet. We could walk upright without being seen.

I felt the shingle under my feet at the least move I made.

I took a coil of rope in each hand and picked them up with great care. Gimenez did the same with the shoes and coats. We stood there waiting for a train: it was five, perhaps even ten minutes coming.

Gimenez became impatient. I was just about to move when the sound of a locomotive reached us from the distance. It grew louder and louder; presently the train steamed past on the nearby track. We managed to get ten feet forward before it vanished into the distance again. The stretch of line which runs past Montluc joins the two main stations of Lyons. As a result it carries very heavy traffic, which had hardly slackened off even at this stage of the war.

We had nearly reached the middle of the roof now. We found ourselves standing by the far end of the penthouse. A little farther on a second penthouse appeared, which stretched away towards the other side of the roof. My eyes were beginning to get accustomed to the dark. I could see the large glass dome above the penthouse; that meant we were standing above the central well. I thought then for a moment of our friends below in their cells: some asleep, lost in wonderful dreams; others, who knew of our plan, awake, waiting in frightful suspense, ears straining for any suspicious noises.

We had advanced with extreme care, putting each foot down as lightly as possible, bent double as if the weight of our apprehension and of the dangers we had to face was too heavy to be supported. Gimenez kept close behind me. I could hear his slow, regular breathing, and glimpse his dark silhouette against the night sky. We had to wait some time before another train came to our assistance. But this time it was a slow goods train. It enabled us to reach our objective—the side of the roof opposite the infirmary—in one quick move.

We put down our various packages. I turned back and whispered to Gimenez: 'Lie down and wait for me here. Don't move.'

'Where are you going?'

'To see what's happening.'

Gimenez obediently dropped to his knees, and remained as motionless as the equipment stacked round him. I crept slowly round the corner of the roof, raised myself cautiously, and peered over the parapet. Below me I could see the stretch of the perimeter which flanked the Rue du Dauphiné. I lifted my head a little farther, and quickly drew it back again at the sight of a sentry. He was standing in one corner near the wash-house. I had known he would be there; yet in my present situation he scared me nearly out of my wits.

Of course, he could not see me. I told myself not to be a fool.

I pressed my cheek against the rough concrete surface and slowly raised my head once more. Unfortunately, the wide shelf outside the parapet cut off my view of the part of the courtyard immediately below. As this was where we would have to climb down, it was essential to find a better observation-post.

But before moving I took another quick look at the soldier in the far corner. He seemed very wide awake. Soon a second sentry walked over to join him—probably the one who guarded the wooden barrack-block on the other side. I saw the glowing tips of their cigarettes. The lamps in the courtyard gave off so weak a light that the men themselves were mere shadows against the surrounding gloom.

Occasionally a twinkling reflection from buckle or bayonet hinted at their movements. I knew that the best way of remaining unseen was to keep absolutely still. If I had to move, it must be done as slowly as possible, with long and frequent pauses. It took me some time to get back to Gimenez, tell him to stay put, climb over the parapet, and crawl along the outer cat-walk till I was once more opposite the infirmary. A train passed by at exactly the right moment; I scrambled along as fast as I could to the corner of the wall. A loose piece of shingle, even a little sand going over the edge would have given me away. I would feel ahead with my hands, then slowly pull myself forward like a slug, breathing through my mouth.

In front of me the perimeter was clearly visible. Beyond it the tobacco factory and the buildings of the military court formed a broken outline against the horizon. Above them the stars shone out in a moonless sky. After a little I could just make out the roof of the covered gallery over which we had to pass. Gradually our whole route became visible. I spotted a familiar landmark—the fanlight of my old cell—and then, on the left, the workshop and women's quarters. Close by was the low wall between the infirmary and the courtyard. Soon, I thought, we should be climbing that wall. One room in the infirmary was still lit up; the light shone behind the wall in the direction of the covered gallery. I was, I realized, directly above cell 45, where my first few weeks of detention had been spent.

I wriggled forward inch by inch, so as to reach the outer edge of the cat-walk and get into a position from which I could observe the whole area of the courtyard. The two sentries were now out of sight round the corner of the block, smoking and chatting. I could see no one below me. The way was clear. My heart beat excitedly. A little farther and I would be certain. My face against the rough surface, I peered cautiously over the edge.

I was horrified at the gulf stretching down below me; I could not help feeling that my rope must be too short.

Nothing was stirring. I examined every danger-point in turn—the shadowy corners by the wash-house and workshop, the women's quarters, the alley between the infirmary wall and the main block, the half-open doors leading from court to court, every conceivable hole or corner where a sentry might be lurking. Nothing. The cell windows were patterned on the façade like black squares in a crossword puzzle. Occasionally the sound of a cough drifted out from one or other of them. This, and the recurrent trains, alone broke the silence. Farther down, on the left, some of the windows seemed to be open. The stillness was almost tangible.

Still I scrutinized the courtyard with minute care. Suddenly a dark shape caught my eye, in a corner near the door of the main block. I stared closely at it. After a moment I realized it was a sentry, asleep on the steps. The weight of this alarming discovery filled me with a sudden vast depression. How on earth were we to get past him? How could we even be certain he was asleep? How—in the last resort—could we surprise him without being seen?

At this point the sentry sat up and lit a cigarette. The flame from his lighter gave me a quick glimpse of his steel helmet and the sub-machine gun he carried. He got up, walked a little way in the direction of the infirmary, and then came back again.

Midnight struck.

It must have been the time when the guard was changed. The soldier passed directly beneath me, between the infirmary and the main block, and vanished in the direction of the guard-house. Four or five minutes later his relief appeared. His footsteps crunched grimly over the cobbles.

A frightful inner conflict racked me as I studied his every movement, like a wild beast stalking its prey. We could not retreat. The way had to be cleared.

The sentry's beat took him away into the shadows at the far end of the court, then back to the main door, where the lamp shone for a moment on his helmet and the barrel of his sub-machine gun.

I watched him for a whole hour, memorizing the pattern of his movements. Then I raised myself on knees and elbows, climbed quietly over the parapet, and returned to Gimenez.

He was asleep. I woke him gently. 'Time to move on,' I said.

He got up without making any noise. I was busy untying the knot of the string lashed round the big rope.

'All set now,' I whispered. 'As soon as a train comes, we'll lower the rope.'

I stood with one foot on the roof and the other on the cat-walk, the low parapet between my legs. This way I could control the rope with both hands and pay it out without it touching the edge. I left Gimenez to control the coil and see the rope was free from entanglements.

An eternity of time seemed to pass before the train came. At the first distant panting of the engine I began to lower away, slowly at first, then with increasing speed. When I felt the reinforced stretch near the end passing through my fingers I stopped, and lowered the rope onto the concrete. Then I hooked the grappling-iron onto the inner side of the parapet. It seemed to hold firm enough. The rope stretched away into the darkness below us.

Gimenez would sling the parcels containing our shoes and coats round his neck, and follow me down when I gave him the signal. I knew that the moment I swung out from the roof into open space the last irrevocable decision would have been taken. By so doing I would either clinch my victory or sign my own death-warrant. While I remained on the roof it was still possible to return to my cell. Once I had begun the descent there was no way back. Despite the cool night air, my face and shirt were soaked with sweat.

'Hold onto the grappling-iron while I'm going down,' I told Gimenez. I took hold of his hands and set them in position.

Then I crouched down the outer ledge, facing him, ready to go down the rope at the first possible moment, and waited for a train to pass. Gimenez leant over and hissed nervously in my ear: 'There's someone down below!'

'Don't worry.'

Then I looked at the sky and the stars and prayed that the rope might be strong enough, that the German sentry would not come round the corner at the wrong moment, that I would not make any accidental noise.

The waiting strained my nerves horribly. Once I began my descent there would be no more hesitation, I knew; but dear God, I thought, let that train come quickly, let me begin my descent into the abyss now, at once, before my strength fails me.

The stroke of one o'clock cut through the stillness like an axe.

Had an hour passed so quickly? The sentries' footsteps, echoing up to us with monotonous regularity, seemed to be counting out the seconds. There could not be so very many trains at this time of night.

Gimenez was showing signs of impatience. I told him to keep still. The words were hardly out of my mouth when a distant whistle broke the silence. Quickly it swelled in volume.

'This is it,' I said.

I shuffled back towards the edge of the cat-walk. Then, holding my breath, I slid myself over, gripping the rope between my knees, and holding the ledge with both hands to steady myself. At last I let go. The rope whirred upwards under my feet, the wire binding tore at my hands. I went down as fast as I could, not even using my legs.

As soon as I touched the ground I grabbed the parcel containing the second rope, and doubled across the courtyard to the low wall. I released the rope, swung the grappling-iron up, hauled myself over, and dropped down on the other side, behind the doorway, leaving the rope behind for Gimenez.

The train was fading away into the distance now, towards the station. The drumming of its wheels seemed to be echoed in my heaving chest. I opened my mouth and breathed deeply to ease the pressure on my lungs. Above me I saw the dark swinging line of rope, and the sharp outline of the roof against the sky.

I stood motionless, getting my breath back and accustoming my eyes to the darkness. The sentry's footsteps rang out behind the wall, scarcely six feet away. They passed on, only to return a moment later. I pressed both hands against my beating heart. When all was quiet again I worked round to the doorway, and flattened myself against it. I felt all my human reactions being swallowed up by pure animal instinct, the instinct for self-preservation which quickens the reflexes and gives one fresh reserves of strength.

I slid myself over, gripping the rope between my knees.

It was my life or his.

As his footsteps approached I tried to press myself into the wood against which my back was resting. Then, when I heard him changing direction, I risked a quick glance out of my hiding-place to see exactly where he was.

He did exactly the same thing twice, and still I waited.

I got a good grip on the ground with my heels; I could not afford to slip. The footsteps moved in my direction, grew louder. The sentry began to turn. . . .

I sprang out of my recess like a panther, and got my hands round his throat in a deadly grip. With frantic violence I began to throttle him. I was no longer a man, but a wild animal. I squeezed and squeezed, with the terrible strength of desperation. My teeth were gritting against each other, my eyes bursting out of my head. I threw back my head to exert extra pressure, and felt my fingers bite deep into his neck. Already half-strangled, the muscles of his throat torn and engorged, only held upright by my vice-like grip, the sentry still feebly raised his arms as if to defend himself; but an instant later they fell back, inert. But this did not make me let go. For perhaps three minutes longer I maintained my pressure on his throat, as if afraid that one last cry, or even the death-rattle, might give me away. Then, slowly, I loosened my blood-stained fingers, ready to close them again at the least movement; but the body remained slack and lifeless. I lowered it gently to the ground.

I stared down at the steel helmet which, fortunately perhaps, concealed the sentry's face; at the dark hunched shape of the body itself, at the sub-machine gun and the bayonet. I thought for a moment, then quickly drew the bayonet from its scabbard, gripped it by the hilt in both hands, and plunged it down with one straight, hard stroke into the sentry's back.

I raised my head, and saw that I was standing immediately below the window of cell 45. Old memories fireworked up in my mind: hunger and thirst, the beatings I had suffered, the handcuffs, the condemned man in the next cell. . . .

I went back to the doorway, near the infirmary, and whistled twice, very softly. A dark shape slid down the rope. It creaked under his weight. I went to meet him. Gimenez climbed the low wall, detached the light rope with its grappling-iron, passed them down to me, and jumped. In his excitement, or nervousness, he had left our coats and shoes on the roof. At the time I said nothing about this. Clearly his long wait had depressed him; he was shivering all over. He gave a violent start when he saw the corpse stretched out near our feet.

I clapped him on the back. 'You'll really have something to shiver about in a moment. Come on, quick.'

Our troubles had only begun. We still had to cross the courtyard in order to reach the wall between it and the infirmary. Then there was the roof of the covered gallery to surmount, and, finally, the crossing of the perimeter walls.

I carried the rope and the fixed grappling-iron; Gimenez had the loose one. We doubled across to the wall. It was essential for us to get up here as quickly as possible. The light left on in the infirmary was shining in our direction, and a guard could easily have spotted us from a first-floor window of the central block as we made our way towards the inner wall of the perimeter.

Gimenez gave me a leg up, and I managed to reach the top of the wall and hang on. But I was quite incapable by now of pulling myself up; all my strength had drained away. I came down again, wiped my forehead and regained my breath. If I had been alone I should in all probability have stuck at this point. As it was, I bent down against the wall in my turn, and Gimenez got up without any trouble. I undid the bundle of rope and passed him the end with the grappling-iron attached. He fixed it securely. Then I tried again, with the rope to help me this time. Somehow I scrambled up, using hands, knees and feet, thrusting and straining in one last desperate effort. Gimenez lay down flat on his belly to give himself more purchase, and managed to grasp me under the arms. Eventually I made it.

My heart was hammering against my ribs and my chest felt as if it was going to burst. My shirt clung damply to my body. But there was not a minute to lose. We coiled up the rope again and crawled along to the covered gallery. From here it was a short climb up the tiles to the ridge of the roof. We had to hurry because of that damned light; once we had got over the other side of the roof we were in shadow again.

Unfortunately I made a noise. Two tiles knocked against each other under the sliding pressure of my knee. Gimenez reproved me sharply.

'For God's sake take care what you're doing!' he hissed.

'It wasn't my fault—'

'I haven't the least desire to be caught, even if you have!'

Since this was a sloping roof, we only needed to climb a little way down the far side to be completely hidden. If we stood upright we could easily see over the wall. Soon we were both crouching in position at the end of the covered gallery, our equipment beside us.

I was not acquainted with the exact details of the patrols in the perimeter. When I went out to be interrogated, I had observed a sentry-box in each corner, but these were always unoccupied. Perhaps the guards used them at night, however: it was vital to find out. We already knew that one guard rode round and round the whole time on a bicycle; he passed us every two or three minutes, his pedals squeaking.

We listened carefully, Gimenez was just saying that the cyclist must be alone, when the sound of voices reached us. We had to think again.

Perhaps there was a sentry posted at each corner of the square, in the angle formed by the outer wall. If this turned out to be so, it would be extremely difficult to get across; nothing but complete darkness would give us a chance. That meant we must cut the electric cable, which ran about two feet below the top of the inner wall, on the perimeter side.

I half-rose from my cramped position and took a quick look. The walls seemed much higher from here, and the lighting system enhanced this impression. A wave of despair swept over me. Surely we could never surmount this obstacle?

From the roof it had all looked very difficult. The yawning gulf had been hidden. But the perimeter was well lit, and the sight of it—deep as hell and bright as daylight—almost crushed my exhausted determination.

I craned forward a little farther. The sentry-box below on our left was empty. I ducked back quickly as the cyclist approached. He ground round the corner and started another circuit. A moment later I was enormously relieved to hear him talking to himself; it was this curious monologue we had intercepted a moment earlier. He was alone, after all.

Behind us rose the dark shape of the main block. We had come a long way since ten o'clock. Another six yards, and we were free. Yet what risks still remained to be run!

Little by little determination flowed back into me. One more effort would do it. Don't look back, I thought. Keep your eyes in front of you till it's all over.

Bitter experience had taught me that over-hastiness could be fatal; that every precipitate action was liable to bring disaster in its train. Gimenez was eager to get on and finish the operation, but I firmly held him back. I was as well aware as he was of the dangers that threatened us; I knew that every moment we delayed increased our risk of recapture. I thought of the open cell, the rope we had left hanging from the wall, the dead sentry in the courtyard, the possibility of his body being discovered by a patrol or his relief. Nevertheless, I spent more than a quarter of an hour watching that cyclist. Every four or five circuits he turned round and went the other way. We were well placed in our corner: he was busy taking the bend, and never looked up. We were additionally protected by the three shaded lights fixed on each wall. All their radiance was thrown down into the perimeter itself, leaving us in shadow. We could watch him without fear of discovery.

Three o'clock.

Gimenez was becoming desperate. At last I decided to move. Holding the end of the rope firmly in one hand, I coiled it across my left arm like a lasso. With the other hand I grasped the grappling-iron. As soon as the sentry had pedalled past, I threw the line as hard as I could towards the opposite wall. The rope snaked up and out, and the grappling-iron fell behind the parapet. I tugged very gently on it, trying to let it find a natural anchorage. Apparently I had been successful; it held firm. A strand of barbed wire, which I had not previously noticed, rattled alarmingly as the rope jerked over it. After a little, however, it was pressed down to the level of the wall.

I gave one violent pull, but the rope did not budge. It had caught first time. I breathed again.

'Give me the other hook,' I muttered to Gimenez. I could feel him trembling.

The cyclist was coming round again now. I froze abruptly. For the first time he passed actually under the rope. When he had gone I threaded the rope through the wire loop and pulled it as tight as we could. While Gimenez held it firm to prevent it slipping, I knotted it tightly, and fixed the grappling-iron in a crevice on the near side of the parapet. In my fear of running things too fine I had actually over-calculated the amount of rope necessary; over six feet were left trailing loose on the roof. That thin line stretching across the perimeter looked hardly less fragile than the telephone-wires which followed a similar route a few yards away.

I made several further tests when the cyclist was round the other side. I unanchored the grappling-iron on our side, and then we both of us pulled on the rope as hard as we could to try out its strength.

If the truth must be told, I was horribly afraid that it would snap, and I would be left crippled in the perimeter. When I pulled on it with all my strength I could feel it stretch. One last little effort and the whole thing would be over; but I had reached the absolute end of my courage, physical endurance, and will-power alike. All the time the cyclist continued to ride round beneath us.

Four o'clock struck.

In the distance, towards the station, the red lights on the railway line still shone out. But the first glimmer of dawn was already creeping up over the horizon, and the lights showed less bright every moment. We could wait no longer.

'Over you go, Gimenez. You're lighter than I am.'

'No. You go first.'

'It's your turn.'

'I won't.'

'Go on, it's up to you.'

'No,' he said desperately, 'I can't do it.'

The cyclist turned the corner again. I shook Gimenez desperately, my fingers itching to hit him.

'Are you going, yes or no?'

'No,' he cried, 'no, *no*!'

'Shut up, for God's sake!' I said. I could not conquer his fear; I said no more. Still the German pedalled round his beat. Once he stopped almost directly beneath us, got off his machine, and urinated against the wall. It was at once a comic and terrifying sight. As time passed and the dawn approached, our chances of success grew steadily less. I knew it, yet I still hesitated. Gimenez shivered in silence.

Abruptly, as the sentry passed us yet again, I stooped forward, gripped the rope with both hands, swung out into space, and got my legs up in position. Hand over hand, my back hanging exposed above the void, I pulled myself across with desperate speed. I reached the far wall, got one arm over it, and scrambled up.

I had done it. I had escaped.

A delirious feeling of triumph swept over me. I forgot how exhausted I was; I almost forgot Gimenez, who was still waiting for the sentry to pass under him again before following me. I was oblivious to my thudding heart and hoarse breath; my knees might tremble, my face be dripping with sweat, my hands scored and bleeding, my throat choked, my head bursting, but I neither knew nor cared. All I was conscious of was the smell of life, the freedom I had won against such desperate odds. I uttered a quick and thankful prayer to God for bringing me through safely.

I moved along the top of the wall towards the courthouse buildings, where it lost height considerably. I stopped just short of a small gateway. Workmen were going past in the street outside, and I waited a few moments before jumping down. This gave Gimenez time to catch up with me.

At five o'clock we were walking down the street in our socks and shirt-sleeves—free men.

SPRINGING THE TRAP

Anthony Hope

As the citizens of Streslau, capital of Ruritania, celebrate the coronation of their new king, only a handful of people know the truth: the head on which the crown rests is that of the king's distant kinsman, Rudolf Rassendyll, who looks exactly like him. For the king has been kidnapped by his treacherous half-brother, Duke Michael.

Although the duke's plan to usurp the throne and announce his betrothal to Princess Flavia has been foiled, the king is in grave danger. He is imprisoned at Zenda, in a castle surrounded by a moat and connected to Duke Michael's chateau by a drawbridge. He is closely guarded by four of Black Michael's followers: Rupert Hentzau, Detchard, De Gautet and Bersonin. In the event of an attack on the castle, the king is to be killed and his body disposed of by means of a chute called 'Jacob's Ladder', which leads directly from his cell to the moat.

Under cover of darkness, Rudolf swims across the moat one night to investigate 'Jacob's Ladder' as an escape route, but it is clear that cunning is the only key to success. His second plan depends on three men loyal to the king—Colonel Sapt, Fritz von Tarlenheim and Strakencz—and on two willing helpers within the duke's chateau—Johann, who is bribed to open the door, and Antoinette de Mauban, who loves Michael but is horrified at his villainy. The plan also depends on Rupert Hentzau, though he does not know it. Everything turns on the fact that Antoinette has caught Hentzau's roving eye. . . .

Here is the plan I had made. A strong party under Sapt's command was to steal up to the door of the chateau. If discovered prematurely, they were to kill anyone who found them—with their swords, for I wanted no noise of firing. If all went well, they would be at the door when Johann opened it. They were to rush in and secure the servants if their mere presence and the use of the King's name were not enough. At the same moment—and on this hinged the plan—a woman's cry was to ring out loud and shrill from Antoinette de Mauban's chamber. Again and again she was to cry: 'Help, help! Michael, help!' and then to utter the name of young Rupert Hentzau. Then, as we hoped, Michael, in fury, would rush out of his apartments opposite, and fall alive into the hands of Sapt. Still the cries would go on; and my men would let down the drawbridge; and it would be strange if Rupert, hearing his name thus taken in vain, did not descend from where he slept and seek to cross. De Gautet might or might not come with him: that must be left to chance.

And when Rupert set his foot on the drawbridge? There was my part: for I was minded for another swim in the moat; and, lest I should grow weary, I had resolved to take with me a small wooden ladder, on which I could rest my arms in the water—and my feet when I left it. I would rear it against the wall just by the bridge; and when the bridge was across, I would stealthily creep onto it—and then if Rupert or De Gautet crossed in safety, it would be my misfortune, not my fault. They dead, two men only would remain; and for them we must trust to the confusion we had created and to a sudden rush. We should have the keys of the door that led to the all-important rooms. Perhaps they would rush out. If they stood by their orders, then the King's life hung on the swiftness with which we could force the outer door; and I thanked God that not Rupert Hentzau watched, but Detchard. For though Detchard was a cool man, relentless, and no coward, he had neither the dash nor the recklessness of Rupert. Moreover, he, if any one of them, really loved Black Michael, and it might be that he would leave Bersonin to guard the King, and rush across the bridge to take part in the affray on the other side.

So I planned—desperately. And, that our enemy might be the better lulled to security, I gave orders that our residence should be brilliantly lighted from top to bottom, as though we were engaged in revelry; and should so be kept all night, with music playing and people moving to and fro. Strakencz would be there, and he was to conceal our departure, if he could, from Flavia. And if we came not again by the morning, he was to march, openly and in force to the Castle, and demand the person of the King; if Black Michael were not there, as I did not think he would be, the marshal would take Flavia with him, as swiftly as he could, to Strelsau, and there proclaim Black Michael's treachery and the probable death of the King, and rally all that there was honest and true round the banner of the princess. And, to say truth, this was what I thought was most likely to happen. For I had great doubts whether either the King or Black Michael or I had more than a day to live. Well, if Black Michael died, and if I, the play-actor, slew Rupert Hentzau with my own hand, and then died myself, it might be that Fate would deal as lightly with Ruritania as could be hoped, notwithstanding that she demanded the life of the King—and to her dealing thus with me, I was in no temper to make objection.

It was late when we rose from conference, and I betook me to the princess's apartments. She was pensive that evening; yet, when I left her, she flung her arms about me and grew, for an instant, bashfully radiant as she slipped a ring on my finger. I was wearing the King's ring; but I had also on my little finger a plain band of gold engraved with the motto of our family: '*Nil Quae Feci*.' This I took off and put on her, and signed to her to let me go. And she, understanding, stood away and watched me with dimmed eyes.

'Wear that ring even though you wear another when you are queen,' I said.

'Whatever else I wear, this I will wear till I die and after,' said she, as she kissed the ring.

* * * *

The night came fine and clear. I had prayed for dirty weather, such as had favoured my previous voyage in the moat, but Fortune was this time against me. Still I reckoned that by keeping close under the wall and in the shadow I could escape detection from the windows of the chateau that looked out on the scene of my efforts. If they searched the moat, indeed, my scheme must fail; but I did not think they would. They had made 'Jacob's Ladder' secure against attack. Johann had himself helped to fix it closely to the masonry on the under side, so that it could not now be moved from below any more than from above. An assault with explosives or a long battering with picks alone could displace it, and the noise involved in either of these operations put them out of the question. What harm, then, could a man do in the moat? I trusted that Black Michael, putting this query to himself, would answer confidently, 'None'; while, even if Johann meant treachery, he did not know my scheme, and would doubtless expect to see me, at the head of my friends, before the front entrance to the chateau. There, I said to Sapt, was the real danger.

'And there,' I added, 'you shall be. Doesn't that content you?'

But it did not. Dearly would he have liked to come with me, had I not utterly refused to take him. One man might escape notice, to double the party more than doubled the risk; and when he ventured to hint once again that my life was too valuable, I, knowing the secret thought he clung to, sternly bade him be silent, assuring him that unless the King lived through the night, I would not live through it either.

At twelve o'clock, Sapt's command left the chateau of Tarlenheim and struck off to the right, riding by unfrequented roads, and avoiding the town of Zenda. If all went well, they would be in front of the Castle by about a quarter to two. Leaving their horses half a mile off, they were to steal up to the entrance and hold themselves in readiness for the opening of the door. If the door were not opened by two, they were to send Fritz von Tarlenheim round to the other side of the Castle. I would meet him there if I were alive, and we would consult whether to storm the Castle or not. If I were not there, they were to return with all speed to Tarlenheim, rouse the marshal, and march in force to Zenda. For if not there, I should be dead; and I knew that the King would not be alive five minutes after I had ceased to breathe.

I must now leave Sapt and his friends, and relate how I myself proceeded on this eventful night. I went out on the good horse which had carried me, on the night of the coronation, back from the hunting-lodge to Strelsau. I carried a revolver in the saddle and my sword. I was covered with a large cloak, and under this I wore a warm, tight-fitting woollen jersey, a pair of knickerbockers, thick stockings, and light canvas shoes. I had rubbed myself thoroughly with oil, and I carried a large flask of whisky. The night was warm, but I might probably be immersed a long while, and it was necessary to take every precaution against cold: for cold not only saps a man's courage if he has to die, but impairs his energy if others have to die, and, finally, gives him rheumatics, if it be God's will that he lives. Also I tied round my body a length of thin but stout cord, and I did not forget my ladder. I, starting after Sapt, took a shorter route, skirting the town to the left, and found myself in the outskirts of the forest at about half-past twelve. I tied my horse up in a thick clump of trees, leaving the revolver in its pocket in the saddle—it would be no use to me,—and, ladder in hand, made my way to the edge of the moat. Here I unwound my rope from about my waist, bound it securely round the trunk of a tree on the bank, and let myself down. The Castle clock struck a quarter to one as I felt the water under me and began to swim round the keep, pushing the ladder before me, and hugging the Castle wall. Thus voyaging, I came to my old friend, 'Jacob's Ladder', and felt the ledge of the masonry under me. I crouched down in the shadow of the great pipe—I tried to stir it, but it was quite immovable—and waited. I remember that my predominant feeling was, neither anxiety for the King nor longing for Flavia, but an intense desire to smoke; and this craving, of course, I could not gratify.

The drawbridge was still in its place. I saw its airy, slight framework above me, some ten yards to my right, as I crouched with my back against the wall of the King's cell. I made out a window two yards my side of it and nearly on the same level. That, if Johann spoke true, must belong to the duke's apartments; and on the other side, in about the same relative position, must be Madame de Mauban's window. Women are careless, forgetful creatures. I prayed that she might not forget that she was to be the victim of a brutal attempt at two o'clock precisely. I was rather amused at the part I had assigned to my young friend Rupert Hentzau; but I owed him a stroke,—for, even as I sat, my shoulder ached where he had, with an audacity that seemed half to hide his treachery, struck at me, in the sight of all my friends, on the terrace at Tarlenheim.

Suddenly the duke's windows grew bright. The shutters were not closed, and the interior became partially visible to me as I cautiously raised myself till I stood on tiptoe. Thus placed, my range of sight embraced a yard or more inside the window, while the radius of light did not reach me. The window was flung open and someone looked out. I marked Antoinette de Mauban's graceful figure, and, though her face was in shadow, the fine outline of her head was revealed against the light behind. I longed to cry softly, 'Remember!' but I dared not—and happily, for a moment later a man came up and stood by her. He tried to put his arm round her waist, but with a swift motion she sprang away and leant against the shutter, her profile towards me. I made out who the new-comer was: it was young Rupert. A low laugh from him made me sure, as he leant forward, stretching out his hand towards her.

'Gently, gently!' I mumured. 'You're too soon, my boy!'

His head was close to hers. I suppose he whispered to her, for I saw her point to the moat, and I heard her say, in slow and distinct tones:

'I had rather throw myself out of this window!'

He came close up to the window and looked out.

'It looks cold,' said he. 'Come Antoinette, are you serious?'

She made no answer so far as I heard; and he, smiting his hand petulantly on the windowsill, went on, in the voice of some spoilt child:

'Hang Black Michael! Isn't the princess enough for him? Is he to have everything? What the devil do you see in Black Michael?'

'If I told him what you say—' she began.

'Well, tell him,' said Rupert, carelessly; and, catching her off her guard, he sprang forward and kissed her, laughing, and crying, 'There's something to tell him!'

If I had kept my revolver with me, I should have been very sorely tempted. Being spared the temptation, I merely added this new score to his account.

'Though, faith,' said Rupert, 'it's little he cares. He's mad about the princess, you know. He talks of nothing but cutting the play-actor's throat.'

Didn't he, indeed?

'And if I do it for him, what do you think he's promised me?'

The unhappy woman raised her hands above her head, in prayer or in despair.

'But I detest waiting,' said Rupert; and I saw that he was about to lay his hand on her again, when there was a noise of a door in the room opening, and a harsh voice cried:

'What are you doing here, sir?'

Rupert turned his back to the window, bowed low, and said, in his loud, merry tones:

'Apologizing for your absence, sir. Could I leave the lady alone?'

The new-comer must be Black Michael. I saw him directly, as he advanced towards the window. He caught young Rupert by the arm.

'The moat would hold more than the King!' said he, with a significant gesture.

'Does your Highness threaten me?' asked Rupert.

'A threat is more warning than most men get from me.'

'Yet,' observed Rupert, 'Rudolph Rassendyll has been threatened, and yet lives!'

'Am I in fault because my servants bungle?' asked Michael scornfully.

'Your Highness has run no risk of bungling!' sneered Rupert.

It was telling the duke that he shirked danger as plain as ever I have heard a man told. Black Michael had self-control. I daresay he scowled —it was a great regret to me that I could not see their faces better,— but his voice was even and calm, as he answered:

'Enough, enough! We mustn't quarrel, Rupert. Are Detchard and Bersonin at their posts?'

'They are, sir.'

'I need you no more.'

'Nay, I'm not oppressed with fatigue,' said Rupert.

'Pray, sir, leave us,' said Michael, more impatiently. 'In ten minutes the drawbridge will be drawn back, and I presume you have no wish to swim to your bed.'

Rupert's figure disappeared. I heard the door open and shut again. Michael and Antoinette de Mauban were left together. To my chagrin, the duke laid his hand on the window and closed it. He stood talking to Antoinette for a moment or two. She shook her head, and he turned impatiently away. She left the window. The door sounded again, and Black Michael closed the shutters.

'De Gautet, De Gautet, man!' sounded from the drawbridge. 'Unless you want a bath before your bed, come along!'

It was Rupert's voice, coming from the end of the drawbridge. A moment later he and De Gautet stepped out on the bridge. Rupert's arm was through De Gautet's, and in the middle of the bridge he detained his companion and leant over. I dropped behind the shelter of 'Jacob's Ladder'.

Then Master Rupert had a little sport. He took from De Gautet a bottle which he carried, and put it to his lips.

'Hardly a drop!' he cried discontentedly, and flung it in the moat.

It fell, as I judged from the sound and the circles on the water, within a yard of the pipe. And Rupert, taking out his revolver, began to shoot at it. The first two shots missed the bottle, but hit the pipe. The third shattered the bottle. I hoped that the young ruffian would be content; but he emptied the other barrels at the pipe, and one, skimming over the pipe whistled through my hair as I crouched on the other side.

''Ware-bridge!' a voice cried, to my relief.

Rupert and De Gautet cried, 'A moment!' and ran across. The bridge was drawn back, and all became still. The clock struck a quarter-past one. I rose and stretched myself and yawned.

I think some ten minutes had passed when I heard a slight noise to my right. I peered over the pipe, and saw a dark figure standing in the gateway that led to the bridge. It was a man. By the careless, graceful poise, I guessed it to be Rupert again. He held a sword in his hand, and he stood motionless for a minute of two. Wild thoughts ran through me. On what mischief was the young fiend bent now? Then he laughed low to himself; then he turned his face to the wall, took a step in my direction, and, to my surprise, began to climb down the wall. In an instant I saw that there must be steps in the wall; it was plain. They were cut into or affixed to the wall, at intervals of about eighteen inches. Rupert set his foot on the lower one. Then he placed his sword between his teeth, turned round, and noiselessly let himself down into the water. Had it been a matter of my life only, I would have swum to meet him. Dearly would I have loved to fight it out with him then and there—with steel, on a fine night, and none to come between us. But there was the King! I restrained myself, but I could not bridle my swift breathing, and I watched him with the intensest eagerness.

He swam leisurely and quietly across. There were more footsteps up on the other side, and he climbed them. When he set foot in the gateway, standing on the drawn-back bridge, he felt in his pocket and took something out. I heard him unlock the door. I could hear no noise of its closing behind him. He vanished from my sight.

Abandoning my ladder—I saw I did not need it now,—I swam to the side of the bridge and climbed half-way up the steps. There I hung, with my sword in my hand, listening eagerly. The duke's room was shuttered and dark. There was a light in the window on the opposite side of the bridge. Not a sound broke the silence, till half-past one chimed from the great clock in the tower of the chateau.

There were other plots than mine afoot in the Castle that night.

* * * *

The position wherein I stood does not appear very favourable to thought; yet for the next moment or two I thought profoundly. I had, I told myself, scored one point. Be Rupert Hentzau's errand what it might, and the villainy he was engaged on what it would, I had scored one point. He was on the other side of the moat from the King, and it would be by no fault of mine if ever he set foot on the same side again. I had three left to deal with: two on guard, and De Gautet in his bed. Ah, if I had the keys! I would have risked everything and attacked Detchard and Bersonin before their friends could join them. But I was powerless. I must wait till the coming of my friends enticed someone to cross the bridge—someone with the keys. And I waited, as it seemed, for half an hour, really for about five minutes, before the next act in the rapid drama began.

All was still on the other side. The duke's room remained inscrutable behind its shutters. The light burnt steadily in Madame de Mauban's window. Then I heard the faintest, faintest sound: it came from behind the door which led to the drawbridge on the other side of the moat. It but just reached my ear, yet I could not be mistaken as to what it was. It was made by a key being turned very carefully and slowly. Who was turning it? And of what room was it the key? There leapt before my eyes the picture of young Rupert, with the key in one hand, his sword in the other, and an evil smile on his face. But I did not know what door it was, nor on which of his favourite pursuits young Rupert was spending the hours of that night.

I was soon to be enlightened, for the next moment—before my

friends could be near the chateau door—before Johann the keeper would have thought to nerve himself for his task—there was a sudden crash from the room with the lighted window. It sounded as though someone had flung down a lamp; and the window went dark and black. At the same instant a cry rang out, shrill in the night: 'Help, help! Michael, help!' and was followed by a shriek of utter terror.

I was tingling in every nerve. I stood on the topmost step, clinging to the threshold of the gate with my right hand and holding my sword in my left. Suddenly I perceived that the gateway was broader than the bridge; there was a dark corner on the opposite side where a man could stand. I darted across and stood there. Thus placed, I commanded the path, and no man could pass between the chateau and the old Castle till he had tried conclusions with me.

There was another shriek. Then a door was flung open and clanged against the wall, and I heard the handle of a door savagely twisted.

'Open the door! In God's name, what's the matter?' cried a voice—the voice of Black Michael himself.

He was answered by the very words I had written in my letter:

'Help, Michael—Hentzau!'

A fierce oath rang out from the duke, and with a loud thud he threw himself against the door. At the same moment I heard a window above my head open, and a voice cried: 'What's the matter?' and I heard a man's hasty footsteps. I grasped my sword. If De Gautet came my way. . . .

Then I heard the clash of crossed swords and a tramp of feet, and—I cannot tell the thing so quickly as it happened, for all seemed to come at once. There was an angry cry from madame's room, the cry of a wounded man; the window was flung open; young Rupert stood there sword in hand. He turned his back, and I saw his body go forward to the lunge.

'Ah, Johann, there's one for you! Come on, Michael!'

Johann was there, then—come to the rescue of the duke! How would he open the door for me? For I feared that Rupert had slain him.

'Help!' cried the duke's voice, faint and husky.

I heard a step on the stairs above me; and I heard a stir down to my left, in the direction of the King's cell. But, before anything happened on my side of the moat, I saw five or six men round young Rupert in the embrasure of madame's window. Three or four times he lunged with incomparable dash and dexterity. For an instant they fell back, leaving a ring round him. He leapt on the parapet of the window, laughing as he leapt, and waving his sword in his hand. He was drunk with blood, and he laughed again wildly as he flung himself headlong into the moat.

What became of him then? I did not see: for as he leapt, De Gautet's lean face looked out through the door by me, and, without a second's hesitation, I struck at him with all the strength God has given me, and he fell dead in the doorway without a word or a groan. I dropped on my knees by him. Where were the keys? I found myself muttering: 'The keys, man, the keys?' as though he had been yet alive and could listen; and when I could not find them, I—God forgive me!—I believe I struck a dead man's face.

At last I had them. There were but three. Seizing the largest, I felt the lock of the door that led to the cell. I fitted in the key. It was right! The lock turned. I drew the door close behind me and locked it as noiselessly as I could, putting the key in my pocket.

I found myself at the top of a flight of steep stone stairs. An oil-lamp burnt dimly in the bracket. I took it down and held it in my hand; and I stood and listened.

'What in the devil can it be?' I heard a voice say.

It came from behind a door that faced me at the bottom of the stairs.

And another answered:

'Shall we kill him?'

I strained to hear the answer, and could have sobbed with relief when Detchard's voice came grating and cold:

'Wait a bit. There'll be trouble if we strike too soon.'

There was a moment's silence. Then I heard the bolt of the door cautiously drawn back. Instantly I put out the light I held, replacing the lamp in the bracket.

'It's dark—the lamp's out. Have you a light?' said the other voice—Bersonin's.

No doubt they had a light, but they should not use it. It was come to the crisis now, and I rushed down the steps and flung myself against the door. Bersonin had unbolted it and it gave way before me. The Belgian stood there sword in hand, and Detchard was sitting on a couch at the side of the room. In astonishment at seeing me, Bersonin recoiled; Detchard jumped to his sword. I rushed madly at the Belgian: he gave way before me, and I drove him up against the wall. He was no swordsman, though he fought bravely, and in a moment he lay on the floor before me. I turned—Detchard was not there. Faithful to his orders, he had not risked a fight with me, but had rushed straight to the door of the King's room, opened it and slammed it behind him. Even now he was at his work inside.

And surely he would have killed the King, and perhaps me also, had it not been for one devoted man who gave his life for the King. For when I forced the door, the sight I saw was this. The King stood in the corner of the room: broken by his sickness, he could do nothing; his fettered hands moved uselessly up and down, and he was laughing horribly in half-mad delirium. Detchard and the doctor were together in the middle of the room; and the doctor had flung himself on the murderer, pinning his hands to his sides for an instant. Then Detchard wrenched himself free from the feeble grip, and, as I entered, drove his sword through the hapless man.

Then he turned on me, crying:

'At last!'

We were sword to sword. By blessed chance neither he nor Bersonin had been wearing their revolvers. I found them afterwards, ready loaded, on the mantlepiece of the outer room: it was hard by the door, ready to their hands, but my sudden rush in had cut off access to them. Yes, we were man to man: and we began to fight, silently, sternly, and hard. Yet I remember little of it, save that the man was my match with the sword—nay, and more, for he knew more tricks than I; and that he forced me back against the bars that guarded the entrance to 'Jacob's Ladder'. And I saw a smile on his face, and he wounded me in the left arm.

No glory do I take for that contest. I believe that the man would have mastered me and slain me, and then done his butcher's work, for he was the most skilful swordsman I have ever met; but even as he pressed me hard, the half-mad, wasted, wan creature in the corner leapt high in lunatic mirth, shrieking:

'It's cousin Rudolf! Cousin Rudolf! I'll help you cousin Rudolf!'

We were sword to sword.

and catching up a chair in his hands (he could but just lift it from the ground and hold it uselessly before him) he came towards us. Hope came to me.

'Come on!' I cried. 'Come on! Drive it against his legs.'

Detchard replied with a savage thrust. He all but had me.

'Come on! Come on, man!' I cried. 'Come and share the fun!'

And the King laughed gleefully, and came on, pushing his chair before him.

With an oath Detchard skipped back, and, before I knew what he was doing, had turned his sword against the King. He made one fierce cut at the King, and the King, with a piteous cry, dropped where he stood. The stout ruffian turned to face me again. But his own hand had prepared his destruction: for in turning he trod in the pool of blood that flowed from the dead physician. He slipped; he fell. Like a dart I was upon him. I caught him by the throat, and before he could recover himself I drove my point through his neck, and with a stifled curse he fell across the body of his victim.

Was the King dead? It was my first thought. I rushed to where he lay. Ay, it seemed as if he were dead, for he had a great gash across his forehead, and he lay still in a huddled heap on the floor. I dropped on my knees beside him, and leant my ear down to hear if he breathed. But before I could, there was a loud rattle from the outside. I knew the sound: the drawbridge was being pushed out. A moment later it rang home against the wall on my side of the moat. I should be caught in a trap and the King with me, if he yet lived. He must take his chance, to live or to die. I took my sword, and passed into the outer room. Who were pushing the drawbridge out—my men? If so, all was well. My eye fell on the revolvers, and I seized one; and paused to listen in the doorway of the outer room. To listen, say I? Yes, and to get my breath: and I tore my shirt and twisted a strip of it round my bleeding arm; and stood listening again. I would have given the world to hear Sapt's voice. For I was faint, spent, and weary. And that wild-cat Rupert Hentzau was yet at large in the Castle. Yet, because I could better defend the narrow door at the top of the stairs than the wider entrance to the room, I dragged myself up the steps, and stood behind it listening.

What was the sound? Again a strange one for the place and the time. An easy, scornful, merry laugh—the laugh of young Rupert Henzau! I could scarcely believe that a sane man would laugh. Yet the laugh told me that my men had not come; for they must have shot Rupert ere now, if they had come. And the clock struck half-past two! My God! The door had not been opened! They had gone to the bank! They had not found me! They had gone by now back to Tarlenheim, with the news of the King's death—and mine. Well, it would be true before they got there. Was not Rupert laughing in triumph?

For a moment I sank, unnerved, against the door. Then I started up alert again, for Rupert cried scornfully:

'Well, the bridge is there! Come over it! And in God's name, let's see Black Michael. Keep back, you curs! Michael, come and fight for her!'

If it were a three-cornered fight, I might yet bear my part. I turned the key in the door and looked out.

* * * *

For a moment I could see nothing, for the glare of lanterns and torches caught me full in the eyes from the other side of the bridge. But soon the scene grew clear: and it was a strange scene. The bridge was in its place. At the far end of it stood a group of the duke's servants; two or three carried the lights which had dazzled me, three or four held pikes in rest. They were huddled together; their weapons were protruded before them; their faces were pale and agitated. To put it plainly, they looked in as arrant a fright as I have seen men look, and they gazed apprehensively at a man who stood in the middle of the bridge, sword in hand. Rupert Hentzau was in his trousers and shirt; the white linen was stained with blood, but his easy, buoyant pose told me that he was himself either not touched at all or merely scratched. There he stood, holding the bridge against them, and daring them to come on; or, rather, bidding them send Black Michael to him; and they, having no firearms, cowered before the desperate man and dared not attack him. They whispered to one another; and, in the backmost rank, I saw my friend Johann, leaning against the portal of the door and stanching with a handkerchief the blood which flowed from a wound in his cheek.

By marvellous chance, I was master. The cravens would oppose me no more than they dared attack Rupert. I had but to raise my revolver, and I sent him to his account with his sins on his head. He did not so much as know that I was there. I did nothing—why I hardly know to this day. I had killed one man stealthily that night, and another by luck rather than skill—perhaps it was that. Again, villain as the man was, I did not relish being one of a crowd against him—perhaps it was that. But stronger than either of these restrained feelings came a curiosity and a fascination which held me spellbound, watching for the outcome of the scene.

'Michael, you dog! Michael! If you can stand, come on!' cried Rupert; and he advanced a step, the group shrinking back a little before him. 'Michael, you bastard! come on!'

The answer to his taunts came in the wild cry of a woman:

'He's dead! My God, he's dead!'

'Dead!' shouted Rupert. 'I struck better than I knew!' and he laughed triumphantly. Then he went on: 'Down with your weapons there! I'm your master now! Down with them, I say!'

I believe they would have obeyed, but as he spoke came new things. First, there arose a distant sound, as of shouts and knockings from the other side of the chateau. My heart leapt. It must be my men, come by a happy disobedience to seek me. The noise continued, but none of the rest seemed to heed it. Their attention was chained by what now happened before their eyes. The group of servants parted and a woman staggered onto the bridge. Antoinette de Mauban was in a loose white robe, her dark hair streamed over her shoulders, her face was ghastly pale, and her eyes gleamed wildly in the light of the torches. In her shaking hand she held a revolver, and, as she tottered forward, she fired it at Rupert Hentzau. The ball missed him, and struck the woodwork over my head.

'Faith, madame,' laughed Rupert, 'had your eyes been no more deadly than your shooting, I had not been in this scrape—nor Black Michael in hell—tonight!'

She took no notice of his words. With a wonderful effort, she calmed herself till she stood still and rigid. Then very slowly and deliberately she began to raise her arm again, taking most careful aim.

He would be mad to risk it. He must rush on her chancing the bullet, or retreat towards me. I covered him with my weapon.

He did neither. Before she had got her aim, he bowed in his most graceful fashion, cried 'I can't kill where I kissed,' and before she or I could stop him, laid his hand on the parapet of the bridge, and lightly leapt into the moat.

At the very moment I heard a rush of feet, and a voice I knew—Sapt's cry: 'God! it's the duke—dead!' Then I knew that the King needed me no more, and throwing down my revolver, I sprang out on the bridge. There was a cry of wild wonder, 'The King!' and then I, like Rupert Hentzau, sword in hand, vaulted over the parapet, intent on finishing my quarrel with him where I saw his curly head fifteen yards off in the water of the moat.

He swam swiftly and easily. I was weary and half-crippled with my wounded arm. I could not gain on him. For a time I made no sound, but as we rounded the corner of the old keep I cried:

'Stop, Rupert, stop!'

I saw him look over his shoulder, but he swam on. He was under the bank now, searching, as I guessed, for a spot that he could climb. I knew there to be none—but there was my rope, which would still be hanging where I had left it. He would come to where it was before I could. Perhaps he would miss it—perhaps he would find it; and if he drew it up after him, he would get a good start of me. I put forth all my remaining strength and pressed on. At last I began to gain on him; for he, occupied with his search, unconsciously slackened his pace.

Ah, he had found it! A low shout of triumph came from him. He laid hold of it and began to haul himself up. I was near enough to hear him mutter: 'How the devil comes this here?' I was at the rope, and he, hanging in mid-air, saw me; but I could not reach him.

'Hullo! who's here?' he cried in startled tones.

For a moment, I believe, he took me for the King—I daresay I was pale enough to lend colour to the thought; but an instant later he cried:

'Why, it's the play-actor! How came you here, man?'

And so saying he gained the bank.

I laid hold of the rope, but I paused. He stood on the bank, sword in hand, and he could cut my head open or spit me through the heart as I came up. I let go the rope.

'Never mind,' said I; 'but as I am here, I think I'll stay.'

He smiled down on me.

'These women are the deuce—' he began; when suddenly the great bell of the Castle started to ring furiously, and a loud shout reached us from the moat.

Rupert smiled again, and waved his hand to me.

'I should like a turn with you, but it's a little too hot!' said he, and he disappeared from above me.

In an instant, without thinking of danger, I laid my hand to the rope. I was up. I saw him thirty yards off, running like a deer towards the shelter of the forest. For once Rupert Henzau had chosen discretion for his part. I laid my feet to the ground and rushed after him, calling to him to stand. He would not. Unwounded and vigorous, he gained on me at every step; but, forgetting everything in the world except him and my thirst for his blood, I pressed on, and soon the deep shades of the forest of Zenda engulfed us both, pursued and pursuer.

It was three o'clock now, and day was dawning. I was on a long straight grass avenue, and a hundred yards ahead ran young Rupert, his curls waving in the fresh breeze. I was weary and panting; he looked over his shoulder and waved his hand again to me. He was mocking me, for he saw he had the pace of me. I was forced to pause for breath. A moment later, Rupert turned sharply to the right and was lost from my sight.

I thought all was over, and in deep vexation sank to the ground. But I was up again directly, for a scream rang through the forest—a woman's scream. Putting forth the last of my strength, I ran on to the place where he had turned out of my sight, and, turning also, I saw him again. But alas! I could not touch him. He was in the act of lifting a girl down from her horse; doubtless it was her scream that I heard. She looked like a small farmer's or a peasant's daughter, and she carried a basket on her arm. Probably she was on her way to the early market at Zenda. Her horse was a stout, well-shaped animal. Master Rupert lifted her down amid her shrieks—the sight of him frightened her; but he treated her gently, laughed, kissed her, and gave her money. Then he jumped on the horse, sitting sideways like a woman; and then he waited for me. I, on my part, waited for him.

Presently he rode towards me, keeping his distance, however. He lifted up his hand, saying:

'What did you in the Castle?'

'I killed three of your friends,' said I.

'What! You got to the cells?'

'Yes.'

'And the King?'

'He was hurt by Detchard before I killed Detchard, but I pray that he lives.'

'You fool!' said Rupert, pleasantly.

'One thing more I did.'

'And what's that?'

'I spared your life. I was behind you on the bridge, with a revolver in my hand.'

'No? Faith, I was between two fires!'

'Get off your horse,' I cried, 'and fight like a man.'

'Before a lady!' said he, pointing to the girl. 'Fie, your Majesty!'

Then in my rage, hardly knowing what I did, I rushed at him. For a moment he seemed to waver. Then he reined his horse in and stood waiting for me. On I went in my folly. I seized the bridle and I struck at him. He parried and thrust at me. I fell back a pace and rushed in at him again; and this time I reached his face and laid his cheek open, and darted back almost before he could strike me. He seemed almost mazed at the fierceness of my attack; otherwise I think he must have killed me. I sank on my knee panting, expecting him to ride at me. And so he would have done, and then and there, I doubt not, one or both of us would have died; but at the moment there came a shout from behind us, and, looking round, I saw, just at the turn of the avenue, a man on a horse. He was riding hard, and he carried a revolver in his hand. It was Fritz von Tarlenheim, my faithful friend. Rupert saw him, and knew that the game was up. He checked his rush at me and flung his leg over the saddle, but yet for just a moment he waited. Leaning forward, he tossed his hair off his forehead and smiled, and said:

'*Au revoir*, Rudolf Rassendyll!'

Then, with his cheek streaming blood, but his lips laughing and his body swaying with ease and grace, he bowed to me; and he bowed to the farm-girl, who had drawn near in trembling fascination, and he waved his hand to Fritz, who was just within range and let fly a shot at him. The ball came nigh doing its work, for it struck the sword he held, and he dropped the sword with an oath, wringing his fingers, and clapped his heels hard on his horse's belly, and rode away at a gallop.

And I watched him go down the long avenue, riding as though he rode for his pleasure and singing as he went, for all there was that gash in his cheek.

Once again he turned to wave his hand, and then the gloom of the thickets swallowed him and he was lost from our sight. Thus he vanished—reckless and wary, graceful and graceless, handsome, debonair, vile, and unconquered. And I flung my sword passionately on the ground and cried to Fritz to ride after him. But Fritz stopped his horse, and leapt down and ran to me, and knelt, putting his arm about me. And indeed it was time, for the wound that Detchard had given me was broken forth afresh, and my blood was staining the ground.

'Then give me the horse!' I cried, staggering to my feet and throwing his arms off me. And the strength of my rage carried me so far as where the horse stood, and then I fell prone beside it. And Fritz knelt by me again.

'Fritz!' I said.

'Ay, friend—dear friend!' he said, tender as a woman.

'Is the King alive?'

He took his handkerchief and wiped my lips, and bent and kissed me on the forehead.

'Thanks to the most gallant gentleman that lives,' said he softly, 'the King is alive!'

CEREMONIES OF THE HORSEMEN

P.L. Frankson

Autumn came with a strange texture, that year, in England. Woodsmoke curling against the drifting copper skies echoed a more radical burning. In East Anglia two cities had been shelled and bombed and burnt, their skeletons sticking charred fingers into the long sunsets over the flatlands, where the wild geese were already strung out in thin patterns of departure against the flaring sky. It was against their cries, and the cries of the rooks, in the gathering but indecisive winds of October, that England awoke from the mad dream of the war. The Third Army was still fighting in the west towards Bristol, but the disappearance of the martins and the crackle of the wasted fallen leaves, the smoke suddenly acrid in the nostrils, were like heralds announcing the breaking of an enchantment. People awoke to the sober, ordinary, appalling and exhilarating realization that life was going on just the same. The country became preoccupied once more with the plain business of living. It was not simply that the end of the Government was so plainly in sight, which added an element of wonder to everyday life. There was also a certain awe which people felt, that they had allowed themselves to put up with the Government for so long—and a feeling that in seeing the Third Army put it down without losing still more freedom, yet more lives, they had perhaps escaped with less suffering than they deserved. As the year darkened, the country enjoyed a kind of moral springtime—but enjoyed it cautiously, as if the pleasure were stolen, and folk might at any moment be called to account. Only the fact that people were still dying in battles in the west prevented the inevitable lapse into self-righteousness, indignation, and pedantic ingratitude towards Alexander 'Pirate' Waters, the Third Army's general who had started it all by sending his tanks rolling down from the North on to London to depose the Patriotic Front.

So at least it seemed to Captain Mark Lennon, bouncing a jeep across the metal plates that covered the shell holes, past a column of tanks. The fat, ungainly, curiously vulnerable creatures chewed unreflectingly on the scored road as they ground up hill. In the late afternoon the way seemed dark between the tall hedges. Lennon tried not to be distracted by the green light spinning above the windshield, or the whoop of the siren, tried not to think that something might be stuck round the next bend, and tried to imagine that they were driving on the proper side of the road. Dusty soldiers walked in straggling groups on the verges. Most wore their round helmets and camouflage dress untidily but cheerfully, their stubby rifles slung at odd angles. As the tanks slowly overtook them, men laughed and waved at each other, or gave rude signs.

'Reckon that's it,' said Lennon's driver, a large sergeant called George, who seemed constantly to bear on his brow the whole weight of humanity's waywardness and imperfection. He nodded towards some tall chimneys on their left.

Lennon looked. Clutching the heavy windshield, he half stood, looking back at the pick-up following. He jabbed a finger at the building that was emerging above the hedges. The driver behind stuck a thumb in the air. Lennon sat down as fast as he could before George slung the jeep into the drive. On the gate was a sign which read: Darkwood.

Leonard James was waiting, slowly loading a rifle magazine, as they drove up beside his parked vehicle. Apparently casually, his driver was leaning on the bonnet, an automatic rifle cradled up towards the house. It was high, grey, and laden with gables.

'Watcher, Ben,' said Lennon, saluting vaguely as he swung himself out of the jeep. 'What are you doing here so soon?'

'Ah, Mark, a good intelligence officer must be everywhere. As a matter of fact I took a short cut. Just waiting for you to turn up and look over this Victorian pile.'

Behind them the pick-up ground across the gravel and stopped. Soldiers began to climb out.

'Bonzo!' called Lennon. A young, fair lieutenant looked round. 'Bring the black bag, we're going in. And a gas gun.' He turned back to Leonard James. 'Coming in, colonel? After you.'

'Yes, but *you* go in first like a good scout captain, if you please, and make sure we don't all get blown up by some peasant's booby.'

George ambled up from somewhere. 'Even got the 'phone lines still up,' he said in an awed voice. Anything in working order amazed George.

'Quite,' said Lennon. 'Not a shell hole near the place. I bet it's as clean as a whistle. There hasn't been a peasant here for weeks.'

'Well, ha ha, that may be strictly true. But do you know who it belongs to?' enquired James.

'Yeah, it's old Blackbeard's new command post, and it's got to be clean and tidy for when he moves in tonight. Silver all polished and that.'

'Yes, quite. But it also happens to have title deeds. In the name of the Front's Home Secretary.'

'*Really?* What did Gosse do to deserve a place like this?'

'Indeed, my boy. And as a humble CO-3 you would not know what we in CO-2 know. Which is that this morning a patrol of the, er, enemy was picked up but two miles from here. Somewhat off their beaten track. They seemed to be heading this way.'

'Peasants or Guards?'

'Oh, real soldiers, Guards. They stood up very well for themselves. Made quite a mess.'

'And won't talk.'

'I'm afraid there weren't very many left *to* talk. And they are a little exhausted after their set-to, I'm told. But there would seem to be *something* here that is really very dear to the Front. Or the Front's so-called Home Secretary, whichever. Otherwise they wouldn't have sent proper soldiers to poke about the place, would they? So when you go in, look sharp about you.'

'Nobody tells you anything, do they? I thought we were just going to make sure nobody had been pinching the claret. Come on, Bonzo. Let's get on with it.'

There were no traps in the house. Lennon and his expert assistant, Bonzo Edwards, went through its well-proportioned rooms in just over an hour. Lennon called the colonel in to the well-lit, panelled dining room. Soldiers began to move crates and boxes into the house from the vehicles.

'George,' said James to Lennon's sergeant, as he lumbered by. 'Get CO-1 on the radio and tell them they can come when they are ready.'

'Time for a brew-up, Ben?' said Lennon.

'There's some rather nice *madeira* in the cellar,' mused Bonzo Edwards loudly.

'Later, later,' said the colonel. 'Why don't you be mother and make some tea, Lennon?'

Lennon stepped out into the passage towards the kitchen. It was a wide, stone-floored room, now full of the last evening light.

Then he saw the foot. Or rather toecap, of someone's shoe. It was plainly no casually dropped piece of footwear, since it had moved. If it had not moved, he wouldn't have seen it. Lennon promptly began to walk backwards, hardly breaking his stride. The large .45 automatic had never seemed larger, nor so heavy, as he lugged it out. He walked forward again to where he could see the foot. He held the gun in both hands, aimed at where a stomach ought to be, and said: 'Come out of there quick, whoever you are. With your hands on your head. If you don't I'll gas you. I'll count to five, okay?'

'Don't shoot,' said a girl's voice. Not frightened: almost as if to reassure him. He realized how icy his own voice must have been.

The girl stepped out. She was pale, frail, dark-haired, and did not look in the least afraid. Lennon found this assurance somewhat disturbing.

'It's all right,' she said.

'Leonard!' he bawled.

James stepped into the passage, 'Oh, dear me,' he said. He had a gas gun.

'I'm sorry,' pleaded the girl, once a foot, now a prisoner.

'Bonzo!' called James, raising his gun casually. 'Get George and

'Come out of there quick, whoever you are.'

Henry to cover the kitchen, quick! Now, Mark, walk her back in.'

'Stuff that. You cover her.'

'Oh, all right. Come on then, young lady, walk towards me, past the captain, and in that door. Don't muck about or he'll shoot you, and so might I.'

Bonzo Edwards charged out into the passage clutching a submachine gun, sailed straight into the colonel, and jabbed the barrel into his ribs. James gasped and the prisoner blenched.

'Oh, hell,' breathed Lennon. He holstered his pistol and turned grimly to the girl. 'Get by me, and go into the dining-room past those two.'

She moved wearily past him. Edwards amiably pointed the submachine gun into her face. She stopped.

'Mark,' called James, a trifle breathlessly, 'better gas it. Much as her looks will delight the general, she may have less gentle friends.'

He tossed the gun to Lennon, who caught it, pumped it, and fired the bulbous grey cartridge into the kitchen. Then he slammed the door.

'That's going to make dinner late,' remarked Edwards. The girl stared in astonishment.

'Ah, Bonzo, you see, you do have domestic instincts. Now, you'd better take charge of the prisoner and search her. I think that's your department. And do please put that ferocious gun away. You have a perfectly good pistol.'

'Aren't you going to ask her name first?'

'I don't think so,' said James lightly. 'We in intelligence could hardly fail to recognize her. This is Rachel Gosse, daughter of this house. Miss Gosse, this is Lieutenant Barbara Edwards, who will see to your needs—and ours—for the time being.'

'Hullo,' said Rachel Gosse weakly. Her large brown eyes gazed at each of them in turn, as if all three of them were quite mad.

* * * *

Mark Lennon lay on a dusty bed in a back room upstairs, waiting for General Waters to arrive. It had been only in the last few weeks, he reflected, that the war had come home to him, even as it had slipped into some category of normality for the country at large. In Lincolnshire and the Fens, seeing the smoke of shellbursts drift across the flat landscape, staring forgetful over the harsh sea, watching the orange scampering of flame at the base of the pall when they had burnt Peterborough, it had been easier to think how much subtlety of colour and tone one might have absorbed, had one the time, than it was to recognize in those weird bloomings actual smoke and flame, the actual destruction of real English cities under the onrush of Waters's advancing Third Army. But this campaign in the west had shown Lennon the nature of his trade. Waters, infuriated with the hacking, bloody pace of the advance, an entanglement of tiny battles for farmsteads and market towns, had insisted again and again on being driven into the lines. There he would stand, with a chill face, emptying magazine after magazine into some resistant house, or streetcorner, or wood, urging on his soldiers, shouting into a radio, carting ammunition, impervious to the racket or the danger about him. At the same time as Lennon learned to accept what it was in himself that had drawn him to his calling as a soldier, he recognized how Waters had built his relentless, loyal, yet informal, almost obsessively jocular army.

Waters had acquired Third Army not because the Government trusted him, nor because they wanted Third Army to fight, but because he was renowned for getting people to work for him. And work was what the government wanted from its new army. It had been conscripted as a legion of navvies.

Waters's army was, in fact, the invention of the very people it was now fighting, and had come into being as a direct result of the drift to the right that had occurred in British politics over the previous decade and a half. The number of racist and extreme nationalist 'independents' in Parliament had grown until, after one frantic and indecisive general election, there had emerged a misshapen alliance between what had been a conservative party, and the New Right. Known as the Patriotic Front, this grotesque collection of opportunists and out-patients *manqués* gave every indication of using parliamentary power as a stepping stone to absolute power. Once welcomed into Cabinet posts, the New Right dictated the terms of their support—and so dictated the terms of government in Britain.

In many ways Waters represented everything that the government was not. In that light, the reasons why he had overturned a fundamental principle of the British military tradition, and had taken power for himself, were quite clear. Waters was that strange creature, a liberal authoritarian, a successful career soldier who demanded absolute obedience in defending the consitutional freedoms which he cherished. No one could have been more adamant that the army had no place in politics. And the only kind of politics worth having was a freely elected parliamentary democracy, and preferably under a respected constitutional monarch. Waters was completely loyal to the King. On the day he sent Third Army's columns rolling towards London, Waters played the national anthem on the forces' radio and repeated his allegiance to the Crown. At the same time he announced his dedication to the freedom of the press, and renounced any political ambitions of his own once the Front had been ousted. His support of NATO and other international agreements was undeviating. In this way he both isolated the Front at home, and prevented foreign intervention in the war. Thereafter, he took great pleasure in reading the correspondence columns of the national dailies, as Third Army trundled inexorably southward and the Government fled, equally inexorably, into the west.

The military success of Third Army had been due to more than the clandestine training it had had with modern weapons. To begin with, Waters made no secret of his opinion that racism was a vulgarity, beneath the interest of a gentleman. And believing that every soldier under his command was unique, he treated every one as an equal. Then, with a combination of cajolery, extravagant speech, foul language, and the example of his own remorseless energy, Waters began to work on his divisions of dispirited, resentful, and unwilling recruits. Until, their self-respect restored, they had become proud, self-reliant soldiers, glad to be led by their swashbuckling general because they knew that he was equally proud to lead them.

Such things, thought Mark Lennon, hearing the distant yelp of sirens from the general's approaching convoy, were what made his own fascination with carnage and destruction somehow bearable: such things, and such principles, and the hope of freedom.

* * * *

Dinner that evening had an air of slight abandon: after interviewing

Rachel Gosse, Waters introduced her to his staff, and announced that she would be joining them at the table. Conscious of the girl's ambiguous position, no one discussed the war. Instead, Waters contrived to start a conversation on architecture, about which, it was noticed, Rachel knew a great deal. The relaxed way she defended her opinions, and the apparent ease with which she adjusted to being held prisoner in her own family house, soon had Leonard James and Bonzo Edwards trading wisecracks with her on some unrelated subject. Waters's blue eyes twinkled as he presided over the success of his party, helping others to the plain French cooking and offering round the excellent wines. A faint air of euphoria had come over the gathering by the time it was announced that coffee was waiting in the next room.

'Miss Gosse and I will take ours here,' declared the general. 'But I will join you presently. We have an order group at 2200 hours, you will recall, ladies and gentlemen.'

A few half-knowing looks passed around the table, but in a few minutes they were alone, and Alexander Waters was pouring Rachel Gosse a generous brandy.

'So,' he said, leaning back in his chair, and stroking his beard, as he watched her savour the vintage. 'Rachel, it is time to discuss your future.'

She smiled. 'You make it sound like the Facts of Life.'

'Well, and it may be, at that. Your being here presents me with something of a problem. I'm sure you understand that. What I am not really sure about is quite why you came here.'

Rachel looked taken aback. 'But I told you, before.'

'You *said* you wanted to get away from your father. And his, ah, circle.'

'Yes, and everything my parents stand for. It was—like a gesture—only more than that. I wanted to show that someone in their, in their circle, as you put it, wasn't going to be associated with all that—that ugliness.'

'But did you mean to come to *me*?'

'Someone in Third Army was bound to take over Darkwood eventually.'

Waters's eyes did not leave her face as he considered this remark. Then he shrugged. 'One's sense of humour does rather give one away.

I suppose it was obvious that I'd enjoy moving into Sir Geoffrey's rural retreat.'

'If sense of humour is what it really is. But I didn't expect to come face to face with you quite so promptly.'

He shook his head, perplexed. 'But surely you expected to be arrested? You still don't quite seem to realize you are a prisoner.' He paused. 'Why the helpless face?'

'I suppose,' she faltered, 'because I didn't think of it like that. And—I was half-prepared for you to be an ogre, the way they say you are. And not too scrupulous towards defenceless young women. And instead you've been nothing but kind, and thoughtful, and entertaining. But I still half-fear what I seem to have found. What I wanted to find.'

'Your mother might have used the very same words,' sighed Waters. 'Rachel, this is not a haven. You are a prisoner. But—I am going to let you go.'

'What's my mother got to do with it?'

'Don't you want to know where you're going?'

Rachel Gosse stared at him, blinking once or twice.

'I'm sending you back to your father. He sent a detachment of Guards to winkle you out of here before we turned up. He wants you back. I expect he will want to know why you came here in the first place, but I leave that to you to answer.'

'But I came here to get away from—'

'Yes, I know. But there is more to it than that. Someone else in my position might have used you differently. Your defection might have had some value as propaganda. You might have been worth a ransom. Even now you might be a spy. You might.'

'But it's nothing to *do* with any of that. I was trying—' She gave up. 'I don't know. I don't know what to think. And I thought—I thought I was getting to know you.'

'Well, here are some facts. I said there was something more. Now listen. About twenty-five years ago, before I settled on the cavalry as the place I really belonged, I was a humble teacher of history—at your mother's university, as a matter of fact. And indeed your mother was one of my students. Yes, of course, you must know that already. I fell in love with her. Madly. Passionately. I did my best not to let very many people know about it. She was not in love with me, after all.

One did not wish to impose. I liked to imagine that Juliet herself knew nothing of it. But in one or two ways she cheated me—cheated me as a friend. Our friendship wasn't a secret at all. But because of that, her dishonesties were somehow less forgivable than the casual deceits that pass as normal in human intercourse. To think of her still causes me pain, even after so many years. Not least because her own deceit, which was both cruel and uncaring, was a sign that she *did* know. She must have known too that nothing mattered more to me than that she should have what she wanted. That for her sake I would overlook, ignore, put entirely to one side my own feelings for her. And, you know, it was like a pain, an aching. For some form of comfort that I thought she could give. And in doing what she did, she seemed to show that she despised me for it. For both wanting her and being prepared to forgo what I wanted. You look very like her, you know. That dark English beauty. She was less fragile perhaps than you. And, I should like to think, less honest. So you are difficult and dangerous for me to have about. You share your mother's air . . . of the victim. More than anyone, you renew that ancient, foolish, obsessive pain.'

Waters stopped, got up, and walked across the room. Staring at the floor under her lashes, Rachel said: 'Why don't you just let me go? Or send me north? You know I don't have any reason to go west. And obviously I don't want to stay here either—not if you don't want me.'

Waters turned sharply. 'Well, that raises some interesting questions, doesn't it? If you had wanted to go north, you should have gone straight. Under another name. Vanished. Not left tracks or messages or whatever it was you did leave, big enough for a snatch squad of Guards to get killed trying to follow them. And as for staying *here*—'

He flung out a hand in anger. Then, collecting himself, paced slowly back to his chair.

'Yes, of course,' he even gave a crooked smile, 'I could give in to wild fantasies. So much would be reconciled. So many old voices silenced. And the irony, the strange justice of it would please me. But there is a way in which you will free me of that pain, kinder and more cruel that the way in which you *could* free me. And I am not going to give you the chance to refuse.'

She looked up, into his face. 'Whatever you had suggested, I probably wouldn't have refused,' she said in a clear voice.

'Then the way I choose to send you home will be all the more poignant,' answered Waters harshly. His voice was like an arm, fending her off. They were silent for a time. Then the girl, pushing away her cold coffee, asked wearily:

'What are you going to do, then?'

'It will be put about,' he said, slowly twirling his brandy, 'that, perhaps rather than be ransomed or kept prisoner, you bought your freedom. In the most obvious way that a young woman of your attractions might. We will have the good taste not to go into details when we let this rumour escape. Everything will depend on what people care to imagine. In the eyes of your father and his unspeakable cronies, I will appear to be the degenerate lecher of mongrel blood which they already believe me to be. The troops of Third Army will be delighted at my irrepressible opportunism, my contempt for prudence, and will rejoice in the ways of Alexander Pirate Waters. And the country at large will either swallow or spurn the story, each according to his prejudice. But *I* will have the satisfaction of knowing that I did not use you as a pawn of the war. I shall also be gratified by the knowledge that I *could* have demanded your body as the price of your freedom. I may allow myself to speculate that in any case you might have offered it. And not for such a freedom as you are about to be given. In fact, it does not matter that I have enjoyed no more than your company at dinner. Another wound will still be healed. And I shall have laid your mother's ghost. Lord, to be free of that torment! Even though—' his voice dropped '—I realize that you do not wish to be sent out into the dark night, onto the edge of a battlefield, to find your cold way home. But I send my love to your mother. Hollow—dead—as that now is. Tell her the truth if you like.'

By the time he finished speaking, there seemed hardly anything left of the man Waters. There was only a voice and a hard purpose, hypnotically fused together. Perhaps the girl felt this. Certainly, when he stopped, there was a tranced silence.

Eventually she said: 'Then there's nothing more to discuss. You leave me no way out.'

Waters looked at her distantly, as if no longer recognizing who she was. 'You sound like your mother again.'

'What else did you expect?' She was helpless, near tears, even.

Waters held her gaze, and slowly shook his head. Quietly he said, 'No, no. That won't do. I am not a hero, Rachel. I offer no shelter from the storm. And it is no good appealing to me. Everyone does what he or she chooses to do, nothing less. You came here of your own free will. You might have known what would come of it.'

'Yes,' she blinked, and swallowed. 'My mother said you had been kind to her.'

Then Rachel Gosse shrugged, and lowered her eyes, to look into the dark pattern of the carpet.

★ ★ ★ ★

According to reports that were later published by Fleet Street, the daughter of the former Patriotic Front's Home Secretary had been found by a Third Army patrol behind their lines, and on being taken to General Waters, had bought her freedom with the only currency at her disposal. The *Guardian* raked up some evidence from among the county set that Miss Gosse was by no means averse to such pastimes, but commented that whatever had passed between the young lady and the general, it was preferable to the sordidness of a ransom demand, 'a terrorist tactic which would, so to speak, make an odd bedfellow with the General's stated principles and his restrained, even liberal, conduct of the war so far.' The *Telegraph*, on the other hand, condemned Waters as a brute and a savage, and portrayed Rachel Gosse as a bruised and abused heroine, fortunate indeed to find her way back to the bosom of her family. However, it was *The Times'* leader which found its way into the folklore of every unit in Third Army. In a long article reviewing the course of the war, *The Times* remarked that whichever of the two had initiated such a strange bargain, 'the fact remains that even if he were surrounded by an entire harem, General Waters would still be a better man for the country than the whole of the Patriotic Front under a cold shower'.

But no one suggested that in the first place Rachel Gosse had been trying to escape from her parents, or that she might have been sorry to get away from the general who was so intent on destroying everything that the Gosses stood for.

THE PIT AND THE PENDULUM

Edgar Allan Poe

When the power of the Spanish Inquisition was at its height, it was a dangerous thing for a man to voice his opinions too loudly if they did not match exactly with the teachings of the Church. For the task of the Inquisition was to seek out and punish anyone who might be considered a heretic—and the tribunal showed little mercy. Trials were conducted in secret, and suspected heretics were often tortured until they confessed their guilt. Those who refused to confess were imprisoned or condemned to death by burning, a sentence which was executed at a ceremony known as an auto-da-fé.

I was sick—sick unto death with that long agony; and when they at length unbound me, and I was permitted to sit, I felt that my senses were leaving me. The sentence—the dread sentence of death—was the last of distinct accentuation which reached my ears. After that, the sound of the inquisitorial voices seemed merged in one dreamy indeterminate hum. This only for a brief period; for presently I heard no more. Yet, for a while, I saw; but with how terrible an exaggeration! I saw the lips of the black-robed judges. They appeared to me white—whiter than the sheet upon which I trace these words—and thin even to grotesqueness; thin with the intensity of their expression of firmness—of immovable resolution—of stern contempt of human torture. . . . And then my vision fell upon the seven tall candles upon the table. At first they wore the aspect of charity, and seemed white slender angels who would save me; but then, all at once, there came a most deadly nausea over my spirit, and I felt every fibre in my frame thrill as if

I had touched the wire of a galvanic battery, while the angel forms became meaningless spectres, with heads of flame, and I saw that from them there would be no help. And then there stole into my fancy, like a rich musical note, the thought of what sweet rest there must be in the grave. The thought came gently and stealthily, and it seemed long before it attained full appreciation; but just as my spirit came at length properly to feel and entertain it, the figures of the judges vanished, as if magically, from before me; the tall candles sank into nothingness; their flames went out utterly; the blackness of darkness supervened; all sensations appeared swallowed up in a mad rushing descent as of the soul into Hades. Then silence, and stillness, and night were the universe. . . .

★ ★ ★ ★

So far, I had not opened my eyes. I felt that I lay upon my back, unbound. I reached out my hand, and it fell heavily upon something damp and hard. There I suffered it to remain for many minutes, while I strove to imagine where and *what* I could be. I longed, yet dared not to employ my vision. I dreaded the first glance at objects around me. It was not that I feared to look upon things horrible, but that I grew aghast lest there should be *nothing* to see. At length, with a wild desperation at heart, I quickly unclosed my eyes. My worst thoughts, then, were confirmed. The blackness of eternal night encompassed me. I struggled for breath. The intensity of the darkness seemed to oppress and stifle me. The atmosphere was intolerably close. I still lay quietly, and made effort to exercise my reason. I brought to mind the inquisitorial proceedings, and attempted from that point to deduce my real condition. The sentence had passed; and it appeared to me that a very long interval of time had since elapsed. Yet not for a moment did I suppose myself actually dead. Such a supposition, notwithstanding what we read in fiction, is altogether inconsistent with real existence—but where and in what state was I? The condemned to death, I knew, perished usually at the *autos-da-fé*, and one of these had been held on the very night of the day of my trial. Had I been remanded to my dungeon, to await the next sacrifice, which would not take place for many months? This I at once saw could not be.

Victims had been in immediate demand. Moreover, my dungeon, as well as all the condemned cells at Toledo, had stone floors, and light was not altogether excluded.

A fearful idea now suddenly drove the blood in torrents upon my heart, and for a brief period I once more relapsed into insensibility. Upon recovering, I at once started to my feet, trembling convulsively in every fibre. I thrust my arms wildly above and around me in all directions. I felt nothing; yet dreaded to move a step, lest I should be impeded by the walls of a *tomb*. Perspiration burst from every pore, and stood in cold big beads upon my forehead. The agony of suspense grew at length intolerable, and I cautiously moved forward, with my arms extended, and my eyes straining from their sockets, in the hope of catching some faint ray of light. I proceeded for many paces; but still all was blackness and vacancy. I breathed more freely. It seemed evident that mine was not, at least, the most hideous of fates.

And now, as I still continued to step cautiously onward, there came thronging upon my recollection a thousand vague rumours of the horrors of Toledo. Of the dungeons there had been strange things narrated—fables I had always deemed them—but yet strange, and too ghastly to repeat, save in a whisper. Was I left to perish of starvation in this subterranean world of darkness; or what fate, perhaps even more fearful, awaited me? That the result would be death, and a death of more than customary bitterness, I knew too well the character of my judges to doubt. The mode and the hour were all that occupied or distracted me.

My outstretched hands at length encountered some solid obstruction. It was a wall, seemingly of stone masonry—very smooth, slimy, and cold. I followed it up, stepping with all the careful distrust with which certain antique narratives had inspired me. This process, however, afforded me no means of ascertaining the dimensions of my dungeon; as I might make its circuit, and return to the point whence I set out, without being aware of the fact; so perfectly uniform seemed the wall. I therefore sought the knife which had been in my pocket, when led into the inquisitorial chamber, but it was gone; my clothes had been exchanged for a wrapper of coarse serge. I had thought of forcing the blade in some minute crevice of the masonry, so as to identify my point of departure. The difficulty, nevertheless, was but trivial; although, in the disorder of my fancy, it seemed at first insuperable. I tore a part of the hem from the robe and placed a fragment at full length, and at right angles to the wall. In groping my way around the prison, I could not fail to encounter this rag upon completing the circuit. So, at least, I thought; but I had not counted upon the extent of the dungeon, or upon my own weakness. The ground was moist and slippery. I staggered onward for some time, when I stumbled and fell. My excessive fatigue induced me to remain prostrate; and sleep soon overtook me as I lay.

Upon awaking, and stretching forth an arm, I found beside me a loaf and a pitcher with water. I was too much exhausted to reflect upon this circumstance, but ate and drank with avidity. Shortly afterward I resumed my tour around the prison, and, with much toil, came at last upon the fragment of the serge. Up to the period when I fell, I had counted fifty-two paces, and, upon resuming my walk, I had counted forty-eight more—when I arrived at the rag. There were in all, then, a hundred paces; and, admitting two paces to the yard, I presumed the dungeon to be fifty yards in circuit. I had met, however, with many angles in the wall, and thus I could form no guess at the shape of the vault; for vault I could not help supposing it to be.

I had little object—certainly no hope—in these researches; but a vague curiosity prompted me to continue them. Quitting the wall, I resolved to cross the area of the enclosure. At first, I proceeded with extreme caution, for the floor, although seemingly of solid material, was treacherous with slime. At length, however, I took courage, and did not hesitate to step firmly—endeavouring to cross in as direct a line as possible. I had advanced some ten or twelve paces in this manner, when the remnant of the torn hem of my robe became entangled between my legs. I stepped on it, and fell violently on my face.

In the confusion attending my fall, I did not immediately apprehend a somewhat startling circumstance, which yet, in a few seconds afterward, and while I still lay prostrate, arrested my attention. It was this: my chin rested upon the floor of the prison, but my lips, and the upper portion of my head, although seemingly at a less elevation than the chin, touched nothing. At the same time, my forehead seemed bathed in a clammy vapour, and the peculiar smell of decayed fungus arose to my nostrils. I put forward my arm, and shuddered to find that I had fallen at the very brink of a circular pit, whose extent, of course, I had no means of ascertaining at the moment. Groping about the masonry just below the margin, I succeeded in dislodging a small fragment, and let it fall into the abyss. For many seconds I hearkened to its reverberations as it dashed against the sides of the chasm in its descent. At length, there was a sullen plunge into water, succeeded by loud echoes. At the same moment, there came a sound resembling the quick opening, and as rapid closing of a door overhead, while a faint gleam of light flashed suddenly through the gloom, and as suddenly faded away.

I saw clearly the doom which had been prepared for me, and congratulated myself upon the timely accident of which I had escaped. Another step before my fall, and the world had seen me no more. And the death just avoided was of that very character which I had regarded as fabulous and frivolous in the tales respecting the Inquisition. To the victims of its tyranny, there was the choice of death with its direst physical agonies, or death with its most hideous moral horrors. I had been reserved for the latter. By long suffering my nerves had been unstrung, until I trembled at the sound of my own voice, and had become in every respect a fitting subject for the species of torture which awaited me.

Shaking in every limb, I groped my way back to the wall—resolving there to perish rather than risk the terrors of the wells, of which my imagination now pictured many in various positions about the dungeon. In other conditions of mind, I might have had courage to end my misery at once, by a plunge into one of these abysses; but now I was the veriest of cowards. Neither could I forget what I had read of these pits—that the *sudden* extinction of life formed no part of their most horrible plan.

Agitation of spirit kept me awake for many long hours; but at length I again slumbered. Upon arousing, I found by my side, as before, a loaf and a pitcher of water. A burning thirst consumed me, and I emptied the vessel at a draught. It must have been drugged—for scarcely had I drunk, before I became irresistibly drowsy. A deep sleep fell upon me—a sleep like that of death. How long it lasted, of course, I know not; but when, once again, I unclosed my eyes, the objects around me were visible. By a wild sulphurous lustre, the origin of which I could not at first determine, I was enabled to see the extent and aspect of the prison.

In its size I had been greatly mistaken. The whole circuit of its walls did not exceed twenty-five yards. For some minutes this fact occasioned me a world of vain trouble; vain indeed—for what could be of less importance, under the terrible circumstances which environed me, than the mere dimensions of my dungeon? But my soul took a wild interest in trifles, and I busied myself in endeavours to account for the error I had committed in my measurement. The truth at length flashed upon me. In my first attempt at exploration I had counted fifty-two paces, up to the period when I fell; I must have then been within a pace or two of the fragment of serge; in fact, I had nearly performed the circuit of the vault. I then slept—and, upon awaking, I must have returned upon my steps—thus supposing the circuit nearly double what it actually was. My confusion of mind prevented me from observing that I began my tour with the wall to the left, and ended it with the wall to the right.

I had been deceived, too, in respect to the shape of the enclosure. In feeling my way, I had found many angles, and thus deduced an idea of great irregularity; so potent is the effect of total darkness upon one arousing from lethargy or sleep! The angles were simply those of a few slight depressions, or niches, at odd intervals. The general shape of the prison was square. What I had taken for masonry seemed now to be iron, or some other metal, in huge plates, whose sutures or joints occasioned the depression. The entire surface of this metallic enclosure was rudely daubed in all the hideous and repulsive devices to which the charnel superstition of the monks has given rise. The figures of fiends in aspects of menace, with skeleton forms, and other more really fearful images, overspread and disfigured the walls. I observed that the outlines of the monstrosities were sufficiently distinct, but that the colours seemed faded and blurred, as if from the effects of a damp atmosphere. I now noticed the floor, too, which was of stone. In the centre yawned the circular pit from whose jaws I had escaped; but it was the only one in the dungeon.

All this I saw indistinctly and by much effort—for my personal condition had been greatly changed during slumber. I now lay upon my back, and at full length, on a species of low framework of wood.

To this I was securely bound by a long strap resembling a surcingle. It passed in many convolutions about my limbs and body, leaving at liberty only my head and my left arm to such extent, that I could, by dint of much exertion, supply myself with food from an earthen dish which lay by my side on the floor. I saw, to my horror, that the pitcher had been removed. I say, to my horror—for I was consumed with intolerable thirst. This thirst it appeared to be the design of my persecutors to stimulate—for the food in the dish was meat pungently seasoned.

Looking upward, I surveyed the ceiling of my prison. It was some thirty or forty feet overhead, and constructed much as the side walls. In one of its panels a very singular figure riveted my whole attention. It was the painted figure of Time as he is commonly represented, save that, in lieu of a scythe, he held what, at a casual glance, I supposed to be the pictured image of a huge pendulum, such as we see on antique clocks. There was something, however, in the appearance of this machine which caused me to regard it more attentively. While I gazed directly upward at it (for its position was immediately over my own), I fancied that I saw it in motion. In an instant afterwards the fancy was confirmed. Its sweep was brief, and, of course, slow. I watched it for some minutes, somewhat in fear, but more in wonder. Wearied at length with observing its dull movement, I turned my eyes upon the other objects in the cell.

A slight noise attracted my notice, and looking to the floor, I saw several enormous rats traversing it. They had issued from the well, which lay just within view to my right. Even then, while I gazed, they came up in troops, hurriedly, with ravenous eyes, allured by the scent of the meat. From this it required much effort and attention to scare them away.

It might have been half an hour, perhaps even an hour (for I could take but imperfect note of time), before I again cast my eyes upward. What I then saw, confounded and amazed me. The sweep of the pendulum had increased in extent by nearly a yard. As a natural consequence, its velocity was also much greater. But what mainly disturbed me, was the idea that it had perceptibly *descended*. I now observed—with what horror it is needless to say—that its nether extremity was formed of a crescent of glittering steel, about a foot in length from horn to horn; the horns upward, and the under edge evidently as keen as that of a razor. Like a razor also, it seemed massy and heavy, tapering from the edge into a solid and broad structure above. It was appended to a weighty rod of brass, and the whole *hissed* as it swung through the air.

I could no longer doubt the doom prepared for me by monkish ingenuity in torture. My cognizance of the pit had become known to the inquisitorial agents—*the pit*, whose horrors had been destined for so bold a recusant as myself—*the pit*, typical of hell, and regarded by rumour as the Ultima Thule of all their punishments. The plunge into this pit I had avoided by the merest of accidents, and I knew that surprise, or entrapment into torment, formed an important portion of all the grotesquerie of these dungeon deaths. Having failed to fall, it was no part of the demon plan to hurl me into the abyss; and thus (there being no alternative) a different and a milder destruction awaited me. Milder! I half smiled in my agony as I thought of such application of such a term.

What boots it to tell of the long, long hours of horror more than mortal, during which I counted the rushing oscillations of the steel! Inch by inch—line by line—with a descent only appreciable at intervals that seemed ages—down and still down it came. Days passed—it might have been that many days passed—ere it swept so closely over me as to fan me with its acrid breath. The odour of the sharp steel forced itself into my nostrils. I prayed—I wearied heaven with my prayer for its more speedy descent. I grew frantically mad, and struggled to force myself upward against the sweep of the fearful scimitar. And then I fell suddenly calm, and lay smiling at the glittering death, as a child at some rare bauble.

There was another interval of utter insensibility; it was brief; for, upon again lapsing into life, there had been no perceptible descent in the pendulum. But it might have been long—for I knew there were demons who took note of my swoon, and who could have arrested the vibration at pleasure. Upon my recovery, too. I felt very—oh, inexpressibly—sick and weak, as if through long inanition. Even amid the agonies of that period the human nature craved for food. With painful effort I outstretched my left arm as far as my bonds permitted, and took possession of the small remnant which had been spared me by the rats. As I put a portion of it within my lips, there rushed to my mind a half-formed thought of joy—of hope. Yet what business had *I* with hope? It was, as I say, a half-formed thought—man has many such, which are never completed. I felt that it was of joy—of hope; but I felt also that it had perished in its formation. In vain I struggled to perfect—to regain it. Long suffering had nearly annihilated all my ordinary powers of mind. I was an imbecile—an idiot.

The vibration of the pendulum was at right angles to my length. I saw that the crescent was designed to cross the region of the heart. It would fray the serge of my robe—it would return and repeat its operations—again—and again. Notwithstanding its terrifically wide sweep (some thirty feet or more), and the hissing vigour of its descent, sufficient to sunder these very walls of iron, still the fraying of my robe would be all that, for several minutes, it would accomplish. And at this thought I paused. I dared not go farther than this reflection. I dwelt upon it with a pertinacity of attention—as if, in so dwelling, I could arrest *here* the descent of the steel. I forced myself to ponder upon the sound of the crescent as it should pass across the garment—upon the peculiar thrilling sensation which the friction of cloth produces on the nerves. I pondered upon all this frivolity until my teeth were on edge.

Down—steadily down it crept. I took a frenzied pleasure in contrasting its downward with its lateral velocity. To the right—to the left—far and wide—with the shriek of a damned spirit! to my heart, with the stealthy pace of the tiger! I alternately laughed and howled, as the one or the other idea grew predominant.

Down—certainly, relentlessly down! It vibrated within three inches of my bosom! I struggled violently—furiously—to free my left arm. This was free only from the elbow to the hand. I could reach the latter, from the platter beside me, to my mouth, with great effort, but no farther. Could I have broken the fastenings above my elbow, I would have seized and attempted to arrest the pendulum. I might as well have attempted to arrest an avalanche!

Down—still unceasingly—still inevitably down! I gasped and struggled at each vibration. I shrunk convulsively at its every sweep. My eyes followed its outward or upward whirls with the eagerness of the most unmeaning despair; they closed themselves spasmodically at the descent, although death would have been a relief, oh, how unspeakable! Still I quivered in every nerve to think how slight a sinking of the machinery would precipitate that keen, glistening axe upon my bosom. It was *hope* that prompted the nerve to quiver—the frame to shrink. It was *hope*—the hope that triumphs on the rack—that whispers to the death-condemned even in the dungeons of the Inquisition.

I saw that ten or twelve vibrations would bring the steel in actual contact with my robe—and with this observation there suddenly came over my spirit all the keen, collected calmness of despair. For the first time during many hours—or perhaps days—I *thought*. It now occurred to me, that the bandage, or surcingle, which enveloped me, was *unique*. It was tied by no separate cord. The first stroke of the razor-like crescent athwart any portion of the band, would so detach it that it might be unwound from my person by means of my left hand. But how fearful, in that case, the proximity of the steel! The result of the slightest struggle, how deadly! Was it likely, moreover, that the minions of the torturer had not foreseen and provided for this possibility? Was it probable that the bandage crossed my bosom in the track of the pendulum? Dreading to find my faint, and, as it seemed, my last hope frustrated, I so far elevated my head as to obtain a distinct view of my breast. The surcingle enveloped my limbs and body close in all directions—*save in the path of the destroying crescent.*

Scarcely had I dropped my head back into its original position, when there flashed upon my mind what I cannot better describe than as the unformed half of that idea of deliverance to which I have previously alluded, and of which a moiety only floated indeterminately through my brain when I raised food to my burning lips. The whole thought was now present—feeble, scarcely sane, scarcely definite—but still entire. I proceeded at once, with the nervous energy of despair, to attempt its execution.

For many hours the immediate vicinity of the low framework upon which I lay had been literally swarming with rats. They were wild, bold, ravenous—their red eyes glaring upon me as if they waited but for motionlessness on my part to make me their prey. 'To what food,' I thought, 'have they been accustomed in the well?'

They had devoured, in spite of all my efforts to prevent them, all but a small remnant of the contents of the dish. I had fallen into an habitual see-saw, or wave of the hand, about the platter; and at length the unconscious uniformity of the movement deprived it of effect. In their voracity, the vermin frequently fastened their sharp fangs in my fingers. With the particles of the oily and spicy viand which now remained, I thoroughly rubbed the bandage wherever I could reach it; then, raising my hand from the floor, I lay breathlessly still.

At first, the ravenous animals were startled and terrified at the change—at the cessation of movement. They shrank alarmedly back; many sought the well. But this was only for a moment. I had not counted in vain upon their voracity. Observing that I remained without motion, one or two of the boldest leaped upon the framework, and smelt at the surcingle. This seemed the signal for a general rush. Forth from the well they hurried in fresh troops. They clung to the wood—they overran it, and leaped in hundreds upon my person. The measured movements of the pendulum disturbed them not at all. Avoiding its strokes, they busied themselves with the anointed bandage. They pressed—they swarmed upon me in ever accumulating heaps. They writhed upon my throat; their cold lips sought my own; I was half stifled by their thronging pressure; disgust, for which the world has no name, swelled my bosom, and chilled, with a heavy clamminess, my heart. Yet one minute, and I felt that the struggle would be over. Plainly I perceived the loosening of the bandage. I knew that in more than one place it must be already severed. With a more than human resolution I lay *still*.

Nor had I erred in my calculations—nor had I endured in vain. I at length felt that I was *free*. The surcingle hung in ribands from my body. But the stroke of the pendulum already pressed upon my bosom. It had divided the serge of the robe. It had cut through the linen beneath. Twice again it swung, and a sharp sense of pain shot through every nerve. But the moment of escape had arrived. At a wave of my hand my deliverers hurried tumultuously away. With a steady movement—cautious, sidelong, shrinking, and slow—I slid from the embrace of the bandage and beyond the reach of the scimitar. For the moment, at least, *I was free*.

Free!—and in the grasp of the Inquisition! I had scarcely stepped from my wooden bed or horror upon the stone floor of the prison,

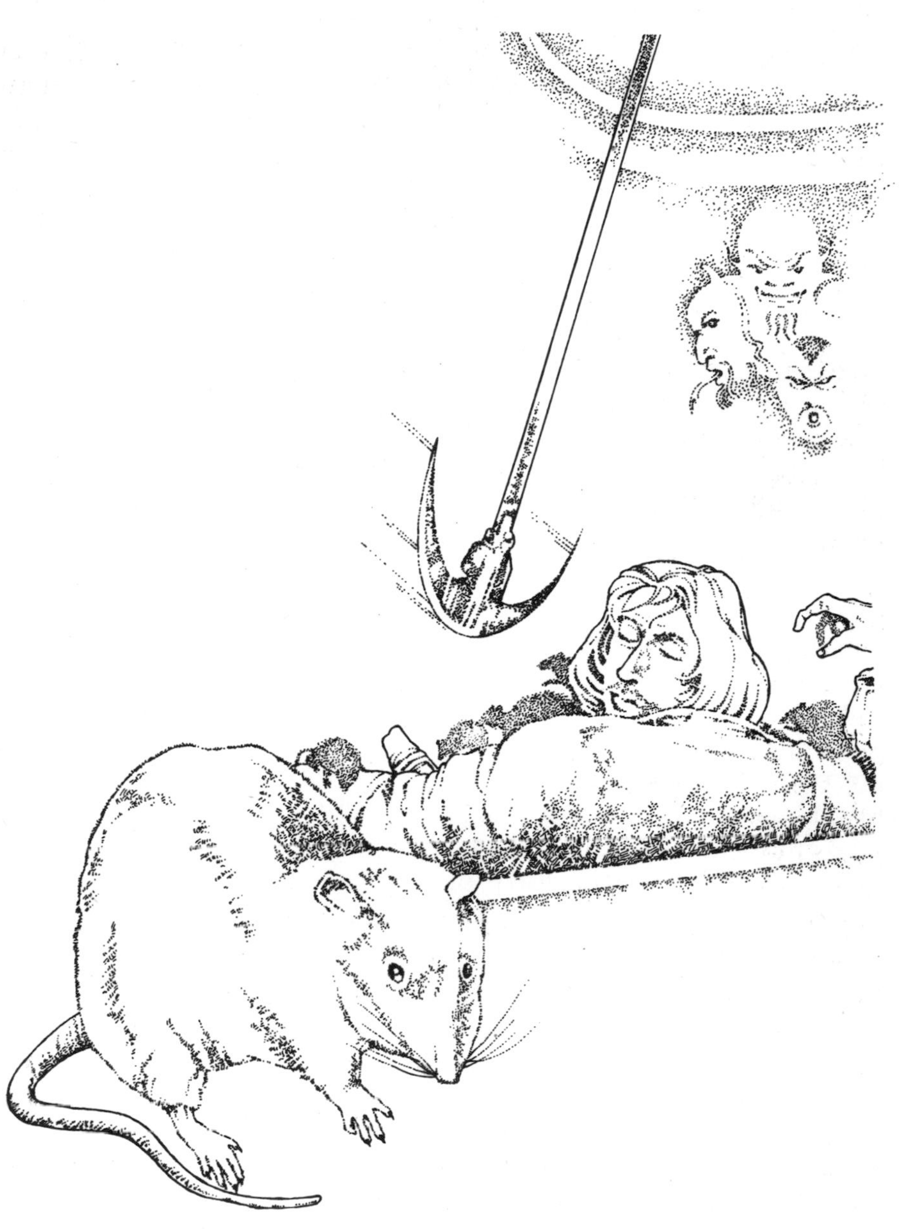

They were wild, bold, ravenous rats.

when the motion of the hellish machine ceased, and I beheld it drawn up, by some invisible force, through the ceiling. This was a lesson which I took deperately to heart. My every motion was undoubtedly watched. Free!—I had escaped death in one form of agony, to be delivered unto worse than death in some other. With that thought I rolled my eyes nervously around on the barriers of iron that hemmed me in. Something unusual—some change which, at first, I could not appreciate distinctly—it was obvious, had taken place in the apartment. For many minutes of a dreamy and trembling abstraction, I busied myself in vain, unconnected conjecture. During this period, I became aware, for the first time, of the origin of the sulphurous light which illumined the cell. It proceeded from a fissure, about half an inch in width, extending entirely around the prison at the base of the walls, which thus appeared, and were completely separated from the floor. I endeavoured, but of course in vain, to look through the aperture.

As I arose from the attempt, the mystery of the alteration in the chamber broke at once upon my understanding. I have observed that, although the outlines of the figures upon the walls were sufficiently distinct, yet the colours seemed blurred and indefinite. These colours had now assumed, and were momentarily assuming, a startling and most intense brilliancy, that gave to the spectral and fiendish portraitures an aspect that might have thrilled even firmer nerves than my own. Demon eyes, of a wild and ghastly vivacity, glared upon me in a thousand directions, where none had been visible before, and gleamed with the lurid lustre of a fire that I could not force my imagination to regard as unreal.

Unreal! Even while I breathed there came to my nostrils the breath of the vapour of heated iron! A suffocating odour pervaded the prison! A deeper glow settled each moment in the eyes that glared at my agonies! A richer tint of crimson diffused itself over the pictured horrors of blood. I panted! I gasped for breath! There could be no doubt of the design of my tormentors—oh! most unrelenting! oh! most demoniac of men! I shrank from the glowing metal to the centre of the cell. Amid the thought of the fiery destruction that impended, the idea of the coolness of the well came over my soul like balm. I rushed to its deadly brink. I threw my straining vision below. The glare from the enkindled roof illumined its inmost recesses. Yet, for a wild moment, did my spirit refuse to comprehend the meaning of what I saw. At length it forced—it wrestled its way into my soul—it burned itself in upon my shuddering reason. Oh! for a voice to speak!—oh! horror! —oh! any horror but this! With a shriek, I rushed from the margin, and buried my face in my hands—weeping bitterly.

The heat rapidly increased, and once again I looked up, shuddering as with a fit of the ague. There had been a second change in the cell—and now the change was obviously in the *form*. As before, it was in vain that I at first endeavoured to appreciate or understand what was taking place. But not long was I left in doubt. The inquisitorial vengeance had been hurried by my twofold escape, and there was to be no more dallying with the King of Terrors. The room had been square. I saw that two of its iron angles were now acute—two, consequently, obtuse. The fearful difference quickly increased with a low rumbling or moaning sound. In an instant the apartment had shifted its form into that of a lozenge. But the alteration stopped not here—I neither hoped nor desired it to stop. I could have clasped the red walls to my bosom as a garment of eternal peace. 'Death,' I said, 'any death but that of the pit!' Fool! might I not have known that *into the pit* it was the object of the burning iron to urge me? Could I resist its glow? or even if that, could I withstand its pressure? And now, flatter and flatter grew the lozenge, with a rapidity that left me no time for comtemplation. Its centre, and of course, its greatest width, came just over the yawning gulf. I shrank back—but the closing walls pressed me resistlessly onward. At length for my scared and writhing body there was no longer an inch of foothold on the firm floor of the prison. I struggled no more, but the agony of my soul found vent in one loud, long, and final scream of despair. I felt that I tottered upon the brink—I averted my eyes—

There was a discordant hum of human voices! There was a loud blast as of many trumpets! There was a harsh grating as of a thousand thunders! The fiery walls rushed back! An outstretched arm caught my own as I fell, fainting, into the abyss. It was that of General Lasalle. The French army had entered Toledo. The Inquisition was in the hands of its enemies.

LORD NITHSDALE'S ESCAPE

John Buchan

The first of the great Jacobite rebellions, that of 1715, was grossly mismanaged from the start. The invasion of England by the Scottish Catholic lords and the Northumbrian Jacobites came to a dismal close at Preston, and the Tower of London was soon full of exalted personages —the English Earl of Derwentwater, who was a grandson of Charles II, and the Scottish Earls of Wintoun, Nithsdale, and Carnwath, and Lord Kenmure, who was head of the Galloway Gordons. The trial of the Jacobite lords was not a masterpiece of English justice. The method followed was impeachment, and it was clear from the start that with a Protestant House of Commons Catholic rebels had no kind of chance. Without proper proof they were condemned—a political, rather than a legal verdict. They were advised to plead guilty, which as it turned out was an unwise course, for thereby they trusted their lives to the Crown and not to the English law, and King George's Government were determined to make an example of them as a matter of policy. Wintoun alone refused to plead.

But the people of England were more merciful than their Government, and the popular feeling in favour of leniency was so strong that Walpole was unable to send all the lords to the scaffold. For Derwentwater there could be no mercy; he was too near in blood to the royal house. Nithsdale and Kenmure were also marked for death, partly because they were devouter Catholics than the others, and partly because of their great power in the Lowlands. On Thursday, 23 February, 1716, the Lord Chancellor signed the warrants for the execution on the Saturday.

Derwentwater and Kenmure duly lost their heads, and two famous houses were brought to ruin. But when the guards arrived to summon Nithsdale to the scaffold they found that he was gone. This is the story of his escape.

* * * *

The Countess of Nithsdale had been Lady Winifred Herbert, the youngest daughter of the first Marquis of Powis. At the time she was twenty-six years of age, a slim young woman with reddish hair and pale blue eyes. Her family had always been Catholic and Royalist, and she had shown herself one of the most ardent of Jacobite ladies.

When the news came of the rout at Preston she was at Terregles, the home of the Maxwells in Nithsdale. She realized at once that her husband could expect no mercy, and that his death must follow his imprisonment as certainly as night follows day. It was a bitter January, with snowdrifts on every road. Without wasting an hour she set off for the south after burning incriminating papers. Her only attendant was a Welsh girl called Evans, from the Powis estates, who had been her maid since childhood.

The two women and a groom rode through the wintry country to Newcastle, where they took the coach for York. Presently the coach stuck in the snow and word came that all the roads were blocked. But by offering a large sum Lady Nithsdale managed to hire horses, and pushed on into the Midlands. The little company suffered every kind of disaster, but the lady's resolute spirit overcame them all, and after some days of weary travel they reached London.

Lady Nithsdale went straight to some of the Scottish great ladies, such as the Duchess of Buccleuch and the Duchess of Montrose, and heard from them that the worst might be expected. She realized that no appeal could save the prisoner, and that, unless he could break bar and bolt, in a week she would be a widow. The first step was to get admission to the Tower. Walpole refused to let her see her husband unless she was prepared to share his captivity to the end. She declined the condition, for she understood that if she was to do anything she must be free. At last she succeeded in bribing the keepers, and found herself in her husband's chamber. As she looked round she saw that there was no chance of an ordinary escape. One high barred window gave on the ramparts and Water Lane, and a sentry was on guard in front. If Lord Nithsdale were to leave the Tower he must leave it by the door. That in turn was stongly guarded. A halberdier stood outside and two sentries with fixed bayonets, and the stairs and the outer door were equally well held. Force was out of the question. The only hope lay in ingenuity.

The weak part of any prison is to be found in the human warders, more especially in a place so strong as the Tower, where the ordinary avenues of escape are few and difficult. The Lieutenant, trusting in his walls, was inclined to be negligent. The prison rules were often disregarded, and the wives and children of the officials wandered about the passages at will. This gave Lady Nithsdale her plan. She proposed to her husband to dress him up in cap and skirt and false curls and pass him as a woman through the soldiers. Very soon she had worked out the details. She had women friends who would assist: a Miss Hilton, and the landlady, Mrs Mills, at her lodging in Drury Lane. The latter was tall and inclined to be stout, and a riding-hood that fitted her would fit Lord Nithsdale, while a red wig would counterfeit Mrs Mill's hair. The prisoner's black eyebrows could be painted out, his chin shaved and his skin rouged.

Lord Nithsdale stubbornly refused. The scheme seemed to him crazy. How could a stalwart soldier with a rugged face and a martial stride imitate any woman? He might do something with a sword in his hand, but, raddled and painted, he would only be a laughing-stock. Far better let his wife get a petition from him placed in the royal hands. There might be some hope in that.

Lady Nithsdale pretended to agree, though she knew well that the King's clemency was a broken reed. For George had given his strict orders that no petition from Lord Nithsdale should be received, and she found her friends very unwilling to disobey the King and act as intermediary. Her only hope was to see George himself; so she dressed herself in deep black, and accompanied by Miss Hilton, who knew the King by sight, went to Court. They reached the room between the King's apartment and the main drawing-room, and when George appeared she flung herself before him. 'I am the wretched Countess of Nithsdale,' she cried. The King stepped back, refusing to take the petition; but she caught him by the skirt of his coat and poured out her story in French. George lost his temper, but she would not let go, and suffered herself to be dragged along the floor to the drawing-room door. There the officials unclasped her fingers and released his angry Majesty.

Lord Nithsdale now turned his hopes to the House of Lords. The Countess went from peer to peer; but once again she failed. Lord Pembroke, indeed, who was a kinsman, spoke in favour of the prisoner, but the thing was hopeless from the start. Nithsdale was utterly intractable and impenitent, and would never beg for his life.

Her husband's counsels having failed, it remained to follow her own. She drove to the Tower and told all the guards and keepers that Lord Nithsdale's last petition to the House of Lords had been favourably received, and that His Majesty was about to listen to their prayer. The officials congratulated her, for she had made herself very popular amongst them, and their friendliness was increased by her gifts. But to her husband she told the plain truth. The last moment had come. Next day was Friday, when the King would answer the petition. If he refused, as he was certain to do, on Saturday the prisoner would go to the scaffold.

On that Friday morning she completed her plans with Mrs Mills, and as the January dusk drew in Miss Hilton joined them in Drury Lane and the details were finally settled. Miss Hilton was to be a friend, 'Mrs Catherine', and Mrs Mills another friend, 'Mrs Betty'. With the maid Evans all three would drive to the Tower, where Evans would wait inconspicuously near the Lieutenant's door, and the other three women would go to the earl's chamber. Miss Hilton, being slim, was to wear two riding-hoods, her own and that of Mrs Mills. When she was in the room she was to drop her extra clothes and leave at once. Mrs Mills was then to go in as 'Mrs Betty', wearing a riding-hood to fit the earl. She was to be weeping bitterly and holding a handkerchief to her face. Everything depended upon Miss Hilton being able to slip away quietly; then Mrs Mills, having diminished in size, was to depart as 'Mrs Catherine', while the earl was to go out as 'Mrs Betty'. The vital point was to get the sentries thoroughly confused as to who had gone in and out.

They drove in a coach to the Tower, and Lady Nithsdale, in order to keep the others from doleful anticipations, chattered the whole way. When they reached the Tower they found several women in the Council Chamber who had come to see Lady Nithsdale pass, for they had a suspicion, in spite of her cheerfulness, that this was the last occasion on which she would see her husband alive. The presence of these women, who were all talking together, helped to confuse the sentries. Lady Nithsdale took in Miss Hilton first, naming her 'Mrs Catherine'. Miss Hilton at once shed her extra clothing and then left, Lady Nithsdale accompanying her to the staircase and crying, 'Send my maid to me at once. I must be dressed without delay or I shall be too late for my petition.' Then Mrs. Mills came up the stairs, a large fat woman sobbing bitterly and apparently all confused with grief. She was greeted by the Countess as 'Mrs Betty' and taken into Lord Nithsdale's room. There she changed her clothes, dried her tears, and went out with her head up and a light foot 'Goodbye, my dear Mrs Catherine,' Lady Nithsdale cried after her. 'Don't omit to send my maid. She cannot know how late it is. She has forgotten that I am to present the petition tonight.' The women in the Council Chamber watched Mrs Mills's departure with sympathy, and the sentry opened the door for her to pass.

Now came the great moment. If any single keeper in the outer room had kept his wits about him the plot must be discovered. Everything depended upon their being confused among the women, and believing that 'Mrs Betty' was still with the Countess in Lord Nithsdale's chamber. It was nearly dark and in a few minutes lights would be brought in, and a single candle would betray them. The Countess took off all her petticoats save one and tied them round her husband. There was no time to shave him, so she wrapped a muffler round his chin. His cheeks were rouged; false ringlets were tied around his brow; and a great riding-hood was put on. Then the Countess opened the door and led him by the hand. Her voice was now sharp with anxiety. 'For the love of God,' she cried, 'my dear Mrs Betty, run and bring her with

The sentries in the dim light were unsuspicious and let them pass.

you. You know my lodgings, and if ever you hurried in your life hurry now. I am driven mad with this delay.'

The sentries in the dim light were unsuspicious and let them pass; indeed, one of them opened the chamber door. The Countess slipped behind her husband in the passage, so that no one looking after him should see his walk, which was unlike that of any woman ever born. 'Make haste, make haste,' she cried, and then, almost before she had realized it, they had passed the last door and the sentries.

Evans, the maid, was waiting, and, seizing Lord Nithsdale, *alias* 'Mrs Betty', by the arm, hurried him off to a house near Drury Lane. There he was dressed in the livery of a servant of the Venetian Minister, and started for the coast.

The Countess, dreading lest some keeper should enter her husband's room and find him gone, rushed back there with a great appearance of distress and slammed the door. Then for a few minutes she strolled about with the step of a heavy man, and carried on an imaginary conversation, imitating his gruff replies. Now came the last stage. She raised the latch, and, standing in the doorway so that all the crowd in the Council Chamber could hear, bade her husband goodnight with every phrase of affection. She declared that something extraordinary must have happened to Evans, and that there was nothing for it but to go herself and see. She added that if the Tower were open she would come back that night. Anyhow, she hoped to be with him early in the morning, bringing him good news. As she spoke she drew the latch-string through the hole and banged the door. 'I pray you, do not disturb my lord,' she said in passing. 'Do not send him candles till he calls for them. He is now at his prayers.' The unsuspicious sentries saluted her with sympathy. Beyond the outer gate was a waiting coach in which she drove at once to tell the Duchess of Montrose what had been done. Meantime Lord Nithsdale, dressed as an Italian servant, was posting along the road to Dover, where, next morning, he found a boat for Calais. It was not long before his wife rejoined him in Rome.

Lady Nithsdale's bold escapade was received by the people of England with very general approval. Even the Government, who were beginning to have doubts about the wisdom of their policy, were not disposed to be too severe on the heroic wife. When the Duchess of

Montrose went to Court next day she found the King very angry. But the royal anger was short-lived. Presently he began to laugh. 'Upon my soul,' he said, 'for a man in my lord's situation it was the very best thing he could have done.'

THE STORY OF THE BAGMAN'S UNCLE

Charles Dickens

'My uncle, gentlemen,' said the bagman, 'was one of the merriest, pleasantest, cleverest fellows that ever lived. I wish you had known him, gentlemen. If any two of his numerous virtues predominated over the many that adorned his character, I should say they were his mixed punch, and his after-supper song. Excuse my dwelling on these melancholy recollections of departed worth; you won't see a man like my uncle every day in the week.

'In personal appearance, my uncle was a trifle shorter than the middle size; he was a thought stouter, too, than the ordinary run of people, and perhaps his face might be a shade redder. He had the jolliest face you ever saw, gentlemen: something like Punch, with a handsomer nose and chin; his eyes were always twinkling and sparkling with good humour; and a smile—not one of your unmeaning, wooden grins, but a real merry, hearty, good-tempered smile—was perpetually on his countenance. He was pitched out of his gig once, and knocked, head first, against a milestone. There he lay, stunned, and so cut about the face with some gravel which had been heaped up alongside it, that, to use my uncle's own strong expression, if his mother could have revisited the earth, she wouldn't have known him. However, there he lay, and I have heard my uncle say, many a time, that the man said who picked him up that he was smiling as merrily as if he had tumbled out for a treat, and that after they had bled him, the first faint glimmerings of returning animation were, his jumping up in bed, bursting out into a loud laugh, kissing the young woman who held the basin, and demanding a mutton chop and a pickled walnut instantly. He was very fond of pickled walnuts, gentlemen. He said he always found that, taken without vinegar, they relished the beer.

'My uncle's great journey was in the fall of the leaf, at which time he collected debts for Tiggin and Welps, and took orders, in the north: going from London to Edinburgh, from Edinburgh to Glasgow, from Glasgow back to Edinburgh, and thence to London by the smack. You are to understand that his second visit to Edinburgh was for his own pleasure. He used to go back for a week, just to look up his old friends; and what with breakfasting with this one, lunching with that, dining with a third, and supping with another, a pretty tight week he used to make of it. I don't know whether any of you gentlemen ever partook of a real substantial hospitable Scotch breakfast, and then went out to a slight lunch of a bushel of oysters, a dozen or so of bottled ale, and a noggin or two of whiskey to close up with. If you ever did, you will agree with me that it requires a pretty strong head to go out to dinner and supper afterwards.

'But bless your hearts and eyebrows, all this sort of thing was nothing to my uncle! He was so well seasoned, that it was mere child's play. I have heard him say that he could see the Dundee people out any day, and walk home afterwards without staggering; and yet the Dundee people have as strong heads and as strong punch, gentlemen, as you are likely to meet with between the poles. I have heard of a Glasgow man and a Dundee man drinking against each other for fifteen hours at a sitting. They were both suffocated, as nearly as could be ascertained, at the same moment, but with this trifling exception, gentlemen, they were not a bit the worse for it.

'One night, within four-and-twenty hours of the time when he had settled to take shipping for London, my uncle supped at the house of a very old friend of his, a Baillie Mac something, and four syllables after it, who lived in the old town of Edinburgh. There were the baillie's wife and the baillie's three daughters, and baillie's grown-up son, and three of four stout, bushy-eyebrowed, canty old Scotch fellows, that the baillie had got together to do honour to my uncle, and help to make merry. It was a glorious supper. There were kippered salmon, and Finnan haddocks, and a lamb's head, and a haggis—a celebrated Scotch dish, gentlemen, which my uncle used to say always looked to him, when it came to table, very much like a cupid's stomach—and a great many other things besides, that I forget the names of, but very good things notwithstanding. The lassies were pretty and agreeable; the baillie's wife, one of the best creatures that ever lived; and my uncle in thoroughly good cue: the consequences of which was, that the young ladies tittered and giggled, and the old lady laughed out loud, and the baillie and the other fellows roared till they were red in the face, the whole mortal time. I don't quite recollect how many tumblers of whiskey toddy each man drank after supper; but this I know, that about one o'clock in the morning, the baillie's grown-up son became insensible while attempting the first verse of "Willie brewed a peck o'maut"; and he having been, for half an hour before, the only other man visible above the mahogany, it occurred to my uncle that it was almost time to think about going: especially as drinking had set in at seven o'clock, in order that he might get home at a decent hour. But, thinking it might not be quite polite to go just then, my uncle voted himself into the chair, mixed another glass, rose to propose his own health, addressed himself in a neat and complimentary speech, and drank the toast with great enthusiasm. Still nobody woke; so my uncle took a little drop more—neat this time, to prevent the toddy disagreeing with him—and, laying violent hands on his hat, sallied forth into the street.

'It was a wild gusty night when my uncle closed the baillie's door, and setting his hat firmly on his head, to prevent the wind from taking it, thrust his hands into his pockets, and looking upwards, took a short survey of the state of the weather. The clouds were drifting over the moon at their giddiest speed: at one time wholly obscuring her: at another, suffering her to burst forth in full splendour and shed her light on all the objects around: anon, driving over her again with increased velocity, and shrouding everything in darkness. "Really, this won't do," said my uncle, addressing himself to the weather, as if he felt himself personally offended. "This is not at all the kind of thing for my voyage. It will not do at any price," said my uncle very impressively. Having repeated this several times, he recovered his balance with some difficulty—for he was rather giddy with looking up into the sky so long—and walked merrily on.

'The baillie's house was in the Canongate, and my uncle was going to the other end of Leith Walk, rather better than a mile's journey. On either side of him, there shot up against the dark sky, tall, gaunt, straggling houses, with time-stained fronts, and windows that seemed to have shared the lot of eyes in mortals, and to have grown dim and sunken with age. Six, seven, eight stories high, were the houses; story piled above story, as children build with cards—throwing their dark shadows over the roughly paved road, and making the dark night darker. A few oil lamps scattered at long distances, but they only served to mark the dirty entrance to some narrow close, or to show where a common stair communicated, by steep and intricate windings, with the various flats above. Glancing at all these things with the air of a man who had seen them too often before to think them worthy of much notice now, my uncle walked up the middle of the street, with a thumb in each waistcoat pocket, indulging, from time to time, in various snatches of song, chanted forth with such good-will and spirit, that the quiet honest folk started from their first sleep, and lay trembling in bed till the sound died away in the distance; when, satisfying themselves that it was only some drunken ne'er-do-weel finding his way home, they covered themselves up warm and fell asleep again.

'I am particular in describing how my uncle walked up the middle of the street, with his thumbs in his waistcoat pockets, gentlemen, because, as he often used to say (and with great reason too), there is nothing at all extraordinary in this story, unless you distinctly understand at the beginning that he was not by any means of a marvellous or romantic turn.

'Gentlemen, my uncle walked on with his thumbs in his waistcoat pockets, taking the middle of the street to himself, and singing, now a verse of a love song, and then a verse of a drinking one, and when he was tired of both, whistling melodiously, until he reached the North Bridge, which, at this point, connects the old and new towns of Edinburgh. Here he stopped for a minute, to look at the strange irregular clusters of lights piled one above the other, and twinkling afar off, so high in the air, that they looked like stars, gleaming from the castle walls on the one side, and then Calton Hill on the other, as if they illuminated veritable castles in the air: while the old picturesque town slept heavily on, in gloom and darkness below: its palace and chapel of Holyrood, guarded day and night, as a friend of my uncle's used to say, by old Arthur's Seat, towering, surly and dark, like some gruff genius, over the ancient city he has watched so long. I say, gentlemen, my uncle stopped here, for a minute, to look about him; and then paying a compliment to the weather, which had a little cleared up, though the moon was sinking, walked on again, as royally as before: keeping the middle of the road with great dignity, and looking as if he should very much like to meet with somebody who would dispute possession of it with him. There was nobody at all disposed to contest the point, as it happened; and so, on he went, with his thumbs in his waistcoat pockets, like a lamb.

'When my uncle reached the end of Leith Walk, he had to cross a pretty large piece of waste ground, which separated him from a short street which he had to turn down, to go direct to his lodging. Now, in this piece of waste ground, there was, at that time, an enclosure belonging to some wheelwright, who contracted with the Post Office for the purchase of old worn-out mail-coaches; and my uncle, being very fond of coaches, old, young, or middle-aged, all at once took it into his head to step out of his road for no other purpose than to peep between the palings at these mails; about a dozen of which he remembered to have seen, crowded together in a very forlorn and dismantled state, inside. My uncle was a very enthusiastic, emphatic sort of person, gentlemen; so, finding that he could not obtain a good peep between the palings, he got over them, and sitting himself quietly down on an old axletree, began to contemplate the mail-coaches with a deal of gravity.

'There might be a dozen of them, or there might be more—my uncle was never quite certain on this point, and being a man of very scrupulous veracity about numbers, didn't like to say—but there they stood, all huddled together in the most desolate condition imaginable. The doors had been torn from their hinges and removed; the linings had been stripped off: only a shred hanging here and there by a rusty nail; the lamps were gone, the poles had long since vanished, the iron-work was rusty, the paint worn away; the wind whistled through the chinks in the bare woodwork; and the rain which had collected on the roofs, fell, drop by drop, into the insides with a hollow and melancholy sound. They were the decaying skeletons of departed mails, and in that lonely place, at that time of night, they looked chill and dismal.

'My uncle rested his head upon his hands, and thought of the busy bustling people who had rattled about, years before, in the old coaches, and were now as silent and changed: he thought of the numbers of people to whom one of those crazy, mouldering vehicles had borne, night after night, for many years, and through all weathers, the anxiously expected intelligence, the eagerly looked-for remittance, the promised assurance of health and safety, the sudden announcement of sickness and death. The merchant, the lover, the wife, the widow, the mother, the schoolboy, the very child who tottered to the door at the postman's knock—how had they all looked forward to the arrival of the old coach! And where were they all now?

'Gentlemen, my uncle used to *say* that he thought all this at the time, but I rather suspect he learnt it out of some book afterwards, for he distinctly stated that he fell into a kind of a doze as he sat on the old axletree looking at the decaying mail-coaches, and that he was suddenly awakened by some deep church bell striking two. Now, my uncle was never a fast thinker, and if he had thought all these things, I am quite certain it would have taken him till full half-past two o'clock, at the very least. I am, therefore, decidedly of opinion, gentlemen, that my uncle fell into a kind of doze, without having thought about anything at all.

'Be this as it may, a church bell struck two. My uncle woke, rubbed his eyes, and jumped up in astonishment.

'In one instant after the clock struck two, the whole of this deserted and quiet spot had become a scene of most extraordinary life and animation. The mail-coach doors were on their hinges, the lining was replaced, the iron-work was as good as new, the paint was restored, the lamps were alight, cushions and great coats were on every coach-box, porters were thrusting parcels into every boot, guards were stowing away letter-bags, hostlers were dashing pails of water against the renovated wheels; numbers of men were rushing about, fixing poles into every coach; passengers arrived, portmanteaus were handed up, horses were put to; and, in short, it was perfectly clear that every mail there was to be off directly. Gentlemen, my uncle opened his eyes so wide at all this, that, to the very last moment of his life, he used to wonder how it fell out that he had ever been able to shut 'em again.

'"Now then!" said a voice, as my uncle felt a hand on his shoulder. "You're booked for one inside. You'd better get in."

'"*I* booked!" said my uncle, turning round.

'"Yes, certainly."

'My uncle, gentlemen, could say nothing; he was so very much astonished. The queerest thing of all was, that although there was such a crowd of persons, and although fresh faces were pouring in every moment, there was no telling where they came from; they seemed to start up, in some strange manner, from the ground or the air, and disappear in the same way. When a porter had put his luggage in the coach, and received his fare, he turned round and was gone; and before my uncle had well begun to wonder what had become of him, half-a-dozen fresh ones started up, and staggered along under the weight of parcels which seemed big enough to crush them. The passengers were all dressed so oddly too—large, broad-skirted, laced coats with great cuffs, and no collars; and wigs, gentlemen,—great formal wigs and a tie behind. My uncle could make nothing of it.

'"Now, *are* you going to get in?" said the person who had addressed my uncle before. He was dressed as a mail guard, with a wig on his head, and most enormous cuffs to his coat, and had a lantern in one hand, and a huge blunderbuss in the other, which he was going to stow away in his little arm-chest. "*Are* you going to get in, Jack Martin?" said the guard, holding the lantern to my uncle's face.

'"Hallo!" said my uncle, falling back a step or two. "That's familiar!"

'"It's so on the way-bill," replied the guard.

'"Isn't there a 'Mister' before it?" said my uncle—for he felt, gentlemen, that for a guard he didn't know to call him Jack Martin, was a liberty which the Post Office wouldn't have sanctioned if they had known it.

'"No; there is not," rejoined the guard coolly.

'"Is the fare paid?" inquired my uncle.

'"Of course it is," rejoined the guard.

'"It is, is it?" said my uncle. "Then here goes—which coach?"

'"This," said the guard, pointing to an old-fashioned Edinburgh and London Mail, which had the steps down, and the door open. "Stop—here are the other passengers. Let them get in first."

'As the guard spoke, there all at once appeared, right in front of my uncle, a young gentleman in a powdered wig, and a sky-blue coat trimmed with silver, made very full and broad in the skirts, which were lined with buckram. Tiggin and Welps were in the printed calico and waistcoat-piece line, gentlemen, so my uncle knew all the materials at once. He wore knees breeches, and a kind of leggings rolled up over his silk stockings, and shoes with buckles; he had ruffles at his wrists, a three-cornered hat on his head, and a long taper sword by his side. The flaps of his waistcoat came half-way down his thighs, and the ends of his cravat reached to his waist. He stalked gravely to the coach door, pulled off his hat, and held it above his head at arm's length: cocking his little finger in the air at the same time, as some affected people do when they take a cup of tea. Then he drew his feet together, and made a low grave bow, and then put out his left hand. My uncle was just going to step forward, and shake it heartily, when he perceived that these attentions were directed, not towards him, but to a young lady, who just then appeared at the foot of the steps, attired in an old-fashioned green velvet dress, with a long waist and stomacher. She had no bonnet on her head, gentlemen, which was muffed in a black silk hood, but she looked round for an instant as she prepared to get into the coach, and such a beautiful face as she discovered, my uncle had never seen—not even in a picture. She got into the coach, holding up her dress with one hand; and, as my uncle always said with a round oath, when he told the story, he wouldn't have believed it possible that legs and feet could have been brought to such a state of perfection, unless he had seen them with his own eyes.

'But, in this one glimpse of the beautiful face, my uncle saw that the young lady had cast an imploring look upon him, and that she appeared terrified and distressed. He noticed, too, that the young fellow in the powdered wig, notwithstanding his show of gallantry, which was all very fine and grand, clasped her tight by the wrist when she got in, and followed himself immediately afterwards. An uncommonly ill-looking fellow in a close brown wig and a plum-coloured suit, wearing a very large sword, and boots up to his hips, belonged to the party; and when he sat himself down next to the young lady, who shrunk into a corner at his approach, my uncle was confirmed in his original impression that something dark and mysterious was going forward, or, as he always said himself, that "there was a screw loose somewhere." It's quite surprising how quickly he made up his mind to help the lady at any peril, if she needed help.

'"Death and lightning!" exclaimed the young gentleman, laying his hand upon his sword, as my uncle entered the coach.

'"Blood and thunder!" roared the other gentleman. With this, he whipped his sword out, and made a lunge at my uncle without further ceremony. My uncle had no weapon about him, but with great dexterity he snatched the ill-looking gentleman's three-cornered hat from his head, and receiving the point of his sword right through the crown, squeezed the sides together, and held it tight.

'"Pink him behind!" cried the ill-looking gentleman to his companion, as he struggled to regain his sword.

'"He had better not," cried my uncle, displaying the heel of one of his shoes in a threatening manner. "I'll kick his brains out if he has any, or fracture his skull if he hasn't." Exerting all his strength at this moment, my uncle wrenched the ill-looking man's sword from his grasp, and flung it clean out of the coach window; upon which the younger gentleman vociferated "Death and lightning!" again, and laid his hand upon the hilt of his sword in a very fierce manner, but didn't draw it. Perhaps, gentlemen, as my uncle used to say, with a smile, perhaps he was afraid of alarming the lady.

'"Now, gentlemen," said my uncle, taking his seat deliberately, "I don't want to have any death, with or without lightning, in a lady's presence, and we have had quite blood and thundering enough for one journey; so, if you please, we'll sit in our places like quiet insides. Here, guard, pick up that gentleman's carving knife."

'As quickly as my uncle said the words, the guard appeared at the coach window, with the gentleman's sword in his hand. He held up his lantern and looked earnestly in my uncle's face, as he handed it in: when, by its light, my uncle saw, to his great surprise, that an

A young lady appeared at the foot of the steps.

immense crowd of mail-coach guards swarmed round the window, every one of whom had his eyes earnestly fixed upon him too. He had never seen such a sea of white faces, and red bodies, and earnest eyes, in all his born days.

'"This is the strangest sort of thing I ever had anything to do with," thought my uncle. "Allow me to return you your hat, sir."

'The ill-looking gentleman received his three-cornered hat in silence; looked at the hole in the middle with an inquiring air; and finally stuck it on the top of his wig, with a solemnity the effect of which was a trifle impaired by his sneezing violently at the moment, and jerking it off again.

'"All right!" cried the guard with the lantern, mounting into his little seat behind. Away they went. My uncle peeped out of the coach window as they emerged from the yard, and observed that the other mails, with coachmen, guards, horses, and passengers, complete, were driving round and round in circles, at a slow trot of about five miles an hour. My uncle burnt with indignation, gentleman. As a commercial man, he felt that the mail-bags were not to be trifled with, and he resolved to memorialize the Post Office on the subject, the very instant he reached London.

'At present, however, his thoughts were occupied with the young lady who sat in the farthest corner of the coach, with her face muffled closely in her hood: the gentleman with the sky-blue coat sitting opposite to her: and the other man in the plum-coloured suit at her side: and both watching her intently. If she so much as rustled the folds of her hood, he could hear the ill-looking man clap his hand upon his sword, and could tell by the other's breathing (it was so dark he couldn't see his face) that he was looking as big as if he were going to devour her at a mouthful. This roused my uncle more and more, and he resolved, come what come might, to see the end of it. He had a great admiration for bright eyes, and sweet faces, and pretty legs and feet; in short, he was fond of the whole sex. It runs in our family, gentlemen—so am I.

'Many were the devices which my uncle practised to attract the lady's attention, or, at all events, to engage the mysterious gentleman in conversation. They were all in vain; the gentleman wouldn't talk, and the lady didn't dare. He thrust his head out of the coach window at intervals, and bawled out to know why they didn't go faster. But he called till he was hoarse—nobody paid the least attention to him. He leant back in the coach, and thought of the beautiful face, and the feet, and legs. This answered better; it whiled away the time, and kept him from wondering where he was going, and how it was he found himself in such an odd situation. Not that this would have worried him much, anyway—he was a mighty free and easy, roving, devil-may-care sort of person, was my uncle, gentlemen.

'All of a sudden the coach stopped. "Hallo!" said my uncle, "what's in the wind now?"

'"Alight her," said the guard, letting down the steps.

'"Here!" cried my uncle.

'"Here," rejoined the guard.

'"I'll do nothing of the sort," said my uncle.

'"Very well, then stop where you are," said the guard.

'"I will," said my uncle.

'"Do," said the guard.

'The other passengers had regarded this colloquy with great attention; and, finding that my uncle was determined not to alight, the younger man squeezed past him, to hand the lady out. At this moment, the ill-looking man was inspecting the hole in the crown of his three-corned hat. As the young lady brushed past, she dropped one of her gloves into my uncle's hand, and softly whispered with her lips so close to his face, that he felt her warm breath on his nose, the single word "Help!" Gentlemen, my uncle leaped out of the coach at once, with such violence that it rocked on the springs again.

'"Oh! you've thought better of it, have you?" said the guard, when he saw my uncle standing on the ground.

'My uncle looked at the guard for a few seconds, in some doubt whether it wouldn't be better to wrench his blunderbuss from him, fire it in the face of the man with the big sword, knock the rest of the company over the head with the stock, snatch up the young lady, and go off in the smoke. On second thoughts, however, he abandoned this plan, as being a shade too melodramatic in the execution, and followed the two mysterious men, who, keeping the lady between them, were now entering an old house, in front of which the coach had stopped. They turned into the passage, and my uncle followed.

'Of all the ruinous and desolate places my uncle had ever beheld, this was the most so. It looked as if it had once been a large house of entertainment; but the roof had fallen in in many places, and the stairs were steep, rugged, and broken. There was a huge fire-place in the room into which they walked, and the chimney was blackened with smoke; but no warm blaze lighted it up now. The white feathery dust of burnt wood was still strewed over the hearth, but the stove was cold, and all was dark and gloomy.

'"Well," said my uncle, as he looked about him, "a mail travelling at the rate of six and half an hour, and stopping for an indefinite time at such a hole as this, is rather an irregular sort of proceeding, I fancy. This shall be made known; I'll write to the papers."

'My uncle said this in a pretty loud voice, and in an open unreserved sort of manner, with the view of engaging the two strangers in conversation if he could. But, neither of them took any more notice of him than whispering to each other, and scowling at him as they did so. The lady was at the farther end of the room, and once she ventured to wave her hand, as if beseeching my uncle's assistance.

'At length the two strangers advanced a little, and the conversation began in earnest.

'"You don't know this is a private room, I suppose, fellow?" said the gentleman in sky-blue.

'"No, I do not, fellow," rejoined my uncle. "Only if this is a private room specially ordered for the occasion, I should think the public room must be a *very* comfortable one." With this my uncle sat himself down in the high-backed chair, and took such an accurate measure of the gentlemen with his eyes, that Tiggin and Welps could have supplied him with printed calico for a suit, and not an inch too much or too little, from that estimate alone.

'"Quit this room," said both the men together, grasping their swords.

'"Eh?" said my uncle, not at all appearing to comprehend their meaning.

'"Quit the room, or you are a dead man," said the ill-looking fellow with the large sword, drawing it at the same time, and flourishing it in the air.

'"Down with him!" cried the gentleman in sky-blue, drawing his sword also, and falling back two or three yards. "Down with him!" The lady gave a loud scream.

'Now, my uncle was always remarkable for great boldness, and great presence of mind. All the time that he had appeared so indifferent to what was going on, he had been looking slily about for some missile or weapon of defence, and at the very instant when the swords were drawn, he espied, standing in the chimney-corner, and old basket-hilted rapier in a rusty scabbard. At one bound, my uncle caught it in his hand, drew it, flourished it gallantly above his head, called aloud to the lady to keep out of the way, hurled the chair at the man in sky-blue, and the scabbard at the man in plum-colour, and taking advantage of the confusion, fell upon them both, pell-mell.

'Gentlemen, there is an old story—none the worse for being true—regarding a fine young Irish gentleman, who being asked if he could play the fiddle, replied he had no doubt he could, but he couldn't exactly say for certain, because he had never tried. This is not inapplicable to my uncle and his fencing. He had never had a sword in his hand before, except once when he played Richard the Third at a private theatre: upon which occasion it was arranged with Richmond that he was to be run through from behind, without showing fight at all; but here he was, cutting and slashing with two experienced swordsmen, thrusting, and guarding, and poking, and slicing, and acquitting himself in the most manful and dexterous manner possible, although up to that time, he had never been aware that he had the least notion of the science. It only shows how true the old saying is, that a man never knows what he can do till he tries, gentlemen.

'The noise of the combat was terrific; each of the three combatants swearing like troopers, and their swords clashing with as much noise as if all the knives and steels in Newport Market were rattling together at the same time. When it was at its very height, the lady, to encourage my uncle most probably, withdrew her hood entirely from her facc, and disclosed a countenance of such dazzling beauty, that he would have fought against fifty men, to win one smile from it, and die. He had done wonders before, but now he began to powder away like a raving mad giant.

'At this very moment, the gentleman in sky-blue turning round, and seeing the young lady with her face uncovered, vented an exclamation of rage and jealousy; and turning his weapon against her beautiful bosom, pointed a thrust at her heart, which caused my uncle to utter a cry of apprehension that made the building ring. The lady stepped aside, and snatching the young man's sword from his hand before he had recovered his balance, drove him to the wall, and running it through him, and the panelling, up to the very hilt, pinned him there, hard and fast. It was a splendid example. My uncle, with a loud shout of triumph, and a strength that was irresistible, made his adversary retreat in the same direction, and plunging the old rapier into the very centre of a large red flower in the pattern of his waistcoat, nailed him beside his friend. There they both stood, gentlemen: jerking their arms and legs about in agony, like the toy-shop figures that are moved by a piece of packthread. My uncle always said, afterwards, that this was one of the surest means he knew of for disposing of an enemy; but it was liable to one objection on the ground of expense, inasmuch as it involved the loss of a sword for every man disabled.

'"The mail, the mail!" cried the lady, running up to my uncle and throwing her beautiful arms around his neck; "we may yet escape."

'"*May!*" cried my uncle; "why, my dear, there's nobody else to kill, is there?" My uncle was rather disappointed, gentlemen, for he thought a little quiet bit of love-making would be agreeable after the slaughtering, if it were only to change the subject.

'"We have not an instant to lose here," said the young lady. "He (pointing to the young gentleman in sky-blue) is the only son of the powerful Marquess of Filletoville."

'"Well, then my dear, I'm afraid he'll never come to the title," said my uncle, looking coolly at the young gentleman as he stood fixed up against the wall, in the cockchafer fashion I have described. "You have cut off the entail, my love."

'"I have been torn from my home and friends by these villains," said the young lady, her features glowing with indignation. "That wretch would have married me by violence in another hour."

'"Confound his impudence!" said my uncle, bestowing a very contemptuous look on the dying heir of Filletoville.

'"As you may guess from what you have seen," said the young lady, "the party were prepared to murder me if I appealed to anyone for assistance. If their accomplices find us here, we are lost. Two minutes hence may be too late. The mail!" With these words, overpowered by her feelings, and the exertion of sticking the young Marquess of Filletoville, she sunk into my uncle's arms. My uncle caught her up, and bore her to the house-door. There stood the mail, with four long-tailed, flowing-maned, black horses, ready harnessed; but no coachman, no guard, no hostler even, at the horses' heads.

'Gentlemen, I hope I do no injustice to my uncle's memory, when I express my opinion, that although he was a bachelor, he *had* held some ladies in his arms before this time; I believe, indeed, that he had rather a habit of kissing barmaids; and I know that, in one or two instances, he had been seen by credible witnesses to tug a landlady in a very perceptible manner. I mention the circumstances to show what a very uncommon sort of person this beautiful young lady must have been, to have affected my uncle in the way she did; he used to say, that as her long dark hair travelled over his arm, and her beautiful dark eyes fixed themselves upon his face when she recovered, he felt so strange and nervous, that his legs trembled beneath him. But, who can look in a sweet soft pair of dark eyes without feeling queer? *I* can't, gentlemen. I am afraid to look at some eyes I know, and that's the truth of it.

'"You will never leave me," murmured the young lady.

'"Never," said my uncle. And he meant it too.

'"My dear preserver!" exclaimed the young lady. "My dear, kind, brave preserver!"

'"Don't," said my uncle, interrupting her.

'"Why?" inquired the young lady.

'"Because your mouth looks so beautiful when you speak," rejoined my uncle, "that I am afraid I shall be rude enough to kiss it."

'The young lady put up her hand as if to caution my uncle not to do so, and said—no, she didn't say anything—she smiled. When you are looking at a pair of the most delicious lips in the world, and see them gently break into a roguish smile—if you are very near them, and nobody else by—you cannot better testify your admiration of their beautiful form and colour by kissing them at once. My uncle did so, and I honour him for it.

'"Hark!" cried the young lady, starting. "The noise of wheels and horses!"

'"So it is," said my uncle, listening. He had a good ear for wheels and the tramping of hoofs; but there appeared to be so many horses and carriages rattling towards them from a distance, that it was impossible to form a guess at their number. The sound was like that of fifty brakes, with six blood cattle in each.

'"We are pursued!" cried the young lady, clasping her hands. "We are pursued. I have no hope but in you!"

'There was such an expression of terror in her beautiful face, that my uncle made up his mind at once. He lifted her into the coach, told her not to be frightened, pressed his lips to hers once more, and then advising her to draw up the window to keep the cold air out, mounted to the box.

'"Stay, love," cried the young lady.

'"What's the matter?" said my uncle, from the coachbox.

'"I want to speak to you," said the young lady; "only a word—only a word, dearest."

'"Must I get down?" inquired my uncle. The lady made no answer, but she smiled again. Such a smile, gentlemen!—it beat the other one to nothing. My uncle descended from his perch in a twinkling.

'"What is it, my dear?" said my uncle, looking in at the coach window. The lady happened to bend forward at the same time, and my uncle thought she looked more beautiful than she had done yet. He was very close to her just then, gentlemen, so he really ought to know.

'"What is it, my dear?" said my uncle.

'"Will you never love anyone but me—never marry anyone besides?" said the young lady.

'My uncle swore a great oath that he would never marry anybody else, and the young lady drew in her head, and pulled up the window. He jumped upon the box, squared his elbows, adjusted the ribbons, seized the whip which lay on the roof, gave one flick to the off leader, and away went the four long-tailed, flowing-maned black horses, at fifteen good English miles an hour, with the mail-coach behind them. Whew! how they tore along!

'The noise behind grew louder. The faster the old mail went, the faster came the pursuers—men, horses, dogs, were leagued in the pursuit. The noise was frightful, but, above all, rose the voice of the young lady, urging my uncle on, and shrieking "Faster! faster!"

'They whirled past the dark trees, as feathers would be swept before a hurricane. Houses, gates, churches, haystacks, objects of every kind they shot by, with a velocity and noise like roaring waters suddenly let loose. Still the noise of pursuit grew louder, and still my uncle could hear the young lady wildly screaming "Faster! faster!"

'My uncle plied whip and rein; and the horses flew onward till they were white with foam; and yet the noise behind increased; and yet the young lady cried "Faster! faster!" My uncle gave a loud stamp on the boot in the energy of the moment, and—found that it was grey morning, and he was sitting in the wheelwright's yard, on the box of an old Edinburgh mail, shivering with cold and wet, and stamping his feet to warm them! He got down, and looked eagerly inside for the beautiful young lady. Alas! there was neither door nor seat to the coach—it was a mere shell.

'Of course, my uncle knew very well that there was some mystery in the matter, and that everything had passed exactly as he used to relate it. He remained staunch to the great oath he had sworn to the beautiful young lady: refusing several eligible landladies on her account, and dying a bachelor at last. He always said, what a curious thing it was that he should have found out, by such a mere accident as his clambering over the palings, that the ghosts of mail-coaches and horses, guards, coachmen, and passengers, were in the habit of making journeys regularly every night; he used to add, that he believed he was the only living person who had ever been taken as a passenger on one of these excursions; and I think he was right, gentlemen—at least I never heard of any other.'

AN AWKWARD SORTIE

Antoine de Saint-Exupéry

The time is 1940. France is occupied by German forces, French resources are scarce, and morale is low. One sunny morning Captain de Saint-Exupéry and Lieutenant Dutertre report to their commanding officer, Major Alias, who instructs them to prepare for a reconnaissance sortie. Their task is to take some aerial photographs at thirty thousand feet and then drop down to two thousand feet above the German tank parks scattered around the town of Arras. The major describes the mission as 'awkward'. The two men know exactly what that means: their chances of getting back alive are two to one against. . . .

It takes a long time to dress for a sortie that you know is a hopeless one. A long time to harness yourself only for the fun of being blasted to bits. There are three thicknesses of clothing to be put on, one over the other: that takes time. And this cluster of accessories that you carry about like an itinerant pedlar! All this complication of oxygen tubes, heating equipment, these speaking tubes that form the 'inter-com' running between the members of the crew, this mask through which I breathe. I am attached to the plane by a rubber tube as indispensable as an umbilical cord. The plane is plugged in to the circulation of my blood. Organs have been added to my being, and they seem to intervene between me and my heart. From one minute to the next I grow heavier, more cumbrous, harder to handle. I turn round all of a piece, and when I bend down to tighten my straps or pull at buckles that resist, all my joints creak aloud. My old fractures begin to hurt again.

'Hand me another helmet. I've told you twenty times that my own won't do. It's too tight.'

God knows why, but a man's skull swells at high altitude. A helmet that fits perfectly on the ground becomes a vice pressing on the skull at thirty thousand feet.

'But this is another helmet, sir. I sent back your old one.'

'Huh!'

I cannot stop grousing, and I grouse without remorse. A lot of good it does! Not that it is important. This is the moment of timelessness. This is the crossing of the inner desert of anguish. There is no god here. There is no face to love. There is no France, no Europe, no civilization. There are particles, detritus, nothing more. I feel no shame at this moment praying for a miracle that should change the course of this afternoon. The miracle, for instance, of a speaking tube out of order. Speaking tubes are always going out of order. Trashy stuff! A speaking tube out of order would preserve us from the holocaust.

Captain Vezin came in with a gloomy look. No pilot ever got off the ground without a dose of Captain Vezin's gloom. His job was to report upon the position of the German air outposts. To tell us where they were. Vezin is my friend and I am very fond of him; but he is a bird of ill omen. I prefer not to meet him when I am about to take off.

'Looks bad, old boy,' said Vezin. 'Very bad. Very bad indeed.'

* * * *

We climbed in. I had still to test the inter-com.

'Can you hear me, Dutertre?'

'I hear you, Captain.'

'You Gunner! Hear me?'

'I . . . Yes, sir. Clearly.'

'Dutertre! Can you hear the gunner?'

'Clearly, Captain.'

'Gunner! Can you hear Lieutenant Dutertre?'

'I . . . er . . . Yes, sir. Clearly.'

'What makes you stutter back there? What are you hesitating about?'

'Sorry, sir. I was looking for my pencil.'

The speaking tubes were not out of order.

'Gunner! Have a look at your oxygen bottles. Air-pressure normal?'

'I . . . Yes, sir. Normal.'

'In all three bottles?'

'All three, sir.'

'All set, Dutertre?'

'All set, Captain.'

'All set, gunner?'

'All set, sir.'

We took off.

* * * *

For me, piloting my plane, time has ceased to run sterile through my fingers. Now, finally, I am installed in my function. Time is no longer a thing apart from me. I have stopped projecting myself into the future. I am no longer he who may perhaps dive down the sky in a vortex of flame. The future is no longer a haunting phantom, for from this moment on I shall myself create the future by my own successive acts. I am he who checks the course and holds the compass at 313°. Who controls the revolutions of the propeller and the temperature of the oil. These are healthy and immediate cares. These are household cares, the little duties of the day that take away the sense of growing older. The day becomes a house brilliantly clean, a floor well waxed, oxygen prudently doled out. . . . Thinking which, I checked the oxygen flow, for we have been rising fast and are at twenty-two thousand feet already.

'Oxygen all right, Dutertre? How do you feel?'

'First rate, Captain.'

'You, gunner! How's your oxygen?'

'I . . . er . . . Shipshape, sir.'

'Haven't you found that pencil yet?'

And I am he who checks his machine-guns, putting a finger on button S, on button A. . . . Which reminds me.

'Gunner! No good-sized town behind you, in your cone of fire?'

'Er . . . all clear, sir.'

'Check your guns. Let fly.'

I hear the blast of the guns.

'Work all right?'

'Worked fine, sir.'

'All of them?'

'Er . . . yes, sir. All of them.'

I test my own and wonder what becomes of all the bullets we scatter so heedlessly over our home territory. They never kill anyone. The earth is vast. . . .

I count the dials, the levers, the buttons, the knobs of my kingdom. I count one hundred and three objects to check, pull, turn, or press. (Perhaps I have cheated in counting my machine-gun controls as two—one for the fire-button, and another for the safety-catch.) Tonight when I get back I shall amaze the farmer with whom I am billeted. I shall say to him:

'Do you know how many instruments a pilot has to keep his eye on?'

'How do you expcct me to know that?'

'No matter. Guess. Name a figure.'

'What figure?'

My farmer is not a man of tact.

'Any figure. Name one.'

'Seven.'

'One hundred and three!'

And shall smile with satisfaction.

Another thing contributes to my peace of mind—it is that all the instruments that were an encumbrance while I was dressing have now settled into place and acquired meaning. All that tangle of tubes and wiring has become a circulatory network. I am an organism integrated into the plane. I turn this switch, which gradually heats up my overall and my oxygen, and the plane begins to generate my comfort. The oxygen, incidentally, is too hot. It burns my nose. A complicated mechanism releases it in proportion to the altitude at which I fly, and I am flying high. The plane is my wet-nurse. Before we took off, this thought seemed to me inhuman; but now, suckled by the plane itself, I feel a sort of filial affection for it. The affection of a nursling.

My weight, meanwhile, is comfortably distributed over a variety of points of support. I am like a feeble convalescent stripped of bodily consciousness and lying in a chaise-longue. The convalescent exists only as a frail thought. My triple thickness of clothing is without weight in my seat. My parachute, slung behind, lies against the back of

I am an organism integrated into the plane.

my seat. My enormous boots rest on the bar that operates the rudder. My hands that are so awkward when first I slip on the thick stiff gloves, handle the wheel with ease. Handle the wheel. Handle the wheel. . . .

'Dutertre!'

'. . . t'n?'

'Something's wrong with the inter-com. I can't hear you. Check your contacts.'

'I can . . . you . . . ctly.'

'Shake it up! Can you still hear me?'

Dutertre's voice comes through clearly.

'Hear you prefectly, Captain.'

'Good! Dutertre, the confounded controls are frozen again. The wheel is stiff and the rudder is stuck fast.'

'That's great! What altitude?'

'Thirty-two thousand.'

'Temperature?'

'Fifty-five below zero. How's your oxygen?'

'Coming fine.'

'Gunner! How's your oxygen?'

No answer.

'Hi! Gunner!'

No answer.

'Do you hear the Gunner, Dutertre?'

'No.'

'Call him.'

'Gunner, Gunner!'

No answer.

'He must have passed out, Captain. We shall have to dive.'

I didn't want to dive unless I had to. The gunner might have dropped off to sleep. I shook up the plane as roughly as I could.

'Captain, sir?'

'That you, gunner?'

'I . . . er . . . yes, sir.'

'Not sure it's you?'

'Yes, sir.'

'Why the devil didn't you answer before?'

'I had pulled the plug, sir. I was testing the radio.'

'You're a bloody fool! Do you think you're alone in this plane? I was just about to dive. I thought you were dead.'

'Er . . . no, sir.'

'I'll take your word for it. But don't play that trick on me again! Damn it! Let me know before you cut.'

'Sorry, sir. I will. I'll let you know, sir.'

Had his oxygen flow stopped working, he wouldn't have known it. The human body receives no warning. A vague swooning comes over you. In a few seconds you have fainted. In a few minutes you are dead. The flow has constantly to be tested—particularly by the pilot. I pinched my tube lightly a few times and felt the warm life-bringing puffs blow round my nose.

★ ★ ★ ★

'Captain!'

'Yes?'

'Six German fighters on the port bow.'

The words rang in my ears like a thunderclap. . . .

'Gunner!'

'Sir?'

'D'you hear the lieutenant? Six German fighters. Six, on the port bow.'

'I heard the lieutenant, sir.'

'Dutertre! Have they seen us?'

'They have, Captain. Banking towards us. Fifteen hundred feet below us.'

'Hear that, gunner? Fifteen hundred feet below us. Dutertre! How near are they?'

'Say ten seconds.'

'Hear that, gunner? On our tail in a few seconds.'

There they are. I see them. Tiny. A swarm of poisonous wasps.

'Gunner! They're crossing broadside. You'll see them in a second. There!'

'Don't see them yet, sir. . . . Yes, I do!'

I no longer see them myself.

'They after us?'

'After us, sir.'

'Rising fast?'

'Can't say sir. Don't think so. . . . No, sir.'

Dutertre spoke. 'What do you say, Captain?'

'What do you expect me to say?'

Nobody said anything. There was nothing to say. We were in God's hands. If I banked, I should narrow the space between us. Luckily, we were flying straight into the sun. At high altitude you cannot go up fifteen hundred feet higher without giving a couple of miles to your game. It was possible therefore that they might lose us entirely in the sun by the time they had reached our altitude and recovered their speed.

'Still after us, gunner?'

'Still after us, sir.'

'We gaining on them?'

'Well, sir. No. . . . Perhaps.'

It was God's business—and the sun's.

Fighters do not fight, they murder. Still, it might turn into a fight, and I made ready for it. I pressed with both feet as hard as I could, trying to free the frozen rudder. A wave of something strange went over me. But my eyes were still on the Germans, and I bore with all my weight down upon the rigid bar.

Once again I discovered that I was in fact much less upset in this moment of action—if 'action' was the word for this vain expectancy—than I had been while dressing. A kind of anger was going through me. A beneficient anger. God knows, no ecstasy of sacrifice. Rather an urge to bite hard into something.

'Gunner! Are we losing them?'

'We are losing them, sir.'

Good job.

'Dutertre! Dutertre!'

'Captain?'

'I . . . nothing.'

'Anything the matter?'

'Nothing. I thought. . . . Nothing.'

* * * *

I decided not to mention it. No good worrying them. If I went into a dive they would know it soon enough. They would know that I had gone into a dive.

It was not natural that I should be running with sweat in a temperature sixty degrees below zero. Not natural. I knew perfectly well what was happening. Gently, very gently, I was fainting.

I could see the instrument panel. Now I couldn't. My hands were losing their grip on the wheel. I hadn't even the strength to speak. I was letting myself go. So pleasant, letting oneself go. . . .

Then I squeezed the rubber tube. A gust of air blew into my nose and brought me to life. The oxygen supply was not out of order! Then it must be. . . . Of course! How stupid I had been! It was the rudder. I had exerted myself like a man trying to pick up a grand piano. Flying thirty-three thousand feet in the air, I had struggled like a professional wrestler. The oxygen was being doled out to me. It was my business to use it up economically. I was paying for my orgy.

I began to inhale in swift repeated gasps. My heart beat faster and faster. It was like a faint tinkle. What good would it do to speak of it? If I went into a dive, they would know soon enough. Now I could see my instrument panel. . . . No, that wasn't true. I couldn't see it. Sitting there in my sweat, I was sad.

* * * *

Life came back as gently as it had flowed out of me.

'Dutertre!'

'Captain?'

I should have liked to tell him what had happened.

'I . . . I thought. . . . No.'

I gave it up. Words consume oxygen too fast. Already I was out of breath. I was very weak. A convalescent.

'You were about to say something, Captain?'

'No . . . nothing.'

'Quite sure, Captain? You puzzle me.'

I puzzle him. But I am alive.

'We are alive.'

'Well, yes. For the time being.'

For the time being. There was still Arras.

For us in the plane life was losing its edge, blunted by a slow wearing away of ourselves. We were ageing. The sortie was ageing. What price high altitude? An hour of life spent at thirty-three thousand feet is equivalent to what? To a week? three weeks? a month of organic life, of the work of the heart, the lungs, the arteries? Not that it signifies. My semi-swoonings have added centuries to me: I float in the serenity of old age.

How far away now is the agitation in which I dressed! In what a distant past it is lost! And Arras is infinitely far in the future. The adventure of war? Where is there adventure in war? I have this day taken an even chance to disappear, and I have nothing to report unless it is that passage of tiny wasps seen for three seconds. The real adventure would have lasted but the tenth of a second; and those among us who go through it do not come back, never come back, to tell the story.

'Give her a kick to starboard, Captain.'

Dutertre has forgotten that my rudder is frozen. I was thinking of a picture that used to fascinate me when I was a child. Against the background of an aurora borealis it showed a graveyard of fantastic ships, motionless in the Antarctic seas. In the ashen glow of an eternal night the ships raised their crystallized arms. The atmosphere was of death, but they still spread sails that bore the impress of the wind as a bed bears the impress of a shoulder, and the sails were stiff and cracking.

Here too everything was frozen. My controls were frozen. My machine-guns were frozen. And when I had asked the gunner about his, the answer had come back, 'Nothing doing, sir.'

Into the exhaust pipe of my mask I spat icicles fine as needles. From time to time I had to crush the stopper of frost that continued to form inside the flexible rubber, lest it suffocate me. When I squeezed the tube I felt it grate in my palm.

'Gunner! Oxygen all right?'

'Yes, sir.'

'What's the pressure in the bottles?'

'Er . . . seventy. Falling, sir.'

Time itself had frozen for us. We were three old men with white beards. Nothing was in motion. Nothing was urgent. Nothing was cruel.

The adventure of war. Major Alias had thought it necessary to say to me one day, 'Take it easy, now!'

Take what easy, Major Alias? The fighters come down on you like lightning. Having spotted you from fifteen hundred feet above you, they take their time. They weave, they orient themselves, take careful aim. You know nothing of this. You are the mouse lying in the shadow of the bird of prey. The mouse fancies that it is alive. It goes on frisking in the wheat. But already it is the prisoner of the retina of the hawk, glued tighter to that retina than to any glue, for the hawk will never leave it now.

And thus you, continuing to pilot, to daydream, to scan the earth, have already been flung outside the dimension of time because of a tiny black dot on the retina of a man.

The nine planes of the German fighter group will drop like plummets in their own good time. They are in no hurry. At five hundred and fifty miles an hour they will fire their prodigious harpoon that never misses its prey. A bombing squadron possesses enough firing power to offer a chance for defence; but a reconnaissance crew, alone in the wide sky, has no chance against the seventy-two machine-guns that first make themselves known to it by the luminous spray of their bullets. At the very instant when you first learn of its existence, the fighter, having spat forth its venom like a cobra, is already neutral and inaccessible, swaying to and fro overhead. Thus the cobra sways, sends forth its lightning, and resumes its rhythmical swaying.

Each machine-gun fires fourteen hundred bullets a minute. And when the fighter group has vanished, still nothing has changed. The faces themselves have not changed. They begin to change now that the sky is empty and peace has returned. The fighter has become a mere impartial onlooker when, from the severed carotid in the neck of the reconnaissance pilot, the first jets of blood spurt forth. When from the hood of the starboard engine the hesitant leak of the first tongue of flame rises out of the furnace fire. And the cobra has returned to its folds when the venom strikes the heart and the first muscle of the face twitches. The fighter group does not kill. It sows death. Death sprouts after it has passed.

Take what easy, Major Alias? When we flew over those fighters I had no decision to make. I might as well not have known they were there. If they had been overhead, I should never have known it.

Take what easy? The sky is empty. . . .

* * * *

'Are the anti-aircraft firing, Dutertre?'

'I believe they are firing, Captain.'

Dutertre cannot tell. The bursts are too distant and the smoke is blended in with the ground. They cannot hope to bring us down by such vague firing. At thirty-three thousand feet we are virtually invulnerable. They are firing in order to gauge our position, and probably also to guide the fighter groups towards us. A fighter group diluted in the sky like invisible dust.

The German on the ground knows us by the pearly white scarf which every plane flying at high altitude trails behind like a bridal veil. The disturbance created by our meteoric flight crystallizes the watery vapour in the atmosphere. We unwind behind us a cirrus of icicles. If the atmospheric conditions are favourable to the formation of clouds, our wake will thicken bit by bit and become an evening cloud over the countryside.

The fighters are guided towards us by their radio, by the bursts on the ground, and by the ostentatious luxury of our white scarf. Nevertheless we swim in an emptiness almost interplanetary. Everything round us and within us is total immobility. . . .

Very far ahead lie Dunkerque and the sea. To the left and right I see nothing. The sun has dropped too low, now, and I command the view of a vast glittering sheet.

'Dutertre! Can you see anything at all in this mess?'

'Straight down, yes.'

'Gunner! Any sign of the fighters?'

'No sign, sir.'

The fact is, I have absolutely no idea whether or not we are being pursued, and whether from the ground they can or cannot see us trailed by the collection of gossamer threads we sport.

Gossamer threads sets me day-dreaming again. An image comes into my mind which for the moment seems to me enchanting. '. . . As inaccessible as a woman of exceeding beauty, we follow our destiny, drawing slowly behind us our train of frozen stars.'

'A little kick to port, Captain.'

There you have reality. But I go back to my shoddy poetry: 'We bank, and a whole sky of suitors banks in our wake.'

Kick to port, indeed! Try it.

The woman of exceeding beauty has fumbled her bank.

Is it true that I was humming?

For Dutertre has spoken again. 'Hum like that, Captain, and you'll pass out.'

He has certainly killed my taste for humming.

'I've just about got all the photos I want, Captain. Another few minutes and we can make for Arras.'

We can make for Arras. Why, of course. Since we're half way there, we might as well.

Phew! My throttles are frozen!

★ ★ ★ ★

I am doing my job like a conscientious workman. Which does not alter the fact that I feel myself to be a pilot of defeat. I feel drenched in defeat. Defeat oozes out of every pore, and in my hands I hold a pledge of it.

For my throttle controls are frozen. The cold has turned them into two stumps of useless metal and has involved me in a serious predicament. For, whatever happens, I am forced to go on flying full throttle. Meanwhile, the pitch of my propellers, which serves in a sense as a brake on the revolution of my engines, is limited by an automatic check. If for any reason I am forced to dive, I shall be unable to reduce the speed of my engines, and unable also to increase my pitch. As I fall through space the torrential rush of air through my propellers will very likely increase the rotation of my engines to the point at which they blow up.

I could, if I had to, switch off my engines; but in that case I should never be able to start them again. I should then be stalled for good and all, which would mean the failure of the sortie and the crack-up of the machine. Not every terrain is favourable to the landing of a plane at one hundred and twenty miles an hour—and this, by manoeuvring and gliding, is about the minimum speed at which I could hope to set the machine down. Therefore I must succeed in unlocking my throttles.

I was able to unlock the throttle of the port engine: the starboard throttle would not budge.

Now if I were forced down, I could reduce the speed of the port engine. But if I cut down the port engine, over which I had regained control, I should need to be able to offset the lateral traction exercised by the starboard engine—for the accelerated rotation of the starboard engine would obviously tend to pivot the plane to port. There is a way of offsetting this tendency. I could do it by the play of my rudder. But the bar that governs my rudder has long been frozen stiff. Therefore I should be able to offset nothing at all. The moment I cut down my port engine I must go into a spin. . . .

'You may drop down now, Captain.'

I may drop down. I shall drop down. I shall drop down upon Arras. I shall carry out the second half of our mission—the low altitude sortie. Behind me I have a thousand years of civilization to help me. But they have not helped me yet. I dare say this is not the moment for rewards.

* * * *

At five hundred miles an hour I lose altitude. Banking, I have left behind me a polar sun exaggeratedly red. Ahead and three or four miles below me, I see the broad surface of a rectilinear mass of cloud that looks like an ice-floe. A whole province of France lies buried in its shadow. Arras lies shadowed by it. Beneath my ice-floe, I imagine, the world has a blackish tinge. The war must be stewing there as in the belly of a giant soup-kettle. Jammed roads, flaming houses, tools lying where they were flung down, villages in ruins, muddle, endless muddle. . . .

* * * *

'172°.'

'Right! 172°.'

Call it one seventy-two. Epitaph: 'Maintained his course accurately on 172°.' How long will this crazy challenge go on? I am flying now at two thousand three hundred feet beneath a ceiling of heavy clouds. If I were to rise a mere hundred feet Dutertre would be blind. Thus we are forced to remain visible to the anti-aircraft batteries and play the part of an archer's target for the Germans. Two thousand feet is a forbidden altitude. Your machine serves as a mark for the whole plain. You drain the cannonade of a whole army. You are within range of every calibre. You dwell an eternity in the field of fire of each successive weapon. You are not shot at with cannon but beaten with a stick. It is as if a thousand sticks were used to bring down a single walnut.

I had given a bit of thought to this problem. There is no question of a parachute. When the stricken plane dives to the ground the opening of the escape hatch takes more seconds than the dive of the plane allows. Opening the hatch involves seven turns of a crank that sticks. Besides, at full speed the hatch warps and refuses to slide.

That's that. The medicine had to be swallowed some day. I always knew it. Meanwhile, the formula is not complicated: stick to 172°. I was wrong to grow older. Pity. I was so happy as a child. . . .

Now is the time when childhood seems sweet. Not only childhood, but the whole of my past life. I see it in perspective as if it were a landscape.

And it seems to me that I myself am unalterable. I have always felt what I now feel. Doubtless my joys and sadness changed object from time to time. But the feelings were always the same. I have been happy and unhappy. I have been punished and forgiven. I have worked well and badly. That depended on the days.

What is my earliest memory? I had a Tyrolian governess whose name was Paula. But she is not even a memory: she is the memory of a memory. Paula was already no more than a legend when at the age of five I sat marooned in the dim hall. Year after year my mother would say to us round the New Year, 'There is a letter from Paula.' That made all the children happy. But why were we happy? None of us remembered Paula. She had gone back long before to her Tyrol. . . .

'One seventy-four.'

'Right! One seventy-four.'

Call it one seventy-four. Must change that epitaph.

Strange, how of a sudden life has collected in a heap. I have packed up my memories. They will never be of use to me again. Nor to anyone else. I remember a great love. My mother would say to us: 'Paula sends kisses to you all.' And my mother would kiss us all for Paula.

'Does Paula know I am bigger?'

'Naturally.'

Paula knew everything.

'Captain, they are beginning to fire.'

Paula they are firing at me! I glanced at the altimeter: two thousand one hundred and fifty feet. Clouds at two thousand three hundred. Well. Nothing to be done about it. What astonishes me is that beneath my cloud-bank the world is not black, as I had thought it would be. It is blue. Marvellously blue. Twilight has come, and all the plain is blue. Here and there I see rain failing. Rain-blue.

'One sixty-eight.'

'Right! One sixty-eight.'

Call it one sixty-eight. Interesting, that the road to eternity should be zigzag. And so peaceful. The earth here looks like an orchard. A moment ago it seemed to me skeletal, inhumanly desiccated. But I am flying low in a sort of intimacy with it. There are trees, some standing isolated, others in clusters. You meet them. And green fields. And houses with red tile roofs and people out of doors. And lovely blue showers pouring all round them. The kind of weather in which Paula must have hustled us rapidly indoors.

'One seventy-five.'

My epitaph has lost a good deal of its laconic dignity: 'Maintained his course on 172°, 174°, 168°, 175°. . . .' I shall seem a very versatile fellow. What's that? Engine coughing? Growing cold. I shut the ventilators of the hood. Good. Time to change over to the reserve tanks. I pull the lever. Have I forgotten anything? I glance at the oil gauge. Everything shipshape. . . .

'Captain! Firing very fast to port. Hard down!'

I kicked my rudder.

'Getting worse!'

Worse?

Getting worse; but I am seated at the heart of the world. All my memories, all my needs, all my loves are now available to me. My childhood, lost in darkness like a root, is at my disposal. My life here begins with the nostalgia of a memory. Yes, it is getting worse; but I feel none of those things I thought I should feel when facing the claws of these shooting stars.

'Arras!'

Yes. Very far ahead. But Arras is not a town. Arras thus far is no more than a red plume against a blue background of night; against a background of storm. For unmistakably, forward on the left, an awful squall is collecting. Twilight alone would not explain this half-light. It wants blocks of clouds to filter a glow so sombre. . . .

★ ★ ★ ★

Something in this countryside suddenly exploded. So a log that seemed burnt out crackles suddenly and shoots forth its sparks. How did it happen that the whole plain started up at the same moment? When spring comes, all the trees at once drop their seed. Why this sudden springtime of arms? Why this luminous flood rising towards us and, of a sudden, universal?

My first feeling was that I had been careless. I had ruined everything. A wink, a single gesture is enough to topple you from the tight-rope. A mountain climber coughs, and he releases an avalanche. Once he has released the avalanche, all is over. . . .

Each burst of a machine-gun or a rapid-fire cannon shot forth hundreds of these phosphorescent bullets that followed one another like the beads of a rosary. A thousand elastic rosaries strung themselves out towards the plane, drew themselves out to the breaking point and burst at our height. When, missing us, the string went off at a tangent, its speed was dizzying. The bullets were transformed into lightning. And I flew drowned in a crop of trajectories as golden as the stalks of wheat. I flew at the centre of a thicket of lance strokes. I flew threatened by a vast and dizzying flutter of knitting needles. All the plane was now bound to me, woven and wound round me, a coruscating web of golden wire. . . .

What's that!

I was jolted nearly a foot out of my seat. The plane has been rammed hard; I thought, It has burst, been ground to bits. . . . But it hasn't; it hasn't . . . I can still feel it responsive to the controls. This was but the first blow of a deluge of blows. Yet there was no sign of explosion below. The smoke of the heavy guns had probably blended into the dark ground.

I raised my head and stared. What I saw was without appeal.

I had been looking on at a carnival of light. The ceiling had risen little by little and I had been unaware of an intervening space between the clouds and me. I had been zigzagging along a line of flight dotted by ground batteries. Their tracer bullets had been spraying the air with wheat-coloured shafts of light. I had forgotten that at the top of their flight the shells of those batteries must burst. And now, raising my head, I saw around and before me those rivets of smoke and steel driven into the sky in the pattern of towering pyramids.

I was quite aware that those rivets were no sooner driven than all danger went out of them, that each of those puffs possessed the power of life and death only for a fraction of a second. But so sudden and simultaneous was their appearance that the image flashed into my mind of conspirators intent upon my death. . . .

Muffled as those explosions reached me, their sound covered by the roar of my engines, I had the illusion of an extraordinary silence. Those vast packets of smoke and steel moving soundlessly upward and behind me with the lingering flow of icebergs, persuaded me that, seen in their perspective, I must be virtually motionless. I was motionless in the dock before an immense assize. The judges were deliberating my fate, and there was nothing I could plead. Once again the timelessness of suspense seized me. I thought—I was still able to think—'They are aiming too high,' and I looked up in time to see straight overhead, swinging away from me as if with reluctance, a swarm of black flakes that glided like eagles. Those eagles had given me up. I was not to be their prey. But even so, what hope was there for me?

The batteries that continued to miss me continued also to readjust their aim. New walls of smoke and steel continued to be built up round me as I flew. The ground-fire was not seeking me out, it was closing me in.

'Dutertre! How much more of this is there?'

'Stick it out three minutes, Captain. Looks bad, though.'

'Think we'll get through?'

'Not on your life!'

There never was such muck as this murky smoke, this mess as grimy as a heap of filthy rags. The plain was blue. Immensely blue. Deep-sea blue.

What was a man's life worth between this blue plain and this foul sky? Ten seconds, perhaps; or twenty. The shock of the exploding shells set all the sky shuddering. When a shell burst very near, the explosion rumbled along the plane like rock dropping through a chute. And when for a moment the roar stopped, the plane rang with a sound that was almost musical. Like a sigh, almost; and the sigh told us that the plane had been missed. Those bursts were like the thunder: the closer they came, the simpler they were. A rumble meant distance, a clean *bang*! meant that we had been squarely hit by a shell fragment. The tiger does not do a messy job on the ox it brings down. The tiger sinks its claws into the ox without skidding. It takes possession of the ox. Each square hit by a fragment of shell sank into the hull of the plane like a claw into living flesh.

*　　*　　*　　*

'Captain!'

'What's up?'

'Getting hot!'

'Gunner!'

'Er . . . yes, sir.'

'What—'

My question vanished in the shock of another explosion.

'Dutertre!'

'Captain?'

'Hurt?'

'No.'

'You, gunner!'

'Yes, sir.'

'I wa—'

I seemed to be running the plane into a bronze wall. A voice in my ear said: 'Boy? oh, boy!' as I looked up to measure the distance to the overhanging clouds. The sharper the angle at which I stared, the more densely the murky tufts seemed to be piled up. Seen straight overhead, the sky was visible between them, and they hung curved and scattered, forming a gigantic coronet in the air.

A man's thigh muscles are incredibly powerful. I bore down upon the rudder bar with all my strength and sent the plane shuddering and skidding at right-angles to our line of flight. The coronet swung overhead and slid down on my right. I had got away from one of the batteries and left it firing wasted packets of shell. But before I could bring my other thigh into play the ground battery had set straight what hung askew—the coronet was back again. Once more I bore down, and again the plane groaned, and swayed in the swampy sky. All the weight of my body was on that bar, and the machine had swung, had skidded squarely to starboard. The coronet curved now above me on the left.

Would we last it out? But how could we? Each time that I brought this ship brutally round, the deluge of lance-strokes followed me before I could jerk back again. Each time the coronet was set back into place and the shell bursts shook up the plane anew. And each time when I looked down, I saw again that same dizzyingly slow ascension of golden bubbles that seemed to be accurately centred upon my plane. How did it happen that we were still whole? I began to believe in us. 'I am invulnerable, after all,' I said to myself, 'I am winning. From second to second, I am more and more the winner.'

'Anybody hurt yet?'

'Nobody.'

They were unhurt. They were invulnerable. They were victorious. I was the owner of a winning team. And from that moment each explosion seemed to me not to threaten us but to temper us. Each time, for a fraction of a second, it seemed to me that my plane had been blown to bits; but each time it responded anew to the controls and I nursed it along like a coachman pulling hard on the reins. I began to relax, and a wave of jubilation went through me. There was just time enough for me to feel fear as no more than a physical stiffening induced by a loud crash, when instantly after each buffet a wave of relief went through me. I ought to have felt successively the shock, then the fear, then the relief; but there wasn't time. What I felt was the shock, then instantly the relief. Shock, relief. Fear, the intermediate step, was missing. And during the second that followed the shock I did not live in the expectancy of death in the second to come, but in the conviction of resurrection born of the second just passed. I lived in a sort of slipstream of joy, in the wake of my jubilation. A prodigiously unlooked for pleasure was flowing through me. It was as if, with each second that passed, life was being granted me anew. As if with each second that passed my life became a thing more vivid to me. I was living. I was alive. I was still alive. . . .

All my tanks had been pierced, both gas and oil. Otherwise we seemed to be sound. Dutertre called out that he was through, and once again I looked up and calculated the distance to the clouds. I raised the nose of the ship, and once again I sent the plane zigzagging as I climbed. Once again I cast a glance earthwards. What I saw I shall not forget. The plain was crackling everywhere with short wicks of spurting flame—the rapid-fire cannon. The coloured balls were still floating upward through an immense blue aquarium of air. Arras was glowing dark red like iron on the anvil. . . .

Already I was flying through the first packets of mist. Golden arrows still rose and pierced the belly of the cloud, and just as the cloud closed round me I caught through an opening my last glimpse of that scene. For a single instant the flame over Arras rose up glowing in the night like a lamp in the nave of a cathedral. The lamp that was Arras was burning in the service of a cult, but at a price. By tomorrow it would have consumed Arras and itself have been consumed.

'Everything all right, Dutertre?'

'First rate, Captain. Two-forty, please. We shan't be able to come down out of this cloud for about twenty minutes. Then I'll pick up a landmark along the Seine somewhere.'

'Everything all right, gunner?'

'Everything fine, sir.'

'Not too hot for you, was it?'

'No, I guess not, sir.'

* * * *

I flew on, drawing deep slow breaths. I filled my lungs to the bottom. It was wonderful to breathe again. There were many things I was going to find out about. First I thought of Alias. No, that's not true, I thought first of my host, my farmer. I still looked forward to asking him how many instruments he thought a pilot had to watch. Sorry, but I am stubborn about some things. One hundred and three. He would never guess. Which reminds me: when your tanks have been pierced, it does no harm to have a look at your gauges. Wonderful tanks! Their rubber coatings have done their job; automatically, they had contracted and plugged the holes made by bullets and shell splinters. I had a look at my stabilizers too. This cloud we flew in was a storm cloud. It shook us up pretty badly.'

'Think we can come down now?'

'Ten minutes more. Better wait another ten minutes.'

Of course I could wait another ten minutes. . . .

★ ★ ★ ★

'Ninety-four, Captain.'

Dutertre had picked up a landmark along the Seine, and we were down now to four hundred feet. Flowing beneath me at three hundred miles an hour, the earth was dragging great rectangles of wheat and alfalfa, great triangles of forest, across my glass windscreen. Divided by the stern of the plane, the flow of the broken landscape to left and right filled me with a curious satisfaction. The Seine shone below, and when I crossed its winding course at an angle it seemed to speed past and pivot upon itself. The swirl of the river was as lovely in my sight as the curve of a sickle in a field. I felt restored to my element. I was captain of my ship. The fuel tanks were holding out. I should certainly win a drink at poker dice from Pénicot and then beat Lacordaire at chess. That was how I was when my team had won.

'Captain! Firing at us! We are in forbidden territory.'

Forbidden, that is, by our own people. A rectangle in which our own people fired on any plane, friend or enemy. We had orders to fly round it, but the Group never bothered to observe these traffic regulations. Well, it was Dutertre who set the course, not I. Nobody could blame me.

'Firing hard?'

'Doing as well as they can.'

'Want to go back and round?'

'Oh, no.'

His tone was matter-of-fact. We had been through our storm. For men like us, this anti-aircraft fire was a mere April shower. Still. . . .

'Dutertre, wouldn't it be silly to be brought down by our own guns?'

'They won't bring anything down. Just giving themselves a little exercise.'

Dutertre was in a sarcastic mood. Not I. I was happy. I was impatient to be back with the Group again.

'They are, for a fact. Firing like . . .'

The gunner! Come to, has he? This is the first time on board that he has opened his mouth without being spoken to. He took in the whole jaunt without feeling the need of speech. Unless that was he who muttered. 'Boy! oh, boy!' when the shells were thickest. But you wouldn't call that blabbing, exactly. He spoke now because machine-guns are his speciality—and how can you keep a specialist quiet about his speciality?

It was impossible for me not to contrast in my mind the two worlds of plane and earth. I had led Dutertre and my gunner this day beyond the bourne at which reasonable men would stop. We had seen France in flames. We had seen the sun shining on the sea. We had grown old in the upper altitudes. We had bent our glance upon a distant earth as over the cases of a museum. We had sported in the sunlight with the dust of enemy fighter planes. Thereafter we had dropped earthward again and flung ourselves into the holocaust. What we could offer up we had sacrificed. And in that sacrifice we had learnt even more about ourselves than we should have done after ten years in a monastery. We had come forth again after ten years in a monastery.

* * * *

When I got back to my billet I found my farmer at table with his wife and niece.

'Tell me,' I said to him; 'how many instruments do you think a pilot has to look after?'

'How should I know! Not my trade,' he answered. 'Must be some missing, though, to my way of thinking. The ones you win a war with. Have some supper?'

CUTIE PIE

Nicholas Fisk

Some of the highest minds on Earth combined to build *Questar,* the spaceship that accidentally captured a creature living on the planet Quta-pi.

Some of the lowest minds on Earth gave the creature its popular name: Cutie Pie. You see how these minds worked. 'From Quta-pi we bring you—Cutie Pie!' Great. Fantastic. Listen, men, we've got a *property* here. Get out there and sell.

Heaven knows, the creature was 'cute'. So cute that all over Earth, millions of human eyes, glued to millions of colour TV sets, goggled rapturously at the irridescent 'feathers' (pearly down on the belly, radiant and shimmering patterns elsewhere) that covered Cutie Pie's curved, cosy, rounded body. Human hearts doted on his dark, liquid eyes; on the gentle mouth that seemed to smile; on the busy little 'hands', complete with thumbs, that Cutie Pie used with such astonishing speed and skill.

'Aaah . . .!' crooned the world, 'Aaah! Just look at him now! He's making his bed!'

'Oh!' The colours! I could just cuddle him to death!'

'Oo, mummy do look! He's cleaning his whiskers again!'

Almost at once there were Cutie Pie dolls, colouring books, tee

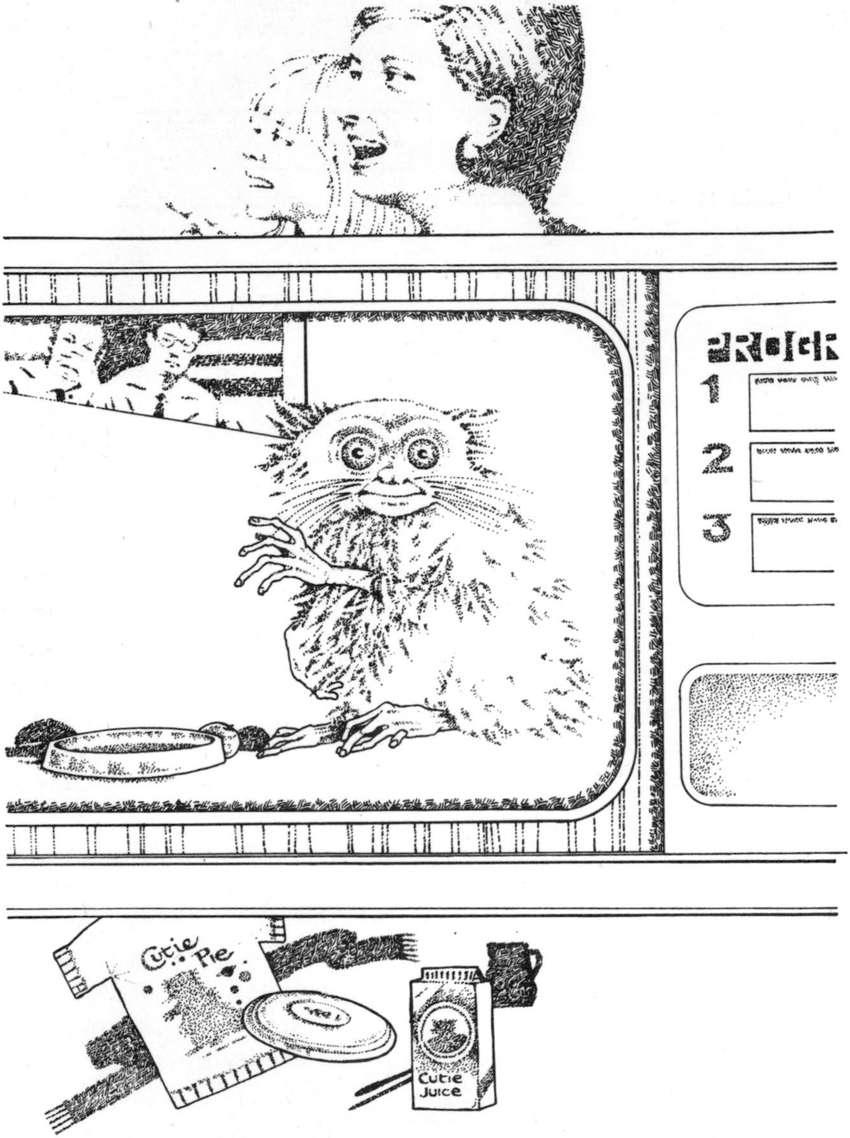

Heaven knows, the creature was 'cute'.

shirts, fan clubs, cereal cartons, cartoon serials—anything, everything. Fortunes were made instantly. How could the promoters fail? The creature was adorable. 'Oh, he's just too sweet to *live*!' the world said.

How right the world was. Every day, Cutie Pie nearly died.

'If only I could actually *see* him—*touch* him—*hold* him!' people mewed. They could not. Cutie Pie—no, this is too much, let us give him his own, proper name, Ch-tsal—Ch-tsal was hermetically sealed. He lived in a glass prison, a scientific tomb. Temperature—exactly 180°F; humidity—precisely 98 per cent; atmosphere—hydrogen, oxygen and careful proportions of a dozen exotic gases. This atmosphere imitated that of Quta-pi, the place where Ch-tsal had been captured. So, the Earth scientists agreed, it must be right.

Ch-tsal knew better. For him, every day was an agonizing fight for life. The 180°F temperature roasted him. The 98 per cent humidity stifled him. The so carefully proportioned atmosphere choked him.

For although Ch-tsal was captured on Quta-pi, that planet was not his home. He merely chanced to be there. For Ch-tsal was, in our terms, an adolescent. The elders had sent him out to undertake what we would call an initiation: he went out as a 'boy', to return with the dignity of a 'man', having faced difficulties and dangers in strange places. Quta-pi was the strangest, most hostile place he had to visit. However, his stay there was to be brief.

Or so it was planned. But on Quta-pi the sky had split and thundered (that was our spaceship *Questar*). A *thing* had descended and scarred the planet's surface (that was *Questar's* scoop, a sort of rake gathering samples of soil, rock, shale). Ch-tsal, stunned, was scooped up too.

He shudderingly remembered silver creatures with bubble faces (those were the crew of *Questar*). He glimpsed them briefly, then lost consciousness. Now he was a prisoner of white-clad men with tube-and-goggle faces. They came into his glass prison fast and went out faster. They wore gas masks to protect themselves against the atmosphere they had created for Ch-tsal.

He knew these jailers did not mean to torture him. They were not wicked; he could feel that they meant well. But he could not talk to them, could not explain. Ch-tsal had no vocal chords; his race does not speak as we do. He could only look past the goggleglasses into the eyes, begging them to understand. But they could not, did not.

If Ch-tsal's eyes seemed liquid to the watching world, it was probably because of the endless tears he shed.

* * * *

'Aaaah!' the world said, 'Look! He's doing it again! He's *grooming* himself!' 'Combing his lovely silky whiskers with his darling little hands!' 'Cleaning his *booful* feathers!'

He was indeed. Ch-tsal unceasingly groomed his feathers because they were filters, temperature-controllers, respirators and much else. As for his whiskers—they were his receivers, antennae, language-carriers, voice, lifeline. They linked him to his people. So even at home, these precious whiskers were groomed frequently. They had to be kept working perfectly.

In the glass prison they did not work.

So Ch-tsal, to add to his physical miseries, was deaf, dumb and cut off. Alone. Alone, alone, alone. . . .

He fought his despair with all the courage and complex experience of his race (far older than ours). His five stomachs and numerous organic filters just about allowed him to stomach the food and atmosphere supplied him. His mind and hands could sometimes be forced for whole hours to entertain him ('Aaah, look! He's making something! A sort of game! Can you understand it? I can't. . . .').

Best of all there was sleep—and dreams; he was home again, free again, loved and loving again. Such dreams!

* * * *

On the nineteenth day, Earth time, of his captivity, Ch-tsal woke from a beautiful dream to an appalling reality.

Lying on the floor of his glass prison were—feathers. Jewelled feathers from his back, the longer, more boldly patterned feathers from his sides, and down from his belly. They had fallen out in the night.

To Ch-tsal, this calamity was what sudden growths of hair would be to a human. Imagine. You wake one morning to find your face, the backs of your hands, your arms, your body, covered with tufts of coarse hair! Unthinkable!

And even worse for Ch-tsal. He had dreamed of his mother: her beauty—the shapes and patterns and colours of her feathers—were largely of her own creation. Like all those of her race, she had created her own style of beauty; willed her own individual, self-expressive loveliness. So, in his different way, had Ch-tsal. His feathers said, 'This is me, Ch-tsal. As you can see simply by looking at me, I am such-and-such an individual, with certain definite tastes and hopes and beliefs.' To him, his feathers were what clothes may be to humans—but more.

To lose his feathers was to lose himself.

To become naked was to become a monster.

He wept, prayed and attended to himself incessantly but without hope. His feathers continued to fall, and his whiskers. The scientists attending him peered through the glass walls and creased their brows. The world at large at first said, 'Oh, the poor thing!' 'Surely something can be done?' 'Poor Cutie Pie!'

Soon the pity soured. 'Really, it's not nice!' 'I think it's disgusting.' 'What's on the other channels?'

And then a baby panda was born—and the Olympic games came round and a new girl singer arrived who wore a one-piece glitter swimsuit back to front. The Cutie Pie tee shirts and badges and books were thrown away. Ch-tsal was forgotten.

By now he was hideous and near to death. Naked, he crouched in a corner of his glass prison, his dull eyes staring back at the bright eyes of the TV cameras. His little hands plucked at the naked flesh or picked at his muzzle, where his whiskers had been. There was nothing left for him. He had long realized that the glass walls prevented him from sending or receiving messages. Now he realized that even if he escaped, he would be powerless. Without his whiskers, he could no longer contact home. And if the impossible happened—if he could find a way of reaching home—how could he reappear there naked, without his feathers?

His scientist-jailers were sympathetic, but they too were powerless. They were also a little annoyed with him. His sickness accused them of incompetence; his survival was an embarrassment. 'Cutie Pie' were words they flinched from.

They did their best. One day, two scientists came into the prison to examine the slack, naked, ugly body of Ch-tsal. 'We could try a change of diet,' one said. 'What, again? We've tried everything,' the other replied. They put down the food bowl and examined Ch-tsal through the glass of their gas-mask goggles. They looked at him hard and long —too long: 'We'd better get out!' they said and hastened from the glass cell, feeling the strange gases beginning to seep through the masks and into their noses. 'Quick! The decontamination centre!'

One of them pressed the button that closed the glass wall. The food bowl jammed it. It could not close, not completely. The food bowl squashed into a figure of eight and a small gap was left.

Ch-tsal thought, 'I can get through that gap. Escape. But I am too tired and I no longer care.' But then he thought of the heavens and the stars and planets—and among them, the little planet that was his home.

So he left his prison and escaped into the world of Earth.

* * * *

Earth astonished him.

The air—he could breathe it! The temperature—it was pleasant! There was even a sun (only one—his planet had three) to warm his decaying body, tingle his naked skin! Then shadow again, and coolness, and delight!

It rained; and Ch-tsal knew ecstasy. For the first time, his body was less than agony to him. For whole moments, as the raindrops beat on his tortured flesh, he felt even the gates of his mind open. He would have sent a message of thanks to his God, but of course he could not: his whiskers, his 'voice', were gone. He gave thanks all the same, beaming his mind as hard as he could. Then alone, still alone, he enjoyed the rain.

He knew he had to hide and how to hide. He was efficient in everything, though deadly tired. His clever hands explored the facts and things of Earth and found them easy. You turn this knob or push this handle . . . you slide this up or pull this down. Everything was big and crude and simple. Child's play.

He found food in the extension to Mrs Chatsworth's house on Cedar Avenue. She grew cacti. They tasted unpleasant but they were food, definitely food, not the poisonous stuff of the prison cell. He ate plants, made himself a carrying bag, cut himself a store of food and carried it off.

Now all he wanted was a friend: a creature, however simple or alien, to give him comfort. He had been alone so long.

* * * *

He found a creature asleep. It was a handsome thing with fur that reminded Ch-tsal of his own feathers. The fur was coloured and patterned, very elaborately; surely not by accident?

The creature awoke and opened golden eyes. It arched its back—saw Ch-tsal—and attacked, fast and viciously. It had white hooks set in its head and brown-black hooks at the end of its limbs.

It took all Ch-tsal's mental power to quieten the creature. When it was quiet, it turned out to be useless. It had only the simplest and crudest thoughts—comfort, hunting, mating, food, territory. It could not link its thoughts. He left the thing purring and went on his way.

After the cat, a dog. Ch-tsal, ashamed of his nakedness, was frightened to approach the well covered, furry animal which radiated the sort of uncertain silly niceness that some of the creatures on Ch-tsal's own planet displayed. The dog growled and wagged its tail. Ch-tsal sensed that it might attack him, or adore him, or both. The dog licked him. Disgusted, Ch-tsal left it. The dog stared after him wagging its tail. It did not follow.

It rained again and Ch-tsal lay on his back, limbs spread, blessing every cold, clear, clean drop. He rubbed the wetness into his skin—and felt stubby prickles!

He felt his muzzle. Tiny, wiry projections tickled his fingers! His heart leapt with hope. He gave thanks. But still he had nobody to turn to. He was still alone.

* * * *

He met the one he needed. The name of this person was Christopher

Harry Winters. His age, at the first meeting, was six weeks and three days.

C. H. Winters was a good happy baby. Ch-tsal first saw him lying on a rug in a garden warmed by early summer sun. He was just the same size as Ch-tsal. Better still, he was completely naked. Ch-tsal did not have to feel ashamed in his company.

The baby kicked its legs and waved its clenched fists and made sounds. From his hiding place, a rhododendron bush, Ch-tsal could see that it leaked water from its mouth. Later, he learned that it was quite a leaky little creature altogether (which confirmed Ch-tsal's suspicion that this was an ungrown specimen of the senior species of Earth; babies were much the same on his home planet).

A big creature, not naked, came out to attend the baby. This, as Ch-tsal quickly deduced, was the mother. Ch-tsal could pick up the strong, thick waves of loving emotions that flowed between mother and baby. He remembered them from his own childhood.

He stayed in or near the rhododendron bush for three days, constantly gathering strength, often eating (by now he had the choice of a dozen foods), and always observing Christopher. Obviously he could not approach the baby in the daytime, his ugly, naked shape would be seen by the mother. In any case, the daytime Christopher was not what Ch-tsal wanted. Awake, the baby was just an active, healthy blob of animal matter, without reason or logic in its excellent mind.

It was the night-time Christopher he needed.

One night, Ch-tsal made his way into Christopher's nursery and lay down on the cot by the sleeping baby, who was almost exactly his size.

'Talk to me!' Ch-tsal said, probing with his mind. The baby stirred.

'Please talk!' Ch-tsal said and laid his whiskery muzzle against the plump hand.

The baby smiled in its sleep. Its mind began talking.

* * * *

It did not talk of what it knew now (which was next to nothing) but of what it had always known; its race memories. Ch-tsal learned what it was like for a human to plunge through a great wave, green and icy; to hunt down animals in dark forests; to let fly an arrow and somehow know for certain, as it left the bow, that it would hit its mark. He learned of the glories of battle, the terrors of defeat, the chill wickedness of snakes, the smell of wood smoke.

In his turn, Ch-tsal told the baby of the building of crystal cities, of creatures in caves, of the pioneer ships that opened up the galaxy, of the Venus invaders and how they were repulsed, of the five ways of knowing God, and of the taste of a certain food that grew only when his planet's three moons were full.

At last, both fell into the true sleep, when the mind closes itself to all but dreams. When morning came, Ch-tsal was gone. The mother fussed over her baby. By now he often laughed. He was made happier than ever by his talks with Ch-tsal. As he gurgled and bubbled, part of his unformed mind romped among the jewels of last night. He chuckled, and his mother nuzzled his neck. He laughed out loud and pulled her hair. His own hair grew longer and curlier each day.

* * * *

So, too, did Ch-tsal's feathers and whiskers. He forced them to grow, mostly by will, but also by careful attention to them and to his person. He energetically searched for food, ate with careful greed, exercised furiously, groomed his plumage continuously. His feathers were still ugly, but this did not worry him. The important thing was that his whiskers grew. He took to crouching rigidly, for hours on end, head up, staring into the night sky, whiskers vibrating, reaching out to home; and trying not to despair when no answer came.

When Christopher was four months old, and the summer was fading, Ch-tsal's feathers were so splendid that he had to be still more careful about hiding himself. He glittered in the darkness; and knew that not all humans slept all night. Some were hunters, as Christopher had told him. They had killing weapons.

But one particular night when Ch-tsal was reaching out to the sky, he heard his mother's voice, very faintly and brokenly. He replied: she heard. There came all sorts of marvellous, tearful, joyous words. . . .

Ch-tsal forgot caution and went mad. In the dewy moonlight of the woods, he became a firework, a bombshell, a Catherine wheel, spinning and zooming and bouncing off tree trunks. He whizzed and somersaulted and flashed and looped the loop on the wet leaves.

Two young men, hopefully poaching with airguns, saw him. But Ch-tsal saw them first and beamed a single pulse of ecstasy so powerful that the young men fell over backwards. They shook their heads and gaped.

They never mentioned the incident to each other or anyone else, fearing to be thought fools.

Nor did they ever mention the spaceship.

* * * *

SPACESHIP LANDS IN HERTS VILLAGE!

The newspaper yelled it. TV followed it up. It seemed a big story: bigger than a baby panda, bigger than the girl singer, a real sensation.

It soon fizzled out. You can get only so much mileage from talking heads on TV screens—from long shots of scientists staring at burnt grass in a roped-off area—from a patch of burnt field with a furrow leading to a dimple like a '!'

WHATEVER BECAME OF CUTIE PIE?

seemed a better story. Was there a link between the alien creature and the spaceship? But this faded too. The questions were fine—but where were the answers?

Only one person on Earth knows them and he is still too young to tell them to anyone but his mother. . . .

'He come. He did come.'

'Did he, darling? I'm glad. Hold your mug properly.'

'He did come last night, oh yes. It was nice.'

'Drink up, darling. More. More.'

'Telling stories he was, oh yes. And come again soon.'

'You're sure *you're* not telling stories, darling? Drink it all up, there's a big boy.'

Christopher sticks out his lower lip and stares at his mother. Why should she think him a liar? Why won't she accept a simple truth—that quite often, in the night, someone else is there beside him in bed (not actually there, only in his mind, but there all the same)—and that they tell each other stories—and that this friendship will last all his life?

His mother kisses C. H. Winters.

C. H. Winters forgives his mother and finishes his milk.

LOVE OF LIFE

Jack London

They limped painfully down the bank, and once the foremost of the two men staggered among the rough-strewn rocks. They were tired and weak, and their faces had the drawn expression of patience which comes of hardship long endured. They were heavily burdened with blanket packs which were strapped to their shoulders. Head straps, passing across the forehead, helped support these packs. Each man carried a rifle. They walked in a stooped posture, the shoulders well forward, the head still farther forward, the eyes bent upon the ground.

'I wish we had just about two of them cartridges that's layin' in that cache of ourn,' said the second man.

His voice was utterly and drearily expressionless. He spoke without enthusiasm; and the first man, limping into the milky stream that foamed over the rocks, vouchsafed no reply.

The other man followed at his heels. They did not remove their footgear, though the water was icy cold—so cold that their ankles ached and their feet went numb. In places the water dashed against their knees, and both men staggered for footing.

The man who followed slipped on a smooth boulder, nearly fell, but recovered himself with a violent effort, at the same time uttering a sharp exclamation of pain. He seemed faint and dizzy and put out his free hand while he reeled, as though seeking support against the air. When he had steadied himself he stepped forward, but reeled again and nearly fell. Then he stood still and looked at the other man, who had never turned his head.

The man stood still for fully a minute, as though debating with himself. Then he called out:

'I say, Bill, I've sprained my ankle.'

Bill staggered on through the milky water. He did not look around. The man watched him go, and though his face was expressionless as ever, his eyes were like the eyes of a wounded deer.

The other man limped up the farther bank and continued straight on without looking back. The man in the stream watched him. His lips trembled a little, so that the rough thatch of brown hair which covered them was visibly agitated. His tongue even strayed out to moisten them.

'Bill!' he cried out.

It was the pleading cry of a strong man in distress, but Bill's head did not turn. The man watched him go, limping grotesquely and lurching forward with stammering gait up the slow slope towards the soft skyline of the low-lying hill. He watched him go till he passed over the crest and disappeared. Then he turned his gaze and slowly took in the circle of the world that remained to him now that Bill was gone.

Near the horizon the sun was smouldering dimly, almost obscured by formless mists and vapours, which gave an impression of mass and density without outline or tangibility. The man pulled out his watch, the while resting his weight on one leg. It was four o'clock, and as the season was near the last of July or first of August—he did not know the precise date within a week or two—he knew that the sun roughly marked the north-west. He looked to the south and knew that somewhere beyond those bleak hills lay the Great Bear Lake; also he knew that in that direction the Arctic Circle cut its forbidding way across the Canadian Barrens. This stream in which he stood was a feeder to the Coppermine River, which in turn flowed north and emptied into Coronation Gulf and the Arctic Ocean. He had never been there, but he had seen it, once, on a Hudson's Bay Company chart.

Again his gaze completed the circle of the world about him. It was not a heartening spectacle. Everywhere was soft sky line. The hills were all low-lying. There were no trees, no shrubs, no grasses—naught but a tremendous and terrible desolation that sent fear swiftly dawning into his eyes.

'Bill!' he whispered, once and twice. 'Bill!'

He cowered in the midst of the milky water, as though the vastness were pressing in upon him with overwhelming force, brutally crushing him with its complacent awfulness. He began to shake as with an ague fit, till the gun fell from his hand with a splash. This served to rouse him. He fought with his fear and pulled himself together, groping in the water and recovering the weapon. He hitched his pack farther over on his left shoulder, so as to take a portion of its weight from off the injured ankle. Then he proceeded, slowly and carefully, wincing with pain, to the bank.

He did not stop. With a desperation that was madness, unmindful of the pain, he hurried up the slope to the crest of the hill over which his comrade had disappeared—more grotesque and comical by far than that limping, jerking comrade. But at the crest he saw a shallow valley, empty of life. He fought his fear again, overcame it, hitched the pack still farther over on his left shoulder, and lurched on down the slope.

The bottom of the valley was soggy with water, which the thick moss held, spongelike, close to the surface. This water squirted out from under his feet at every step, and each time he lifted a foot the action culminated in a sucking sound as the wet moss reluctantly released its grip. He picked his way from muskeg to muskeg, and followed the other man's footsteps along and across the rocky ledges which thrust like islets through the sea of moss.

Though alone, he was not lost. Farther on, he knew, he would come to where dead spruce and fir, very small and wizened, bordered the shore of a little lake, the *titchin-nichilie*, in the tongue of the country, the 'land of little sticks'. And into that lake flowed a small stream, the water of which was not milky. There was rush grass on that stream—this he remembered well—but no timber, and he would follow it till its first trickle ceased at a divide. He would cross this divide to the first trickle of another stream, flowing to the west, which he would follow until it emptied into the river Dease, and here he would find a cache under an upturned canoe and piled over with many rocks. And in this cache would be ammunition for his empty gun, fishhooks and lines, a small net—all the utilities for the killing and snaring of food. Also he would find flour—not much—a piece of bacon, and some beans.

Bill would be waiting for him there, and they would paddle away south down the Dease to the Great Bear Lake. And south across the lake they would go, ever south, till they gained the Mackenzie. And south, still south, they would go, while the winter raced vainly after them, and the ice formed in the eddies, and the days grew chill and crisp, south to some warm Hudson's Bay Company post, where timber grew tall and generous and there was grub without end.

These were the thoughts of the man as he strove onward. But hard as he strove with his body, he strove equally hard with his mind, trying to think that Bill had not deserted him, that Bill would surely wait for him at the cache. He was compelled to think this thought, or else there would not be any use to strive, and he would have lain down and died. And as the dim ball of the sun sank slowly into the northwest he covered every inch—and many times—of his and Bill's flight south before the downcoming winter. And he conned the grub of the cache and the grub of the Hudson's Bay Company post over and over again. He had not eaten for two days; for a far longer time he had not had all he wanted to eat. Often he stooped and picked pale muskeg berries, put them into his mouth, and chewed and swallowed them. A muskeg berry is a bit of seed enclosed in a bit of water. In the mouth the water melts away and the seed chews sharp and bitter. The man knew there was no nourishment in the berries, but he chewed them patiently with a hope greater than knowledge and defying experience.

At nine o'clock he stubbed his toe on a rocky ledge, and from sheer weariness and weakness staggered and fell. He lay for some time, without movement, on his side. Then he slipped out of the pack straps and clumsily dragged himself into a sitting posture. It was not yet dark, and in the lingering twilight he groped about among the rocks for shreds of dry moss. When he had gathered a heap he built a fire—a smouldering, smudgy fire—and put a tin pot of water on to boil.

He unwrapped his pack and the first thing he did was to count his matches. There were sixty-seven. He counted them three times to make sure. He divided them into several portions, wrapping them in oil paper, disposing of one bunch in his empty tobacco pouch, of another bunch in the inside band of his battered hat, of a third bunch under his shirt on the chest. This accomplished, a panic came upon him, and he unwrapped them all and counted them again. There were still sixty-seven.

He dried his wet footgear by the fire. The moccasins were in soggy shreds. The blanket socks were worn through in places, and his feet were raw and bleeding. His ankle was throbbing, and he gave it an examination. It had swollen to the size of his knee. He tore a long strip from one of his two blankets and bound the ankle tightly. He tore other strips and bound them about his feet to serve for both moccasins and socks. Then he drank the pot of water, steaming hot, wound his watch, and crawled between his blankets.

He slept like a dead man. The brief darkness around midnight came and went. The sun arose in the north-east—at least the day dawned in that quarter, for the sun was hidden by grey clouds.

At six o'clock he awoke, quietly lying on his back. He gazed straight up into the grey sky and knew that he was hungry. As he rolled over on his elbow he was startled by a loud snort, and saw a bull caribou regarding him with alert curiosity. The animal was not more than fifty feet away, and instantly into the man's mind leaped the vision and the savour of a caribou steak sizzling and frying over a fire. Mechanically he reached for the empty gun, drew a bead, and pulled the trigger. The bull snorted and leaped away, his hoofs rattling and clattering as he fled across the ledges.

The man cursed and flung the empty gun from him. He groaned aloud as he started to drag himself to his feet. It was a slow and arduous task. His joints were like rusty hinges. They worked harshly in their sockets, with much friction, and each bending or unbending was accomplished only through a sheer exertion of will. When he finally gained his feet, another minute or so was consumed in straightening up, so that he could stand erect as a man should stand.

He crawled up a small knoll and surveyed the prospect. There were no trees, no bushes, nothing but a grey sea of moss scarcely diversified

Mechanically he reached for the empty gun.

by grey rocks, grey lakelets, and grey streamlets. The sky was grey. There was no sun nor hint of sun. He had no idea of north, and he had forgotten the way he had come to this spot the night before. But he was not lost. He knew that. Soon he would come to the land of the little sticks. He felt that it lay off to the left somewhere, not far—possibly just over the next low hill.

He went back to put his pack into shape for travelling. He assured himself of the existence of his three separate parcels of matches, though he did not stop to count them. But he did linger, debating, over a squat moose-hide sack. It was not large. He could hide it under his two hands. He knew that it weighed fifteen pounds—as much as all the rest of the pack—and it worried him. He finally set it to one side and proceeded to roll the pack. He paused to gaze at the squat moose-hide sack. He picked it up hastily with a defiant glance about him, as though the desolation were trying to rob him of it; and when he rose to his feet to stagger on into the day, it was included in the pack on his back.

He bore away to his left, stopping now and again to eat muskeg berries. His ankle had stiffened, his limp was more pronounced, but the pain of it was as nothing compared with the pain of his stomach. The hunger pangs were sharp. They gnawed and gnawed until he could not keep his mind steady on the course he must pursue to gain the land of the little sticks. The muskeg berries did not allay this gnawing, while they made his tongue and the roof of his mouth sore with their irritating bite.

He came upon a valley where rock ptarmigan rose on whirring wings from the ledges and muskegs. *Ker—ker—ker* was the cry they made. He threw stones at them but could not hit them. He placed his pack on the ground and stalked them as a cat stalks a sparrow. The sharp rocks cut through his pants legs till his knees left a trail of blood; but the hurt was lost in the hurt of his hunger. He squirmed over the wet moss, saturating his clothes and chilling his body; but he was not aware of it, so great was his fever for food. And always the ptarmigan rose, whirring, before him, till their *ker—ker—ker* became a mock to him, and he cursed them and cried aloud at them with their own cry.

Once he crawled upon one that must have been asleep. He did

not see it till it shot up in his face from its rocky nook. He made a clutch as startled as was the rise of the ptarmigan, and there remained in his hand three tail feathers. As he watched its flight he hated it, as though it had done him some terrible wrong. Then he returned and shouldered his pack.

As the day wore along he came into valleys or swales where game was more plentiful. A band of caribou passed by, twenty and odd animals, tantalizingly within rifle range. He felt a wild desire to run after them, a certitude that he could run them down. A black fox came towards him, carrying a ptarmigan in his mouth. The man shouted. It was a fearful cry, but the fox, leaping away in fright, did not drop the ptarmigan.

Late in the afternoon he followed a stream, milky with lime, which ran through sparse patches of rush grass. Grasping these rushes firmly near the root, he pulled up what resembled a young onion sprout no larger than a shingle nail. It was tender, and his teeth sank into it with a crunch that promised deliciously of food. But its fibres were tough. It was composed of stringy filaments saturated with water, like the berries, and devoid of nourishment. He threw off his pack and went into the rush grass on hands and knees, crunching and munching, like some bovine creature.

He was very weary and often wished to rest—to lie down and sleep; but he was continually driven on, not so much by his desire to gain the land of little sticks as by his hunger. He searched little ponds for frogs and dug up the earth with his nails for worms, though he knew in spite that neither frogs nor worms existed so far north.

He looked into every pool of water vainly, until, as the long twilight came on, he discovered a solitary fish, the size of a minnow, in such a pool. He plunged his arm in up to the shoulder, but it eluded him. He reached for it with both hands and stirred up the milky mud at the bottom. In his excitement he fell in, wetting himself to the waist. Then the water was too muddy to admit of his seeing the fish, and he was compelled to wait until the sediment had settled.

The pursuit was renewed, till the water was again muddied. But he could not wait. He unstrapped the tin bucket and began to bail the pool. He bailed wildly at first, splashing himself and flinging the water so short a distance that it ran back into the pool. He worked more carefully, striving to be cool, though his heart was pounding against his chest and his hands were trembling. At the end of half an hour the pool was nearly dry. Not a cupful of water remained. And there was no fish. He found a hidden crevice among the stones through which it had escaped to the adjoining and larger pool—a pool which he could not empty in a night and a day. Had he known of the crevice, he could have closed it with a rock at the beginning and the fish would have been his.

Thus he thought, and crumpled up and sank down upon the wet earth. At first he cried softly to himself, then he cried loudly to the pitiless desolation that ringed him around; and for a long time after he was shaken by great dry sobs.

He built a fire and warmed himself by drinking quarts of hot water, and made camp on a rocky ledge in the same fashion he had the night before. The last thing he did was to see that his matches were dry and to wind his watch. The blankets were wet and clammy. His ankle pulsed with pain. But he knew only that he was hungry, and through his restless sleep he dreamed of feasts and banquets and of food served and spread in all imaginable ways.

He awoke chilled and sick. There was no sun. The grey of earth and sky had become deeper, more profound. A raw wind was blowing, and the first flurries of snow were whitening the hilltops. The air about him thickened and grew white while he made a fire and boiled more water. It was wet snow, half rain, and the flakes were large and soggy. At first they melted as soon as they came in contact with the earth, but ever more fell, covering the ground, putting out the fire, spoiling his supply of moss fuel.

This was a signal for him to strap on his pack and stumble onward, he knew not where. He was not concerned with the land of little sticks, nor with Bill and the cache under the upturned canoe by the river Dease. He was mastered by the verb *to eat*. He was hunger-mad. He took no heed of the course he pursued, so long as that course led him through the swale bottoms. He felt his way through the wet snow to the watery muskeg berries, and went by feel as he pulled up the rush grass by the roots. But it was tasteless stuff and did not satisfy. He found a weed that tasted sour and he ate all he could find of it, which was not much, for it was a creeping growth, easily hidden under the several inches of snow.

He had no fire that night, nor hot water, and crawled under his blanket to sleep the broken hunger sleep. The snow turned into a cold rain. He awakened many times to feel it falling on his upturned face. Day came—a grey day and no sun. It had ceased raining. The keenness of his hunger had departed. Sensibility, as far as concerned the yearning for food, had been exhausted. There was a dull, heavy ache in his stomach, but it did not bother him so much. He was more rational, and once more he was chiefly interested in the land of little sticks and the cache by the river Dease.

He ripped the remnant of one of his blankets into strips and bound his bleeding feet. Also he recinched the injured ankle and prepared himself for a day of travel. When he came to his pack he paused long over the squat moose-hide sack, but in the end it went with him.

The snow had melted under the rain, and only the hilltops showed white. The sun came out, and he succeeded in locating the points of the compass, though he knew now that he was lost. Perhaps, in his previous days' wanderings, he had edged away too far to the left. He now bore off to the right to counteract the possible deviation from his true course.

Though the hunger pangs were no longer so exquisite, he realized that he was weak. He was compelled to pause for frequent rests, when he attacked the muskeg berries and rush-grass patches. His tongue felt dry and large, as though covered with a fine hairy growth, and it tasted bitter in his mouth. His heart gave him a great deal of trouble. When he had travelled a few minutes it would begin a remorseless thump, thump, thump, and then leap up and away in a painful flutter of beats that choked him and made him go faint and dizzy.

In the middle of the day he found two minnows in a large pool. It was impossible to bail it, but he was calmer now and managed to catch them in his tin bucket. They were no longer than his little finger, but he was not particularly hungry. The dull ache in his stomach had been growing duller and fainter. It seemed almost that his stomach was dozing. He ate the fish raw, masticating with painstaking care, for the eating was an act of pure reason. While he had no desire to eat, he knew that he must eat to live.

In the evening he caught three more minnows, eating two and saving the third for breakfast. The sun had dried stray shreds of moss, and he was able to warm himself with hot water. He had not covered more than ten miles that day; and the next day, travelling whenever his heart permitted him, he covered no more than five miles. But his stomach did not give him the slightest uneasiness. It had gone to sleep. He was in a strange country, too, and the caribou were growing more plentiful, also the wolves. Often their yelps drifted across the desolation, and once he saw three of them slinking away before his path.

Another night; and in the morning, being more rational, he untied the leather string that fastened the squat moose-hide sack. From its open mouth poured a yellow stream of coarse gold dust and nuggets. He roughly divided the gold in halves, caching one half on a prominent ledge, wrapped in a piece of blanket, and returning the other half to the sack. He also began to use strips of the one remaining blanket for his feet. He still clung to his gun, for there were cartridges in that cache by the river Dease.

This was a day of fog, and this day hunger awoke in him again. He was very weak and was afflicted with a giddiness which at times blinded him. It was no uncommon thing now for him to stumble and fall; and stumbling once, he fell squarely into a ptarmigan nest. There were four newly hatched chicks, a day old—little specks of pulsating life no more than a mouthful; and he ate them ravenously, thrusting them alive into his mouth and crunching them like eggshells between his teeth. The mother ptarmigan beat about him with great outcry. He used his gun as a club with which to knock her over, but she dodged out of reach. He threw stones at her and with one chance shot broke a wing. Then she fluttered away, running, trailing the broken wing, with him in pursuit.

The little chicks had no more than whetted his appetite. He hopped and bobbed clumsily along on his injured ankle, throwing stones and screaming hoarsely at times; at other times hopping and bobbing silently along, picking himself up grimly and patiently when he fell, or rubbing his eyes with his hand when the giddiness threatened to overpower him.

The chase led him across swampy ground in the bottom of the valley, and he came upon footprints in the soggy moss. They were not his own—he could see that. They must be Bill's. But he could not stop, for the mother ptarmigan was running on. He would catch her first, then he would return and investigate.

He exhausted the mother ptarmigan; but he exhausted himself. She lay panting on her side. He lay panting on his side, a dozen feet away, unable to crawl to her. And as he recovered she recovered, fluttering out of reach as his hungry hand went out to her. The chase was resumed. Night settled down and she escaped. He stumbled from weakness and pitched head foremost on his face, cutting his cheek, his pack upon his back. He did not move for a long while; then he rolled over on his side, wound his watch, and lay there until morning.

Another day of fog. Half of his last blanket had gone into foot-wrappings. He failed to pick up Bill's trail. It did not matter. His hunger was driving him too compellingly—only—only he wondered if Bill, too, were lost. By midday the irk of his pack became too oppressive. Again he divided the gold, this time merely spilling half of it on the ground. In the afternoon he threw the rest of it away, there remaining to him only the half blanket, the tin bucket, and the rifle.

A hallucination began to trouble him. He felt confident that one cartridge remained to him. It was in the chamber of the rifle and he had overlooked it. On the other hand, he knew all the time that the chamber was empty. But the hallucination persisted. He fought it off for hours, then threw his rifle open and was confronted with emptiness. The disappointment was as bitter as though he had really expected to find the cartridge.

He plodded on for half an hour, when the hallucination arose again. Again he fought it, and still it persisted, till for very relief he opened his rifle to unconvince himself. At times his mind wandered farther afield, and he plodded on, a mere automaton, strange conceits and whimsicalities gnawing at his brain like worms. But these excursions out of the real were of brief duration, for ever the pangs of the hunger bite called him back. He was jerked back abruptly once from such an excursion by a sight that caused him nearly to faint. He reeled and swayed, doddering like a drunken man to keep from falling. Before him stood a horse. A horse! He could not believe his eyes. A thick mist was in them, intershot with sparkling points of light. He rubbed his eyes savagely to clear his vision, and beheld not a horse but a great brown bear. The animal was studying him with bellicose curiosity.

The man had brought his gun halfway to his shoulder before he realized. He lowered it and drew his hunting knife from its beaded sheath at his hip. Before him was meat and life. He ran his thumb along the edge of his knife. It was sharp. The point was sharp. He would fling himself upon the bear and kill it. But his heart began its warning thump, thump, thump. Then followed the wild upward leap and tattoo of flutters, the pressing as of an iron band about his forehead, the creeping of the dizziness into his brain.

His desperate courage was evicted by a great surge of fear. In his weakness, what if the animal attacked him? He drew himself up to his most imposing stature, gripping the knife and staring hard at the bear. The bear advanced clumsily a couple of steps, reared up, and gave vent to a tentative growl. If the man ran, he would run after him; but the man did not run. He was animated now with the courage of fear. He, too, growled, savagely, terribly, voicing the fear that is to life germane and that lies twisted about life's deepest roots.

The bear edged away to one side, growling menacingly, himself appalled by this mysterious creature that appeared upright and unafraid. But the man did not move. He stood like a statue till the danger was past, when he yielded to a fit of trembling and sank down into the wet moss.

He pulled himself together and went on, afraid now in a new way. It was not the fear that he should die passively from lack of food, but that he should be destroyed violently before starvation had exhausted the last particle of the endeavour in him that made towards surviving. There were the wolves. Back and forth across the desolation drifted their howls, weaving the very air into a fabric of menace that was so tangible that he found himself, arms in the air, pressing it back from him as it might be the walls of a wind-blown tent.

Now and again the wolves, in packs of two and three, crossed his path. But they sheered clear of him. They were not in sufficient numbers, and besides, they were hunting the caribou, which did not battle, while this strange creature that walked erect might scratch and bite.

In the late afternoon he came upon scattered bones where the wolves had made a kill. The debris had been a caribou calf an hour before, squawking and running and very much alive. He contemplated the bones, clean-picked and polished, pink with the cell life in them which had not yet died. Could it possibly be that he might be that ere the day was done! Such was life, eh? A vain and fleeting thing. It was only life that pained. There was no hurt in death. To die was to sleep. It meant cessation, rest. Then why was he not content to die?

But he did not moralize long. He was squatting in the moss, a bone in his mouth, sucking at the shreds of life that still dyed it faintly pink. The sweet meaty taste, thin and elusive almost as a memory, maddened him. He closed his jaws on the bones and crunched. Sometimes it was the bone that broke, sometimes his teeth. Then he crushed the bones between rocks, pounding them to a pulp, and swallowed them. He pounded his fingers, too, in his haste, and yet found a moment in which to feel surprise at the fact that his fingers did not hurt much when caught under the descending rock.

Came frightful days of snow and rain. He did not know when he made camp, when he broke camp. He travelled in the night as much as in the day. He rested wherever he fell, crawled on whenever the dying life in him flickered up and burned less dimly. He, as a man, no longer strove. It was the life in him, unwilling to die, that drove him on. He did not suffer. His nerves had become blunted, numb, while his mind was filled with weird visions and delicious dreams.

But ever he sucked and chewed on the crushed bones of the caribou calf, the least remnants of which he had gathered up and carried with him. He crossed no more hills or divides, but automatically followed a large stream which flowed through a wide and shallow valley. He did not see this stream nor this valley. He saw nothing save visions. Soul and body walked or crawled side by side, yet apart, so slender was the thread that bound them.

He awoke in his right mind, lying on his back on a rocky ledge. The sun was shining bright and warm. Afar off he heard the squawking of caribou calves. He was aware of vague memories of rain and wind and snow, but whether he had been beaten by the storm for two days or two weeks he did not know.

For some time he lay without movement, the genial sunshine pouring upon him and saturating his miserable body with its warmth. A fine day, he thought. Perhaps he could manage to locate himself. By a painful effort he rolled over on his side. Below him flowed a wide and sluggish river. Its unfamiliarity puzzled him. Slowly he followed it with his eyes, winding in wide sweeps among the bleak, bare hills, bleaker and barer and lower-lying than any hills he had yet encountered. Slowly, deliberately, without excitement or more than the most casual interest, he followed the course of the strange stream towards the sky line and saw it emptying into a bright and shining sea. He was still unexcited. Most unusual, he thought, a vision or a mirage—more likely a vision, a trick of his disordered mind. He was confirmed in this by sight of a ship lying at anchor in the midst of the shining sea. He closed his eyes for a while, then opened them. Strange how the vision persisted! Yet not strange. He knew there were no seas or ships in the heart of the barren lands, just as he had known there was no cartridge in the empty rifle.

He heard a snuffle behind him—a half-choking gasp or cough. Very slowly, because of his exceeding weakness and stiffness, he rolled over on his other side. He could see nothing near at hand, but he waited patiently. Again came the snuffle and cough, and outlined between two jagged rocks not a score of feet away he made out the grey head of a wolf. The sharp ears were not pricked so sharply as he had seen them on other wolves; the eyes were bleared and bloodshot, the head seemed to droop limply and forlornly. The animal blinked continually in the sunshine. It seemed sick. As he looked it snuffled and coughed again.

This, at least, was real, he thought, and turned on the other side so that he might see the reality of the world which had been veiled from him before by the vision. But the sea still shone in the distance and the ship was plainly discernible. Was it reality after all? He closed his eyes for a long while and thought, and then it came to him. He had been making north by east, away from the Dease Divide and into the Coppermine Valley. This wide and sluggish river was the Coppermine. That shining sea was the Arctic Ocean. That ship was a whaler, strayed east, far east, from the mouth of the Mackenzie, and it was lying at anchor in Coronation Gulf. He remembered the

Hudson's Bay Company chart he had seen long ago, and it was all clear and reasonable to him.

He sat up and turned his attention to immediate affairs. He had worn through the blanket wrappings, and his feet were shapeless lumps of raw meat. His last blanket was gone. Rifle and knife were both missing. He had lost his hat somewhere, with the bunch of matches in the band, but the matches against his chest were safe and dry inside the tobacco pouch and oil paper. He looked at his watch. It marked eleven o'clock and was still running. Evidently he had kept it wound.

He was calm and collected. Though extremely weak, he had no sensation of pain. He was not hungry. The thought of food was not even pleasant to him, and whatever he did was done by his reason alone. He ripped off his pants legs to the knees and bound them about his feet. Somehow he had succeeded in retaining the tin bucket. He would have some hot water before he began what he foresaw was to be a terrible journey to the ship.

His movements were slow. He shook as with a palsy. When he started to collect dry moss he found he could not rise to his feet. He tried again and again, then contented himself with crawling about on hands and knees. Once he crawled near to the sick wolf. The animal dragged itself reluctantly out of his way, licking its chops with a tongue which seemed hardly to have the strength to curl. The man noticed that the tongue was not the customary healthy red. It was a yellowish brown and seemed coated with a rough and half-dry mucus.

After he had drunk a quart of hot water the man found he was able to stand, and even to walk as well as a dying man might be supposed to walk. Every minute or so he was compelled to rest. His steps were feeble and uncertain, just as the wolf's that trailed him were feeble and uncertain; and that night, when the shining sea was blotted out by blackness, he knew he was nearer to it by no more than four miles.

Throughout the night he heard the cough of the sick wolf, and now and then the squawking of the caribou calves. There was life all around him, but it was strong life, very much alive and well, and he knew the sick wolf clung to the sick man's trail in the hope that the man would die first. In the morning, on opening his eyes, he beheld it regarding him with a wistful and hungry stare. It stood crouched, with tail between its legs, like a miserable and woebegone dog. It shivered in the chill morning wind and grinned dispiritedly when the man spoke to it in a voice that achieved no more than a hoarse whisper.

The sun rose brightly, and all morning the man tottered and fell towards the ship on the shining sea. The weather was perfect. It was the brief Indian summer of the high latitudes. It might last a week. Tomorrow or the next day it might be gone.

In the afternoon the man came upon a trail. It was of another man, who did not walk, but who dragged himself on all fours. The man thought it might be Bill; but he thought in a dull, uninterested way. He had no curiosity. In fact sensation and emotion had left him. He was no longer susceptible to pain. Stomach and nerves had gone to sleep. Yet the life that was in him drove him on. He was very weary, but it refused to die. It was because it refused to die that he still ate muskeg berries and minnows, drank his hot water, and kept a wary eye on the sick wolf.

He followed the trail of the other man who dragged himself along, and soon came to the end of it—a few fresh-picked bones where the soggy moss was marked by the foot pads of many wolves. He saw a squat moose-hide sack, mate to his own, which had been torn by sharp teeth. He picked it up, though its weight was almost too much for his feeble fingers. Bill had carried it to the last. Ha-ha! He would have the laugh on Bill. He would survive and carry it to the ship in the shining sea. His mirth was hoarse and ghastly, like a raven's croak, and the sick wolf joined him, howling lugubriously. The man ceased suddenly. How could he have the laugh on Bill if that were Bill; if those bones, so pinky-white and clean, were Bill?

He turned away. Well, Bill had deserted him; but he would not take the gold, nor would he suck Bill's bones. Bill would have, though, had it been the other way around, he mused as he staggered on.

He came to a pool of water. Stooping over in quest of minnows, he jerked his head back as though he had been stung. He had caught sight of his reflected face. So horrible was it that sensibility awoke long enough to be shocked. There were three minnows in the pool, which was too large to drain; and after several ineffectual attempts to catch them in the tin bucket he forbore. He was afraid, because of his great weakness, that he might fall in and drown. It was for this reason that he did not trust himself to the river astride one of the many drift logs which lined its sandspits.

That day he decreased the distance between him and the ship by three miles; the next day by two—for he was crawling now as Bill had crawled; and the end of the fifth day found the ship still seven miles away and him unable to make even a mile a day. Still the Indian summer held on, and he continued to crawl and faint, turn and turn about; and ever the sick wolf coughed and wheezed at his heels. His knees had become raw meat like his feet, and though he padded them with the shirt from his back it was a red track he left behind him on the moss and stones. Once, glancing back, he saw the wolf licking hungrily his bleeding trail, and he saw sharply what his own end might be—unless—unless he could get the wolf. Then began as grim a tragedy of existence as was ever played—a sick man that crawled, a sick wolf that limped, two creatures dragging their dying carcasses across the desolation and hunting each other's lives.

Had it been a well wolf, it would not have mattered so much to the man; but the thought of going to feed the maw of that loathsome and all but dead thing was repugnant to him. He was finicky. His mind had begun to wander again and to be perplexed by hallucinations, while his lucid intervals grew rarer and shorter.

He was awakened once from a faint by a wheeze close in his ear. The wolf leaped lamely back, losing its footing and falling in its weakness. It was ludicrous, but he was not amused. Nor was he even afraid. He was too far gone for that. But his mind was for the moment clear, and he lay and considered. The ship was no more than four miles away. He could see it quite distinctly when he rubbed the mists out of his eyes, and he could see the white sail of a small boat cutting the water of the shining sea. But he could never crawl those four miles. He knew that, and was very calm in the knowledge. He knew that he could not crawl half a mile. And yet he wanted to live. It was unreasonable that he should die after all he had undergone. Fate asked too much of him. And, dying, he declined to die. It was stark madness, perhaps, but in the very grip of death he defied death and refused to die.

He closed his eyes and composed himself with infinite precaution. He steeled himself to keep above the suffocating languor that lapped like a rising tide through all the wells of his being. It was very like a sea, this deadly languor that rose and rose and drowned his consciousness bit by bit. Sometimes he was all but submerged, swimming through oblivion with a faltering stroke; and again, by some strange alchemy of soul, he would find another shred of will and strike out more strongly.

Without movement he lay on his back, and he could hear, slowly drawing near and nearer, the wheezing intake and output of the sick wolf's breath. It drew closer, ever closer, through an infinitude of time, and he did not move. It was at his ear. The harsh dry tongue grated like sandpaper against his cheek. His hands shot out—or at least he willed them to shoot out. The fingers were curved like talons, but they closed on empty air. Swiftness and certitude require strength, and the man had not this strength.

The patience of the wolf was terrible. The man's patience was no less terrible. For half a day he lay motionless, fighting off unconsciousness and waiting for the thing that was to feed upon him and upon which he wished to feed. Sometimes the languid sea rose over him and he dreamed long dreams; but ever through it all, waking and dreaming, he waited for the wheezing breath and the harsh caress of the tongue.

He did not hear the breath, and he slipped slowly from some dream to the feel of the tongue along his hand. He waited. The fangs pressed softly; the pressure increased; the wolf was exerting its last strength in an effort to sink teeth in the food for which it had waited long. But the man had waited long, and the lacerated hand closed on the jaw. Slowly, while the wolf struggled feebly and the hand clutched feebly, the other hand crept across to a grip. Five minutes later the whole weight of the man's body was on top of the wolf. The hands had not sufficient strength to choke the wolf, but the face of the man was pressed close to the throat of the wolf and the mouth of the man was full of hair. Later the man rolled over on his back and slept.

* * * *

There were some members of a scientific expedition on the whale ship

Bedford. From the deck they remarked a strange object on the shore. It was moving down the beach towards the water. They were unable to classify it, and, being scientific men, they climbed into the whaleboat alongside and went ashore to see. And they saw something that was alive but which could hardly be called a man. It was blind, unconscious. It squirmed along the ground like some monstrous worm. Most of its efforts were ineffectual, but it was persistent, and it writhed and twisted and went ahead perhaps a score of feet an hour.

★ ★ ★ ★

Three weeks afterwards the man lay in a bunk on the whale ship *Bedford*, and with tears streaming down his wasted cheeks told who he was and what he had undergone. He also babbled incoherently of his mother, of sunny southern California, and a home among the orange groves and flowers.

The days were not many after that when he sat at table with the scientific men and ship's officers. He gloated over the spectacle of so much food, watching it anxiously as it went into the mouths of others. With the disappearance of each mouthful an expression of deep regret came into his eyes. He was quite sane, yet he hated those men at mealtime. He was haunted by a fear that the food would not last. He inquired of the cook, the cabin boy, the captain, concerning the food stores. They reassured him countless times; but he could not believe them, and pried cunningly about the lazaret to see with his own eyes.

It was noticed that the man was getting fat. He grew stouter with each day. The scientific men shook their heads and theorized. They limited the man at his meals, but still his girth increased and he swelled prodigiously under his shirt.

The sailors grinned. They knew. And when the scientific men set a watch on the man they knew. They saw him slouch for'ard after breakfast, and, like a mendicant, with outstretched palm, accost a sailor. The sailor grinned and passed him a fragment of sea biscuit. He clutched it avariciously, looked at it as a miser looks at gold, and thrust it into his shirt bosom. Similar were the donations from other grinning sailors.

The scientific men were discreet. They let him alone. But they privily examined his bunk. It was lined with hardtack; the mattress was stuffed with hardtack; every nook and cranny was filled with hardtack. Yet he was sane. He was taking precautions against another possible famine—that was all. He would recover from it, the scientific men said; and he did, ere the *Bedford's* anchor rumbled down in San Francisco Bay.

BID FOR FREEDOM

W. B. Thomas

Lieutenant Thomas, badly wounded, is captured by invading German forces on the island of Crete. He is sent to a military hospital on the Greek mainland. His attempts to escape cause the hospital so much trouble that the decision is finally made to transfer him to a prisoner of war camp in Germany. On the first stage of the journey, he leaves Athens on board a hospital ship bound for the port of Salonika, where there is a transit camp. . . .

Soon after midday on 30 October with snow-capped Olympus on our left, we steamed up the Gulf of Salonika to tie up in that historic port.

Above the harbour the old stone city walls, the towers and the fortresses standing out on the hill gave a medieval atmosphere, but around the docks things were modern enough. There was a small amount of German and Italian shipping about, with here and there a cruiser or a destoyer from Mussolini's fleet. German Marines, none of whom seemed more than eighteen years old, paraded on the wharves, constantly saluting their smart-looking officers. Everybody seemed busy, but all were very interested in the Englanders as we were off-loaded and shepherded into Red Cross vans. We were driven along the water-front, past the great circular tower of Salonika and in a few minutes were at the gates of the prison camp.

My heart sank at the sight. Here was no hospital wire. This was a real prison camp. High mazes of barbed wire ran at all angles. Throughout the camp were great towers on which sentries could be seen fondling their machine-guns. From behind the wire near the gate a crowd of unkempt and undernourished prisoners gathered to gape forlornly as we were formed into ranks and our luggage checked.

It was almost dark by the time all our personal belongings had been strewn on the gravel and the Guard Officer satisfied that we carried no implements for escape. The great gates opened and we poured in, to be ushered into various buildings.

In a large dormitory I met again quite a few of the officers who had come up from Athens in the hospital ship. We all fell to exchanging experiences, and I felt quite at home amongst them. Two in particular I came to respect immensely. Lieutenant-Colonel Le Soeuf, tall, dark, and quietly spoken, had been captured with his unit, the 7th Australian Field Ambulance, when they were overrun at Heraklion in Crete; Major Richard Burnett, a regular officer, had been CO of his unit on Crete and had been captured while making a reconnaissance in the dark.

Salonika was a bad camp in every way. In the past many shocking atrocities had been committed by guards who had been former members of the Nazi Youth Movement. Burnett was even then investigating a horrible case—a German sentry had thrown a grenade into a latrine packed with dysentery cases and the carnage had been frightful. The only explanation given on Burnett's protest was that the men were whispering in a suspicious manner. The authorities supported the sentry's action.

In a recent unsuccessful attempt at escape, three men had been shot out of hand and their bodies left for days in the hot sun, while for other escapes soldiers had been bound with barbed wire and whipped as a warning to all. Drunken guards had been known to walk into the compound and cruelly maul unarmed prisoners, while it was said that the officer in charge of the young Nazis would ask daily of his guard how many English swine they had killed and congratulate the murderer effusively.

It was an alarming picture, quite different from the treatment I had experienced in Athens. Listening to it all I regretted much that I had ever left the hospital.

The camp had been an old Greek Artillery barracks, but the Germans had allowed it to deteriorate badly, so that now it was in a terrible state of sanitation, with practically no drainage at all. Millions of flies swarmed around the latrines and cookhouses and formed ugly black heaps where refuse was dropped. Scores of mangy cats slunk among the barrack-rooms.

The prisoners in the compound were the stragglers of the large army which had already passed through to Germany. There were thirty officers and some two hundred men, one hundred and fifty of whom were maimed in some way.

About fifteen were men who had lately been caught in and around Salonika. These were a grand crowd of fellows, and I made a point of talking to them and gaining much valuable information.

Some had been out and recaptured four or five times; indeed, the greatest joke amongst them was the case of the Australian who was picked up as a matter of course by a German patrol each Friday at a house of ill fame. Others with higher motives for escape had been free for long periods, only to be recaptured either on the very borders of Turkey or at sea moving south to freedom.

One, a tall New Zealand sergeant with a sense of humour, had seen his chance on a day of pouring rain, when a German officer had visited the camp hospital. The officer had walked into the lobby, and hung up his dripping coat and hat before entering the German guard-room. The sergeant had donned these quickly and marched out into the rain. The sentries had all, one by one, frozen into a salute. Thereafter, he walked down into the streets of Salonika. It was truly an escape to fire the imagination.

A long-haired lad from Sussex had clung to the bottom of one of the contractor's drays and had been carried out of the camp. A very young Cockney told us of his adventure in going out in a bag of rubbish.

The prisoners were even then working on a mass escape plan. But they had the shrewdness of experienced escapists. It was some days before I was to be allowed into their confidence.

Meanwhile, the atmosphere in the officers' mess was unpleasantly strained. There were bickerings over food all round, and quarrels between the Medical Corps and the combatants over such futile things as seniority and the post of Senior British Officer in Captivity. On one occasion feeling ran so high that one side actually asked a German NCO to consider and settle the dispute.

It was not a pleasant place. Consequently I was pleased when Dick Burnett asked me to share a room accorded him because of his rank.

Burnett was keen on escape. He had been free on more than one occasion in Crete and in spite of his forty years was determined to risk all the hazards to get back to his regiment. For as long as he was to be a prisoner he was firmly resolved to cause as much trouble for his captors as possible.

For the first three or four days, I think, he was weighing me up as a possible partner for the months we might have to spend together before reaching British lines.

Then we began to lay our plans.

The section of the camp we were concerned with was only a small part, a sub-section, of the main Salonika Prison Camp. Most of the other sub-sections were now empty and unguarded, with the exception of the one immediately to the west of ours. This held political prisoners from Greece and Yugoslavia. In there one day we had seen an old lady awaiting execution for aiding British escapers.

The sub-section was an oblong, some three hundred yards by two hundred, containing seven large barrack huts, a cookhouse and a large new building. The only exit was the gate at the north-west corner, and apart from the roving sentries within the compound, the Germans relied mainly on the guard posts immediately outside it. At the southern end these consisted of two twenty-foot towers, each with two sentries, a machine-gun and a movable searchlight. At the northern end there were the sentries on the gate, those on a tower by the gate, and two sentries with machine-gun and searchlight on the roof of a small shed used for storing horse fodder. The south and west sides were bounded by other sub-sections, the north by an open space and the Salonika road, and the east side had a wide gravel road which separated the compound from rubbish and salvage and which led along to the stables.

A whole morning spent watching guards, drawing innumerable diagrams and getting annoyed with one another disposed of the front, the west and rear sides as quite impossible. Only the east side was left, and we had little hope that it would produce the answer. In common with the others it had some three hundred yards of wire tangle, ten feet high, ten feet wide, but there was one difference. There were two buildings which broke the obstacle, that is, the wire tangle ran in between them, and rambled up and over them. It did not run along the back.

One of these was the cookhouse. It had a thick cement wall for a back and, furthermore, was less than a stone's throw from the southern sentry tower. We mooched around it for half an hour after lunch and rejected it as impracticable.

The second building was a fairly new three-storied building. A preliminary examination revealed no possibilities; all the windows facing out were heavily barred with steel and barbed wire, while even if work could free them it would be too dangerous to be lowered to the road below in full view of the searchlights at either end.

But just as we were deciding dejectedly that a tunnel was the only solution, we espied a staircase winding down from the ground floor to hide what must be a back doorway onto the gravel road below. The passage down was blocked by large empty crates. The door was of itself unimportant. There were still the searchlight and machine-guns covering the road outside. But Dick had an idea and we climbed again onto the first floor to discuss it.

The two searchlights which concerned us covered the road very efficiently. The one at the south end from the tower had an unobstructed view, while the one on the roof of the hay shed was only limited by its position from seeing the actual back of the building in question. But, and on this our plan depended, these posts had the additional task of covering the south and north wire respectively: their searchlights were on swivels and they would swing from one task to the other every few seconds. For the most part one or other of the posts would have its light focused on the gravel road, occasionally both would play together along it for minutes on end. But with an understandable human error, often for a few seconds, both crews would switch simultaneously onto their secondary task. This would leave the road in darkness until either of them realized the position and swung his searchlight back. Burnett and I considered that, given luck, this erratic few seconds would give us a chance to make the initial dash across the road and use the scant cover of a shallow culvert before the searchlights swung back.

And so we examined the door.

The crates barring the steps down from the first floor were really no obstacle and would afford good cover for any work we should do. The steps ran down in two short flights onto a very small landing, and the door-frame was set firmly in stone. There were steel and wooden bars across it, both bolted and nailed, and the whole was covered with barbed wire on staples. Formidable certainly, but, provided we were not hurried, we thought it could be done.

One remarkable thing about our work on this project was the complete absence of the adventure spirit and the elation of imaginary success. Every step we took in this venture was coldly methodical. We took very few into our confidence.

Amazingly enough, the tools for the work were no trouble at all. I brought a pair of excellent pliers from a Greek electrician working in the barracks; Burnett made some useful crowbars from sections of our beds; and Fred Moodie, a camp doctor, provided a strong pair of plaster cutters. Fred also arranged for me a good supply of the German cod liver oil salve which had proved very soothing and beneficial to my wound.

We started work that night. Immediately after the evening check we made our way to the building with innocent unconcern and talked to various orderlies until curfew, when we slipped behind the crates under the first flight of stairs until all was quiet.

The work was necessarily slow, and not a little nerve-racking. Each nail, each bolt had to be worked out slowly and with great caution; a loud squeak would leave us perspiring and fearful for long minutes. Every now and then the crunch of heavy feet on the gravel outside would hold us up, and on three occasions during the first night two of the guards talked for a long time just outside the door.

By four o'clock we had removed all the wooden bars and two of the six more formidable steel bars. We tacked the bars back loosely into their old positions and generally tidied up the evidence before setting off on the quite hazardous trip back to our barracks. The two sentries detailed to prowl round inside the compound had orders to shoot on sight after curfew, and though the twenty minutes they took on their regular rounds provided ample time for us there were the searchlights to pin us down occasionally and always the chance that the sentries might vary their tactics.

We reached our room without incident and were sound asleep for the six o'clock room check. Having previously convinced the Germans that it was less trouble not to order us out to stand by our beds each morning (as laid down), we were left to slumber on until almost lunch time.

Our progress on the second night did not compare with the first night. There were too many interruptions—stable-hands coming home late from leave and arguing out on the road, restless sentries and irregular changing of guards. And we were discovered at work by a group of Australian and British medical orderlies, and it took us some little time to impress on them the need for absolute secrecy. However, we worked out two more steel bars and managed to loosen a third before an early rooster, crowing beyond the stables, warned us of approaching day.

On the third night we made very good progress indeed; by eleven o'clock the last of the steel bars was disposed of. We had brought a rough chisel and a screwdriver to remove the lock, but, to our amazement, we found that it was not, in fact, locked. A few nails had been hammered at random around the edges, however, and just after midnight the last was worked out and we were able to move the door.

It opened two or three inches and then stuck. We realized that there was an apron of barbed wire stapled onto the outside. With some difficulty it would be possible to worm a wrist with pliers through the opening. After a short consultation we decided to leave it as it was until the night of the break, knowing that it would only take a few minutes to open it.

We made our way carefully back to our room, secreted our tools under our mattresses and in the stove, and undressed in the dark. It was only about one o'clock and, tired as we were, the prospect of a few extra hours' sleep was very pleasing.

No sooner had we said good night, however, than we were suddenly startled by the tread of heavy feet in the passageway outside. There was a guttural order, our door burst open, and three soldiers rushed in. Torches flashed in our faces, our blankets were pulled off roughly, and the room quickly but not throughly searched. Then, as if satisfied, the officer barked an order and the party clattered out and away, leaving two very shaken men behind.

Now that visit was unfortunate. The explanation was quite beyond us, particularly as ours was the only room searched. Perhaps someone had discovered and reported that we had not been sleeping in our beds at night; or perhaps it was merely a check on me as a known 'bad lad'. But the effect was this: Burnett decided not to come. Three nights' work had taxed his nerves badly and now he thought our whole plan was discovered. Even when daylight proved that no attempt was made to re-fix the door, Burnett saw the possibility of a trap—a machine-gun covering the exit to make an example of anyone who attempted to escape. He was still as determined as ever, but with the caution of forty years he weighed the chances as too dangerous, and started straight away on a new plan to throw ourselves from the train on the way through Yugoslavia.

His pessimism shook me not a little. I spent the morning watching the area near the cookhouse, and after lunch sat down and tried to come to some decision. His arguments were very sound; the plan had been hazardous enough without the new threat. Yet at the back of my mind was a conviction, however unfounded, that the plan was still secret.

Finally I took out a piece of paper, and ruling a line down the centre, wrote in two columns all the pros and cons I could think of.

That was a poignant half-hour. I knew well that the wrong decision might cost me my life. Yet I felt very strongly that it was a case of 'now or never', that, if I let this opportunity pass, I might never be presented with another.

As the page filled up, Burnett sat quietly watching me. I knew that he was apprehensive, but, having stated his arguments once, he made no attempt to dissuade me further.

Before I could make up my mind we were beseiged by some five or six of the more hardened card players and I was quite willing to procrastinate an hour for a game of pontoon. Perhaps it was my abstraction, but within half an hour, without effort, I had taken every *drachma* off the whole school. After a drink of cocoa from my Red Cross parcel they all departed very disgruntled, threatening that they would come back on the morrow to get it all back. As soon as they had gone, at Burnett's suggestion, I entered under the 'Pros' the fact that I now had 8,000 *drachmae* for escape purposes.

At six o'clock I made my decision. It was, I am sure, the decision of my life. Our original plan had been to get some greatly needed rest that night, Saturday, and escape on Sunday about nine when the guards not on duty were on leave. But now, as things appeared to be moving rapidly and because my nerves were so tense that I could not sleep, I decided to go on my own that night.

When Burnett saw that I was determined, he gave me everything he had; all his bread, condensed Red Cross food, a civilian coat, and all his savings, including some English money. He cooked me up a wonderful farewell meal and set himself to do a thousand and one little things to help me to get ready.

It was now after curfew. It was therefore necessary to move with great care over to the building. Soon after eight-thirty, I said goodbye to Burnett. He was terribly apprehensive of the risk I was taking and heartily miserable that he was not coming with me. I realized I was going to miss his company very much.

It took me almost an hour to go the two hundred yards from our barracks. The searchlights seemed particularly restless and the roving patrol sat down and talked for nearly half an hour while I lay in what shade a wire-netting fence afforded. When finally they moved off I ran quickly up the steps and through the door into the hall of the medical building. As soon as I latched the door behind me a startled voice greeted me.

'Are you *mad*? Surely you know that it's dangerous to be out at curfew?'

It was an Australian medical orderly. When I told him of my plans he immediately offered his help.

We moved onto the first landing, from where we could look through the barred window down onto the road. Everything seemed quite normal. We watched for half an hour, but, with the exception of a team of horses being taken out from the stables, only the usual movement was apparent.

The orderly and a friend appointed themselves to keep watch while I worked. We arranged a code of signals whereby, should they wish to warn me, they would throw something small down the steps leading to the escape door. The 'all-clear' would be one or the other whistling from *Rigoletto*.

The door was as we had left it. I removed all the loosely held bars and convinced myself that no one had tampered with them. The door opened noiselessly some three inches and even with great caution it only took me twenty minutes to cut the eight or nine restraining wires on the outside.

As I cut the last one and felt the door suddenly swing easily towards me, the first alarm signal in the form of a leather slipper clattered down the stairs behind me. I closed the door quickly, my heart in my mouth. Outside I could hear heavy feet crunching slowly down the road. As they approached the door I held my breath in apprehension. With the searchlights full on I felt that no one could miss the tell-tale loose ends of wire. But, although I could have sworn there was a slight pause just level with the door, the danger passed and in a few seconds I heard a soft but unmusical attempt to whistle the arranged all clear.

I opened the door a few inches and studied the ground. The road was only some fifteen feet across, but I realized that unless the searchlights settled down I would never get over without being seen. The sentry in the tower on the south end was unusually restless; his light was flickering to and fro every few seconds. I decided, as it was then nine-thirty, to wait until the ten o'clock change of sentries with the hope of getting someone more placid. During the wait I worked out each step across the road, and the point where I should get over the low wall into the rubbish on the other side.

Just before ten the team of horses, which had gone out earlier, returned noisely up the road, and, although I did not look, I imagined they were towing some vehicle. When they had passed up towards the German stables I stole a look out. I thought for a moment that the opportunity was ideal, for one of the searchlights was playing on the stable yard, probably to help the unhitching of the horses. I had just made the decision to go and was in the act of opening the door when some object clattered down the stairs behind me. A second later came the sharp order of the Corporal of the guard as he turned his ten o'clock relief up the road—I shivered as I realized how very nearly I had run right into them.

For fifteen minutes after the old guard had clattered past the door on their way to the guard-room, the searchlights on both ends were seldom still for more than a few seconds, but soon after that the new sentries began to tire of their vigilance. Sitting back on the stairs I could count up to four seconds while no light shone through the keyhole or under the door. So I opened the door cautiously and looked out.

Looking across the road, I realized that although the tower at the south end shone direct onto the exit, it would be the light from the roof of the hay shed which would be most dangerous, as it shone over the rubbish. I started counting the irregular breaks of darkness. Sometimes there would be one or other searchlight shining on the road for over ten minutes, then for an erratic five minutes it would be in darkness every few seconds.

'One—two—three,' I counted, 'one—two—three—four getting better now, one—two—three—four—my word, I could have made it that time, one—two—three—phew, just as well I didn't then . . .' and then there would be another period of light. The most unnerving thing about it all was the fact that there was no way of knowing how long any particular period of darkness was going to be. I knew that whenever I made the decision it would be final. The success or failure of the whole plan depended on nothing more than luck.

I think perhaps I must have been poised there for half an hour. But it seemed years to me. I alternated between self-reproach for having missed a good chance and a chill of horror when a period of darkness lasted only one second.

And then I went. Not running, but carefully over the road, my stocking-covered shoes making little noise on the gravel. But as I prepared to throw myself over the low wall on the other side of the road, I sensed the return of one of the lights and involuntarily dropped to the ground, realizing instantly that I must present an ideal target to either sentry post.

First the light from the hay shed played idly up and down the road, and so brilliant was it that it shone right into the gravel where my face was buried. Then I sensed the other one flashing over my shoulder. My body tingled with terror and for the first time in my life I felt the hairs on the nape of my neck pricking and rising.

I could hear two of the sentries talking quite clearly. They did not sound at all excited and yet surely they must have seen me. My body began to flinch and cringe as I imagined a bullet striking home. My

My body tingled with terror.

mind went numb, and I had no idea how long I lay there, but at last, one after the other, the lights swung away.

I sprang up. Instead of vaulting the low wall I passed along it, turned into the courtyard of an MT garage. I dropped behind a large oil drum as the first light swung back. Here I was not so frightened, for the low wall now shielded me completely from the one searchlight and the drum from the other. I must have been pinned there for all of ten minutes. It was uncomfortably cramped, and I was apprehensive lest some driver or later-returning guard should discover me.

But when darkness came I was able to slip over the wall, and worm through the rubbish towards the outer ring of wire. There was no need to stop even when both lights were playing down the road, for there was sufficient shadow amongst the rubbish and small scrub to mask cautious movement. There was thirty yards of this cover stretching over to the outer ring of doubled apron barbed wire. This presented no problem with my wire-cutters. But I was surprised when I was through it to run into a wire-netting fence. Following it along, I came to a break covered by a sheet of iron, which I crawled through to find myself in a small cleared space littered with large boxes. I was just passing one of the latter when a movement somewhere near stopped me. I hugged the ground, my heart in my mouth. All was quiet for a few minutes, then just as I prepared to continue, again came the small movement, much closer this time. I placed it as just behind the box. I was becoming really scared when from inside the box came the unmistakable clucking of a disturbed hen. I was inside the guards' chicken run.

I crossed the run to the rear corner of the garage and cut a small square to let myself out. I found myself in a grass enclosure, bounded by two very high stone walls, which ran into a corner some two hundred yards away. Very clearly I could hear the rumbling of the trams on the main Salonika road.

The wall bounding the road was about ten feet high and I could see glass glistening along its length. But it didn't present any great obstacle—the Germans had attempted to make it more formidable by giving it an apron of barbed wire—thus making an ideal ladder.

I climbed up it carefully. The road was still very busy for that time of night. In addition to the trams and army vehicles there was a steady stream of civilians and soldiers on both sides of the street. I waited ten minutes and was thinking of retiring for a few hours to let things settle down when I fancied I heard a single shot from back in camp. I listened for a full minute. Although I heard nothing further and was almost convinced that it was my over-taxed mind playing tricks, I decided to push on and take the chance of discovery.

With the glare from the lights of the prison camp there was quite a shadow on the road side of the wall, and as soon as there was a perceptible break in the traffic below I lowered myself so far as the lowest strand of barbed wire would allow me and dropped the remaining four feet, falling in a heap on the footpath.

My first reaction was one of acute pain. The jar was considerable. But almost immediately I became aware of two figures standing some fifteen paces away arguing volubly. They were both soldiers and I saw by the rifle he had slung over his shoulder that one of them was on duty. But as I picked myself up I knew I had not been seen. The second soldier was obviously very drunk and was abusing the sentry roundly.

I moved quickly up the street for two or three hundred yards, stopped and removed the spare pair of socks which I had worn over my shoes, and walked very quietly into Salonika.

The whole of the venture up to this stage had been cool and methodical. A desperate fear of the risks had numbed my mind against any anticipation of success. But now at every step I felt welling within me a glorious exhilaration, an ecstasy so sweet that my eyes pricked with tears of gratitude. All the oppression, all the worry and boredom, which had so weighed me down, seemed to disappear as though they were taken like a heavy cloak off my shoulders. The air was pure and free.

For perhaps an hour I let my exuberance lead me drunkenly up and down strange streets. Every unsuspecting soldier I passed was a boost to my confidence. As each approached, I weighed up his size, darted a glance right and left for possible flight and then, as we drew level, either made a great play of blowing my nose or whistled the one Greek tune I knew in what I hoped was a nonchalant manner. But soon I realized there was no need to regard each as a suspicious enemy—each was going about his own business whether leave or duty;

probably the last thought anyone had was that the stream of pedestrians might include an English officer.

Although there was some attempt at a black-out the streets were full of gaiety. From every restaurant and wine-shop came the laughter and music of the conquerors. Happy, and here and there inebriated, couples thronged the alleyways. At one street corner a lone violinist was playing old music rather sweetly. I felt wonderfully at ease, confident and vastly superior to all those in field-grey uniforms who had not the sense to recognize an enemy in their midst.

However, somewhere in the centre of Salonika, the exhilaration quietened and allowed reason to prevail. I turned reluctantly to follow my plan of being well clear of the city by dawn. With some difficulty I oriented myself. Striking south, I moved through a suburb full of cheerful chatter and houses that glowed with homely light until I came to the foot of the great Salonika Hill. I followed up the same zigzag path trod by many a conqueror, sitting down occasionally on the stone steps to rest and marvel at the beauty of the subdued lighting fringed by the sea below me. One by one the lights in the nearby houses went out as the city quietened down. By the time I reached the old Salonika wall with its massive gateways all was quiet.

I sat down fifty yards from the gateway and watched for a while. All the exits to Salonika were under guard. Occasionally every civilian would be forced to produce his identity card, but this particular gate divided the city from one of its more modern suburbs. From somewhere in the prison camp had come the information that, with the large numbers passing to and fro, the sentries had become very slack.

The sentry on duty moved out of the shadow of the archway and shifted his slung rifle from one shoulder to the other. A group of civilians, coming from a side street near the wall passed through quietly, so I braced myself and slouched through after them, blowing my nose noisily; indeed, so interested was I in appearing nonchalant that I almost collided with a sentry who was moving across the archway. But he hardly glanced at me. And so I went through the last suburb and down to the outskirts of the town. I drew my coat close around me, for the wind was bitterly cold.

Soon there loomed ahead of me a massive grey building, and the path I was following took me quite close to it. Just as I passed from the moonlight into its shadow, without warning and so suddenly that it froze me to the spot, a harsh order rang out and there before me in the dark I could see the glint of a bayonet some five inches from my throat.

Slowly I raised my hands to my shoulders, and as my fear was replaced by an overwhelming disappointment, muttered miserably:

'English—*Engländer—Englezi*.'

What happened then was typical of any adventures in Greece, the land of 'you-never-know'. The rifle clattered to the ground, two hands reached up and grasped mine, and before my startled wits could register what was happening a bristly face had planted a kiss on both my cheeks. In the dark I could see my new friend was in uniform. Looking again at the silhouette of the imposing building, in whose shadow we stood, some memory of a conversation in the camp convinced me that I had run into a Greek policeman guarding the civilian jail. It was the first indication, and a surprise after my other experiences, to find that the Greek police were not necessarily pro-German.

But after the first emotional outburst had spent itself fear seized him and immediately he fell to gesticulating violently and whispering urgent instructions. I gathered he wanted me to make myself scarce and also not to continue along the track I had been following. When I shrugged my shoulders in an expression of hopelessness he seized my arms and pointed to some lights in the far distance with repeated whispers 'Bon, kala, goot, bon, kala, goot'.

Half an hour, over a bare and stony hillock, brought me to the lights, a group of perhaps thirty poor houses. Most of them were in darkness and quiet, but the lights I had followed indicated that someone was still afoot. I moved in to try my luck, and knocked at the door of the nearest house.

We say an Englishman's home is his castle; so it is with the Greek. He won't let the drawbridge down at night until he recognizes a friend. He peers furtively at you from the window on the left of the door, then from the one on the right, and finally decides through the keyhole and from your foreign jabber that you are no friend. And after that no amount of noise nor knocking, no entreaties, nor threats will affect him. You will hear urgent whispers inside, and movement near the door, but you are lucky indeed if it opens.

I tried every house in the first group whether lights shone or not, but always with the same result. I felt desolate and cold, and the unusual exercise was causing my wound to tug uncomfortably at my thigh. To make things more desperate, suddenly from one of the dark alleyways between two houses bounded a large village dog, fiercely growling and snarling. Three or four of its kind joined it and I was forced to move warily along one of the walls with my boots ready and my heart in my mouth.

At first the brutes showed a certain caution, would move back a yard or two, if I made as though I had something to throw, but gradually, as their numbers swelled, they took confidence and started snapping at the cuffs of my trousers. The situation was ugly. There seemed no possibility of help from the dark, aloof houses, and I knew that to run would only bring them upon me in a ferocity far beyond my strength to combat. But in the end that is just what I did. Panic seized me and I ran full pelt down the rough street with them all at heels, until, seeing a flight of steps leading up to a small house I ran frantically up and hammered on the door. The first of the dogs came half-way up the steps and paused, the remainder stayed snarling and yapping below.

From inside some order was called, then repeated, then foot-steps padded over and the door was flung open. The smallest of men, about five feet high, smiled up at me and spoke rapidly in Greek. With a gesture I said '*Englezi*' and indicated the bristling dark forms below. With that unique fluttering of the hand which is the Greek beckoning, I was waved into a tiny living-room.

In the centre of the room, huddled round a tin of ashes on the top of which were a few live coals, were two more small people—an old lady and a young fellow. On my entry they both stood up and looked over inquiringly. The first one said something, which I took to be an introduction of sorts, and the old lady, dear fragile thing that she was, reached up and patted my arm. She sighed deeply and suddenly I felt in that sigh all the sympathy I had been craving for so long. They indicated a chair, and as I collapsed into it, both body and mind relaxed into a relief that brought me almost to tears.

FACING THE STORM

Joseph Conrad

The Nan-Shan, *under the command of Captain MacWhirr, is sailing south through the China seas to the treaty port of Fu-chau. Her lower holds are full of cargo, and she is carrying two hundred passengers—unskilled Chinese labourers (coolies) who are returning home, with a camphor-wood box of possessions each, after seven years' work in various tropical colonies.*

The captain and Solomon Rout, the chief engineer, are unusually irritable, and Jukes, the chief mate, is disturbed to see the barometer dropping minute by minute. . . .

At its setting the sun had a diminished diameter and an expiring brown, rayless glow, as if millions of centuries elapsing since the morning had brought it near its end. A dense bank of cloud became visible to the northward; it had a sinister dark olive tint, and lay low and motionless upon the sea, resembling a solid obstacle in the path of the ship. She went floundering towards it like an exhausted creature driven to its death. The coppery twilight retired slowly, and the darkness brought out overhead a swarm of unsteady, big stars, that, as if blown upon, flickered exceedingly and seemed to hang very near the earth. At eight o'clock Jukes went into the chart room to write up the ship's log.

He copied neatly out of the rough book the number of miles, the course of the ship, and in the column for 'wind' scrawled the word 'calm' from top to bottom of the eight hours since noon. He was exasperated by the continuous monotonous rolling of the ship. The heavy inkstand would slide away in a manner that suggested perverse intelligence in dodging the pen. Having written in the large space under the head of 'Remarks' 'Heat very oppressive', he stuck the end of the penholder in his teeth, pipe fashion, and mopped his face carefully.

'Ship rolling heavily in a high cross swell,' he began again, and commented to himself, 'Heavily is no word for it.' Then he wrote: 'Sunset threatening with a low bank of clouds to N. and E. Sky clear overhead.'

Sprawling over the table with arrested pen, he glanced out of the door, and in that frame of his vision he saw all the stars flying upwards between the teakwood jambs on a black sky. The whole lot took flight together and disappeared, leaving only a blackness flecked with white flashes, for the sea was as black as the sky and speckled with foam afar. The stars that had flown to the roll came back on the return swing of the ship, rushing downwards in their glittering multitude, not of fiery points, but enlarged to tiny discs brilliant with a clear wet sheen.

Jukes watched the flying big stars for a moment, and then wrote: '8 P.M. Swell increasing. Ship labouring and taking water on her decks. Battened down the coolies for the night. Barometer still falling.' He paused, and thought to himself, 'Perhaps nothing whatever'll come of it.' And then he closed resolutely his entries: 'Every appearance of a typhoon coming on.'

* * * *

Captain MacWhirr opened his eyes.

He thought he must have been asleep. What was that loud noise? Wind? Why had he not been called? The lamp wriggled in its gimbals, the barometer swung in circles, the table altered its slant every moment; a pair of limp seaboots with collapsed tops went sliding past the couch. He put out his hand instantly, and captured one.

Jukes's face appeared in a crack of the door: only his face, very red, with staring eyes. The flame of the lamp leaped, a piece of paper flew up, a rush of air enveloped Captain MacWhirr. Beginning to draw on the boot, he directed an expectant gaze at Jukes's swollen, excited features.

'Came on like this,' shouted Jukes, 'five minutes ago . . . all of a sudden.'

The head disappeared with a bang, and a heavy splash and patter of drops swept past the closed door as if a pailful of melted lead had been flung against the house. A whistling could be heard now upon the deep vibrating noise outside. The stuffy chart room seemed as full of draughts as a shed. Captain MacWhirr collared the other seaboot on its violent passage along the floor. He was not flustered, but he could not find at once the opening for inserting his foot. The shoes he had flung off were scurrying from end to end of the cabin, gambolling playfully over each other like puppies. As soon as he stood up he kicked at them viciously, but without effect.

He threw himself into the attitude of a lunging fencer, to reach after his oilskin coat; and afterwards he staggered all over the confined space while he jerked himself into it. Very grave, straddling his legs far apart, and stretching his neck, he started to tie deliberately the strings of his sou'wester under his chin, with thick fingers that trembled slightly. He went through all the movements of a woman putting on her bonnet before a glass, with a strained, listening attention, as though he had expected every moment to hear the shout of his name in the confused clamour that had suddenly beset his ship. Its increase filled his ears while he was getting ready to go out and confront whatever it might mean. It was tumultuous and very loud—made up of the rush of the wind, the crashes of the sea, with that prolonged deep vibration of the air, like the roll of an immense and remote drum beating the charge of the gale.

He stood for a moment in the light of the lamp, thick, clumsy, shapeless in his panoply of combat, vigilant and red-faced.

'There's a lot of weight in this,' he muttered.

As soon as he attempted to open the door the wind caught it. Clinging to the handle, he was dragged out over the doorstep, and at once found himself engaged with the wind in a sort of personal scuffle whose object was the shutting of that door. At the last moment a tongue of air scurried in and licked out the flame of the lamp.

Ahead of the ship he perceived a great darkness lying upon a multitude of white flashes; on the starboard beam a few amazing stars drooped, dim and fitful, above an immense waste of broken seas, as if seen through a mad drift of smoke.

On the bridge a knot of men, indistinct and toiling, were making great efforts in the light of the wheelhouse windows that shone mistily on their heads and backs. Suddenly darkness closed upon one pane, then on another. The voices of the lost group reached him after the manner of men's voices in a gale, in shreds and fragments of forlorn shouting snatched past the ear. All at once Jukes appeared at his side, yelling, with his head down.

'Watch—put in—wheelhouse shutters—glass—afraid—blown in.'

Jukes heard his commander upbraiding.

'This—come—anything—warning—call me.'

He tried to explain, with the uproar pressing on his lips.

'Light air—remained—bridge—sudden—northeast—could turn—thought—you—sure—hear.'

They had gained the shelter of the weather cloth, and could converse with raised voices, as people quarrel.

'I got the hands along to cover up all the ventilators. Good job I had remained on deck. I didn't think you would be asleep, and so . . . What did you say, sir? What?'

'Nothing,' cried Captain MacWhirr. 'I said—all right.'

'By all the powers! We've got it this time,' observed Jukes in a howl.

'You haven't altered her course?' enquired Captain MacWhirr, straining his voice.

'No, sir. Certainly not. Wind came out right ahead. And here comes the head sea.'

A plunge of the ship ended in a shock as if she had landed her forefoot upon something solid. After a moment of stillness a lofty flight of sprays drove hard with the wind upon their faces.

'Keep her at it as long as we can,' shouted Captain MacWhirr.

Before Jukes had squeezed the salt water out of his eyes all the stars had disappeared.

* * * *

Jukes was as ready a man as any half-dozen young mates that may be caught by casting a net upon the waters; and though he had been somewhat taken aback by the startling viciousness of the first squall, he had pulled himself together on the instant, had called out the hands and had rushed them along to secure such openings about the deck as had not been already battened down earlier in the evening. Shouting in his fresh, stentorian voice, 'Jump, boys, and bear a hand!' he led in the work, telling himself the while that he had 'just expected this'.

But at the same time he was growing aware that this was rather more than he had expected. From the first stir of the air felt on his cheek the gale seemed to take upon itself the accumulated impetus of an avalanche. Heavy sprays enveloped the *Nan-Shan* from stem to stern, and instantly in the midst of her regular rolling she began to jerk and plunge as though she had gone mad with fright.

Jukes thought, 'This is no joke.' While he was exchanging explanatory yells with his captain, a sudden lowering of the darkness came upon the night, falling before their vision like something palpable. It was as if the masked lights of the world had been turned down. Jukes was uncritically glad to have his captain at hand. It relieved him as though that man had, by simply coming on deck, taken most of the gale's weight upon his shoulders. Such is the prestige, the privilege, and the burden of command.

Captain MacWhirr could expect no relief of that sort from anyone on earth. Such is the loneliness of command. He was trying to see, with that watchful manner of a seaman who stares into the wind's eye as if into the eye of an adversary, to penetrate the hidden intention and guess the aim and force of the thrust. The strong wind swept at him out of a vast obscurity; he felt under his feet the uneasiness of his ship, and he could not even discern the shadow of her shape. He wished it were not so; and very still he waited, feeling stricken by a blind man's helplessness.

To be silent was natural to him, dark or shine. Jukes, at his elbow, made himself heard yelling cheerily in the gusts, 'We must have got the worst of it at once, sir.' A faint burst of lightning quivered all round, as if flashed into a cavern—into a black and secret chamber of the sea, with a floor of foaming crests.

It unveiled for a sinister, fluttering moment a ragged mass of clouds hanging low, the lurch of the long outlines of the ship, the black figures of men caught on the bridge, heads forward, as if petrified in the act of butting. The darkness palpitated down upon all this, and then the real thing came at last.

It was something formidable and swift, like the sudden smashing of a vial of wrath. It seemed to explode all round the ship with an overpowering concussion and a rush of great waters, as if an immense dam had been blown up to windward. In an instant the men lost touch of each other. This is the disintegrating power of a great wind: it isolates one from one's kind. An earthquake, a landslip, an avalanche, overtake a man incidentally, as it were—without passion. A furious gale attacks him like a personal enemy, tries to grasp his limbs, fastens upon his mind, seeks to rout his very spirit out of him.

Jukes was driven away from his commander. He fancied himself whirled a great distance through the air. Everything disappeared—even, for a moment, his power of thinking; but his hand had found one of the rail stanchions. His distress was by no means alleviated by an inclination to disbelieve the reality of this experience. Though young, he had seen some bad weather, and had never doubted his ability to imagine the worst; but this was so much beyond his powers of fancy that it appeared incompatible with the existence of any ship whatever. He would have been incredulous about himself in the same way, perhaps, had he not been so harassed by the necessity of exerting a wrestling effort against a force trying to tear him away from his hold. Moreover, the conviction of not being utterly destroyed returned to him through the sensations of being half-drowned, bestially shaken, and partly choked.

It seemed to him he remained there precariously alone with the stanchion for a long, long time. The rain poured on him, flowed, drove in sheets. He breathed in gasps; and sometimes the water he swallowed was fresh and sometimes it was salt. For the most part he kept his eyes shut tight, as if suspecting his sight might be destroyed in the immense flurry of the elements. When he ventured to blink hastily, he derived some moral support from the green gleam of the starboard light shining feebly upon the flight of rain and sprays. He was actually looking at it when its ray fell upon the uprearing sea which put it out. He saw the head of the wave topple over, adding the mite of its crash to the tremendous uproar raging around him, and almost at the same instant the stanchion was wrenched away from his embracing arms. After a crushing thump on his back he found himself suddenly afloat and borne upwards. His first irresistible notion was that the whole China Sea had climbed on the bridge. Then, more sanely, he concluded himself gone overboard. All the time he being tossed, flung, and rolled in great volumes of water, he kept on repeating mentally, with the utmost precipitation, the words: 'My God! My God! My God!'

All at once, in a revolt of misery and despair, he formed the crazy resolution to get out of that. And he began to thresh about with his arms and legs. But as soon as he commenced his wretched struggles he discovered that he had become somehow mixed up with a face, an oilskin coat, somebody's boots. He clawed ferociously all these things in turn, lost them, found them again, lost them once more, and finally was himself caught in the firm clasp of a pair of stout arms. He returned the embrace close round a thick solid body. He had found his captain.

They tumbled over and over, tightening their hug. Suddenly the water let them down with a brutal bang; and, stranded against the side of the wheelhouse, out of breath and bruised, they were left to stagger up in the wind and hold on where they could.

Jukes came out of it rather horrified, as though he had escaped some unparalleled outrage directed at his feelings. It weakened his faith in himself. He started shouting aimlessly to the man he could feel near him in that fiendish blackness, 'Is it you, sir? Is it you, sir?' till his temples seemed ready to burst. And he heard in answer a voice, as if crying far away, as if screaming to him fretfully from a very great distance, the one word 'Yes!' Other seas swept again over the bridge. He received them defencelessly right over his bare head, with both his hands engaged in holding.

The motion of the ship was extravagant. Her lurches had an appalling helplessness: she pitched as if taking a header into a void, and seemed to find a wall to hit every time. When she rolled she fell on her side headlong, and she would be righted back by such a demolishing blow that Jukes felt her reeling as a clubbed man reels before he collapses. The gale howled and scuffled about gigantically in the darkness, as though the entire world were one black gully. At certain moments the air streamed against the ship as if sucked through a tunnel with a concentrated solid force of impact that seemed to lift her clean out of the water and keep her up for an instant with only a quiver running through her from end to end. And then she would begin her tumbling again as if dropped back into a boiling cauldron. Jukes tried hard to compose his mind and judge things coolly.

The sea, flattened down in the heavier gusts, would uprise and overwhelm both ends of the *Nan-Shan* in snowy rushes of foam, expanding wide, beyond both rails, into the night. And on this dazzling sheet, spread under the blackness of the clouds and emitting a bluish glow, Captain MacWhirr could catch a desolate glimpse of a few tiny specks black as ebony, the tops of the hatches, the battened companions, the heads of the covered winches, the foot of a mast. This was all he could see of his ship. Her middle structure, covered by the bridge which bore him, his mate, the closed wheelhouse where a man was steering shut up with the fear of being swept overboard together with the whole thing in one great crash—her middle structure was like a half-tide rock awash upon a coast. It was like an outlying rock with the water boiling up, streaming over, pouring off, beating round—like a rock in the surf to which shipwrecked people cling before they let go—only it rose, it sank, it rolled continuously, without respite and rest, like a rock that should have miraculously struck adrift from a coast and gone wallowing upon the sea.

The *Nan-Shan* was being looted by the storm with a senseless, destructive fury: trysails torn out of the extra gaskets, double-lashed awnings blown away, bridge swept clean, weather cloths burst, rails twisted, light screens smashed—and two of the boats had gone already. They had gone unheard and unseen, melting, as it were, in the shock and smother of the wave. It was only later, when upon the white flash of another high sea hurling itself amidships, Jukes had a vision of two pairs of davits leaping black and empty out of the solid blackness, with one overhauled fall flying and an ironbound block capering in the air, that he became aware of what had happened within about three yards of his back.

He poked his head forward, groping for the ear of his commander. His lips touched it—big, fleshy, very wet. He cried in an agitated tone, 'Our boats are going now, sir.'

And again he heard that voice, forced and ringing feebly, but with a penetrating effect of quietness in the enormous discord of noises, as if sent out from some remote spot of peace beyond the black wastes of the gale; again he heard a man's voice—the frail and indomitable sound that can be made to carry an infinity of thought, resolution, and purpose, that shall be pronouncing confident words on the last day, when heavens fall, and justice is done—again he heard it, and it was crying to him, as if from very, very far—'All right.'

He thought he had not managed to make himself understood. 'Our boats—I say boats—the boats, sir! Two gone!'

The same voice, within a foot of him and yet so remote, yelled sensibly, 'Can't be helped.'

Captain MacWhirr had never turned his face, but Jukes caught some more words in the wind.

'What can—expect—when hammering through—such—Bound to leave—something behind—stands to reason.'

Watchfully Jukes listened for more. No more came. This was all Captain MacWhirr had to say; and Jukes could picture to himself rather than see the broad squat back before him. An impenetrable obscurity pressed down upon the ghostly glimmers of the sea. A dull conviction seized upon Jukes that there was nothing to be done.

If the steering gear did not give way, if the immense volumes of water did not burst the deck in or smash one of the hatches, if the engines did not give up, if way could be kept on the ship against this terrific wind, and she did not bury herself in one of these awful seas, of whose white crests alone, topping high above her bows, he could now and then get a sickening glimpse—then there was a chance of her coming out of it. Something within him seemed to turn over, bringing uppermost the feeling that the *Nan-Shan* was lost.

'She's done for,' he said to himself, with a surprising mental agitation, as though he had discovered an unexpected meaning in this thought. One of these things was bound to happen. Nothing could be prevented now, and nothing could be remedied. The men on board did not count, and the ship could not last. This weather was too impossible.

Jukes felt an arm thrown heavily over his shoulders; and to this overture he responded with great intelligence by catching hold of his captain round the waist.

They stood clasped thus in the blind night, bracing each other against the wind, cheek to cheek and lip to ear, in the manner of two hulks lashed stem to stern together.

And Jukes heard the voice of his commander hardly any louder than before, but nearer, as though, starting to march athwart the prodigious rush of the hurricane, it had approached him, bearing that strange effect of quietness like the serene glow of a halo.

'D'ye know where the hands got to?' it asked, vigorous and evanescent at the same time, overcoming the strength of the wind, and swept away from Jukes instantly.

Jukes didn't know. They were all on the bridge when the real force of the hurricane struck the ship. He had no idea where they had crawled to. Under the circumstances they were nowhere, for all the use that could be made of them. Somehow the captain's wish to know distressed Jukes.

'Want the hands, sir?' he cried, apprehensively.

'Ought to know,' asserted Captain MacWhirr. 'Hold hard.'

They held hard. An outburst of unchained fury, a vicious rush of the wind absolutely steadied the ship; she rocked only, quick and light like a child's cradle, for a terrific moment of suspense, while the whole atmosphere, as it seemed, streamed furiously past her, roaring away from the tenebrous earth.

It suffocated them, and with eyes shut they tightened their grasp. What from the magnitude of the shock might have been a column of water running upright in the dark, butted against the ship, broke short, and fell on her bridge, crushingly, from on high, with a dead burying weight.

A flying fragment of that collapse, a mere splash, enveloped them in one swirl from their feet over their heads, filling violently their ears, mouths, and nostrils with salt water. It knocked out their legs, wrenched in haste at their arms, seethed away swiftly under their chins; and opening their eyes, they saw the piled-up masses of foam dashing to and fro amongst what looked like the fragments of a ship. She had given way as if driven straight in. Their panting hearts yielded, too, before the tremendous blow; and all at once she sprang up again to her desperate plunging, as if trying to scramble out from under the ruins.

The seas in the dark seemed to rush from all sides to keep her back where she might perish. There was hate in the way she was handled, and a ferocity in the blows that fell. She was like a living creature thrown to the rage of a mob: hustled terribly, struck at, borne up, flung down, leaped upon. Captain MacWhirr and Jukes kept hold of each other, deafened by the noise, gagged by the wind; and the great physical tumult beating about their bodies, brought, like an unbridled display of passion, a profound trouble to their souls. One of those wild and appalling shrieks that are heard at times passing mysteriously overhead in the steady roar of a hurricane, swooped, as if borne on wings, upon the ship, and Jukes tried to outscream it.

'Will she live through this?'

The cry was wrenched out of his breast. It was as unintentional as the birth of a thought in the head, and he heard nothing of it himself. It all became extinct at once—thought, intention, effort—and of his cry the inaudible vibration added to the tempest waves of the air.

He expected nothing from it. Nothing at all. For indeed what answer could be made? But after a while he heard with amazement the frail and resisting voice in his ear, the dwarf sound, unconquered in the giant tumult.

'She may!'

It was a dull yell, more difficult to seize than a whisper. And presently the voice returned again, half submerged in the vast crashes, like a ship battling against the waves of an ocean.

'Let's hope so!' it cried—small, lonely, and unmoved, a stranger to the visions of hope or fear; and it flickered into disconnected words: 'Ship . . . This . . . Never—Anyhow . . . for the best.' Jukes gave it up.

Then, as if it had come suddenly upon the one thing fit to withstand the power of a storm, it seemed to gain force and firmness for the last broken shouts:

'Keep on hammering . . . builders . . . good men . . . And chance it . . . engines. . . . Rout . . . good man.'

Captain MacWhirr removed his arm from Jukes's shoulders, and thereby ceased to exist for his mate, so dark it was; Jukes, after a tense stiffening of every muscle, would let himself go limp all over. The gnawing of profound discomfort existed side by side with an incredible disposition to somnolence, as though he had been buffeted and worried into drowsiness. The wind would get hold of his head and try to shake it off his shoulders; his clothes, full of water, were as heavy as lead, cold and dripping like an armour of melting ice: he shivered—it lasted a long time; and with his hands closed hard on his hold, he was letting himself sink slowly into the depths of bodily misery. His mind became concentrated upon himself in an aimless, idle way, and when something pushed lightly at the back of his knees he nearly, as the saying is, jumped out of his skin.

In the start forward he bumped the back of Captain MacWhirr, who didn't move; and then a hand gripped his thigh. A lull had come, a menacing lull of the wind, the holding of a stormy breath—and he felt himself pawed all over. It was the boatswain. Jukes recognized these hands, so thick and enormous that they seemed to belong to some new species of man.

He pulled himself up by Jukes's coat, taking that liberty with the greatest moderation, and only so far as it was forced upon him by the hurricane.

'What is it, boss'n, what is it?' yelled Jukes, impatiently. The typhoon had got on Jukes's nerves.

The boatswain's other hand had found some other body, for he began to inquire: 'Is it you, sir? Is it you, sir?' The wind strangled his howls.

'Yes!' cried Captain MacWhirr.

All that the boatswain, out of a superabundance of yells, could make clear to Captain MacWhirr was the bizarre intelligence that 'All them Chinamen in the fore tween-deck have fetched away, sir.'

Jukes to leeward could hear these two shouting within six inches of his face, as you may hear on a still night half a mile away two men conversing across a field. He heard Captain MacWhirr's exasperated 'What? What?' and the strained pitch of the other's hoarseness. 'In a lump . . . seen them myself. . . . Awful sight, sir . . . thought . . . tell you.'

Jukes remained indifferent, as if rendered irresponsible by the force of the hurricane, which made the very thought of action utterly vain. Besides, being very young, he had found the occupation of keeping his heart completely steeled against the worst so engrossing that he had come to feel an overpowering dislike towards any other form of activity whatever. He was not scared; he knew this because, firmly believing he would never see another sunrise, he remained calm in that belief.

Captain MacWhirr had made Jukes understand that he wanted him to go down below—to see.

'What am I to do then, sir?' And the trembling of his whole wet body caused Jukes's voice to sound like bleating.

'See first . . . Boss'n . . . says . . . adrift.'

'That boss'n is a confounded fool,' howled Jukes, shakily.

The absurdity of the demand made upon him revolted Jukes. He was as unwilling to go as if the moment he had left the deck the ship were sure to sink.

'I must know . . . can't leave. . . .'

'They'll settle, sir.'

'Fight . . . boss'n says they fight. . . . Why? Can't have . . . fighting . . . board ship. . . . Much rather keep you here . . . case . . . I should . . . washed overboard myself. . . . Stop it . . . some way. You see and tell me . . . through engine-room tube. Don't want you . . . come up here . . . too often. Dangerous . . . moving about . . . deck.'

Jukes, held with his head in chancery, had to listen to what seemed horrible suggestions.

'Don't want . . . you get lost . . . so long . . . ship isn't. . . . Rout . . . Good man . . . Ship . . . may . . . through this . . . all right yet.'

All at once Jukes understood he would have to go.

'Do you think she may?' he screamed.

But the wind devoured the reply, out of which Jukes heard only the one word, pronounced with great energy '. . . Always. . . .'

Captain MacWhirr released Jukes, and bending over the boatswain, yelled, 'Get back with the mate.' Jukes only knew that the arm was gone off his shoulders. He was dismissed with his orders—to do what? He was exasperated into letting go his hold carelessly, and on the instant was blown away. It seemed to him that nothing could stop him from being blown right over the stern. He flung himself down hastily, and the boatswain, who was following, fell on him.

'Don't you get up yet, sir,' cried the boatswain. 'No hurry!'

A sea swept over. Jukes understood the boatswain to splutter that the bridge ladders were gone. 'I'll lower you down, sir, by your hands,' he screamed. He shouted also something about the smoke-stack being as likely to go overboard as not. Jukes thought it very possible, and imagined the fires out, the ship helpless. . . .

In the dark, Jukes, unsteady on his legs, listened to a faint thunderous patter. A deadened screaming went on steadily at his elbow, as it were; and from above the louder tumult of the storm descended upon these near sounds. His head swam. To him, too, in that bunker, the motion of the ship seemed novel and menacing, sapping his resolution as though he had never been afloat before.

He had half a mind to scramble out again; but the remembrance of Captain MacWhirr's voice made this impossible. His orders were to go and see. What was the good of it, he wanted to know. Enraged, he told himself he would see—of course. But the boatswain, staggering clumsily, warned him to be careful how he opened that door; there was a blamed fight going on. And Jukes, as if in great bodily pain, desired irritably to know what the devil they were fighting for.

'Dollars! Dollars, sir. All their rotten chests got burst open. Blamed money skipping all over the place, and they are tumbling after it head over heels—tearing and biting like anything. A regular little hell in there.'

Jukes convulsively opened the door. The short boatswain peered under his arm.

One of the lamps had gone out, broken perhaps. Rancorous, gutteral cries burst out loudly on their ears, and a strange panting sound, the working of all these straining breasts. A hard blow hit the side of the ship; water fell above with a stunning shock, and in the forefront of the gloom, where the air was reddish and thick, Jukes saw a head bang the deck violently, two thick calves waving on high, muscular arms twined round a naked body, a yellow face, openmouthed and with a set wild stare, look up and slide away. An empty chest clattered turning over; a man fell head first with a jump, as if lifted by a kick; and farther off, indistinct, others streamed like a mass of rolling stones down a bank, thumping the deck with their feet and flourishing their arms wildly. The hatchway ladder was loaded with coolies swarming on it like bees on a branch. They hung on the steps in a crawling, stirring cluster, beating madly with their fists the underside of the battened hatch, and the headlong rush of the water above was heard in the intervals of their yelling. The ship heeled over more, and they began to drop off: first one, then two, then all the rest went away together, falling straight off with a great cry.

Jukes was confounded. The boatswain, with gruff anxiety, begged him, 'Don't you go in there, sir.'

The whole place seemed to twist upon itself, jumping incessantly the while; and when the ship rose to a sea Jukes fancied that all these men would be shot upon him in a body. He backed out, swung the door to, and with trembling hands pushed at the bolt. . . .

★ ★ ★ ★

'You've got to hurry up,' shouted Mr Rout, as soon as he saw Jukes appear in the stokehold doorway.

Jukes's glance was wandering and tipsy; his red face was puffy, as though he had overslept himself. He had had an arduous road, and had travelled over it with immense vivacity, the agitation of his mind corresponding to the exertions of his body. He had rushed up out of the bunker, stumbling in the dark alleyway amongst a lot of bewildered men who, trod upon, asked 'What's up, sir?' in awed mutters all round him; down the stokehold ladder, missing many iron rungs in his hurry, down into a place deep as a well, black as Tophet, tipping over back and forth like a seesaw. The water in the bilges thundered at each roll, and the lumps of coal skipped to and fro, from end to end, rattling like an avalanche of pebbles on a slope of iron.

Somebody in there moaned with pain, and somebody else could be seen crouching over what seemed the prone body of a dead man; a lusty voice blasphemed; and the glow under each fire door was like a pool of flaming blood radiating quietly in a velvety blackness.

A gust of wind struck the nape of Jukes's neck and next moment he felt it streaming about his wet ankles. The stokehold ventilators hummed: in front of the six fire doors two wild figures, stripped to the waist, staggered and stooped, wrestling with two shovels.

Jukes, after a bewildered moment, had been helped by a roll to dart through; and as soon as his eyes took in the comparative vastness, peace, and brilliance of the engine room, the ship, setting her stern heavily in the water, sent him charging head down upon Mr Rout.

The chief's arm, long like a tentacle, and straightening as if worked by a spring, went out to meet him, and deflected his rush into a spin towards the speaking tubes. At the same time Mr Rout repeated earnestly:

'You've got to hurry up, whatever it is.'

Jukes yelled 'Are you there, sir?' and listened. Nothing. Suddenly the roar of the wind fell straight into his ear, but presently a small voice shoved aside the shouting hurricane quietly.

'You, Jukes?—Well?'

Jukes was ready to talk: it was only time that seemed to be wanting. It was easy enough to account for everything. He could perfectly imagine the coolies battened down in the reeking tween-deck, lying sick and scared between the rows of chests. Then one of these chests—or perhaps several at once—breaking loose in a roll, knocking out others, sides splitting, lids flying open, and all these clumsy Chinamen rising up in a body to save their property. Afterwards every fling of the ship would hurl that tramping, yelling mob here and there, from side to side, in a whirl of smashed wood, torn clothing, rolling dollars. A struggle once started, they would be unable to stop themselves. Nothing could stop them now except main force. It was a disaster. He had seen it, and that was all he could say. Some of them must be dead, he believed. The rest would go on fighting. . . .

He sent up his words, tripping over each other, crowding the narrow tube. They mounted as if into a silence of an enlightened comprehension dwelling alone up there with a storm. And Jukes wanted to be dismissed from the face of that odious trouble intruding on the great need of the ship.

★ ★ ★ ★

He waited. Before his eyes the engines turned with slow labour, that in the moment of going off into a mad fling would stop dead at Mr Rout's shout, 'Look out, Beale!' They paused in an intelligent immobility, stilled in mid-stroke, a heavy crank arrested on the cant, as if conscious of danger and the passage of time. Then, with a 'Now, then!' from the chief, and the sound of a breath expelled through clinched teeth, they would accomplish the interrupted revolution and begin another.

There was the prudent sagacity of wisdom and the deliberation of enormous strength in their movements. This was their work—this patient coaxing of a distracted ship over the fury of the waves and into the very eye of the wind. At times Mr Rout's chin would sink on his breast, and he watched them with knitted eyebrows as if lost in thought.

The voice that kept the hurricane out of Jukes's ear began: 'Take the hands with you . . .' and left off unexpectedly.

'What could I do with them, sir?'

A harsh, abrupt, imperious clang exploded suddenly. The three pairs of eyes flew up to the telegraph dial to see the hand jump from FULL to STOP, as if snatched by a devil. And then these three men in the engine room had the intimate sensation of a check upon the ship, of a strange shrinking, as if she had gathered herself for a desperate leap.

'Stop her!' bellowed Mr Rout.

Nobody—not even Captain MacWhirr, who alone on deck had caught sight of a white line of foam coming on at such a height that he couldn't believe his eyes—nobody was to know the steepness of that sea and the awful depth of the hollow the hurricane had scooped out behind the running wall of water.

It raced to meet the ship, and, with a pause, as of girding the loins, the *Nan-Shan* lifted her bows and leaped. The flames in all the lamps sank, darkening the engine room. One went out. With a tearing crash and a swirling, raving tumult, tons of water fell upon the deck, as though the ship had darted under the foot of a cataract.

Down there they looked at each other, stunned.

'Swept from end to end, by God!' bawled Jukes.

She dipped into the hollow straight down, as if going over the edge of the world. The engine room toppled forward menacingly, like the inside of a tower nodding in an earthquake. An awful racket, of iron things falling, came from the stokehold. She hung on this appalling slant long enough for Beale to drop on his hands and knees and begin to crawl as if he meant to fly on all fours out of the engine room, and for Mr Rout to turn his head slowly, rigid, cavernous, with the lower jaw dropping. Jukes had shut his eyes, and his face in a moment became hopelessly blank and gentle, like the face of a blind man.

The hands were on deck covering up the ventilators.

At last she rose slowly, staggering, as if she had to lift a mountain with her bows.

Mr Rout shut his mouth; Jukes blinked; and little Beale stood up hastily.

'Another one like this, and that's the last of her,' cried the chief.

He and Jukes looked at each other, and the same thought came into their heads. The Captain! Everything must have been swept away. Steering gear gone—ship like a log. All over directly.

'Rush!' ejaculated Mr Rout thickly, glaring with enlarged, doubtful eyes at Jukes, who answered him by an irresolute glance.

The clang of the telegraph gong soothed them instantly. The black hand dropped in a flash from STOP to FULL.

'Now then, Beale!' cried Mr Rout.

The steam hissed low. The piston rods slid in and out. Jukes put his ear to the tube. The voice was ready for him. It said: 'Pick up all the money. Bear a hand now. I'll want you up here.' And that was all.

'Sir?' called up Jukes. There was no answer.

He staggered away like a defeated man from the field of battle. He had got, in some way or other, a cut above his left eyebrow—a cut to the bone. He was not aware of it in the least: quantities of the China Sea, large enough to break his neck for him, had gone over his head, had cleaned, washed, and salted that wound. It did not bleed, but only gaped red; and this gash over the eye, his dishevelled hair, the disorder of his clothes, gave him the aspect of a man worsted in a fight with fists.

'Got to pick up the dollars.' He appealed to Mr Rout, smiling pitifully at random.

'What's that?' asked Mr Rout, wildly. 'Pick up . . . ? I don't care. . . .' Then, quivering in every muscle, but with an exaggeration of paternal tone, 'Go away now, for God's sake. You deck people'll drive me silly. You fellows are going wrong for want of something to do. . . .'

At these words Jukes discovered in himself the beginnings of anger. Want of something to do—indeed. . . .

A frenzy possessed Jukes. By the time he was back amongst the men in the darkness of the alleyway, he felt ready to wring all their necks at the slightest sign of hanging back. The very thought of it exasperated him. *He* couldn't hang back. They shouldn't.

The impetuosity with which he came amongst them carried them along. They had already been excited and startled at all his comings and goings—by the fierceness and rapidity of his movements; and more felt than seen in his rushes, he appeared formidable—busied with matters of life and death that brooked no delay. At his first word he heard them drop into the bunker one after another obediently, with heavy thumps.

They were not clear as to what would have to be done. 'What is it? What is it?' they were asking each other. The boatswain tried to explain; the sounds of a great scuffle surprised them: and the mighty shocks, reverberating awfully in the black bunker, kept them in mind of their danger. When the boatswain threw open the door it seemed that an eddy of the hurricane, stealing through the iron sides of the ship, had set all these bodies whirling like dust; there came to them a confused uproar, a tempestuous tumult, a fierce mutter, gusts of screams dying away, and the tramping of feet mingling with the blows of the sea.

For a moment they glared amazed, blocking the doorway. Jukes pushed through them brutally. He said nothing, and simply darted in. Another lot of coolies on the ladder, struggling suicidally to break through the battened hatch to a swamped deck, fell off as before, and he disappeared under them like a man overtaken by a landslide.

The boatswain yelled excitedly: 'Come along. Get the mate out. He'll be trampled to death. Come on.'

They charged in, stamping on breasts, on fingers, on faces, catching their feet in heaps of clothing, kicking broken wood; but before they could get hold of him Jukes emerged waist deep in a multitude of clawing hands. In the instant he had been lost to view, all the buttons of his jacket had gone, its back had got split up to the collar, his waistcoat had been torn open. The central struggling mass of Chinamen went over to the roll, dark, indistinct, helpless, with a wild gleam of many eyes in the dim light of the lamps.

'Leave me alone—damn you. I am all right,' screeched Jukes. 'Drive them forward. Watch your chance when she pitches. Forward with 'em. Drive them against the bulkhead. Jam 'em up.'

The rush of the sailors into the seething tween-deck was like a splash of cold water into a boiling cauldron. The commotion sank for a moment.

The bulk of Chinamen were locked in such a compact scrimmage that, linking their arms and aided by an appalling dive of the ship, the seaman sent it forward in one great shove, like a solid block. Behind their backs small clusters and loose bodies tumbled from side to side.

The boatswain performed prodigious feats of strength. With his long arms open, and each great paw clutching at a stanchion, he stopped the rush of seven entwined Chinamen rolling like a boulder. His joints cracked; he said, 'Ha!' and they flew apart. But the carpenter showed the greater intelligence. Without saying a word to anybody he went back into the alleyway, to fetch several coils of cargo gear he had seen there—chain and rope. With these lifelines were rigged.

There was really no resistance. The struggle, however it began, had turned into a scramble of blind panic. If the coolies had started up after their scattered dollars they were by that time fighting only for their footing. They took each other by the throat merely to save themselves from being hurled about. Whoever got a hold anywhere would kick at the others who caught at his legs and hung on, till a roll sent them flying together across the deck.

The coming of the white devils was a terror. Had they come to kill? The individuals torn out of the ruck became very limp in the seamen's hands: some, dragged aside by the heels, were passive, like dead bodies, with open, fixed eyes. Here and there a coolie would fall on his knees as if begging for mercy; several, whom the excess of fear made unruly, were hit with hard fists between the eyes, and cowered; while those who were hurt submitted to rough handling, blinking rapidly without a plaint. Faces streamed with blood; there were raw places on the shaven heads, scratches, bruises, torn wounds, gashes. The broken porcelain out of the chests was mostly responsible for the latter. Here and there a Chinaman, wild-eyed, with his tail unplaited, nursed a bleeding sole.

They had been ranged closely, after having been shaken into submission, cuffed a little to allay excitement, addressed in gruff words of encouragement that sounded like promises of evil. They sat on the deck in ghastly, drooping rows, and at the end the carpenter, with two hands to help him, moved busily from place to place, setting taut and hitching the lifelines. The boatswain, with one leg and one arm embracing a stanchion, struggled with a lamp pressed to his breast, trying to get a light, and growling all the time like an industrious gorilla. The figures of seamen stooped repeatedly, with the movements of gleaners, and everything was being flung into the bunker: clothing, smashed wood, broken china, and the dollars, too, gathered up in men's jackets. Now and then a sailor would stagger towards the doorway with his arms full of rubbish; and dolorous, slanting eyes followed his movements. . . .

★ ★ ★ ★

Captain MacWhirr had gone into the chart room. There was no light there; but he could feel the disorder of that place where he used to live tidily. His armchair was upset. The books had tumbled out on the floor; he scrunched a piece of glass under his boot. He groped for the matches and found a box on a shelf with a deep ledge. He struck one, and puckering the corners of his eyes, held out the little flame towards the barometer whose glittering top of glass and metals nodded at him continuously.

It stood very low—incredibly low, so low that Captain MacWhirr grunted. The match went out, and hurriedly he extracted another, with thick, stiff fingers.

Again a little flame flared up before the nodding glass and metal of the top. His eyes looked at it, narrowed with attention, as if expecting an imperceptible sign. With his grave face he resembled a booted and misshapen pagan burning incense before the oracle of a Joss. There was no mistake. It was the lowest reading he had ever seen in his life.

Captain MacWhirr emitted a low whistle. He forgot himself till the flame diminished to a blue spark, burnt his fingers and vanished. Perhaps something had gone wrong with the thing!

There was an aneroid glass screw above the couch. He turned that way, struck another match, and discovered the white face of the other instrument looking at him from the bulkhead, meaningly, not to be gainsaid, as though the wisdom of men were made unerring by the indifference of matter. There was no room for doubt now. Captain MacWhirr pshawed at it and threw the match down.

The worst was to come, then—and if the books were right this worst would be very bad. The experience of the last six hours had enlarged his conception of what heavy weather could be like. 'It'll be terrific,' he pronounced, mentally. He had not consciously looked at anything by the light of the matches except at the barometer; and yet somehow he had seen that his water bottle and the two tumblers had been flung out of their stand. It seemed to give him a more intimate knowledge of the tossing the ship had gone through. 'I wouldn't have believed it,' he thought. And his table had been cleared, too; his rulers, his pencils, the inkstand—all the things that had their safe appointed places—they were gone, as if a mischevious hand had plucked them out one by one and flung them on the wet floor. The hurricane had broken in upon the orderly arrangements of his privacy. This had never happened before, and the feeling of dismay reached the very seat of his composure. And the worst was to come yet! He was glad the trouble in the tweendeck had been discovered in time. If the ship had to go after all, then, at least, she wouldn't be going to the bottom with a lot of people in her fighting teeth and claw. That would have been odious. And in that feeling there was a humane intention and a vague sense of the fitness of things.

These instantaneous thoughts were yet in their essence heavy and slow, partaking of the nature of the man. He extended his hand to put back the matchbox in its corner of the shelf. There were always matches there—by his order. The steward had his instructions impressed upon him long before. 'A box . . . just there, see? Not so very full . . . where I can put my hand on it, steward. Might want a light in a hurry. Can't tell on board ship *what* you might want in a hurry. Mind, now.'

And of course on his side he would be carcful to put it back in its place scrupulously. He did so now, but before he removed his hand it occurred to him that perhaps he would never have occasion to use that box any more. The vividness of the thought checked him and for an infinitesimal fraction of a second his fingers closed again on the small object as though it had been the symbol of all these little habits that chain us to the weary round of life. He released it at last, and letting himself fall on the settee, listened for the first sounds of returning wind.

Not yet. He heard only the wash of water, the heavy splashes, the dull shocks of the confused seas boarding his ship from all sides. She would never have a chance to clear her decks.

But the quietude of the air was startlingly tense and unsafe, like a slender hair holding a sword suspended over his head. By this awful pause the storm penetrated the defences of the man and unsealed his lips. He spoke out in the solitude and the pitch darkness of the cabin, as if addressing another being awakened within his breast.

'I shouldn't like to lose her,' he said half aloud.

He sat unseen, apart from the sea, from his ship, isolated, as if withdrawn from the very current of his own existence, where such freaks as talking to himself surely had no place. His palms reposed on his knees, he bowed his short neck and puffed heavily, surrendering to a strange sensation of weariness he was not enlightened enough to recognize for the fatigue of mental stress.

From where he sat he could reach the door of a washstand locker. There should have been a towel there. There was. Good. . . . He took it out, wiped his face, and afterwards went on rubbing his wet head. He towelled himself with energy in the dark, and then remained motionless with the towel on his knees. A moment passed, of a stillness so profound that no one could have guessed there was a man sitting in that cabin. Then a murmur arose.

'She may come out of it yet.'

When Captain MacWhirr came out on deck, which he did brusquely, as though he had suddenly become conscious of having stayed away too long, the calm had lasted already more than fifteen minutes—long enough to make itself intolerable even to his imagination. Jukes, motionless on the forepart of the bridge, began to speak at once. His voice, blank and forced as though he were talking through hard-set teeth, seemed to flow away on all sides into the darkness, deepening again upon the sea.

'I had the wheel relieved. Hackett began to sing out that he was done. He's lying in there alongside the steering gear with a face like death. At first I couldn't get anybody to crawl out and relieve the poor devil. That boss'n's worse than no good, I always said. Thought

I would have had to go myself and haul out one of them by the neck.'

'Ah, well,' muttered the Captain. He stood watchful by Jukes's side.

'The second mate's in there, too, holding his head. Is he hurt, sir?'

'No—crazy,' said Captain MacWhirr, curtly.

'Looks as if he had a tumble, though.'

'I had to give him a push,' explained the Captain.

Jukes gave an impatient sigh.

'It will come very sudden,' said Captain MacWhirr, 'and from over there, I fancy. God only knows though. It will be bad, and there's an end. If we only can steam her round in time to meet it. . . .'

A minute passed. Some of the stars winked rapidly and vanished. . . .

A hollow echoing noise, like that of a shout rolling in a rocky chasm, approached the ship and went away again. The last star, blurred, enlarged, as if returning to the fiery mist of its beginning, struggled with the colossal depth of blackness hanging over the ship—and went out.

'Now for it!' muttered Captain MacWhirr. 'Mr Jukes.'

'Here, sir.'

The two men were growing indistinct to each other.

'She will be smothered and swept again for hours,' mumbled the Captain. 'There's not much left by this time above deck for the sea to take away—unless you or me.'

'Both, sir,' whispered Jukes, breathlessly.

'You are always meeting trouble halfway, Jukes,' Captain MacWhirr remonstrated quaintly. 'Though it's a fact that the second mate is no good. D'ye hear, Mr Jukes? You would be left alone if . . .'

Captain MacWhirr interrupted himself, and Jukes, glancing on all sides, remained silent.

'Don't you be put out by anything,' the Captain continued, mumbling rather fast. 'Keep her facing it. They may say what they like, but the heaviest seas run with the wind. Facing it—always facing it—that's the way to get through. You are a young sailor. Face it. That's enough for any man. Keep a cool head.'

'Yes, sir,' said Jukes, with a flutter of the heart.

In the next few seconds the Captain spoke to the engine room and got an answer.

For some reason Jukes experienced an access of confidence, a sensation that came from outside like a warm breath, and made him feel equal to every demand. The distant muttering of the darkness stole into his ears. He noted it unmoved, out of that sudden belief in himself, as a man safe in a shirt of mail would watch a point.

The ship laboured without intermission amongst the black hills of water, paying with this hard tumbling the price of her life. She rumbled in her depths, shaking a white plummet of steam into the night, and Jukes's thought skimmed like a bird through the engine room, where Mr Rout—good man—was ready. When the rumbling ceased it seemed to him that there was a pause of every sound, a dead pause in which Captain MacWhirr's voice rang out startlingly.

'What's that? A puff of wind?'—it spoke much louder than Jukes had ever heard it before—'On the bow. That's right. She may come out of it yet.'

The mutter of the winds drew near apace. In the forefront could be distinguished a drowsy waking plaint passing on, and far off the growth of a multiple clamour, marching and expanding. There was the throb as of many drums in it, a vicious rushing note, and like the chant of a tramping multitude.

Jukes could no longer see his captain distinctly. The darkness was absolutely piling itself upon the ship. At most he made out movements, a hint of elbows spread out, of a head thrown up.

Captain MacWhirr was trying to do up the top button of his oilskin coat with unwonted haste. The hurricane, with its power to madden the seas, to sink ships, to uproot trees, to overturn strong walls and dash the very birds of the air to the ground, had found this taciturn man in its path, and, doing its utmost, had managed to wring out a few words. Before the renewed wrath of winds swooped on his ship, Captain MacWhirr was moved to declare, in a tone of vexation, as it were: 'I wouldn't like to lose her.'

He was spared that annoyance.

THE PERFECT RENDEZVOUS

Lawrence Durrell

Methuen, a secret agent, has been sent to Yugoslavia by Dombey, head of Special Operations in London. His mission is to study the activities of a Royalist group, the White Eagles, who have been moving armed units into the mountains of southern Serbia, and to investigate the murder of Anson, a British diplomat who has been killed on a mountain fishing trip. Methuen spends a week in Belgrade, posing as an accountant called Judson. He discovers that treasure hidden in the mountains is to be used to finance a Royalist coup, and that a submarine is lying off the coast nearby.

Methuen leaves for the mountains, having arranged a rendezvous with two embassy officials, Porson and Blair. He is disguised as a Serbian peasant and equipped only with essential provisions, a gun and a fishing rod. The region seems deserted, but one day he finds a man who has been fatally wounded by a bullet and who mistakes Methuen for a Royalist. The man, Marco, instructs Methuen to meet a caravan of mules and to conduct them to Black Peter, leader of the White Eagles, who is waiting for them in a tunnel near the Janko Stone.

Methuen follows his instructions and passes himself off as a rebel. He warns Black Peter that Communist troops are combing the area and that the White Eagles must move soon. Black Peter appears to accept Methuen and offers him food and a bed. . . .

He slept for a good six-hour spell and the sun was high when he awoke on his bed of straw at the end of a long tunnel. As he sat up and yawned he felt a pair of strong arms gripping his shoulders and in a moment his wrists were tightly tied together behind his back. He turned and stared into the hairy face of Branko his jailor. 'What is this?' The old man drew the knots secure and tested them with a grunt before answering with laconic abruptness: 'Order.'

'But Black Peter said—'

'He has changed his mind. Until we can check on you.'

Methuen swore loudly and lay back once more. The old man squatted on his haunches and cut an apple into squares with his knife. He proceeded to eat it noisily. 'This will gain you nothing,' said Methuen. 'Absolutely nothing. Can I talk to Black Peter?' Branko shook his head. 'He is busy.'

Methuen felt the pangs of a gradually dawning despair; he should, he realized now, never have come up here. He should have been content with the knowledge he had gained. Now all his plans might miscarry unless he could gain the confidence of Black Peter.

He requested and was given a long drink of water; and after some thought he stood up and walked to the mouth of the tunnel. Branko followed his every step. The grassy hollows round the great stone obelisk were alive with men and mules engaged in the various activities of a camp. There must have been a good spring somewhere hereabouts, for a long line of men were watering the animals; others were setting up shelters and lighting fires. Immediately opposite was another hollow tunnel, obviously the entrance to some old abandoned working, and here Methuen saw the flash of yellow light from carbide lamps. Two sentries stood on guard at the entrance with tommy-guns. Shadows flapped and staggered inside the mouth of the cave and Methuen made out the giant form of Black Peter. 'There he is,' he said. 'I must talk to him.' His jailor tried to detain him but he shouldered him aside and walked to the cave-mouth where the sentries barred his way. He called out: 'Black Peter! I must talk to you.'

The leader of the White Eagles was seated on a wooden chest, deep in conversation with two ruffianly-looking men. 'What is it?' he said impatiently, and catching sight of Methuen, 'Ah! it is you. Come in.' Methuen pressed himself past the cold muzzles of the tommy-guns and walked into the flapping circle of light. 'Why am I a prisoner?' he said. 'You are not,' said Peter gruffly, 'but I want to be sure about you. Too much is at stake.' He waved his hand vaguely

'Why am I a prisoner?' he said.

in the direction of the inner tunnel and Methuen saw for the first time the long stacks of wooden crates which he presumed must contain the gold bars. 'Is this the treasure?' he said and Black Peter stood up, struggling between his desire for secrecy and an obvious pride. He followed the direction of Methuen's glance and sighed as he said: 'Yes.'

'Gold bars are heavy,' said Methuen.

'I know. But there are other things too. Look here.' Black Peter took him gently by the shoulder and piloted him deeper into the cave. It was rather like a wine-cellar. Hanging from a long chain of racks Methuen saw what at first he took to be inner tubes of car-tyres, but which proved on closer inspection to be rubber coin-bandoliers, each designed to carry five hundred gold coins. 'I see. Each man will carry something. You can't travel fast, then.' A furrow appeared on the forehead of Black Peter. 'That is the problem. And look here.'

Piled in one corner (as bolts of cloth are piled in the corner of a tailor's shop) he saw what at first he took to be a series of strips of sequin-covered material which glittered like fish scales in the yellow light. 'What on earth is it?'

Great blocks of gold coins had been joined together into strips, joined by tiny gold staples. Each piece measured about a square foot and in the centre of each was a hole. 'I don't understand,' said Methuen and Peter gave a hoarse bark of laughter as he picked up one of these glittering sheets and slipped his head through the hole in the centre. It was like a coat of chain-mail, only made of coins. 'Each man will also wear one of these golden shirts; and look, there are others to put over the mules like blankets.' Methuen gave a low whistle. 'But the weight,' he said. 'You can't do a good day's march with this.' Black Peter looked at him for a moment without speaking. 'You will see,' he said confidently. 'You will see.'

There was a ripple of movement outside and the sound of voices. Black Peter cocked his ear and said: 'The scouts are coming in. They will confirm your story about the troops. Come.'

They left the cave and at once a group of bearded peasants rushed across the grass to Black Peter and began to gabble unintelligibly, waving their arms and flourishing weapons of all kinds. For a moment they were inundated with questions and cries and even Black Peter could understand little of what the men had to say. It was useless calling for silence so with admirable presence of mind he lit a cigarette and sat down on the grass; at once he was encircled by the scouts who squatted round him as if round a camp fire, and fell silent. 'Now,' said Black Peter and one felt the authority behind his deep melodious voice, 'let us speak in turn so that we see the true picture of events. You, Bozo: what have you to tell?'

One by one he heard them out, puffing reflectively at his cigarette, betraying no concern and no impatience. Then he turned to Methuen, who sat close beside him, still uncomfortably pinioned and said: 'You are right. We must move tonight.' He dismissed the scouts and sat for a while in deep thought on the grass.

He rose at last and walked to where a shattered fragment of the old wall made an admirable natural dais and climbing onto it, with his back to the cliffside, blew three shrill blasts on a whistle. At once the camp hummed with life, as an ant's nest does if one drops something down it. From all quarters men came running to gather before him, and Black Peter waited for them without any trace of impatience. Methuen could not help admiring his perfect self-possession and calm. When the whole band was assembled silently before him Black Peter stared at them for a full half-minute before beginning to speak. He was obviously a born orator and experienced in his effects.

He began by praising their heroism in facing the danger of guerilla life in a territory as difficult as Yugoslavia; he reminded them that the journey they were about to undertake would be in many ways the most dangerous and exhausting they might ever make. 'The treasure is heavy, we know that. Our march will be slow. And I must warn you that it may be interrupted, for the Communists are approaching this mountain from three sides, hoping to cut us off. One thing we must remember. Usually it is the guerillas who can move fast, and who travel light, while regular troops are encumbured with heavy equipment. But in this case we will be the slow ones, the heavily laden ones. We will be like ants laden with ears of corn too big for them. Therefore we shall need discipline. Therefore we shall need skill in place of speed.'

A hoarse murmur greeted him, and he waited for silence before continuing. 'Many of you know the route I propose to follow; at the head of each column will be a guide who knows the country well. I think we should avoid the cordon easily if we do not lack courage, and by dawn on Saturday we should reach a mountain path known to nobody which runs above the Black Lake. Then to Durmitor and the *karst*.' Everyone spat with pleasure at this and Black Peter went on in a fusillade of sound. 'We shall not lose the King's treasure, that at least is certain. Rather we shall die, rather we shall take it into the Black Lake with us, locked in a death-grip with the enemies who have ruined our country.' A hoarse ragged cheer broke out and some of his audience shouted: 'Well spoken!' and brandished their weapons.

A grim smile played about Black Peter's mouth for a moment. Then he went on seriously: 'One thing makes it difficult for us now —namely aircraft. Some of you saw those planes this morning looking for us. If they should find us they would be able to attack us from the air and who could escape? For this reason I ask you: when the planes come do not all start running about in every direction to hide. Let each man stay absolutely still where he stands. Let him become unmoving as the Janko Stone, for the planes cannot see stillness in men—only movement. This is so important to understand that I have taken an extraordinary measure. Three guards have orders to take up a central position if planes are heard, and to shoot immediately at anyone who is seen moving. Now I don't want anyone to be hurt. But whoever moves endangers the life of each one of us, and he will be shot. Do you agree with me?'

A wild chanting cry went up from the assembled band of ruffians: 'Well spoken, Peter!' 'Well said, Brother Peterkin!'

He waited once more for silence and then in a crisp and altered tone, added: 'That is all I have to say. You have one hour in which to eat and rest, and then we must begin the loading. Each man knows what he must carry and what each mule must carry. Tonight we shall be joined at dusk by a party of our own men from the mountain above Sarajevo. We leave at darkness.'

'At darkness!' he repeated as he stepped down from the dais and shouldered his way through the press to where Methuen sat on the grass. The ropes had begun to cut into his forearms and he was dying for a smoke. Black Peter stood looking down at him for a moment with a smile. 'It is very clumsy,' he said at last, 'and typical Branko.

Here.' He undid the ropes at the back with the aid of his henchman and said: 'We'll tie your hands in front. Then at least you can smoke if you wish.'

'Am I expected to march like this?' asked Methuen testily.

'Yes.'

'I can use a gun far better than most of these ruffians of yours. You may need me.'

'If we do we will release you.'

Methuen stood up and sighed. Black Peter took his arms and said lightly: 'Do not take it too hard. It is a natural precaution. Suppose you were an agent—and I may tell you that we have already had one visitor of the kind. You might escape and take back our position and strength to the Communists in the valley.'

'Do they not know it?'

Black Peter started to walk slowly to his own headquarters, taking Methuen familiarly by the arm as he did so and piloting him along. 'I don't think they do as yet. But we can't be sure. We have been out of touch with Usizce for several days—I suppose because of all this increased activity. I think that the Communists suspect something big afoot; but they don't as yet know what. They think we are planning to start a revolution in Serbia. Ach! I'm tired.' They had entered the room which served him for a battle headquarters, and he slumped down at the table once more. The old man lay asleep in the corner on a tattered-looking couch. Black Peter uncorked a bottle of plum brandy and placed two small glasses on the table. 'Sit,' he said, 'and drink and let us talk about something else apart from this project of ours. I've been six months up here living like a goat. Pretty tiring I can tell you.'

It turned out in conversation that Black Peter was not entirely without culture of a sort. He had been trained as an engineer in both Belgrade and Vienna, and at the outbreak of war with Germany had been in charge of a building project in Bosnia. His wife and child had perished early in the war and he had joined the ill-fated Royalist band of General Mihaelovic which called itself Chetnik, and which had been abandoned to its fate by the Allies. With the disappearance of the Chetnik organization and the murder of its chief by the Communists, Black Peter had gone underground and worked for a spell as a cobbler in Usizce.

Then the *émigrés* in London had started trying to patch together the old Royalist movement from the shreds which remained. Black Peter was called and told of a discovery in south Serbia which set his heart aflame once more. Here was a chance to serve the Royalist cause once more. He spoke with touching simplicity of the dangers undergone and the difficulties surmounted in order to infiltrate a well-armed band into a single mountain area. Many of his comrades had been captured; mistakes had been made. 'The gravest mistake has been hurry,' he said. 'Too many men, too many arms in too short a time. I wanted another six months to do things gradually without awakening suspicion. But they want me to hurry. Always hurry. Now we are in danger, as you know. We may have to fight our way through to the coast.'

'That would be impossible,' said Methuen. 'With the whole army after you?'

'Perhaps. But you do not know the route we are planning to follow. You could not bring an army to bear on us at any place because we travel on the top of the mountains; the only time we come down is tonight, the first valley. The rest of the way you could only bring perhaps two battalions into contact. As far as we are concerned the army can race up and down the roads as much as it wants.'

'And at the coast?'

'You are a pessimist,' said Black Peter impatiently. 'You see all the difficulties; but at the coast, my friend, we have a point of rendezvous so perfect that . . . well, I won't tell you any more. I will only say that there is not a soldier within a dozen miles of our point of embarkation.'

All this, which sounded on the face of it utterly fantastic, was in fact plausible—so Methuen at least thought as he saw in his mind's eye the great hairy chain of groined mountains running westward upon the map like a cluster of spiders; the eyries of barren white limestone known as the *karst* which succeeded the heavily wooded and deeply glaciated chain of hills upon which they now were.

'Drink,' said Black Peter. 'Leave the worries to me.' The old man snorted in the corner and muttered something to himself. Methuen smoked on in silence while Black Peter turned his attention to his papers, carefully burning them in a biscuit-box and sifting the ash with a poker before calling for an orderly to take them away. 'This pistol of yours is a jewel,' he said, taking it up from the table. 'I let you keep your glasses as a special favour.' Methuen smiled. 'Will you tell Branko that?' he said. 'Because he has relieved me of them.'

Branko was summoned and forced to disgorge his loot, which he did with clumsy reluctance, growling under his breath like a mastiff. Black Peter watched him in silence and then curtly dismissed him. 'You see?' he said, turning back to Methuen, 'I am a just man, and an honest one.'

'And my pistol?' said Methuen.

'That is different. I want it.' He gave a harsh laugh and slapped Methuen consolingly on the back. 'Never mind. We will see. Who lives longest shall keep it for himself.'

It seemed a fair enough solution, though Methuen was already busy with plans for escape. Indeed he was beginning to feel that he had committed a cardinal error in coming to the headquarters of the White Eagles. He should have taken the knowledge gained back to Belgrade with him and not ventured his neck in so risky an exploit. But when he started for the Janko Stone he had not realized that he might find himself a virtual prisoner marching to the coast with a column of armed men, an unwitting target for the attentions of Tito's whole army. His blood curdled when he thought of the Ambassador's face. His only hope was to escape and keep the dawn rendezvous on Sunday with Porson; yet as things were it was not going to be easy. One false move and the suspicions of his captors would be aroused. That might lead him to share poor Anson's fate. And then, on the other hand, it was absolutely vital that some knowledge of the treasure should reach Dombey and the Foreign Office. All sorts of diplomatic repercussions might be expected if the Royalists movement abroad were suddenly to come into large funds. Policy might have to be altered to meet this new contingency. And if the White Eagles did not get through with their precious freight? If he himself perished with them nobody would be any the wiser. Only sooner or later Mr Judson's disappearance would have to be accounted for. 'O Lord,' said Methuen despondently to himself. 'I seem to have made an awful mess of things.'

They ate their midday meal at a clumsy table in the sunshine outside the cave as Black Peter wanted to keep a wary eye on the loading of his mule-team. They ate slices of fat pork-meat heavily spiced and a good country wine with it. Such conversation as there was was punctuated by interruptions. Orderlies came backwards and forwards with reports sent in by scouts; the guides clustered round for detailed instructions as to the route which they had difficulty in following on the map—being unused to such civilized amenities as maps and compasses. Meanwhile the loading went forward steadily and Methuen could not help but admire the excellent camp discipline which he observed; for method and order this ragged band of guerillas would not have disgraced a regular army unit.

As the light slanted towards afternoon he watched a breathtaking transformation of the men and mules into glittering armoured knights and their caparisoned steeds. The shirts of gold gleamed in the sunlight. The mules at first showed their fright as the great blankets of gold coins were thrown over them, but their team-leaders soothed them and gradually accustomed them to the new sensation. Panniers were packed, and the great wooden saddles were heaped with the wooden boxes containing the treasure. Black Peter occupied himself tirelessly with details, walking from group to group, admonishing, cajoling and teasing. It was obvious that the men adored him and would follow him anywhere. He was a marvellous natural soldier, thought Methuen with a touch of envy and admiration. It was amazing to watch the whole band a-glitter in gold coats of mail, leading their glittering animals. Once there was an alarm as the sound of planes was heard; but the sound passed away to the east of the camp without anything being spotted in the sky.

As dusk was falling small knots of armed men began to come into camp from several different quarters of the compass. Each new arrival was signalled by sharp cries and whistles, and some two or three were greeted by Black Peter as old friends.

Methuen had braced himself for the arrival of the escort, for surely among this band was someone capable of detecting the falseness of his cover story; someone from headquarters who would give him away. . . . His anxiety mounted as Black Peter advanced to meet some of these new arrivals, to greet them with affectionate tenderness, kissing their faces and hugging them with bearish enthusiasm.

Methuen walked slowly across the grassy depression and climbed the hillock on the other side from where he could just see the upper part of the Janko Stone. A ring of sentries lay in the grass facing inwards towards the depression in which the camp was situated. Nobody was allowed beyond a certain radius, lest he showed himself in the skyline, and in consequence the whole wild panorama of peaks and mountains was out of sight. Methuen would have liked to climb up as far as the obelisk but he was prevented. Branko walked behind him all the way.

Escape was out of the question. And if he were discovered to be an agent sudden death might follow immediately. Methuen braced himself against an ordeal by interrogation which he felt must soon come. In order to compose his mind he examined an old working in detail, admiring the rich and varied seams of rock which the spades of forgotten men had uncovered; snowy quartz, fragments of rich iron ore glittered over by the scales of mica, pale green serpentine, and dappled jasper. He stopped to pick up a beautiful piece of chalcedony, a network of glittering crystals, which he handed to his jailor, saying: 'Look at the riches of the place.' Branko grunted doubtfully as he turned the specimen over in his fingers. 'And look there is gold,' added Methuen, picking up a piece of fractured iron pyrites with its enticing yellowish gleam. 'Gold?' said Branko with interest. 'Yes. Here, take it.'

These pleasantries were interrupted by a guard who sought them out and said curtly: 'Black Peter wants to see you at once in the cave.' Methuen drew a deep breath and braced himself. 'Now it is coming,' he thought as he walked slowly back into the depression which was now swimming with golden warriors and brightly caparisoned mules, turned to a dazzle by the last fainting rays of the sunlight.

The cave had been stripped of everything now, and a huge bonfire burned in one corner on which the old man was putting various oddments of equipment and some papers from a wallet. Black Peter sat at the table with a preoccupied air and motioned Methuen to the chair which faced him.

'Well,' said Methuen.

'I was hoping some of these people might be able to confirm your story.'

'So was I.'

'They can't. They've been in touch with headquarters, but not for a day or two; and their field of operations has been around Sarajevo.'

'O damn!' said Methuen with a wild joy in his heart which he disguised by holding up his tethered wrists for inspection. 'Must I really go about like this? After all the camp is surrounded by sentries. One can't even get up to the Janko Stone to look at the view—much less escape, just supposing I wanted to do so.' Black Peter nodded vigorously, and then shook his head once more. 'I refuse to take chances,' he said with slow obstinate determination.

The room had slowly been filling up with guerillas and it was obvious that he had not more time to spare for Methuen. 'Go and get ready,' he said. 'We march in a little while.'

Methuen walked into the starry darkness with a light step. He was overwhelmed with relief. His shaggy janitor now led him to the cave which contained the treasure, and having first untied his hands, slipped a coat of coins over his head. The weight was really staggering—it could hardly have been less than that of a medieval suit of armour. To this was added a double bandolier of coins which rested on his hips. 'My God,' said Methuen, 'one can't carry ammunition as well as this.' Branko gave a chuckle. 'You won't be expected to use any. As for us we are strong.'

'We shall see,' said Methuen. The latest arrivals were being loaded with their bandoliers and he noticed that ammunition had been cut to the minimum. It did not argue well for any action they might have to fight on their way to the coast; and food? He had noticed a flock of sheep among the mules and presumed that they would drive a few with them and kill them whenever they camped. 'This is going to be some journey,' he said soberly and Branko grunted as he replied: 'Come along man. Our ancestors did as much and more.' Methuen looked suitably shame-faced as he replied: 'Yes. It is well said.'

Outside the cave in the starlit night the mule-teams had formed up and the camp was bustling with life. Having loaded Methuen up Branko took the opportunity of attaching a long piece of rope to his left arm. This would enable the jailor to walk behind his charge in the night and yet keep a secure hold upon him by means of the rope. They were not going to have him slipping away in the darkness.

Now the melodious voice of Black Peter came at them out of the darkness and a great silence fell. 'Men!' said the invisible orator. 'Everything is prepared and we are about to set out. I must remind you that none shall speak, and none shall smoke until I tell you. Tonight and tomorrow night will be dangerous. Say prayers for your loved ones and for the King in whose name we will perform this exploit or perish.'

Branko now led him across the dark grass to join the little group which stood about Black Peter like an unofficial bodyguard. 'We will march with them in front,' he said in a hoarse whisper, and they set their faces to the west, climbing the slopes under the Janko Stone slowly and laboriously, in their coats of mail.

There was a young moon half-hidden by clouds and looking back from the great obelisk Methuen saw the black serpent of the mule-train coiling behind them on that windless mountain. In the darkness around they could see the great clusters of peaks and canyons which surrounded the Janko Stone. The grass was damp from the heavy mountain dew. Black Peter headed the procession with a cluster of armed men round him; then came Methuen and his jailor, closely followed by the leader of the first mule-team.

The path led steadily down towards a watershed and the going was not as even as Methuen had hoped as he stumbled along with Branko tugging at the rope. They walked in complete silence except for an occasional hoarse word of command or a whispered confabulation about their direction among the little party which led the way. For the greater part of the descent they were in the open and it was fortunate that the moon was hidden by clouds, for once or twice they heard the noise of an aircraft overhead—and perhaps the glitter of moonlight on coin might have been visible. Once they had descended into the shadowy watershed visibility became limited and in the inky darkness there were one or two minor accidents—a broken girth, and a man who fell down a steep bank and knocked himself almost insensible with his rifle-butt. But in general their progress was steady and the disciplined behaviour of the men excellent. Methuen kept up as well as he could, glad to be on the move once more, but with his brain swimming with half-formulated plans and hopes which he did not know how to achieve.

They marched through a dark wood and over some rolling dunes of grass reminiscent of the mountain range they had just left. To their left in the darkness they could hear the ripple of water rushing in a stony bed. Once the whole column halted for a while while the scouts went forward to investigate something suspicious. After much whispering they continued bearing sharply to the left and crossing a swift stream at a shallow ford. Methuen was rapidly becoming exhausted both by the weight he carried and by the acute discomfort caused by his pinioned wrists. He repeatedly asked Branko in a whisper if he could talk to Black Peter but each time he was met by a grunt of refusal.

At last, in exasperation, he sat down and refused to walk another step unless he could see the chief. Branko cursed and swore and tugged vigorously at the rope but all to no avail. 'Here I stay,' said Methuen in a low voice, 'until I speak to him.' The column of mules had halted uncertainly. Branko muttered murderously and drew his pistol which he thrust under Methuen's nose in a threatening manner. But Methuen simply said: 'Go on and shoot me, then. I am not moving.' While the argument was still going on in hissing whispers Black Peter and his party retraced their steps hastily to see what was the cause of the hold-up. 'What is it?' he said angrily.

'He won't move,' said Branko.

'Black Peter,' said Methuen, 'I shall not be able to march with you unless I have my hands free. I am already half-dead. Either you give me a chance to march freely or you can kill me now.'

He was in an extremely bad temper by this time, and pouring with sweat. Black Peter paused for a long moment, and then, without a word drew a knife and cut him free. 'But be careful,' he whispered, and turning to Branko added: 'Keep a good hold on the rope.'

It was a prodigious relief and Methuen now found that he could keep up with the forward party with comparative ease. They all seemed to be skilled mountaineers, and at almost every stage of the journey they gave proof of their talents, slipping off to left and right of the road on short reconnaisances, using natural cover like born huntsmen. A small group of four scouts had been pushed out about a mile ahead of the party, and each in turn waited to make contact before moving off ahead again; his place was always taken by another. In this way they had an intelligence relay of runners bringing them information about the country they were traversing. These men were the only ones not cumbered with the coin-coats or bandoliers.

It was after midnight when the order came to halt and the party was allowed half an hour of much-needed rest in a shadowy ravine which made an excellent hiding-place. The moon had long since gone, though the sky was soft and lit with bright stars. Black Peter came and sat for a moment by Methuen, wiping his streaming face and asking: 'How is it going?' Methuen's good humour had returned with his increased freedom. He had spent his time well, by turning pickpocket and stealing back his compass from Branko. This enabled him to keep an eye on the general direction of the party and he noted with satisfaction that they were walking roughly parallel (though of course at a great distance from) the main road down which Porson must drive on his way from Skopje to Belgrade.

He still had hopes of being able to escape and reach the road in time for the next rendezvous. But for the moment he was enjoying himself, watching the extraordinary skill with which these mountaineers piloted their mule-team through enemy territory. Once or twice they passed settlements of straw shacks such as shepherds build in the uplands for summer use and at one of these he noticed a fire burning and the vague outlines of figures sitting round it. In the clear night air, too, he heard the monotonous jigging music of stringed instruments. The column halted in a ravine by a pool and while a scout crept forward to the settlement the mules were watered and washed down with as little noise as possible. Presently low voices sounded in the darkness and they started off once more at the slow plodding pace of somnambulists.

From here their road began to ascend very steeply and the going became much more difficult. The soft path turned rudely to flint under the hooves of their mules and after some time vanished altogether, leaving them on the wooded side of a mountain. They toiled their way upward through a jungle of fern and dwarf-elder, slipping and sliding, and hoisting themselves wherever they could by the help of projecting shrubs. Progress was slowed up a good deal, and it was with some relief that they at last reached the beech-glades of the mountain-top where movement was freer and the surface soft once more.

Through the avenues of great trees they caught an occasional glimpse of the vistas of mountains which stretched out on every side of them, but there were no signs of human habitation anywhere along their path. Dawn was already showing some signs of breaking behind the backcloth of peaks when they reached the final peak of the range, and here they were halted in a fir forest, carpeted with wonderful rich heather already burnt brown by the summer sun. The order to bivouac was given and no sooner were the mules safely tethered than each man lay down and fell asleep in his tracks. Methuen freed himself from his bandoliers and his coin-coat and followed suit, falling almost at once into a deep and dreamless sleep.

He woke to find Black Peter shaking him by the shoulder and saying: 'Wake up now. Get under cover.' Everyone was ordered into the shadow of the trees and elaborate precautions were taken that none of the animals should stray outside the radius of the wood. As the light grew Methuen understood why for they were camped on the crown of a hill which overlooked one of the main roads into Serbia. In this corner of the picture there was also a good deal of activity; frequent cars and lorries rolled along in the dawn light sending up their plumes of dust. They heard, too, a few desultory bangs in the east which might have been the noise of guns, but for the most part the landscape around them seemed as peaceful as a charm.

They lay up here for the whole of that day, eating what food they could lay hands on; those lucky enough to have some bread of their own shared it, and the supply of water was strictly rationed. Black Peter and his little band of sharp-shooters lay at the edge of the wood carefully watching the road for signs of military movement. Methuen for his part spent the day dozing. The constant marching and counter-marching of the last forty-eight hours was beginning to tell on him, and moreover he had been troubled by a nail projecting from the sole of his left boot. He took ample advantage of the long wait to massage his feet and to get what rest he could. Despite the relative freedom of movement he enjoyed the rope on his arm had began to annoy him, chiefly because it meant being tethered to Branko and Branko smelt very strongly. He swore that that night he would untie his end of the rope and lash his jailor to some more appropriate bondsman—a mule.

Twice they were visited by aircraft that day, and the second time a reconnassance plane circled the hill most carefully before flying away to the east. Discipline was perfect and not a soul moved; indeed the cover itself was magnificent and one could lie at ease in the bracken without fear of being detected. Nevertheless these visitations put everyone on the *qui vive*, and Methuen could detect an increase of nervous tension among the men when dusk began to fall. Once more before they set out Black Peter made a short speech reminding them all of the pledge they had taken to win through with the treasure, and Methuen could not help reflecting that this alone betrayed the one weakness of a Balkan soldier—forgetfulness. He must each day be reminded what he is fighting for and exhorted to do his duty.

They set off in the grey dusk and after traversing several shallow ranges all of a sudden reached the foot of a mountain which dominated the whole landscape with its jagged white slopes. The surface had changed again and the noise of the mules' hooves on the loose stones sounded tremendous in the silence. Away to the west they could see a line of bivouac fires—though whether they were troops or shepherds it was impossible to tell. A thin refreshing drizzle fell for an hour and then a wind sprang up and cleared the sky. The young moon looked in on them and they could see the groins and limestone precipices of the mountain they must scale glimmering in the dusky light. They had started on a barren flinty shoulder which climbers would call a glacis; thousands of feet below they could see the tossing woods of Spanish chestnut and wild vine.

At their first resting-point Black Peter came in search of Methuen, full of excitement. 'You see now?' he said. 'We have not seen a soul, and once we reach the top there is a narrow stone path above the Black Lake which will carry us over to the next mountain. Impossible to ambush us there. It will be like swinging from tree to tree, eh? From mountain-top to mountain-top while the troops walk up and down the valleys.' He was tremendously excited. For his own part Methuen did not like it at all; he thought it ominous that so far they had encountered no trace of enemy opposition. But there seemed little point in saying so.

Besides, another and more serious question was beginning to gnaw at him. He must soon make a bid for it if he was to reach the road in time to contact Porson. It was already a long walk as far as he could judge, and a daylight escape would be virtually impossible. He had already experimented with the rope round his arm and found that he could undo it easily enough and tether it to a mule without Branko noticing. But how and when could he slip out of the column and disappear? He would wait, he thought, until dawn when the men were tired.

They trudged on up the mountain for several hours until they reached a large ravine at the top and here, at a bend in the path, an involuntary hoarse cry broke from the throats of the men as they saw the glittering expanse of the Black Lake lying below them. They knew that once they had skirted it the worst part of the journey would be over.

They halted for half an hour and re-formed before entering the gulley which was to lead them by a narrow path along the sides of the lake. The path was of a decent width, allowing two mules to walk abreast for the most part; only in certain spots did it narrow enough to become dangerous. The view from here was indescribably lovely, for they looked down upon the polished surface of the Black Lake from the position of eagles.

Methuen hoped that by dawn they would have finished with this narrow path and emerge into more open country, for his chances of escape were nil under present conditions. Two mules walked ahead of him and two behind, and left no room for someone to squeeze past. The only way out would have been to jump into the Black Lake itself, and that he did not fancy.

Nevertheless he tied Branko to one of the mules without the old man noticing anything and waited for his chance to come. At one of the halts on this rocky staircase Black Peter came back to see if everything was going well. 'I am so happy,' he said. 'I know in my heart that we will get through now. They have missed us.'

Who could know the nature of the ambush into which they were walking?

* * * *

Whenever he thought of the ambush in later years Methuen always recalled the suddenness of it with a shudder. The long march had made them confident of evading capture by the enemy, and their spirits were high as they knew that the path would lead them out on to the crest of a remote mountain-top near Durmitor—far from roads and rivers. Each man felt his spirits rise as he heard his own tramping feet echo against the rocks in a silence punctuated only by the creaking of girths, the occasional snort of a mule, or the faint clink of a weapon touching a coat of coin. Below them slept the lake.

Dawn was already beginning to break, and Methuen was in a fever of impatience to make his bid for freedom. The men marched on in exhausted silence, and as far as he could judge Branko was all but asleep on his feet. At any rate he had not noticed that the rope-end he held was tied to the saddle of a mule.

The path widened now into a rocky defile which gave some space for manoeuvre and the press behind grew greater as the leading mule-section halted—perhaps to tighten a loose girth. All at once there came a rapid rattle of sound from over the rocky hillock—like the sound of a stick being dragged across iron railings. That was all. And in the following silence a flock of geese rose off the surface of the lake and circled nervously a thousand feet below. A man coughed loudly, and there came the sound of running feet. Then once more came that ominous rattle, and this time it swelled into a roar, being echoed from three or four different points of the compass. A group of scouts came running, bent double across the rocky corridors and among them Methuen recognized Black Peter waving a tommy-gun. His face was contorted with rage. He shouted a sharp order and the supports surged forward, leaving the mules with only their guards; they clustered round him as he shouted and then loped off to the end of the defile and were lost to sight. Rapid fire sounded from the entrance and whitish chips of rock began to peel off and fly into the air. It was as if a dozen pneumatic drills had suddenly started up in competition.

Methuen sprang forward and grasped Peter by the arm. 'What has happened?' he said and Black Peter suddenly burst into tears of rage as he answered: 'They are over the path. We must fight our way out.' The rocky cliff prevented any serious estimate of the situation and Methuen shouted: 'Come up the cliff and let us see.' Black Peter was already giving orders to line up the mules under cover of the cliff. A rush of guerillas swept past them towards the firing-point, shouting hoarsely. 'Come,' said Methuen in an agony of impatience and seizing Black Peter's arm he pulled him towards the cliff.

Even though the guerilla leader was cumbered by a heavy automatic weapon he climbed like a goat and Methuen had a job to keep up with him. They climbed to the highest spur and cautiously edged themselves between two great rocks from which point they could look down over the crown of the hill. Methuen gave a groan for it was clear that in another five minutes the path would have led them out into the open, onto a wooded promontory. And it was here that he saw, squinting through his glasses, the long ominous grey line of squatting infantry. 'Machine-guns,' he said gloomily, 'and by God!' There was a faint crash and a puff of smoke which sailed languidly into the air while over to the left of their position, on the rocky crown of the next hill, came a jarrying spout of stone and gravel which whizzed about their ears like a choir of gnats. 'Mortars!' said Methuen.

'Mortars!' echoed Black Peter. 'We must fight our way through. God's death! It's getting light. We must give the word for a general advance.'

They rejoined the guerillas on the ledge below. There was considerable confusion of men coming back and others going forward. Several were wounded.

Methuen rushed across the path and into the defile in order to see for himself what things were like at the point of action. As he turned the corner the air swished and whooped about him and he flopped to his stomach and began to crawl. The path debouched onto the crown of a hill and here he saw the scrambling kicking bundle of wounded men and mules. The advance guard were returning the fire of the troops over this barrier but it was quite clear that there was little chance of a break out of the narrow entrance where the noise of the firing was simply deafening. Some of the guerillas had climbed the sides of the gorge to take up firing positions and the noise of their tommy-guns was like the noise of giant woodpeckers at work. Fragments of stone were flying everywhere.

As he lay, pressed against the side of the cliff, he heard the ragged roar of the supports coming up. They surged over him like a wave and burst out of the opening towards the crest where the troops were entrenched. A blinding smoke hung over everything and the noise redoubled in volume. It was impossible to see, but Methuen could imagine the line of charging figures racing down the slope towards the machine-guns, shouting and firing as they ran. 'What a party to be caught in,' he kept muttering to himself as the seconds ticked away.

A wounded man came crawling back out of the smoke crying something which he could not hear above the roaring of the fusillade. Methuen dragged him to the nearest cover and laid him down beside the path. Then he raced back to the central amphitheatre where the greater part of the mules were. Here confusion reigned. The wounded were lying everywhere groaning and cursing, and the skeleton team of muleteers divided its attention between attempts to quieten the animals and vain attempts to help those who had been hurt. A wave of yellow smoke filled the cave entrance through which occasional figures darted or lurched but it was impossible to know how the battle was going. They were like the comrades of entombed miners waiting at a pit entrance after a heavy fall of rock, thought Methuen grimly; and in the general confusion he shed his bandoliers and coin-coat unnoticed, hoping to retreat down the path and make his way out.

But he had hardly started the path when a new outbreak of firing from the opposite direction set his pulse racing. Were there troops behind them as well as in front? Once more there came the violent scramble of men running for their lives, and stopping to fire short snarling bursts with their tommy-guns before resuming their flight. 'We are cut off,' said Methuen, and sat down despairingly on a pack-saddle. A panic was about to start when suddenly a majestic figure was seen to materialize from the smoke which blocked the first entrance. A shout went up for it was Black Peter. He walked slowly—with the calculated slowness of a drunkard who knows he is drunk and is elaborately anxious to seem sober. He walked with tremendous circumspection, holding his shoulder with his hand. His face was white and his eyes staring. Methuen jumped forward with a cry of 'Black Peter!' but the figure advanced at the same slow speed, giving no sign of having heard.

Black Peter walked towards the group of muleteers like a somnambulist. He threw his whistle from his pocket and slowly put it to his lips to blow a long shrill blast. Once, twice, three times he sounded and a hoarse cry went up for this was the pre-arranged signal which told them that the battle was lost. 'Destroy the treasure!' he shouted once, weakly, but his voice was lost in the rattle of firing.

Now Methuen was swept aside by the press of mules which were driven to the edge of the path and pushed screaming into space. This was by no means an easy operation as the poor animals, already half-crazed by the din, were terrified to see the immense drop before them and fought madly to escape, snorting and screaming. Some had to be shot and some clubbed, and Methuen's gorge rose as he saw them plunging into space.

Black Peter had fallen to his knees and Methuen caught hold of the young giant and dragged him away from the mêlée. It was clear that he was dying. His eyes were rapidly glazing and his breath came in harsh gulps. 'Black Peter,' whispered Methuen as he propped the wounded man's head with a rolled-up coat, 'is the action really finished?' But there was not a shadow of response in those dark eyes.

The firing had become thinner and more spasmodic now, though it sounded nearer, and was definitely coming from two opposite quarters. The muleteers were working like fiends, throwing their bandoliers and coats into the Black Lake, and urging the screaming and reluctant animals forward to their deaths with wild yells. But even in the confusion Methuen could not help noticing the methodical way they worked. Each mule was led to the edge, its front legs were worked over the precipice and while one man held it another cut the girth and the ropes binding the treasure with a knife. Then the animal was pushed over, or if it showed reluctance was clubbed.

For his own part Methuen was filled with a sort of blank indecision. What should he do, since the enemy was both before and behind? As always in moments like these when there seemed to be no way out of a dilemma he was careful not to panic, not to start running—but to wait upon events. They alone could show him a way out, if way there was to be. Accordingly he busied himself by making Black Peter as comfortable as he could. He took back his cherished pistol from the leather sling at Peter's hip, and refilled a clip of cartridges. From a discarded parcel of food lying on the path he took a piece of bread and some cheese. Then he started off down the path in the direction from which they had been marching when the attack started. He had gone perhaps twenty yards along the path, picking his way over the bodies of men and mules, discarded ammunition boxes and derelict saddles, when he reached a point where the path made a steep turn and here he could see the tell-tale cloud of smoke which indicated that the rear guard was still putting up a fight. Methuen halted in indecision for it was clear that he would never find a way both through his own men and through the ranks of the Communists.

Then it was that his luck changed abruptly for the better. A dead mule lay wedged between two rocks at the very edge of the precipice with the body of its muleteer lying dead across it. The man had been killed as he was trying to urge the mule over the edge. From the high wooden saddle Methuen saw a long coil of rope which had untied itself and hung dangling over the edge, and all of a sudden an idea occurred to him. Would it be possible to find a way of climbing out of his present predicament by lowering himself down the cliff a good way?

In a second he was lying beside the mule staring down into the gulf, his eyes hunting keenly for some vestiges of a path, or a fault in the rock-face which might give him a foothold. He could not resist a sharp cry of joy, for there, forty feet below, was a narrow path running parallel to the one upon which he now was, a path graven in the side of the cliff face. It is true that it was narrow—a mere shelf of rock above the gulf. But Methuen was by now desperate and prepared to follow his luck wherever it led.

He tested the rope after giving it an extra turn or two round the wooden saddle-frame and then, to make it even more secure, he passed it round a smooth rock projection. It bore him easily; and with a final glance around him he lowered himself gingerly into the gulf with a prayer on his lips, not daring to look down into the depths of the Black Lake below.

In his younger days he had been a rock-climber of promise and this experience stood him in good stead now, for he reached the rocky ledge below in a matter of moments and saw with relief that it did indeed continue along the side of the mountain, though here and there it was blocked by a projecting shrub or a fault. Above him he could still hear the unearthly racket of the battle and from time to time a shower of boulders or a grotesque dummy-like figure of man or mule fell slowly past him and produced a dull thick splash in the lake below. It was strange to see how slowly objects seemed to fall as they reached the level of the ledge upon which he stood, turning over and over and giving the impression of trying to unfold in space as they travelled towards the dark water below. The noise of the firing, too, seemed to change into a number of different variations of the same sound; one set of guns sounded like woodpeckers, another crisp as whip-strokes, while from above him where the rear guard was still fighting, the firing sounded like a series of dull cracks and hisses—as of a red-hot poker thrust into water.

He was bathed in sweat and trembling with fatigue in every limb, yet he set off at a good pace towards the eastern end of the massif. At times he had to travel with his back pressed to the rock, so narrow did the path become; and at others he was forced to climb out of his way in places where the path abruptly ceased. Once he was forced to take the risk of swinging across a gap on a shrub.

In half an hour he had put the sounds of the battle well behind him and the path at last petered out on the side of a hill made of rugged outcrops where climbing was again possible, and he was able to travel upwards towards the mountain-top along a narrow funnel. By the time he reached the top the sun had already risen and the mists were streaming up from the lowland meadows.

He had emerged on the crown of the mountain and could see, with a thrill of relief, that the scene of the ambush lay well to the west of his present position. As he crouched in a rocky hollow and ate some bread and cheese with a ravenous appetite he combed the country with his precious glasses. The battle was still going on among the cliffs of the mountain-top and he could see lines of infantry taking up position among the beech woods which crowned the range beyond.

In the valley below him he saw a long train of mounted troops deploring across the watershed they had crossed the previous day. The whole operation had been a masterpiece of planning and had caught the White Eagles at the most vulnerable point of the whole journey— the last defile which might lead them to Durmitor and safety.

There was a small reconnaissance plane in the sky hovering over the scene of the battle. As Methuen watched and considered, his heart came into his mouth for he heard the sound of horses' hoofs from near at hand; up the steep mountain path which had been hidden from him by a fold of rock came a cavalcade of troops in the familiar grey uniforms and forage-caps marked with the red star. Methuen flattened himself against the rock and held his breath.

They passed him without seeing him and clattered across the rough paths towards the battle—their weapons at the ready. Methuen drew a breath of relief as he heard their horses' hoofs dying away among the rocky defiles, and he for his part made haste to take the path which would lead him back over the watershed and into the country where —how remote in space and time it seemed—the cave was.

Danger always gave one reserve of unexpected strength he had discovered in the past, and now the narrowness of his escape spurred him on. On the crest of the mountain the cover was not good though the path along which they had so laboriously marched was clearly marked. He forced himself to adopt a regular pace in order not to tire too easily, and every hour he took a three-minute rest during which he checked his course with the compass he had recovered from Branko. A fearful thirst was his only trouble and hereabouts there seemed to be no springs or rivulets; he investigated several ravines which looked as if they might have rivers running in them but without any luck.

Away to the east he could see the great mist-encircled massifs of the range which was crowned by the Janko Stone, and he steered for it, bearing right the whole time so that he could cross the foothills and avoid climbing the central range once more. In this way he hoped to find himself back once more in the valley from which he had started on his journey to contact the mule-teams.

The sun was hot now and he was tempted to shed his heavy coat and hat in order to make his march the lighter, but he thought it wiser to keep these articles for he did not as yet know where he was going to spend the night. At his present pace he calculated that he might reach the cave at dusk—provided he did not meet with any mishap. As far as he could see the countryside was more or less deserted. He caught a glimpse of several roads in the distance and could see the plumes of dust left by wheeled traffic, but it was too far to see clearly.

As far as he could judge the concentrations of troops were in the area he had left behind him, but he took no chances; before crossing each range where the cover was sparse he studied his route carefully. Once he was forced to make a long detour owing to the presence of some sheep and a group of shepherds who sat indolently under a cherry tree, playing on reed pipes—a strangely peaceful and reassuring sound to ears accustomed to the rattle and bark of machine-guns. Methuen listened to them as he crouched under cover in a fir forest and devoured the scanty remains of his bread and cheese.

His detour served a good purpose, too, for it led him to water; he found himself entangled in the debris of a recent forest fire—a steep bank clothed with fern and dwarf elder where the ground was covered with sharp splinters of charred and fractured rock, and where he had to scale high barricades of sooty timber in order to reach a cliff edge from where one could hear the distant ripple of a summer river. He slipped and skidded his way down and was delighted to find a shallow pebbled pool brimming with ice-cold water, and he plunged into it bodily, clothes and all, revelling in the icy sharpness of the water and feeling immediately refreshed.

It was here, while he was drying his clothes that a large and extremely savage sheep-dog spotted him from the hill-top and rushed down upon him, barking. Methuen scrambled for his pistol and covered the beast with it. He was standing in the middle of the stream on a rock, and he hurled a boulder at the animal as a warning to keep off. But it came down the bank and showed every intention of attacking him.

He shot it with great reluctance, for he knew how valuable dogs must be to the peasantry of this remote countryside. But he could not afford to take the chance of being given away; and lest the dog's owner should be anywhere in the vicinity he gathered up his possessions and set about climbing the opposite hill in his squelching and waterlogged boots. It was a full two hours before his clothes had dried out on his body, and the sun by this time was baking. Despite his hunger and weariness he was encouraged to look at the distance he had covered through his glasses—the long shallow spine of the mountain range which backed the stony watershed.

Once or twice he saw small isolated patrols of grey infantry mounted on mules, but they were always a good way off and he was able to pass them by without being seen. Once or twice, too, he happened upon a long line of peasant muleteers carrying wood down to the valleys and was forced to hide in whatever cover was available. Much of the terrain hereabouts was planted with firs and beeches, and the dense growth of heather and fern made hiding easy.

By midday he had reached the second range of mountains which were crowned by the Janko Stone and he took half an hour's rest. His feet had begun to hurt intolerably and despite every precaution he had managed to blister both heels. The flesh was raw and painful. But now he was on the great shelving meadow upland with its carpets of thick grass, like coarse brushed hair, and he started out to walk barefoot, carrying his boots round his neck, tied with string. This relieved him somewhat and as the going was all downhill he made good time along the range, his pulse quickening every time he came upon a familiar landmark pointing the way to the valley of the cave which he had begun to think of almost as home.

The long fatigue of the journey had begun to make itself felt and he found himself falling into a pleasant stupefaction as he walked; it was as if he had detached himself from his body and allowed it to walk on towards the horizon like an automaton, leaving his mind suspended up here on the windless pasture land which buzzed with crickets and shone with butterflies. This, he recognized, was the sort of state in which one became careless and unobservant and he did his best to remain alert and fully wide awake; but in vain. His mind kept wandering off on a tack of its own.

He thought of the Awkward Shop—the rabbit warren of corridors in some corner of which Dombey sat, turned green by his desk-lamp like a mandarin in a stage-spotlight, brooding over his collection of moths; he thought of the companions who usually accompanied him on missions like the present one—the Professor with his absent-minded air, and Danny with his huge hands and yellow hair. And thinking of it all with nostalgia he cursed himself for a fool to have left it all behind, to have given way to an impulse. 'If I get out of this,' he said aloud, 'I'm turning up my cards,' and then he laughed aloud, for he remembered the many occasions when, in the face of strain and fatigue, he had made himself the same idiotic promise—a promise which he had never managed to keep.

He had crossed the whole range by now and the sun was rapidly westering. He had come to familiar country, the soft shallow hills whose limestone curves foretold the passage of a dozen mountain rivers towards the Ebar gorge. He was replete with the excitement of a mission accomplished and the knowledge that he would be in time for the rendezvous at dawn. The path he followed hugged the banks of a stream rising and falling along the curvature of the hillside like a swallow and he walked swiftly and decisively along it, hoping that it would not be too dark by the time he reached the cave to recover and reassemble his cherished fishing-rod. The rushing river below him deadened the sound of his feet on the flinty path. He rested for a few moments on the bank to drink and bathe his face, and made a half-hearted attempt to put his boots on, but his feet were by now too swollen and too painful. It was obvious that he would have to carry on barefoot. He was meditating upon this unlucky chance when a shout from somewhere behind him sent his heart into his mouth. He stood up and turned a dazed face towards the cliff.

A young soldier stood on a spur of rock above him covering him with a carbine. He did not look unduly menacing, and a cigarette hung from the corner of his lip. He waved his hand and shouted: 'You there! Come here for questioning.' Methuen put his hand to his ear as if he did not hear very well and pointed to the river. 'What do you say?' He was thinking rapidly as he moved slowly away from the bank. If there were more troops on the hill behind he was finished. 'What cursed luck,' he exclaimed involuntarily as he obeyed.

* * * *

The soldier stood nonchalantly with his back to the sun, smoking, in an attitude that suggested lazy indecision. Methuen's eyes took in the grey uniform, the mud-spattered gaiters and ugly boots: the flat cap with its lack-lustre star: and lastly the short repeating carbine of Russian pattern which he held at the hip. 'What is it comrade?' he called in a whining tone. The soldier waved the muzzle of his weapon languidly and shouted: 'Come here!' in a more imperious tone. His black eyes had a stupid arrogant expression.

It was clear that he was some peasant conscript from a remote country village rejoicing in the possession of a gun. Methuen nodded and said: 'I come, comrade, I come,' and started to climb the cliff slowly and wearily. His eyes darted hither and thither, attempting to see whether there were other soldiers about, but as far as he could judge this one was quite alone. What should he do? He was almost within pistol-range now. The wisest move would be perhaps to be quite passive and to come in close under the muzzle of the carbine. If he were asked for his identity papers, as he most certainly would be, he could put his hand inside his coat and draw his pistol with one hand while he grabbed the carbine-muzzle with the other. He climbed with an exaggerated slowness up the slope.

When he was half-way up he saw an expression of resolute savagery cross the face of the soldier. His mouth depressed itself in a savage grin as, raising the carbine to shoulder-level, he fired at Methuen at almost point-blank range. Even as the latter felt the hot whistle of the bullet pluck the lapel of his coat he leapt sideways and in less time than it takes to tell, was cowering under the protection of a rock, swearing volubly in a mixture of languages. He was absolutely furious at this dumb treachery.

The earth began to jump and spatter around the rock as the soldier opened up on him, and Methuen with his pistol in hand cowered back against the smooth stone with murder in his heart. He began to feel sorry for the nonchalant young man who was so liberally peppering the landscape with lead. 'You wait, you brute,' muttered Methuen through clenched teeth, and in his mind's eye he had a sudden picture of Vida.

An interval of silence followed while the soldier smartly changed the clip on his carbine. He was obviously under the impression that his prey was unarmed. In the first gust of firing Methuen had felt a sharp stab of pain in the calf of his left leg and for a moment he had explored this feeling of pain with concern, for he could not afford to be incapacitated at this late stage of the game. Now in the silence he cautiously stretched his leg and was relieved to find that it responded normally enough, though it hurt him considerably.

A second burst of firing followed and Methuen tossed his fur hat down the slope as a distraction before worming himself away to the left to where a clump of bushes afforded excellent cover. Here he drew his breath for a moment before climbing gently up the slope at an angle. The soldier was still staring at the rock behind which Methuen had disappeared, attentively smiling. He had thrown his cigarette away now and had the butt of his carbine pressed to his shoulder.

Methuen took him softly on the sights of his pistol—the ugly backless shaven skull surmounted by the blue cap—and pressed the trigger. There was a loud sniff and the figure lurched out of sight, its disappearance being followed by a ragged bumping and scrambling noise. He had fallen down the cliff and rolled down to the bottom. In the silence that followed the noise of the river welled up once more, and Methuen could hear, above the sound his own laboured breathing, birds singing in the trees across the valley.

He waited for a long moment before he set off running across the now familiar valley towards the cave. The path was sheltered here and he raced along it, pausing from time to time to listen for sounds of pursuit. But the valley had returned to its silent beauty. Once he thought he heard the barking of dogs in the forest, but that was all. His leg was extremely painful now but he did not dare to stop and examine his wound, for he knew from experience that wounds are apt to seem worse than they really are if once one sets eyes on them. That it could not be anything vital he knew for, despite the pain which made him limp grotesquely, the limb could still be used normally enough.

Twilight was already upon him when he struck the main branch of the Studenitsa river and followed its silver windings and meanderings through the mulberry orchards and across the slopes beyond the monastery and sawmill. He was almost blind with exhaustion now and he forded the river with difficulty, staggering as he felt the sucking pull of the water around his ankles. Nevertheless he had enough presence of mind to wait for a full quarter of an hour on the hill opposite the cave, watching the entrance, before he climbed the slope to enter it.

It was extraordinary the feeling of affection he felt for this fox's burrow which had sheltered him from his enemies; it was almost like arriving home once more after a perilous journey. Nothing had changed. The snake was not visible, but then it always retired at dusk. The barrier of greenery which he had placed at the mouth was undisturbed. Methuen entered the musty precincts and groped along the stone edges of the sill for the matches which he had placed in a convenient place together with his candle-stump. He lit up and the warm rosy light flickered once more over the veined walls which glimmered like the marbled endpapers of a Victorian ledger.

The dead man still lay on his rude couch of leaves. Methuen hardly gave him a glance as he busied himself in the collection of his possessions. The bed-roll must be sacrificed, but he was not going to lose the other things. He filled his pockets with the most vital of his possessions, and buried the rest in the earth floor. It was too dark and his leg was too painful now to enable him to hunt for his cherished rod. That too would have to be sacrificed, he realized with a pang. He ate a hasty and scrappy meal as he walked up and down. He did not dare to sit down for fear either that he would fall asleep or that his leg would stiffen and prevent him from undertaking the last lap of the journey into the Ebar valley.

Darkness had fallen when he limped out of the cave and with a final glance around him descended the slope to ford the river. He was glad of this, for it increased his chances of escape if he should run into further trouble. By now his route was familiar to him and he had no fear that he would lose his way. His only preoccupation was his wounded leg which had begun to stiffen up in an ugly manner; but he calculated that it was good for an hour's march. A stiff drink had made him feel much better, though he realized that sooner or later the effect of the spirits would induce sleepiness and he was most concerned about this. Suppose he fell asleep and let Porson pass him in the night—at dawn?

It was useless worrying, however, and he plodded on across the soft meadows with determination. There was a feeble glimmer of light from one room in the monastery and he heard the distant barking of a dog. Beyond the trees by the sawmill he heard the sounds of singing from the little tavern where the peasants were drinking their evening glass of plum brandy. He smiled as he crossed the ridge for the last time and entered the dark avenues of pines to feel the soft ferny floor of the hillside under his bare feet.

He arrived at the road after a journey full of falls and slips, due to his leg, and worked his way along the northern end under cover of the trees. When he reached a point almost opposite the white marker stone where Porson should stop by agreement, he climbed into the ditch and was delighted to find it still dry and full of tall ferns which afforded excellent cover. Here he must lie until the car came for him, and it was characteristic that having won his way so far he should begin to worry about the rendezvous. His sleepy mind began playing tricks with him, telling him that today was not Saturday but Friday. He buried his face in the deep grass and, despite himself, fell into a fitful slumber, lulled by the roaring of the water in the valley below him. He had had the presence of mind to slip the leather thong of his pistol round his wrist and to slip the safety catch.

Time passed and the moon rose. He was woken by the whistle of a train which rumbled through the cuttings opposite and disappeared with a succession of shrill grunts and squeaks into the heart of the mountain. It looked more than ever like a toy with its small lighted carriages, and fussing engine. In the silence that followed he could hear the voices of soldiers and plate layers on the railway-line opposite.

His leg had become stiff now, and to ease it he was forced to turn on his back and lie in a more relaxed position. The mosquitoes too were troublesome and Methuen felt the bumps rising on his face and neck from their sharp bites; but he was too far gone with sleep to care, and sinking his head back into the soft bank he fell now into a deep troubled sleep in which the vivid images of the last two days flickered and flashed as if across a cinema screen: Black Peter's glazing eyes, the turning, tossing figures of men in gold coats falling into space, the mule-teams strung out along the mountain like a serpent, the smile on the face of the soldier with the carbine. Then, too, he saw himself picking Branko's pocket, walking along the edge of the cliff, or running bent double among the bracken like a wounded hare. The whole insane jumble of events seemed to have become telescoped in his mind with those other scenes taken from his first days at the cave—the fish rising to his fly, the rain swishing down from the great bare mountains. . . .

It is possible that he would indeed have missed Porson, so deeply did he sleep, had it not been for a lucky chance; for it was already dawn when he was abruptly dragged from his stupor by the rumble of lorries as a convoy burst round the corner and passed the place where he was lying, the yellow headlamps lighting up the cliff-side and the road with their ghastly pale radiance.

He counted seven lorries, and he could dimly see that they were packed with troops and leather-men. They were heading in the southerly direction which must lead them to the nearest road-point from which to climb to the scene of the battle. Methuen breathed a prayer of gratitude as he came full awake, for dawn was fast breaking; and in the choking cloud of dust which followed their passage he rolled once more onto his stomach and settled himself in a position of watchfulness by the road, half-stifled by the dust and petrol fumes.

He had not long to wait. The dust settled slowly and the dawn-light crept along the strides of the hill opposite, scooping great pools of violet shadow in the sides of the mountains. He heard, thin and sweet in the chill morning air, the klaxon of the Mercedes crying down the gorge, and he could not suppress an involuntary cry of joy. 'Good old Porson,' he said over and over again, every muscle tense with expectation, as he waited for the car to appear around the bend.

A thousand yards away Porson himself was swearing volubly as he drove the old car around the curves of the road. He was in a bemused and shaky condition, having nearly been run down by the convoy of lorries a little further down the valley. In addition to this he had spent time mending a puncture, and had twice been stopped by troops at a road-block, and forced to show his papers. If Methuen was still alive, and he had managed to reach the point of rendezvous, perhaps he (Porson) was arriving too late? Perhaps there were troops around the white milestone? If so what should he do? His teeth were chattering with cold and excitement as he gradually throttled down the car and slackened speed, while Blair kept a check on their escort through the back. This time they had kept the hood of the car raised and the side-curtains drawn.

They clattered round the last bend and into the cover of the trees when all of a sudden Porson gave a great yelp of surprise for a battered-looking scarecrow with bare feet suddenly plunged into the road by the white milestone, waving its arms. It limped grotesquely and seemed about to collapse under the wheels of the car. 'He's done it,' said Blair. But for a moment Porson could not believe it was Methuen, so wild and ragged did the figure seem. He pressed the brake and the car slowed down. 'Good show!' shouted Methuen in a thin voice and clutching the handle of the door swung himself by a mighty effort into the back of the car, where Blair immediately threw a rug over him.

'My God,' said Porson in a shaky voice as he accelerated once more, 'Methuen, are you all right?' but Methuen was pressing his cheek to the dusty floor of the car and thinking that he had never felt so glad to hear English voices in all his life. So great was his relief that he was completely bereft of speech. He tried once or twice to say something but only a dull croak came out of his mouth. Perhaps it was sheer fatigue or the dust he had swallowed. But he became conscious now that he was hot, indeed that he had a high temperature.

He heard Porson say: 'Just in time,' and then he heard the rumble of another convoy of lorries. The two young men were too busy to pay much attention to him for a moment or two. The car was fairly speeding along the road when Porson turned a pale face over his shoulder and said: 'Blair, for heaven's sake, see if he is dead.'

Once more Methuen tried to speak but could only utter a dull croak. Blair's white face peered down at him and a hand touched his cheek. 'No. He's not dead. He's smiling,' said Blair academically, and Porson made an impatient movement. 'For goodness' sake Blair,' he said, 'get into the back and see if he's wounded.'

With an heroic effort, Methuen rolled over onto his back and croaked. 'Not dead, Porson, not dead,' and Blair, like a man coming out of a trance, suddenly went into action. He gave Methuen a long shaky drink out of a thermos, and climbing over him on the back seat, examined him roughly for wounds. 'I'm all right,' said Methuen feebly, glad that he was recovering his voice at last. 'My leg is shot up a bit.'

Porson let out an explosive breath of relief. 'Thank God!' he said, and there were tears in his eyes. 'We'd really given you up as lost. The place is swarming with troops and some sort of battle seems to be going on.'

Methuen drank once more, deeply, and spilled some water over the crown of his head. It was wonderfully refreshing. 'I know,' he said, and even *in extremis* he could not prevent a touch of innocent pride creeping into his voice, 'I know. It was going on all round me.'

Blair's methodical examination had by now reached his injured leg and Methuen began to protest at these amateur ministrations with a vigour which showed that he was far from seriously wounded. 'You just leave it alone until we get in,' he said. Blair peered at him gravely. 'But it's bleeding,' he said. 'Colonel, it's bleeding. It may need a tourniquet.'

He was vainly trying to recall a diagram he had once seen in the

Scouts' First Aid Manual of how to apply a tourniquet. You took a pencil and a piece of string. . . . He could not remember exactly. Methuen brushed him aside and repeated: 'You leave it alone until we get to the Embassy doctor. I've walked a good thirty miles on it and it'll last out awhile.'

'But what,' said Porson, jumping up and down in the driving-seat in curiosity, 'what has been happening up there in the mountains? Did you find the White Eagles?'

'They found me,' said Methuen, 'and darned nearly kept me. I've been trotting up the mountains with them, trying to get the Mihaelovic treasure to the coast, believe it or not. But the troops surrounded us.'

'Crumbs,' said Porson solemnly, 'did you really?'

Blair was feeding him slowly and carefully with bread and butter from a paper bag, and after a long gulp of wine Methuen felt sufficiently recovered to prop himself on one elbow. 'The puzzle all fitted together very nicely,' he said, 'once I reached the White Eagles, though they took some finding. They'd unearthed the treasure, you see. We were fools not to think of that.'

Porson blew a great blast on his klaxon in order to express his surprise as he said: 'Of course. There is a whole file about it which I read a few months ago. What idiots we are. But Methuen, will they get it out?' Methuen smiled sadly—for in his mind's eye he saw once more those toppling kicking figures falling into the gulf of the Black Lake. 'Laddie,' he said soberly, 'there's not a hope in hell. We walked into the neatest ambush you've ever seen. Regular troops. Caught us in a defile.'

But it was useless to attempt a connected conversation for he was still far more tired than he himself knew. His voice tailed away into a sleepy mumble. 'I'm going to have a nap now,' he said, and propping his head on his arm he closed his eyes and felt the great car racing on towards Belgrade. 'And I've lost my fishing-rod,' he added as an afterthought.

'His fishing-rod,' said Blair in accents of pious horror, raising his eyes to the sunny sky.

'His fishing-rod,' repeated Porson, wagging his head.

Methuen began to snore.

WAR GAMES

Keith Miles

War dominated the life of Terry Heggotty from the very start. On the night that he was born behind thick, black curtains in an upstairs room, a stray German bomb fell on the house next door and brought it crashing to the ground. The Heggotty dwelling was shaken to its foundations and all its windows were blown out by the blast. Falling plaster from walls and ceiling made the job of the midwife more difficult and the terrified young mother screamed when the electric light bulb exploded above her head. But the baby was delivered safely and came into the world with an amazing eagerness.

'It's a boy, Mrs Heggotty.'

'What?' The mother was distraught with fear.

'It's a boy. A fine, healthy boy.'

The midwife did not have to administer the traditional slap of the baby's bare rump. Right on cue, Terry Heggotty yelled his first welcome to a war-torn city.

'It's a boy,' smiled his mother, dopily, and then she drifted off to sleep.

The air raid was now over and anxious voices could be heard outside as wardens assessed the damage to the house next door. There was a harsh grating noise as shovels began to dig the neighbours out of their shelter. Terry seemed almost to understand what had happened and he added his own cries of defiance at the bombers now heading back towards the Channel.

Photographers came the next morning and the bombed house was given stark fame on the front page of the *South Wales Echo*. The paper also carried a photograph of a tiny child, scarcely twenty-four hours old, wrapped in a blanket but waving his infant fist at the camera. The caption was to be prophetic—MIRACULOUS ESCAPE.

Throughout that year enemy aircraft continued to oppress the people of Cardiff and to send them, at periodic intervals, scuttling to their cellars or their air raid shelters. The main target for the bomber squadrons was the Dowlais, the huge steelworks which stood on East Moors and which was working at full stretch to help the British war effort. Since the Dowlais was less than a mile from Terry's house, his ears grew accustomed very quickly to the menacing drone of German aircraft and to the screech of the sirens.

'Let me take him, Ann.'

'I can manage, Dad.' She was bundling the child into his crib before lifting it up and rushing out of the house.

'Give it to me. It's too heavy for you.'

Tom Heggotty was her father-in-law, a strong, kind, wiry little man who was doing all that he could to help the young mother through testing times. He reached for the crib but his daughter-in-law would not surrender it. As the sirens reached a more strident and insistent note, she hurried down the path of the small garden until she got to the steps at the top of the shelter. Black sky suddenly lit up with dramatic effect as bombs scored marginal hits nearby. Ann was so startled that she missed her footing and pitched head first down the steps onto the hard stone floor. She was knocked senseless at once and the crib almost split in two with the impact.

'Dear God!' cried Tom, going first to the baby.

But Terry Heggotty was in no need of help. As the crib had struck the floor, he had been catapulted clear to make a soft landing on an old carpet that had been put down in one corner. The boy was excited but not alarmed by what had happened and he lay there gurgling happily, kicking his legs in the air. Had he been thrown another six inches further, his head would have been smashed against the damp red brick. It was another miraculous escape and his grandfather could not believe it.

'Come here, boy!'

He hugged the child to his chest then remembered the inert woman behind him. Terry looked on with a kind of amused curiosity as his grandfather tried to revive his mother. Her first words, inevitably, showed concern for the baby.

'Where's Terry? How's Terry?'

'He's fine, girl. It'll take more than a nose-dive down a few steps to upset our Terry. He's fine.'

The months passed and both war and child grew older together. Terry learned to speak and found that he liked the sound of words such as 'gun', 'bomb', 'tank', and 'sub'. As soon as his tongue would let him, he talked about soldiers and hand-grenades and the barrage balloon in nearby Splott Park. By the time he had reached his second birthday, he was quite seasoned in the vocabulary of battle and was already playing his own uncertain war games in the street.

The pattern of the war had changed now and the blitz was a thing of the past. With the allied forces on the offensive, there was little sign of large bomber squadrons over Cardiff and the citizens were enjoying better nights. There was still a kind of suppressed panic in people's faces but there was a feeling that the real crisis on the home front had been weathered and that there would not be many more nasty accidents on the steps of air raid shelters. Newspapers tried to keep morale high by praising every advance by the Allies and by playing down the losses that had been sustained. Wirelesses all over the nation offered crackling reassurances with their daily propaganda.

Like many other Cardiffians, Tom Heggotty put his faith in the skill of the American soldier.

'The Yanks'll show 'em!'

'Gor anythin' for me, Grandad?'

'You watch, son. Ole Jerry won't know what hit him. Just wait till the Yanks really get going.'

'Wor did they give you today?'

While the old man was expecting deliverance at the hands of the Americans, the boy was ready to settle for a good deal less. His grandfather was a docker and he often came home from work with proof of the generosity of American sailors. That very morning, indeed, while helping to unload a US cargo vessel in the Alexandra Dock, Tom had been given three packets of chewing gum by friendly crew members. In a city that suffered the horrors of sweets rationing, chewing gum was like gold dust.

'Thanks, Grandad! Thass great!'

'The Yanks always give something.'

'Don't chew that stuff now, Terry,' warned his mother, uselessly, as the first piece of gum was slipped into his mouth. 'It'll put you off your tea.'

The boy's jaws moved rhythmically and he turned his attention to higher things. As always, war obsessed him.

'Do the Yanks kill lots of Germans?'

'Oh yes, Terry,' grinned Tom. 'They eat 'em for breakfast.'

'Tell me, Grandad.'

The old man spoke with passion on the subject and his grandson's imagination was fired. The lad was still well short of his fourth birthday yet he was already committed to the idea of one day joining the US army so that he could lead a battalion of gum-chewing heroes to some decisive victory.

Ann Heggotty was not at all happy at the way that her son talked about the war all the time but she could do nothing to stop it. A weak and wasted woman, she needed all her strength simply to get through those pinched days. Tom kept advising her to go to the doctor's for a tonic of some sorts, but she could not afford it so she managed without. She just hoped that she would feel better soon. With her husband abroad with the army, she felt that she had to press on and bring up the child as best she could. Even if he presented special problems.

'Where is he, Dad?' Her voice was anxious.

'I thought he was with you in the scullery, Ann.'

'I thought he was with you.'

'No, I haven't seen him since he went out the garden.'

It was a Sunday afternoon and a boy of three had vanished into thin air. They searched the house from top to bottom but there was no trace of him. Terry was in the habit of locking himself into some of the cupboards in order to effect an escape from them but a search of these yielded no results either. Worry became fear and fear turned to hysteria. Ann was trembling.

'Where can he be, Dad? Where on earth can he be?'

'Take it easy, woman. He'll turn up.'

'But *where*?'

'Let's take a look in the street.'

As they opened the front door and stepped out onto the pavement, they were given an immediate clue as to the whereabouts of Terry Heggotty. A cluster of people stood there, staring up at something with helpless amazement. Ann followed the direction of their gaze, then almost fainted when she saw him. Terry was in the bombed house. He had somehow clambered over the garden wall, made his way up the remains of the staircase next door, crawled on past the exposed peeling wallpaper, and climbed up the chimney breast by means of some jagged footholds. He was now clinging to the chimney itself, twenty-five feet above the ground.

'Don't move,' gulped Tom. 'For heaven's sake, don't move.'

'Hello, Grandad,' called the boy, unruffled.

'Stay there,' urged his grandfather, then he despatched one of the bystanders to fetch a ladder.

'It's a job for the Fire Brigade,' opined one woman.

'Or an ambulance,' decided her morbid friend.

Ann was speechless with terror. Her son had only to release his grasp and he would fall to certain death amid the rubble below. There seemed no way that he could escape. What made it more unbearable was the fact that Terry was treating the whole thing as some sort of game. He kept saying something about being an American soldier escaping from a concentration camp.

The ladder was brought and Tom propped it gingerly up against the other side of the chimney, vaguely hoping that he could climb to the top and somehow reach round to grasp the boy. He began to ascend the rings, calling out softly to his grandson.

'Stay right where you are. I'm coming. Stay right there.'

The audience down below had almost trebled in size and it included many of Terry's friends. They were enormously impressed and yelled out words of encouragement before being silenced by grim adults. Terry responded to all this with a wave and his mother felt faint again.

'No! Don't budge from there!' ordered his grandfather.

'Hang on, Terry,' she breathed.

'I'm nearly there,' promised Tom, reaching what had once been a slate roof. 'I'll get you down.'

Terry Heggotty looked quite offended by the suggestion. He did not need any assistance. It was an insult even to suggest it. He was a highly trained member of the US Armed Forces and he knew how to cope with any emergency. He would prove it.

'No! Don't budge from there!' ordered his grandfather.

'Terry!' shrieked his mother.

But the boy ignored them both. With a reckless disregard of his safety, he started to feel his way along the chimney until he found a proper purchase for his feet. Then he lowered himself inch by inch down the vestigial chimney breast, dislodging a half-brick and a lot of dust as he did so.

'He'll fall,' noted the morbid woman.

'Go on, Terry,' laughed a friend in his exhilaration.

'Stop him, someone,' gasped the hapless mother.

Terry kept on coming and another brick fell to its doom. It did not disturb him in the least and his progress, though slow, continued. For a moment it almost looked as if he would gain the first floor of the house without any setback. Then his foot slipped. In a flash he fell from his precarious position on a brick face and landed on the rotting remains of a floor joist that was jutting out at right angles to the wall. The joist sagged, then gave way, but not before it had broken the first part of his fall. Terry was now sent hurtling down on to a pile of bricks in what had once been the living room of the house. A dozen hands came up to help him up but he shrugged them away and stood up with a grin. He was bruised and filthy but otherwise unhurt.

'Wor you doin' up there, Grandad?' he asked, waving up at the old man on the ladder. 'I can ger down easy, see?'

Ann Heggotty was not sure whether to embrace or scold him and so she did both at the same time. The neighbours discussed what they had seen and shook their heads in astonishment. It was his third miraculous escape. Clearly, Terry Heggotty led a charmed life.

The legend of Terry grew quickly in that area of the city and he became something of a celebrity. His friends all insisted on playing games that involved escapes and each time he managed to get away. He was tied up, locked away, even rolled up in a tarpaulin but nothing could hold Terry Heggotty. He celebrated his fifth birthday by tempting fate once more. Before the stunned gaze of his family and friends, he threw a stone at the baker's horse, causing the animal to bolt forward. As it headed straight for him, he threw himself to the ground so that both hooves and wheels passed over him without touching him. The applause he drew from his admirers more than made up for the clout his was given by the baker.

'Thar was fantastic, Terry.' It was his best friend, Glyn Griffiths.

'You've seen nothin' yet.'

'A wild 'orse and you escapes. Fantastic!'

'I can escape from anythin'!' boasted the adventurer.

'Yeah, I know,' conceded Glyn, eyes glowing with pride. 'I know.'

The war came to an end and a pall seemed to lift from the city. Cardiff had been a drab, beleaguered city of old men, dark-eyed women and confused children. Suddenly it was fully alive again, bedecked with flags and bunting and all the paraphernalia of victory. Large messages of welcome were painted on the walls and streets and families who had not seen a father for five years all gathered at the railway station for the first batch of returning soldiers.

'My Dad was a Desert Rat,' said Glyn, knowledgeably, as he was jostled by the crowd.

'Thass nor as good as my Dad,' countered Terry. 'My Dad escaped from 'itler's gas chambers.'

The boys, like hundreds of others present on that occasion, turned ordinary men into conquering heroes and were ready to worship them by the time the train finally arrived. Reunions were tearful and ecstatic and the whole platform seemed to be swarming with khaki. One by one families drifted away to homes that now had fathers.

'Where's *my* Dad?' asked Terry.

'Maybe he wasn't on this train,' suggested his grandfather.

'He should have been,' reminded Ann. 'Eddie's in the same regiment as Ron Griffiths. And Ron was on the train.'

'Yeah. I saw Glyn's Dad. He was no Desert Rat. *My* Dad's better than Glyn's Dad. My Dad is a master of escape.' Certainty deserted him and he became a lost and frightened child. 'Where is he, Mam?'

'Uh, would it be Mrs Heggotty, by any chance?'

The man was wearing the uniform of a lieutenant and he seemed to have some information about Corporal Edward Heggotty. He broke the news to a stricken wife and a numb father in the privacy of the Station Master's office. Terry was left outside in the care of a uniformed sergeant. It transpired that Eddie Heggotty was a casualty of peacetime. After surviving five years of war, he had returned to his native soil only to be killed in an unfortunate accident in the docks at Dover. The shunting had not been scheduled to take place when it did. It was a source of regret to all concerned that there had been no time to contact the family sooner.

Tom Heggotty, musing on the irony of it all, took the grieving widow home. One arm stayed around the shoulders of a puzzled boy. Unlike his son, Eddie Heggotty did not bear a charmed life.

* * * *

'Show 'im your gun, Dad.'

'Terry's seen it twice,' smiled Ron Griffiths, indulgently.

'Aw go on, Dad,' insisted Glyn. 'Lerrim see it again.'

'Please,' added Terry.

'All right.' The demobbed soldier took the gun out from his kit bag. It was a Luger pistol, filched from the belt of a dead German. 'Here, Terry.'

The boy handled the weapon with a fond care, raised it and disposed of ten more Germans with pin-point accuracy. Glyn Griffiths was a true friend. Since Terry had no father, Glyn was keen to share his own with him. Terry was touched by this and yet he felt somehow that he was better off than Glyn. Ron Griffiths could never compare as a father with the figure of Eddie Heggotty. Terry's imagination provided him with a paragon. A boy who had been told nothing about a crushed body beneath a railway wagon devised a story about a thrilling escape bid from the very heart of Hitler's empire. His father, leader of that daring band, had let the others get away first before being shot to death.

'My Dad was one of the best escapers of the war.'

'I knows, Terry.' Glyn believed his friend implicitly.

'He gor away from Rommel when he was captured in the desert.'

'Cor!'

'He always gor away in the end.'

'They should have given him the VC.' Glyn's tone was reverential.

'They did,' bragged Terry, until hard fact caused him to modify the lie. 'Well—almost.'

It was curious. With a real father at home, Glyn Griffiths grew into a shy, nervous boy who could never shake off the hold which his friend had over him. Terry, on the other hand, became self-confident to the point of arrogance and was much bigger and sturdier than the spindly Glyn. Their reliance on each other was total. Glyn needed someone to look up to and idolize, while Terry required someone who would offer complete obedience. Other boys might join in their games but it was always the friendship between these two that was paramount.

The war informed all that Terry Heggotty did. Every game had to have an element of escape in it and he always had to emerge as the hero. Glyn was dragged into all kinds of dangers so that his friend could prove his superiority. He was terrified at some of the risks he was called upon to take but he was even more afraid of disobeying his master. Years passed; the games became more and more sophisticated; Terry yearned for greater challenges.

'You carn, Terry!' For once, Glyn was opposing a plan.

'*Who* carn!' Defiance made his face shine.

'Worrabout the police, like?'

'They'll never catch us.'

'They'd catch me,' admitted the smaller boy, miserably. '*You'd* ger away with it. I wouldn't.'

'Chicken!'

'Please, Ter.'

'Chicken!'

Glyn Griffiths eventually bowed to the pressure and went along with the plan. It made his mind cloud over. Terry had announced that the National Museum of Wales, a superb, neo-Classical building of white stone in the civic centre, was the headquarters of the Nazi regime. Two prisoners had to be held there before finding their way back to freedom under the cover of darkness. All that Glyn could think about were the hazards. The Museum was full of hawk-eyed little men in uniform and it only made it worse when he was told that these attendants were really members of the Gestapo. Full of dread, he went into the building with his friend. He saw none of the thousands of exhibits that they passed.

'Less go 'ome, Ter.'

'We gorru *escape*.'

Glyn could do nothing but follow orders and these—he should have had more faith—were carefully designed to achieve a certain objective. Shortly before closing time, the boys slipped into one of the lavatories and hid there until the attendants had made their rounds. When the Museum was completely locked and guarded by its hypersensitive alarm system, the escape was put into operation. It involved a journey through a ventilation duct, a balancing act along the coping on a part of the roof and a perilous descent down a drainpipe.

'We done it, Ter,' laughed Glyn, shaking with relief. 'We done it.'

'Dead easy.'

The ten-year-old boy had brought off his greatest feat yet.

Glyn's dependence on his friend was now more complete than ever and it worried his parents. There was a manic quality about Terry Heggotty that they distrusted. Glyn did not heed their warnings, however, and the friendship intensified. It excited a lot of envy among other boys and, inevitably, a measure of contempt.

'Liar!'

'We did, Jacko. 'oness!' Glyn turned to his friend. 'Tell 'em, Ter.'

'We did,' shrugged Terry.

'Liar!'

Jacko Armstrong was a tall, sneering boy with a hare-lip. He was two years older than Terry and could not cope with the idea that the latter was in some way braver and better. Jacko's companion, Derek Evans, was equally sceptical when he heard the story about the escape from the Gestapo at the National Museum of Wales. Argument led to blows and blows led to a challenge. Terry was not big enough to fight and beat the two of them but he did know a way to demonstrate his superiority. It involved yet another escape.

'Then we all meets 'ere and tells where we been. Okay?'

'Okay,' accepted Jacko.

'Suits me,' agreed Derek.

'Terry will win,' Glyn piped up, and he collected a reflex cuff from Jacko.

Terry's game was simple. Each of the four boys was a prisoner inside some kind of stockade. His task was to warn his army colleagues by displaying a flag—they each took a scarf—at the highest point they could reach. The boy whose flag fluttered the highest and who had taken the most risks to put it there would be deemed to be the champion. All four of them set out to become the master escaper.

Jacko Armstrong knew at once where he would go. After cycling to Splott Park, he shinned up the ironwork of the bandstand and tied his flag to the ornate pinnacle. Nobody would get higher than that. Derek Evans opted for a set of rugby posts and climbed almost to the top of one of the uprights before leaving his mark. Glyn Griffiths could not compete with either of these. Without the support and encouragement of Terry, he lost all confidence and simply climbed up the nearest lamp post. His scarf would earn the sniggers of Jacko and Derek but he did not mind. He knew that Terry would be supreme.

'Useless!'

'Oh. S'all I could think of, Ter.'

'Flippin' lamp post!' Terry was disgusted by Glyn's lack of courage. 'Follow me. I'll show you.'

With his audience trotting at his heels, Terry set off to show the world and two sneering older boys his true mettle. They went over Beresford Road Bridge and on down to the Royal Oak Hotel. Only when they swung into Newport Road and quickened their pace did Glyn have the slightest idea where they might be going. When he was at length confronted with the enormity of it all, he gaped. Terry, as ever, had set himself something very special.

'Be careful, Ter!'

'Shurrup!'

'But all them volts.'

Terry dismissed his friend's qualms with a wave. He was a boy with a charmed life and nothing could hurt him. After glancing around to make sure that nobody could see him, he padded through the long grass and tackled the first stage of his climb. Thick iron railings stood eight feet out of the ground but he was up and over them in seconds. Without pausing he ran to the second stage of his climb, drawing a gasp of pain from Glyn. The pylon was a tower of metal surmounted by twisted cables that were humming with evil power. Terry Heggotty was going to thread his way past the cables so that he could tie his scarf to the very apex of the pylon. It was an act that would attest his supremacy once and for all and humble two older lads.

'Steady, Ter,' murmured Glyn, watching him rise higher and higher.

A wave from his friend made Glyn feel much better. Terry could and would do it. He was being disloyal in fearing that there could be any slip. A boy who could escape German bombs, a fall down the steps of an air raid shelter and a drop onto a pile of rubble in Railway Street could certainly scale a pylon in the grounds of the power station.

'Go on, Ter. You can do it.'

Glyn began to laugh with pride. Terry had outwitted the Gestapo at the Museum and pulled off dozens of similar escapes. This latest feat was simplicity itself to a person of his rare talents.

'Show 'em, Terry. Show 'em.'

His laughter became almost hysterical as he imagined the looks on the faces of the others when they learned what had happened. Then the laughter stopped. Glyn froze. High above him, moving with the authority and bravery of one who knows exactly what he wants to do in a testing situation, Terry Heggotty had drawn level with the cables. Assured that nothing could harm him, he brushed against one of them as he went past and there was an ominous flash.

'No, Terry! Don't!'

Glyn's warning came too late. The body fell to the ground with a thud and lay there, stiff and tormented.

It was a long time before Glyn could move, but he knew instinctively what he had to do. He had to follow Terry's lead just once more. It took effort and concentration and nerve, but he was spurred on by the memory of a friendship. Fifteen minutes later, Terry's scarf was flying at the very top of the pylon.

No one had witnessed the tragedy. No one was there to see Glyn's slow and painful descent. But as the boy, shaking violently, reached the ground again and bent to take a last look at the anguished face of his friend, he was dimly aware that this had been their greatest escape. He had been released from the tyranny of his own fears—and Terry had escaped forever from war games and all that they had meant.

JEEVES AND THE IMPENDING DOOM

P. G. Wodehouse

It was the morning of the day on which I was slated to pop down to my Aunt Agatha's place at Woollam Chersey in the county of Herts for a visit of three solid weeks; and, as I seated myself at the breakfast table, I don't mind confessing that the heart was singularly heavy. We Woosters are men of iron, but beneath my intrepid exterior at that moment there lurked a nameless dread.

'Jeeves,' I said, 'I am not the old merry self this morning.'

'Indeed, sir?'

'No, Jeeves. Far from it. Far from the old merry self.'

'I am sorry to hear that, sir.'

He uncovered the fragrant eggs and b., and I pronged a moody forkful.

'Why—this is what I keep asking myself, Jeeves,—why has my Aunt Agatha invited me to her country seat?'

'I could not say, sir.'

'Not because she is fond of me.'

'No, sir.'

'It is a well established fact that I give her a pain in the neck. How it happens I cannot say, but every time our paths cross, so to speak, it seems to be a mere matter of time before I perpetrate some ghastly floater and have her hopping after me with her hatchet. The result being that she regards me as a worm and an outcast. Am I right or wrong, Jeeves?'

'Perfectly correct, sir.'

'And yet now she has absolutely insisted on my scratching all previous engagements and buzzing down to Woollam Chersey. She must have some sinister reason of which we know nothing. Can you blame me, Jeeves, if the heart is heavy?'

'No, sir. Excuse me, sir, I fancy I heard the front-door bell.'

He shimmered out, and I took another listless stab at the e. and bacon.

'A telegram, sir,' said Jeeves, re-entering the presence.

'Open it, Jeeves, and read contents. Who is it from?'

'It is unsigned, sir.'

'You mean there's no name at the end of it?'

'That is precisely what I was endeavouring to convey, sir.'

'Let's have a look.'

I scanned the thing. It was a rummy communication. Rummy. No other word.

As follows:

> Remember when you come here absolutely vital meet perfect strangers.

We Woosters are not very strong in the head, particularly at breakfast time; and I was conscious of a dull ache between the eyebrows.

'What does it mean, Jeeves?'

'I could not say, sir.'

'It says "come here". Where's here?'

'You will notice that the message was handed in at Woollam Chersey, sir.'

'You're absolutely right. At Woollam, as you very cleverly spotted, Chersey. This tells us something, Jeeves.'

'What, sir?'

'I don't know. It couldn't be from my Aunt Agatha, do you think?'

'Hardly, sir.'

'No; you're right again. Then all we can say is that some person unknown, resident at Woollam Chersey, considers it absolutely vital for me to meet perfect strangers, Jeeves?'

'I could not say, sir.'

'And yet, looking at it from another angle, why shouldn't I?'

'Precisely, sir.'

'Then what it comes to is that the thing is a mystery which time alone can solve. We must wait and see, Jeeves.'

'The very expression I was about to employ, sir.'

I hit Woollam Chersey at about four o'clock, and found Aunt Agatha in her lair, writing letters. And, from what I know of her, probably offensive letters, with nasty postscripts. She regarded me with not a fearful lot of joy.

'Oh, there you are, Bertie.'

'Yes, here I am.'

'There's a smut on your nose.'

I plied the handkerchief.

'I am glad you have arrived so early. I want to have a word with you before you meet Mr Filmer.'

'Who?'

'Mr Filmer the Cabinet Minister. He is staying in the house. Surely even you must have heard of Mr Filmer?'

'Oh, rather,' I said, though as a matter of fact the bird was completely unknown to me. What with one thing and another, I'm not frightfully up in the personnel of the political world.

'I particularly wish you to make a good impression on Mr Filmer.'

'Right-ho.'

'Don't speak in that casual way, as if you supposed that it was perfectly natural that you would make a good impression upon him. Mr Filmer is a serious-minded man of high character and purpose, and you are just the type of vapid and frivolous wastrel against which he is most likely to be prejudiced.'

Hard words, of course from one's own flesh and blood, but well in keeping with past form.

'You will endeavour, therefore, while you are here not to display yourself in the *rôle* of a vapid and frivolous wastrel. In the first place, you will give up smoking during your visit.'

'Oh, I say!'

'Mr Filmer is president of the Anti-Tobacco League. Nor will you drink alcoholic stimulants.'

'Oh, dash it!'

'And you will kindly exclude from your conversation all that is suggestive of the bar, the billiards-room, and the stage-door. Mr Filmer will judge you largely by your conversation.'

I rose to a point of order.

'Yes, but why have I got to make an impression on this—on Mr Filmer?'

'Because,' said the old relative, giving me the eye, 'I particularly wish it.'

Not, perhaps, a notably snappy come-back as come-backs go; but it was enough to show me that that was more or less that; and I beetled out with an aching heart.

I headed for the garden, and I'm dashed if the first person I saw wasn't young Bingo Little.

Bingo Little and I have been pals practically from birth. Born in the same village within a couple of days of one another, we went through kindergarten, Eton, and Oxford together; and, grown to riper years we have enjoyed in the old metrop, full many a first-class binge in each other's society. If there was one fellow in the world, I felt, who could alleviate the horrors of this blighted visit of mine, that bloke was young Bingo Little.

But how he came to be there was more than I could understand. Some time before, you see, he had married the celebrated authoress, Rosie M. Banks; and the last I had seen of him he had been on the point of accompanying her to America on a lecture tour. I distinctly remembered him cursing rather freely because the trip would mean his missing Ascot.

'Bingo!'

He spun round; and, by Jove, his face wasn't friendly after all. It was what they call contorted. He waved his arms at me like a semaphore.

''Sh!' he hissed. 'Would you ruin me?'

'Eh?'

'Didn't you get my telegram?'

'Was that *your* telegram?'

'Of course it was my telegram.'

'Then why didn't you sign it?'

'I did sign it.'

'No, you didn't. I couldn't make out what it was all about.'

'Well, you got my letter.'

'What letter?'

'My letter.'

'I didn't get any letter.'

'Then I must have forgotten to post it. It was to tell you that I was down here tutoring your Cousin Thomas, and that it was essential that, when we met, you should treat me as a perfect stranger.'

'But why?'

'Because, if your aunt supposed that I was a pal of yours, she would naturally sack me on the spot.'

'Why?'

Bingo raised his eyebrows.

'Why? Be reasonable, Bertie. If you were your aunt, and you knew the sort of chap you were, would you let a fellow you knew to be your best pal tutor your son?'

This made the old head swim a bit, but I got his meaning after a while, and I had to admit that there was much rugged good sense in what he said. Still, he hadn't explained what you might call the nub or gist of the mystery.

'I thought you were in America,' I said.

'Well, I'm not.'

'Why not?'

'Never mind why not. I'm not.'

'But why have you taken a tutoring job?'

'Never mind why. I have my reasons. And I want you to get it into your head, Bertie—to get it right through the concrete—that you and I must not be seen hobnobbling. Your foul cousin was caught smoking in the shrubbery the day before yesterday, and that has made my position pretty tottery, because your aunt said that, if I had exercised an adequate surveillance over him, it couldn't have happened. If, after that, she finds out I'm a friend of yours, nothing can save me from being shot out. And it is vital that I am not shot out.'

'Why?'

'Never mind why.'

At this point he seemed to think he heard somebody coming, for he suddenly leaped with incredible agility into a laurel bush. And I toddled along to consult Jeeves about these rummy happenings.

'Jeeves,' I said, repairing to the bedroom, where he was unpacking my things, 'you remember that telegram?'

'Yes, sir.'

'It was from Mr Little. He's here, tutoring my young Cousin Thomas.'

'Indeed, sir?'

'I can't understand it. He appears to be a free agent, if you know what I mean; and yet would any man who was a free agent wantonly come to a house which contained my Aunt Agatha?'

'It seems peculiar, sir.'

'Moreover, would anybody of his own free-will and as a mere pleasure-seeker tutor my Cousin Thomas, who is notoriously a tough egg and a fiend in human shape?'

'Most improbable, sir.'

'These are deep waters, Jeeves.'

'Precisely, sir.'

'And the ghastly part of it all is that he seems to consider it necessary, in order to keep his job, to treat me like a long-lost leper. Thus killing my only chance of having anything approaching a decent time in this abode of desolation. For do you realize, Jeeves, that my aunt says I musn't smoke while I'm here?'

'Indeed, sir?'

'Nor drink.'

'Why is this, sir?'

'Because she wants me—for some dark and furtive reason which she will not explain—to impress a fellow named Filmer.'

'Too bad, sir. However, many doctors, I understand, advocate such abstinence as the secret of health. They say it promotes a freer circulation of the blood and insures the arteries against premature hardening.'

'Oh, do they? Well, you can tell them next time you see them that they are silly asses.'

'Very good, sir.'

* * * *

And so began what, looking back along a fairly eventful career, I think I can confidently say was the scaliest visit I have ever experienced in the course of my life. What with the agony of missing the life-giving cocktail before dinner; the painful necessity of being obliged, every time I wanted a quiet cigarette, to lie on the floor in my bedroom and puff the smoke up the chimney; the constant discomfort of meeting Aunt Agatha round unexpected corners; and the fearful strain on the morale of having to chum with the Right Hon. A. B. Filmer, it was not long before Bertram was up against it to an extent hitherto undreamed of.

I played golf with the Right Hon. every day, and it was only by biting the Wooster lip and clenching the fists till the knuckles stood out white under the strain that I managed to pull through. The Right Hon. punctuated some of the ghastliest golf I have ever seen with a flow of conversation which, as far as I was concerned, went completely over the top; and, all in all, I was beginning to feel pretty sorry for myself when, one night as I was in my room listlessly donning the soup-and-fish in preparation for the evening meal, in trickled young Bingo and took my mind off my own troubles.

For when it is a question of a pal being in the soup, we Woosters no longer think of self; and that poor old Bingo was knee-deep in the bisque was made plain by his mere appearance—which was that of a cat which has just been struck by a half-brick and is expecting another shortly.

'Bertie,' said Bingo, having sat down on the bed and diffused silent gloom for a moment, 'how is Jeeves's brain these days?'

'Fairly strong on the wing, I fancy. How is the grey matter, Jeeves? Surging about pretty freely?'

'Yes, sir.'

'Thank Heaven for that,' said young Bingo, 'for I require your soundest counsel. Unless right-thinking people take strong steps through the proper channels, my name will be mud.'

'What's wrong, old thing?' I asked, sympathetically.

Bingo plucked at the coverlet.

'I will tell you,' he said. 'I will also now reveal why I am staying in this pest-house, tutoring a kid who requires not education in the Greek and Latin languages but a swift slosh on the base of the skull with a black-jack. I came here, Bertie, because it was the only thing I could do. At the last moment before she sailed to America, Rosie decided that I had better stay behind and look after the Peke. She left me a couple of hundred quid to see me through till her return. This sum, judiciously expended over the period of her absence, would have been enough to keep Peke and self in moderate affluence. But you know how it is.'

'How what is?'

'When someone comes slinking up to you in the club and tells you that some cripple of a horse can't help winning even if it develops lumbago and the botts ten yards from the starting-post. I tell you, I regarded the thing as a cautious and conservative investment.'

'You mean you planked the entire capital on a horse?'

Bingo laughed bitterly.

'If you could call the thing a horse. If it hadn't shown a flash of speed in the straight, it would have got mixed up with the next race. It came in last, putting me in a dashed delicate position. Somehow or other I had to find the funds to keep me going, so that I could win through till Rosie's return without her knowing what had occurred. Rosie is the dearest girl in the world; but if you were a married man, Bertie, you would be aware that the best of wives is apt to cut up rough if she finds that her husband has dropped six weeks' housekeeping money on a single race. Isn't that so, Jeeves?'

'Yes, sir. Women are odd in that respect.'

'It was a moment for swift thinking. There was enough left from the wreck to board the Peke out at a comfortable home. I signed him up for six weeks at the Kosy Komfort Kennels at Kingsbridge, Kent, and tottered out, a broken man, to get a tutoring job. I landed the kid Thomas. And here I am.'

It was a sad story, of course, but it seemed to me that, awful as it might be to be in constant association with my Aunt Agatha and young Thos, he had got rather well out of a tight place.

'All you have to do,' I said, 'is to carry on here for a few weeks more, and everything will be oojah-cum-spiff.'

Bingo barked bleakly.

'A few weeks more! I shall be lucky if I stay two days. You remember I told you that your aunt's faith in me as a guardian of her blighted son was shaken a few days ago by the fact that he was caught smoking. I now find that the person who caught him smoking was the man Filmer. And ten minutes ago young Thomas told me that he was proposing to inflict some hideous revenge on Filmer for having reported him to your aunt. I don't know what he is going to do, but if he does it, out I inevitably go on my left ear. Your aunt thinks the world of Filmer, and would sack me on the spot. And three weeks before Rosie gets back!'

I saw all.

'Jeeves,' I said.

'Sir?'

'I see all. Do you see all?'

'Yes, sir.'

'Then flock round.'

'I fear, sir—'

Bingo gave a low moan.

'Don't tell me, Jeeves,' he said, brokenly, 'that nothing suggests itself.'

'Nothing at the moment, I regret to say, sir.'

Bingo uttered a stricken woofle like a bull-dog that has been refused cake.

'Well, then, the only thing I can do, I suppose,' he said sombrely, 'is not to let the pie-faced little thug out of my sight for a second.'

'Absolutely.' I said, 'Ceaseless vigilance, eh, Jeeves?'

'Precisely, sir.'

'But meanwhile, Jeeves,' said Bingo in a low, earnest voice, 'you will be devoting your best thought to the matter, won't you?'

'Most certainly, sir.'

'Thank you, Jeeves.'

'Not at all, sir.'

* * * *

I will say for young Bingo that, once the need for action arrived, he behaved with an energy and determination which compelled respect. I suppose there was not a minute during the next two days when the kid Thos was able to say to himself, 'Alone at last!' But on the evening of the second day Aunt Agatha announced that some people were coming over on the morrow for a spot of tennis, and I feared that the worst must now befall.

Young Bingo, you see, is one of those fellows who, once their fingers close over the handle of a tennis racket, fall into a sort of trance in which nothing outside the radius of the lawn exists for them. If you came up to Bingo in the middle of a set and told him that panthers were devouring his best friend in the kitchen garden, he would look at you and say, 'Oh, ah?' or words to that effect. I knew that he would not give a thought to young Thomas and the Right Hon. till the last ball had bounced, and, as I dressed for dinner that night, I was conscious of an impending doom.

'Jeeves,' I said, 'have you ever pondered on Life?'

'From time to time, sir, in my leisure moments.'

'Grim, isn't it, what?'

'Grim, sir?'

'I mean to say, the difference between things as they look and things as they are.'

'The trousers perhaps a half-inch higher, sir. A very slight adjustment of the braces will effect the necessary alteration. You were saying, sir?'

'I mean, here at Woollam Chersey we have apparently a happy, care-free country-house party. But beneath the glittering surface, Jeeves, dark currents are running. One gazes at the Right Hon. wrapping himself round the salmon mayonnaise at lunch, and he seems a man without a care in the world. Yet all the while a dreadful fate is hanging over him, creeping nearer and nearer. What exact steps do you think the kid Thomas intends to take?'

'In the course of an informal conversation which I had with the young gentleman this afternoon, sir, he informed me that he had been reading a romance entitled *Treasure Island*, and had been much struck by the character and actions of a certain Captain Flint. I gathered that he was weighing the advisability of modelling his own conduct on that of the Captain.'

'But, good heavens, Jeeves! If I remember *Treasure Island*, Flint was the bird who went about hitting people with a cutlass. You don't think young Thomas would bean Mr Filmer with a cutlass?'

'Possibly he does not possess a cutlass, sir.'

'Well, with anything.'

'We can but wait and see, sir. The tie, if I might suggest it, sir, a shade more tightly knotted. One aims at the perfect butterfly effect. If you will permit me—'

'What do ties matter, Jeeves, at a time like this? Do you realize that Mr Little's domestic happiness is hanging in the scale?'

'There is no time, sir, at which ties do not matter.'

I could see the man was pained, but I did not try to heal the wound. What's the word I want? Preoccupied. I was too preoccupied, don't you know. And distrait. Not to say careworn.

* * * *

I was still careworn when, next day at half past two, the revels commenced on the tennis lawn. It was one of those close, baking days, with thunder rumbling just around the corner; and it seemed to me that there was a brooding menace in the air.

'Bingo,' I said, as we pushed forth to do our bit in the first doubles, 'I wonder what young Thos will be up to this afternoon, with the eye of authority no longer on him?'

'Eh?' said Bingo, absently. Already the tennis look had come into his face, and his eye was glazed. He swung his racket and snorted a little.

'I don't see him anywhere,' I said.

'You don't what?'

'See him.'

'Who?'

'Young Thos.'

'What about him?'

I let it go.

The only consolation I had in the black period of the opening of the tourney was the fact that the Right Hon. had taken a seat among the spectators and was wedged in between a couple of females with parasols. Reason told me that even a kid so steeped in sin as young Thomas would hardly perpetrate any outrage on a man in such a strong strategic position. Considerably relieved, I gave myself up to the game; and was in the act of putting it across the local curate with a good deal of vim when there was a roll of thunder and the rain started to come down in buckets.

We all stampeded for the house, and had gathered in the drawing-room for tea, when suddenly Aunt Agatha, looking up from a cucumber-sandwich, said:

'Has anybody seen Mr Filmer?'

It was one of the nastiest jars I have ever experienced. What with my fast serve zipping sweetly over net and the man of God utterly unable to cope with my slow bending return down the centre-line, I had for some little time been living, as it were, in another world. I now came down to earth with a bang: and my slice of cake, slipping from my nerveless fingers, fell to the ground and was wolfed by Aunt Agatha's spaniel, Robert. Once more I seemed to become conscious of an impeding doom.

For this man Filmer, you must understand, was not one of those men who are lightly kept from the tea-table. A hearty trencherman, and particularly fond of his five o'clock couple of cups and bite of muffin, he had until this afternoon always been well up among the leaders in the race for the food-trough. If one thing was certain, it was that only the machinations of some enemy could be keeping him from being in the drawing-room now, complete with nosebag.

'He must have got caught in the rain and be sheltering somewhere in the grounds,' said Aunt Agatha. 'Bertie, go out and find him. Take a raincoat to him.'

'Right-ho!' I said. My only desire in life now was to find the Right Hon. And I hoped it wouldn't be merely his body.

I put on a raincoat and tucked another under my arm, and was sallying forth, when in the hall I ran into Jeeves.

'Jeeves,' I said, 'I fear the worst. Mr Filmer is missing.'

'Yes, sir.'

'I am about to scour the grounds in search of him.'

'I can save you the trouble, sir. Mr Filmer is on the island in the middle of the lake.'

'In this rain? Why doen't the chump row back?'

'He has no boat, sir.'

'Then how can he be on the island?'

'He rowed there, sir. But Master Thomas rowed after him and set his boat adrift. He was informing me of the circumstances a moment ago, sir. It appears that Captain Flint was in the habit of marooning people on islands, and Master Thomas felt that he could pursue no more judicious course than to follow his example.'

'But, good Lord, Jeeves! The man must be getting soaked.'

'Yes, sir. Master Thomas commented upon that aspect of the matter.'

It was time for action.

'Come wth me, Jeeves!'

'Very good, sir.'

I buzzed for the boathouse.

My Aunt Agatha's husband, Spencer Gregson, who is on the Stock Exchange, has recently cleaned up to an amazing extent in Sumatra Rubber; and Aunt Agatha, in selecting a country estate, had lashed out on an impressive scale. There were miles of what they call rolling parkland, trees in considerable profusion well provided with doves and what not cooing in no uncertain voice, gardens full of roses, and also stables, outhouses, and messuages, the whole forming a rather fruity *tout ensemble*. But the feature of the place was the lake.

It stood to the east of the house, beyond the rose garden, and covered several acres. In the middle of it was an island. In the middle of the island was a building known as the Octagon. And in the middle of the Octagon, seated on the roof and spouting water like a public fountain, was the Right Hon. A. B. Filmer. As we drew nearer, striking a fast clip with self at the oars and Jeeves handling the tiller-ropes, we heard cries of gradually increasing volume, if that's the expression I want; and presently, up aloft, looking from a distance as if he were perched on top of the bushes, I located the Right Hon. It seemed to me that even a Cabinet Minister ought to have had more sense than to stay right out in the open like that when there were trees to shelter under.

I made a neat landing.

'Wait here, Jeeves.'

'Very good, sir. The head gardener was informing me this morning, sir, that one of the swans had recently nested on this island.'

'This is no time for natural history gossip, Jeeves,' I said, a little severely, for the rain was coming down harder than ever and the Wooster trouser-legs were already considerably moistened.

'Very good, sir.'

I pushed my way through the bushes. The going was sticky and took about eight and elevenpence off the value of my Sure-Grip tennis shoes in the first two yards: but I persevered, and presently came out in the open and found myself in a sort of clearing facing the Octagon.

This building was run up somewhere in the last century, I have been told, to enable the grandfather of the late owner to have some quiet place out of earshot of the house where he could practise the fiddle. From what I know of fiddlers, I should imagine that he had produced some fairly frightful sounds there in his time; but they can have been nothing to the ones that were coming from the roof of the place now. The Right Hon. not having spotted the arrival of the rescue-party, was apparently trying to make his voice carry across the waste of waters to the house; and I'm not saying it was not a good sporting effort.

I thought it about time to slip him the glad news that assistance had arrived, before he strained a vocal cord.

'Hi!' I shouted, waiting for a lull.

He poked his head over the edge.

'Hi!' he bellowed, looking in every direction but the right one, of course.

'Hi!'

'Hi!'

'Oh!' he said, spotting me at last.

'What-ho!' I replied, sort of clinching the thing.

I suppose the conversation can't be said to have touched a frightfully high level up to this moment; but probably we should have got a good deal brainier very shortly—only just then, at the very instant when I was getting ready to say something good, there was a hissing noise like a tyre bursting in a nest of cobras, and out of the bushes to my left there popped something so large and white and active that, thinking quicker than I have ever done in my puff, I rose like a rocketing pheasant, and, before I knew what I was doing, had begun to climb for life. Something slapped against the wall about an inch below my right ankle, and any doubts I may have had about remaining below vanished. The lad who bore 'mid snow and ice the banner with the strange device 'Excelsior!' was the model for Bertram.

'Be careful!' yipped the Right Hon.

I was.

The swan gave a sort of jump and charged ahead.

Whoever built the Octagon might have constructed it especially for this sort of crisis. Its wall had grooves at regular intervals which were just right for the hands and feet, and it wasn't very long before I was parked up on the roof beside the Right Hon., gazing down at one of the largest and shortest-tempered swans I had ever seen. It was standing below, stretching up a neck like a hosepipe, just where a bit of brick, judiciously bunged, would catch it amidships.

I bunged the brick and scored a bull's-eye.

The Right Hon. didn't seem any too well pleased.

'Don't tease it!' he said.

'It teased me.' I said.

The swan extended another eight feet of neck and gave an imitation of steam escaping from a leaky pipe. The rain continued to lash down with what you might call indescribable fury, and I was sorry that in the agitation inseparable from shinning up a stone wall at practically a second's notice I had dropped the raincoat which I had been bringing with me for my fellow-rooster. For a moment I thought of offering him mine, but wiser counsels prevailed.

'How near did it come to getting you?' I asked.

'Within an ace,' replied my companion, gazing down with a look of marked dislike. 'I had to make a very rapid spring.'

The Right Hon. was a tubby little chap who looked as if he had been poured into his clothes and had forgotten to say 'When!' and the picture he conjured up, if you know what I mean, was rather pleasing.

'It is no laughing matter,' he said, shifting the look of dislike to me.

'Sorry.'

'I might have been seriously injured.'

'Would you consider bunging another brick at the bird?'

'Do nothing of the sort. It will only annoy him.'

'Well, why not annoy him? He hasn't shown such a dashed lot of consideration for our feelings.'

The Right Hon. now turned to another aspect of the matter.

'I cannot understand how my boat, which I fastened securely to the stump of a willow-tree, can have drifted away.'

'Dashed mysterious.'

'I begin to suspect that it was deliberately set loose by some mischievous person.'

'Oh, I say, no, hardly likely, that. You'd have seen them doing it.'

'No, Mr Wooster. For the bushes form an effective screen. Moreover, rendered drowsy by the unusual warmth of the afternoon, I dozed off for some little time almost immediately I reached the island.'

This wasn't the sort of thing I wanted his mind dwelling on, so I changed the subject.

'Wet, isn't it, what?' I said.

'I had already observed it,' said the Right Hon. in one of those nasty, bitter voices. 'I thank you, however, for drawing the matter to my attention.'

Chit-chat about the weather hadn't gone with much of a bang, I perceived. I had a shot at Bird Life in the Home Counties.

'Have you ever noticed,' I said, 'how a swan's eyebrows sort of meet in the middle?'

'I have had every opportunity of observing all that there is to observe about swans.'

'Gives them a sort of peevish look, what?'

'The look to which you allude has not escaped me.'

'Rummy,' I said, rather warming to my subject, 'how bad an effect family life has on a swan's disposition.'

'I wish you would select some other topic of conversation than swans.'

'No, but, really, it's rather interesting. I mean to say, our old pal down there is probably a perfect ray of sunshine in normal circumstances. Quite the domestic pet, don't you know. But purely and simply because the little woman happens to be nesting—'

I paused. You will scarcely believe me, but until this moment, what with all the recent bustle and activities, I had clean forgotten that, while we were treed up on the roof like this, there lurked all the time in the background one whose giant brain, if notified of the emergency and requested to flock round, would probably be able to think up half a dozen schemes for solving our little difficulties in a couple of minutes.

'Jeeves!' I shouted.

'Sir?' came a faint respectful voice from the great open spaces.

'My man,' I explained to the Right Hon. 'A fellow of infinite resource and sagacity. He'll have us out of this in a minute. Jeeves!'

'Sir?'

'I'm sitting on the roof.'

'Very good, sir.'

'Don't say "Very good". Come and help us. Mr Filmer and I are treed, Jeeves.'

'Very good, sir.'

'Don't keep saying "Very good". It's nothing of the kind. The place is alive with swans.'

'I will attend to the matter immediately, sir.'

I turned to the Right Hon. I even went so far as to pat him on the back. It was like slapping a wet sponge.

'All is well,' I said. 'Jeeves is coming.'

'What can he do?'

'That,' I replied with a touch of stiffness, 'we cannot say until we see him in action. He may pursue one course, or he may pursue another. But on one thing you can rely with the utmost confidence—Jeeves will find a way. See, here he comes stealing through the undergrowth, his face shining with the light of pure intelligence. There are no limits to Jeeve's brain-power. He virtually lives on fish.'

I bent over the edge and peered into the abyss.

'Look out for the swan, Jeeves.'

'I have the bird under close observation, sir.'

The swan had been uncoiling a further supply of neck in our direction; but now he whipped round. The sound of a voice speaking in his rear seemed to affect him powerfully. He subjected Jeeves to a short, keen scrutiny; and then, taking in some breath for hissing purposes, gave a sort of jump and charged ahead.

'Look out, Jeeves!'

'Very good, sir.'

Well, I could have told that swan it was no use. As swans go, he may have been well up in the ranks of the intelligentsia; but, when it came to pitting his brains against Jeeves, he was simply wasting his time. He might just as well have gone home at once.

Every young man starting life ought to know how to cope with an angry swan, so I will briefly relate the proper procedure. You begin by picking up the raincoat which somebody has dropped; and then, judging the distance to a nicety, you simply shove the raincoat over the bird's head; and, taking the boat-hook which you have prudently brought with you, you insert it underneath the swan and heave. The swan goes into a bush and starts trying to unscramble itself; and you saunter back to your boat, taking with you any friends who may happen at that moment to be sitting on roofs in the vicinity. That was Jeeve's method, and I cannot see how it could have been improved upon.

The Right Hon., showing a turn of speed of which I would not have believed him capable, we were in the boat in considerably under two ticks.

'You behaved very intelligently, my man,' said the Right Hon. as we pushed away from the shore.

'I endeavour to give satisfaction, sir.'

The Right Hon. appeared to have said his say for the time being. From that moment he seemed to sort of huddle up and meditate. Dashed absorbed he was. Even when I caught a crab and shot about a pint of water down his neck he didn't seem to notice it.

It was only when we were landing that he came to life again.

'Mr Wooster.'

'Oh, ah?'

'I have been thinking of that matter of which I spoke to you some time back—the problem of how my boat can have got adrift.'

I didn't like this.

'The dickens of a problem,' I said. 'Better not bother about it any more. You'll never solve it.'

'On the contrary, I have arrived at a solution, and one which I think is the only feasible solution. I am convinced that my boat was set adrift by the boy Thomas, my hostess's son.'

'Oh, I say, no! Why?'

'He had a grudge against me. And it is the sort of thing only a boy, or one who is practically an imbecile, would have thought of doing.'

He legged it for the house; and I turned to Jeeves, aghast. Yes, you might say aghast.

'You heard, Jeeves?'

'Yes, sir.'

'What's to be done?'

'Perhaps Mr Filmer, on thinking the matter over, will decide that his suspicions are unjust.'

'But they aren't unjust.'

'No, sir.'

'Then what's to be done?'

'I could not say, sir.'

I pushed off rather smartly to the house and reported to Aunt Agatha that the Right Hon. had been salved; and then I toddled upstairs to have a hot bath, being considerably soaked from stem to stern as the result of my rambles. While I was enjoying the grateful warmth, a knock came at the door.

It was Purvis, Aunt Agatha's butler.

'Mrs Gregson desires me to say, sir, that she would be glad to see you as soon as you are ready.'

'But she has seen me.'

'I gather that she wishes to see you again, sir.'

'Oh, right-ho.'

I lay beneath the surface for another few minutes; then, having dried the frame, went along the corridor to my room. Jeeves was there, fiddling about with underclothing.

'Oh, Jeeves,' I said, 'I've just been thinking. Oughtn't somebody to go and give Mr Filmer a spot of quinine or something? Errand of mercy, what?'

'I have already done so, sir.'

'Good. I wouldn't say I like the man frightfully, but I don't want him to get a cold in the head.' I shoved on a sock. 'Jeeves,' I said, 'I suppose you know that we've got to think of something pretty quick? I mean to say, you realize the position? Mr Filmer suspects young Thomas of doing exactly what he did do, and if he brings home the charge Aunt Agatha will undoubtedly fire Mr Little, and then Mrs Little will find out what Mr Little has been up to, and what will be the upshot and outcome, Jeeves? I will tell you. It will mean that Mrs Little will get the goods on Mr Little to an extent which, though only a bachelor myself, I should say that no wife ought to get the goods on her husband if the proper give and take of married life—what you might call the essential balance, as it were—is to be preserved. Women bring these things up, Jeeves. They do not forget and forgive.'

'Very true, sir.'

'Then how about it?'

'I have already attended to the matter, sir.'

'You have?'

'Yes, sir. I had scarcely left you when the solution of the affair presented itself to me. It was a remark of Mr Filmer's that gave me the idea.'

'Jeeves, you're a marvel!'

'Thank you very much, sir.'

'What was the solution?'

'I conceived the notion of going to Mr Filmer and saying that it was you who had stolen his boat, sir.'

The man flickered before me. I clutched a sock in a feverish grip.

'Saying—what?'

'At first Mr Filmer was reluctant to credit my statement. But I pointed out to him that you had certainly known that he was on the island—a fact which he agreed was highly significant. I pointed out, furthermore, that you were a light-hearted young gentleman, sir, who might well do such a thing as a practical joke. I left him quite convinced, and there is now no danger of his attributing the action to Master Thomas.'

I gazed at the blighter spellbound.

'And that's what you consider a neat solution?' I said.

'Yes, sir. Mr Little will now retain his position as desired.'

'And what about me?'

'You are also benefited, sir.'

'Oh, I am, am I?'

'Yes, sir. I have ascertained that Mrs Gregson's motive in inviting you to this house was that she might present you to Mr Filmer with a view to your becoming his private secretary.'

'What!'

'Yes, sir. Purvis, the butler, chanced to overhear Mrs Gregson in conversation with Mr Filmer on the matter.'

'Secretary to that superfatted bore! Jeeves, I could never have survived it.'

'No, sir. I fancy you would not have found it agreeable. Mr Filmer is scarcely a congenial companion for you. Yet, had Mrs Gregson secured the position for you, you might have found it embarrassing to decline to accept it.'

'Embarrassing is right!'

'Yes, sir.'

'But I say, Jeeves, there's just one point which you seem to have overlooked. Where exactly do I get off?'

'Sir?'

'I mean to say, Aunt Agatha sent word by Purvis just now that she wanted to see me. Probably she's polishing up her hatchet at this very moment.'

'It might be the most judicious plan not to meet her, sir.'

'But how can I help it?'

'There is a good, stout waterpipe running down the wall immediately outside this window, sir. And I could have the two-seater waiting outside the park gates in twenty minutes.'

I eyed him with reverence.

'Jeeves,' I said, 'you are always right. You couldn't make it five, could you?'

'Let us say ten, sir.'

'Ten it is. Lay out some raiment suitable for travel, and leave the rest to me. Where is this waterpipe of which you speak so highly?'

THE FUGITIVE

Maxwell Gray

The day was hot and fiercely bright. The town was full of life. Gay carriages were bearing ladies in light summer bravery to garden parties, afternoon dances on board ships, and other revels; bands were playing on piers; vessels of every kind, some gay with flags, dotted the Solent and the calm blue harbour; colours had been trooped on the common, troops had marched past the convicts; the sweet chimes of St Thomas' had rung a wedding peal; the great guns had thundered out royal salutes to the royal yacht as she bore the sovereign over to the green Wight—there was such a rush and stir of life as quite bewildered Everard, and made to the sharpest contrast to his grey and dreary prison life. To see these freest of free creatures, the street boys, sauntering or springing at will along the hot streets, or, casting off their dirty rags, flinging themselves into the fresh salt sea and revelling there like young Tritons, or, balanced on rails, criticizing the passing troops, was maddening.

The day grew hotter, but pick and barrow had to be plied without respite, though the sweat poured from hot brows, and one man dropped. Everard saw that it was sunstroke, and not malingering, as the warder was inclined to think, and by his earnest representations got the poor creature proper treatment. The brassy sky grew lurid purple, and heavy growls of thunder came rumbling from the distance;

some large drops of rain fell scantily, and then suddenly the sky opened from horizon to horizon and let down a sheet of vivid flame. Darkness followed, and a roar as of all the artillery at Portsmouth firing and all its magazines exploding at once.

'Now or never,' thought Everard, and, dropping his barrow at the end of his plank, he leaped straight ahead down into a waste patch, over which he sprang to the road. He ran for life and liberty with a speed he did not know himself capable of, straight on, blindly aiming at the shore, tearing off his cap and jacket and flinging them wildly in different directions, as he went through the dark curtain of straight rushing rain.

The warders, bewildered by the awful roar of the thunder, blinded by the fierce, quick dazzle of the lightning and the blackness of the all-concealing rain, did not at first miss him. It was only when he leaped the palisade bounding the road, and showed through the rain curtain a bare-headed, fugitive figure, that the grim guardian caught sight of him. Had he possessed the nerve to walk quietly out through the gate, he might have got off unobserved under cover of the storm.

Quick as thought, the warder, on seeing him, lifted his piece to his shoulder and fired. He was a good marksman, and his face lighted up with satisfaction as he hit his flying quarry, in spite of the bad light and confusing storm.

Everard felt a sharp, hot sting in the thigh, but ran on, his course marked with blood, which the friendly storm quickly washed away. The darkness became intenser, the lightning more blinding, the downrush of rain heavier, and the crashing of the thunder more deafening. Nevertheless, the alarm was given, and the pursuers were soon in full chase.

Down the now deserted highroad dashed the fugitive, every faculty he possessed concentrated on flight. With the blind instinct of the hunted, he rushed at the first turning, through a gate, up some steps, along to the bastion which rose behind the powder magazines. He darted along some pleasant green walk under the massy elms, till he reached the first sentry box, in which stood the sentry, a stalwart Highlander, sheltering from the storm.

Instead of firing on him, as the desperate fugitive expected, the man stepped swiftly aside, and the panting runner, divining his friendly purpose, ran into the box.

The soldier swiftly resumed his station.

The soldier swiftly resumed his station, and stood looking out with an immovable face as before, while the hunted convict, in the darkness in the narrow space at his side, stood face inward, close pressed to the wooden wall, soaked to the skin, and panting in hard gasps that were almost groans, yet sufficiently master of himself to press a wad of folded trouser on the bleeding wound which proved to be only a flesh graze, but which might ruin the friendly Scot by its damning stains on the floor of the box.

'Quiet's the word,' said the hospitable sentry, and nothing more.

Some minutes passed. Everard's breathing became less laboured, and his reflections more agonized; the thunder peals grew less tremendous, while the rain became heavier. The pursuers had lost sight of their prey in the road before he reached the gate, and had been thrown off the scent, while still sending searchers in all directions. Two of these turned up through the gate, and one explored all the nooks and crannies of the crescent-shaped space walled by the bastion which sheltered the powder magazines, while the other examined the path itself, and interrogated the sentry.

'Past the Garrison Chapel, towards High Street; out of my range,' he said coolly; and the pursuer, calling his comrade, flew with him along the bastion, not stopping to enquire of the other sentries. 'Gone away,' observed the Highlander to his quivering guest, who had feared lest his light-coloured dress might betray him behind the sentry, whose plaid and kilt and feather bonnet filled up all of the opening not darkened by his tall figure. 'Off the scent. What next, mate?'

'Heaven knows! I only hope I may not ruin you. If I get off, I will not forget you. My friends are well off, and I am—'

'Henry Everard. Seen you often with your gang—recognized at once.'

'Good heavens!' cried Everard, not seeing his host's handsome face, but feeling a vague stir of memory at his voice; 'who are you?'

'Private Walker, 179th Highlanders. Was Balfour of Christ Church.'

'Balfour? What! come to this? What did we not expect of you?'

'Wear a better coat than yours. Manby rough on you—hard lines. Do anything for you.'

'You always were a good-hearted fellow. And I was innocent,

Balfour; I had not the faintest grudge against the poor fellow. But how did you come to this? You took honours.'

'Governor poor—large family—small allowance at Cambridge—debts. Always liked the service—enlisted—Hussar regiment—jolly life—saw service—full sergeant—time expired. Sent into Reserve—not allowed to re-enlist—name of Smith. Tried civil life—down on my luck again—deserted from Reserve—re-enlisted in Highlander—name of Walker—enlisted fraudulent—liable to imprisonment—foreign service soon—all right. Now for you.'

Everard had to confess that he did not in the least know what to do next, unless he could hide till the darkness rendered his dress unobservable. The moment he was seen he would be recognized anywhere as a convict. Various schemes were revolved between them as rapidly as possible, for it was essential that Everard should leave the sentry box for a better hiding place before the rapid diminishing of the storm should once more open the bastion to observers.

The massive foliage of the elms hard by might have hidden a regiment, and Balfour had observed that the branches attracted no suspicion on the part of the pursuers, and, as the forking of the boughs did not begin till many feet off the ground, and the broad, smooth trunk offered not the smallest foothold, it was impossible for a man to climb into them unassisted.

But the sentry remembered that a stout rope had been flung aside there by some gunners busy cleaning the cannon on the bastion that day. If Everard could find this, and fling it over a bough, he might hoist himself up. If he could not find it, the soldier offered to come and lend him his shoulder—an action that might attract attention even in the darkness of the storm, since that part of the bastion was commanded by many windows, and that would, if discovered, bring certain ruin upon both men.

Everard darted swiftly from the box, and groped about in the wet grass till he found the rope. This, in the still blinding rain, he threw over the lowest stout branch, keeping one end, and fearful lest the other would not descend within reach. After a couple of casts, however, he succeeded in bringing the second end, in which he had fastened a stone, within easy reach, and grasping both, and planting his feet against the broad bole, slippery with wet, managed to struggle up with moderate speed. He was halfway up, and pausing a moment to steady himself and look round, saw to his infinite horror that he was exactly opposite to, and in full view and firing range of, the sentry on the opposite end of the bastion, which was roughly crescent-shaped.

Outlined as he was, and almost stationary against the tree trunk, he presented the easiest target for a moderate range shot. The man was in no hurry for his easy prey, he lifted his musket slowly, while Everard paused, transfixed with horror. The sentry seemed as if waiting for him to rise into a still better position for a shot. Everard slipped down, expecting to hear a ball sing over his head, if not into his body; but there was no report, and he stood irresolute a moment, seeking where to fly.

A signal of warning and haste from Balfour made him once more grasp his rope in desperation, and climb through the peril of the sentry's aim. A flash of lightning showed him his foe standing as before, with his musket planted firmly in front of him; he was supporting himself placidly with both hands clasped upon it, and his head bent slightly down, almost as if he had fallen asleep at his post.

But Everard knew that the most careless sentries do not fall asleep in the process of aiming at fugitive prisoners, and he pressed on till he reached the first fork, where he rested, wondering why no shot had been fired. The fact was, the rain was beating straight into the man's face, and he had much ado to see a yard before him, and had raised his musket merely to see if the breech was properly shielded from the wet. Everard, however, hoisting up his rope, climbed higher into his green fortress, expecting nothing less than to have it soon riddled in all directions by a fusillade from below. To his surprise he heard Balfour's signal of safety, and gladly responded to it; for they had framed a little code of signals before parting.

It was comparative luxury to the weary, wounded man to sit astride a branch, with his back against the trunk, and the foot of the wounded limb supported upon a lower bough, and he gave a deep sigh of relief, and reflected that he was at last, after all those dreary years of bondage, free. Balfour could do nothing till he was off guard, which would happen in another half-hour. Nothing could be done during the next sentry's guard, because it would be impossible to get at him and see how far he could be trusted; but if any subsequent sentry proved manageable, and if Balfour could get a pass for the night, he might bring him some sort of clothing, and then, under favourable circumstances, he might get off. And then?

The storm abated, the last, low mutterings of thunder died away in the distance, the rain ceased, and the evening sun shone out with golden clearness. Some of the long, slanting beams pierced the green roof of his airy prison, and fell hopefully upon the fugitive's face. He heard the sentry's measured tread below, and then the change of guard; the hum of the town, and the noises from the vessels at anchor came, mingled with distant bugle calls, to his lonely tower. The light faded, the sun went down in glory, the gun on the bastion fired the sunset, the parish church chimed half-past eight, the sounds from sea and shore came more distinct on the quieting night air, and he heard the band of a Highland regiment begin its skirl of pipes on the Clarence pier. It was probably Balfour's regiment.

Poor Balfour! He fell to thinking of his unfortunate lot, much as he had to occupy his thoughts with regard to his own immediate safety.

*   *   *   *

The air was chill after sunset. Everard, motionless on his airy perch, bareheaded, and in his shirt sleeves, was wet to the skin, and shivered with a double chill after the heat of his hard labour in the sultry afternoon. His wound ached till he began to fear it might lame him, and his hunger waxed keener as the night deepened and the cold increased. The stars came out and looked at him with their friendly, quieting gaze. He could see the sparkle of lights in the water and in the town; he could make out the lights of the admiral's signal station on his housetop above the dockyard.

Which man-of-war was Keppel's, he wondered, knowing nothing even of the outside world that was so near him. The chimes of the parish church told him the hours, and he knew when the guard would be relieved.

It was a weary night; its minutes lagged by leaden paced. He thought their long procession would never end; and yet there was a strange, delicious enchantment in the feeling that he had at last broken the bars of that iron prison, with its terrible bondage of unending routine and drudgery. The thick foliage of the elm still held the wet, which every passing breath of the night wind shook on the grass below in a miniature shower. The moon rose and wandered in pale majesty across the sweet blue sky—such a free, broad night sky as had not blessed his eyes for years and years; its beams hung his green fortress roof with pearls and trembling diamonds, falling ever and anon to the earth. Sentinel after sentinel came on guard below, but there was no friendly signal from beneath. He had descended to the lowest bough to catch the lightest sound. The watch was passing; the early dawn would shine on the next watch, and, if help did not come before the sunrise, he would have to wait till the following night, wet, starved, suffering as he was. But no; there is the welcome signal at last.

Quickly he gave the answering signal; and, bending down in the darkness, heard the following sentence above the sound of the sentinel's backward and forward steps: 'Sentry blind and deaf—sneak off to right. Catch.'

Something flew up to him in the dark, and, after two misses, he caught it; and then, rising to where a rift in the foliage let in a shaft of rays from the waning moon, unfastened his bundle, which was roughly tied with string.

A battered hat, very large, so that it would hide the close-cropped head; a boatman's thick blue jersey; and a pair of wide trousers, worn and stained, with a belt to fasten them; also some second-hand boots,—such was the simple but sufficient wardrobe which Balfour had purchased with his slender means, and brought him at deadly risk.

Everard was able to discard every rag of the tell-tale prison garb, stamped all over as it was with the broad arrow, and securing the dangerous garments to a branch of the tree, invested himself in the contents of the bundle—an occupation that took so long, owing to the inconvenience of his lofty dressing room, that the eastern sky was brightening and the friendly sentinel's watch almost expired by the time he was ready to descend from his perch, which he did noiselessly and apparently unobserved by the sentry.

Then, slowly and painfully,—for his limbs were cramped and chilled, and his wound ached,—he glided behind the dark boles till he reached the steps, and, descending them, found to his dismay that the gate was locked.

There is almost always some small but vitally important hitch in the best-laid human plans, and the hitch in Balfour's arrangement was that he forgot the nightly locking of the gate leading onto the bastion. He had approached the tree from the other side, passing the sentries, being challenged by them and giving the word in reply.

Everard knew the bastion, and had had many a pleasant stroll there in old days, when stopping with his father when in port, and he knew well that his only course was now to climb the gate, which he could not do without noise, and which was in no case an easy feat, the plain board of which the gate was made being high and the top thickly studded with those dreadful crooked nails, which look like alphabets gone wrong, and do dreadful damage to both hands and clothing.

Fortunately, the moon had set, the sun was not yet risen, and the darkness favoured him—a darkness which every moment threatened to dissipate. He struggled up with as little sound as possible, with set teeth and a beating heart, lacerating his hands cruelly. Then, having gained the top—not without some rents in his scanty clothing—he grasped the nail-studded ridge and sprang down. Alas! not to the ground, for one of the crooked nails caught in the back part of the wide trousers, and, with a rending of cloth and a knocking of his feet against the boards, he found himself arrested midway, and suspended by the waist against the gate, like a mole on a keeper's paling.

Had he been caught in front, he might have raised himself and somehow torn himself free; but being hooked thus in the rear, he was almost helpless, and his slightest effort to free himself brought the heels of his boots knocking loudly against the gate as if to obtain admittance, which was the last thing he wanted. Meantime the minutes flew on, the darkness was breaking fast; before long the sun would rise and disclose him hung thus helplessly on his nail to the earliest passer-by, who would probably be a policeman.

A beautiful faint flush of red rose suddenly shot up over the eastern sky, and the brown shadows lessened around him. He heard footsteps echoing through the dewy stillness, and struggled with blind desperation. The rose red turned deep glowing orange, objects became more and more distinct before him, the street lamps sickened, a soft orange ray shot straight from the sea across the common, through the leaves of the tree shadowing the gate, onto the fugitive's cheek. At the same instant he heard the boom of the sunrise guns; it was day.

The footsteps approached nearer and nearer; on the bastion he heard the change of watch. He felt that all was lost, and yet, in his mental tension, his chief consciousness was of the awful beauty of the dawn, the dewy quiet and freshness brooding over the great town, and—strange contrast!—the grotesque absurdity of his situation. He heard the lively twitter of the birds waking in the trees, and admired the soft radiance of the ruddy beams on the sleeping town; and then something gave way and he found himself full length on the pavement.

The echoing footsteps had as yet brought no figure round the corner, and Everard welcomed the hard salute of the paving stones as the first greeting of freedom, and, quickly picking himself up, he fell into the slow, slouching walks he had observed in tramps, and moved on, adjusting his discoloured garments as best he might. The footsteps proved indeed to be those of a policeman, whose eyes were dazzled with the level sunbeam which he faced, and who gave him a dissatisfied but not suspicious glance and passed on.

Everard drew a deep breath, and limped on, trying to disguise the lameness of the wounded limb, which he feared might betray him, and thrust his torn hands into the pockets of the trousers which had so nearly ruined him. His surprise and joy were great on touching with his left hand a substance which proved to be bread and cheese, which he instantly devoured, and with his right a few pence, and, what moved him to tears of gratitude for Balfour's thankful kindness, a short, brier-wood pipe, well seasoned, and doubtless the good fellow's own, a screw of cheap tobacco and some matches. He had not touched tobacco for nine years.

A drinking fountain supplied him with the draught of water which his fevered throat and parched lips craved; it also enabled him to wash off some of the blood and dirt from his torn hand. And then, dragging his stiff and wounded limb slowly along, and eating his stale bread and cheese in the sweet sunshine, he made his morning orisons in the dewy quiet of the yet unawakened town, and felt a glow of intense gratitude, which increased as the food and water strengthened him, and exercise warmed his chill and stiffened frame.

He was glad to see the houses open one by one, and the streets begin to fill; he thought he should attract less attention among numbers. He passed groups of free labourers, hurrying to the dockyards to work, and it gave him an eerie shudder to think that some of them, whose faces he knew, might recognize him. His terror increased when he saw a light on a workman's face—a face he knew well, for the man had slipped over the side of the dock one morning, and was in imminent danger of being jammed by some floating timber, when Everard had promptly sprung after him, regardless of prison discipline, and held him up, for he could not swim, till a rope was brought, and the two men were hauled out, bruised, but otherwise uninjured.

The man stopped; Everard went straight on, not appearing to see him, and, after a few seconds, to his dismay, heard footsteps running after him. He dared not quicken his pace, lest he should attract attention, but the food he was eating stuck in his throat, and his face paled. His pursuer gained his side, and, seizing his hand, pressed some pence into it, saying, in a low tone, 'Mum's the word, mate! All the ready I've got. Simon Jones, 80 King Street, for help. Better not stop.'

Then he turned and resumed his road, telling his companions something about a chum of his down in his luck, and Everard slouched on with a lightened heart and increased gratitude for the pence. He had now nearly two shillings in his pockets, and when he had lighted Balfour's brierwood, he felt like a king. The last time he handled a coin was when he gave pence to a blind man, sitting by the police station at Oldport, just before his arrest. He bought needle and thread to repair the tremendous fissure in the unlucky garments which had played him so ill a trick, and in two hours' time found himself well clear of the town and suburbs. Presently he found a shed used for sheltering cattle, but now empty. This he entered, and, having with some difficulty drawn the chief rents in his clothes together, washed his wound in a trough placed for some cattle to drink from, and bandaged that and the worst hurts in his hand with the handkerchief in which the bread and cheese was wrapped, lay down on some litter behind a turnip-cutting machine, and in a moment was fast asleep, utterly oblivious of prisons, wounds, and hunger.

THE THREE STRANGERS

Thomas Hardy

As friends gather in Shepherd Fennel's cottage one rainy night to celebrate the christening of his daughter, a stranger makes his way across the downs from the town of Casterbridge. He stops to shelter from the rain under the eaves of an outhouse and listens to the sound of the fiddle. When the music stops, he crosses to the door of the cottage and lifts his hand to knock, but then he pauses. . . .

In his indecision he turned and surveyed the scene around. Not a soul was anywhere visible. The garden path stretched downward from his feet, gleaming like the track of a snail; the roof of the little well (mostly dry), the well-cover, the top rail of the garden-gate, were varnished with the same dull liquid glaze; while, far away in the vale, a faint whiteness of more than usual extent showed that the rivers were high in the meads. Beyond all this winked a few bleared lamplights through the beating drops—lights that denoted the situation of the county-town from which he had appeared to come. The absence of all notes of life in that direction seemed to clinch his intentions, and he knocked at the door.

Within, a desultory chat had taken the place of movement and musical sound. The hedge-carpenter was suggesting a song to the company, which nobody just then was inclined to undertake, so that the knock afforded a not unwelcome diversion.

'Walk in!' said the shepherd promptly.

The latch clicked upward, and out of the night our pedestrian appeared upon the door-mat. The shepherd arose, snuffed two of the nearest candles, and turned to look at him.

Their light disclosed that the stranger was dark in complexion and not unprepossessing as to feature. His hat, which for a moment he did not remove, hung low over his eyes, without concealing that they were large, open, and determined, moving with a flash rather than a glance round the room. He seemed pleased with his survey, and, baring his shaggy head, said, in a rich deep voice, 'The rain is so heavy, friends, that I ask leave to come in and rest awhile.'

'To be sure, stranger,' said the shepherd. 'And faith, you've been lucky in choosing your time, for we are having a bit of a fling for a glad cause—though, to be sure, a man could hardly wish that glad cause to happen more than once a year.'

'Nor less,' spoke up a woman. 'For 'tis best to get your family over and done with, as soon as you can, so as to be all the earlier out of the fag o't.'

'And what may be this glad cause?' asked the stranger.

'A birth and christening,' said the shepherd.

The stranger hoped his host might not be made unhappy either by too many or too few of such episodes, and being invited by a gesture to a pull at the mug, he readily acquiesced. His manner, which, before entering, had been so dubious, was now altogether that of a careless and candid man.

'Late to be traipsing athwart this coomb—hey?' said the engaged man of fifty.

'Late it is, master, as you say.—I'll take a seat in the chimney-corner, if you have nothing to urge against it, ma'am; for I am a little moist on the side that was next the rain.'

Mrs Shepherd Fennel assented, and made room for the self-invited comer, who, having got completely inside the chimney-corner, stretched out his legs and his arms with the expansiveness of a person quite at home.

'Yes, I am rather cracked in the vamp,' he said freely, seeing that the eyes of the shepherd's wife fell upon his boots, 'and I am not well fitted either. I have had some rough times lately, and have been forced to pick up what I can get in the way of wearing, but I must find a suit better fit for working-days when I reach home.'

'One of hereabouts?' she inquired.

'Not quite that—further up the country.'

'I thought so. And so be I; and by your tongue you come from my neighbourhood.'

'But you would hardly have heard of me,' he said quickly. 'My time would be long before yours, ma'am, you see.'

This testimony to the youthfulness of his hostess had the effect of stopping her cross-examination.

'There is only one thing more wanted to make me happy,' continued the new-comer. 'And that is a little baccy, which I am sorry to say I am out of.'

'I'll fill your pipe,' said the shepherd.

'I must ask you to lend me a pipe likewise.'

'A smoker, and no pipe about 'ee?'

'I have dropped it somewhere on the road.'

The shepherd filled and handed him a new clay pipe, saying, as he did so, 'Hand me your baccy-box—I'll fill that too, now I am about it.'

The man went through the movement of searching his pockets.

'Lost that too?' said his entertainer, with some surprise.

'I am afraid so,' said the man with some confusion. 'Give it to me in a screw of paper.' Lighting his pipe at the candle with a suction that drew the whole flame into the bowl, he resettled himself in the corner and bent his looks upon the faint steam from his damp legs, as if he wished to say no more.

Meanwhile the general body of guests had been taking little notice of this visitor by reason of an absorbing discussion in which they were engaged with the band about a tune for the next dance. The matter being settled, they were about to stand up when an interruption came in the shape of another knock at the door.

At sound of the same the man in the chimney-corner took up the poker and began stirring the brands as if doing it thoroughly were the one aim of his existence; and a second time the shepherd said, 'Walk in!' In a moment another man stood upon the straw-woven door-mat. He too was a stranger.

This individual was one of a type radically different from the first. There was more of the commonplace in his manner, and a certain jovial cosmopolitanism sat upon his features. He was several years older than the first arrival, his hair being slightly frosted, his eyebrows bristly, and his whiskers cut back from his cheeks. His face was rather full and flabby, and yet it was not altogether a face without power. A few grog-blossoms marked the neighbourhood of his nose. He flung back his long drab greatcoat, revealing that beneath it he wore a suit of cinder-grey shade throughout, large heavy seals, of some metal or other that would take a polish, dangling from his fob as his only personal ornament. Shaking the water-drops from his low-crowned glazed hat, he said, 'I must ask for a few minutes' shelter, comrades, or I shall be wetted to my skin before I get to Casterbridge.'

'Make yourself at home, master,' said the shepherd, perhaps a trifle less heartily than on the first occasion. Not that Fennel had the least tinge of niggardliness in his composition; but the room was far from large, spare chairs were not numerous, and damp companions were not altogether desirable at close quarters for the women and girls in their bright-coloured gowns.

However, the second comer, after taking off his greatcoat, and hanging his hat on a nail in one of the ceiling-beams as if he had been specially invited to put it there, advanced and sat down at the table. This had been pushed so closely into the chimney-corner, to give all available room to the dancers, that its inner edge grazed the elbow of the man who had ensconced himself by the fire; and thus the two strangers were brought into close companionship. They nodded to each other by way of breaking the ice of unacquaintance, and the first stranger handed his neighbour the family mug—a huge vessel of brown ware, having its upper edge worn away like a threshold by the rub of whole generations of thirsty lips that had gone the way of all flesh, and bearing the following inscription burnt upon its rotund side in yellow letters:

THERE IS NO FUN
UNTIL I CUM

The other man, nothing loth, raised the mug to his lips, and drank on, and on, and on—till a curious blueness overspread the countenance of the shepherd's wife, who had regarded with no little surprise the first stranger's free offer to the second of what did not belong to him to dispense.

'I knew it!' said the toper to the shepherd with much satisfaction. 'When I walked up your garden before coming in, and saw the hives all of a row, I said to myself, "Where there's bees there's honey, and where there's honey there's mead." But mead of such a truly comfortable sort as this I really didn't expect to meet in my older days.' He took yet another pull at the mug, till it assumed an ominous elevation.

'Glad you enjoy it!' said the shepherd warmly.

'It is goodish mead,' assented Mrs Fennel, with an absence of enthusiasm which seemed to say that it was possible to buy praise for one's cellar at too heavy a price. 'It is trouble enough to make—and really I hardly think we shall make any more. For honey sells well, and we ourselves can make shift with a drop o' small mead and metheglin for common use from the comb-washings.'

'O, but you'll never have the heart!' reproachfully cried the stranger in cinder-grey, after taking up the mug a third time and setting it down empty. 'I love mead, when 'tis old like this, as I love to go to church o' Sundays, or to relieve the needy any day of the week.'

'Ha, ha, ha!' said the man in the chimney-corner, who, in spite of the taciturnity induced by the pipe of tobacco, could not or would not refrain from this slight testimony to his comrade's humour.

Now the old mead of those days, brewed of the purest first-year or maiden honey, four pounds to the gallon—with its due complement of white of eggs, cinnamon, ginger, cloves, mace, rosemary, yeast, and processes of working, bottling, and cellaring—tasted remarkably strong; but it did not taste so strong as it actually was. Hence, presently, the stranger in cinder-grey at the table, moved by its creeping influence, unbuttoned his waistcoat, threw himself back in his chair, spread his legs, and made his presence felt in various ways.

'Well, well, as I say,' he resumed, 'I am going to Casterbridge, and to Casterbridge I must go. I should have been almost there by this time; but the rain drove me into your dwelling, and I'm not sorry for it.'

'You don't live in Casterbridge?' said the shepherd.

'Not as yet; though I shortly mean to move there.'

'Going to set up in trade, perhaps?'

'No, no,' said the shepherd's wife. 'It is easy to see that the gentleman is rich, and don't want to work at anything.'

The cinder-grey stranger paused, as if to consider whether he would accept that definition of himself. He presently rejected it by answering, 'Rich is not quite the word for me, dame. I do work, and I must work. And even if I only get to Casterbridge by midnight I must begin work there at eight tomorrow morning. Yes, het or wet, blow or snow, famine or sword, my day's work tomorrow must be done.'

'Poor man! Then, in spite o' seeming, you be worse off than we?' replied the shepherd's wife.

''Tis the nature of my trade, men and maidens. 'Tis the nature of my trade more than my poverty. . . . But really and truly I must up and off, or I shan't get a lodging in the town.' However, the speaker did not move, and directly added, 'There's time for one more draught of friendship before I go; and I'd perform it at once if the mug were not dry.'

'Here's a mug o' small,' said Mrs Fennel. 'Small, we call it, though to be sure 'tis only the first wash o' the combs.'

'No,' said the stranger disdainfully. 'I won't spoil your first kindness by partaking o' your second.'

'Certainly not,' broke in Fennel. 'We don't increase and multiply every day, and I'll fill the mug again.' He went away to the dark place under he stairs where the barrel stood. The shepherdess followed him.

'Why should you do this?' she said reproachfully, as soon as they were alone. 'He's emptied it once, though it held enough for ten people; and now he's not contented wi' the small, but must needs call for more o' the strong! And a stranger unbeknown to any of us. For my part, I don't like the look o' the man at all.'

'But he's in the house, my honey; and 'tis a wet night, and a christening. Daze it, what's a cup of mead more or less? There'll be plenty more next bee-burning.'

'Very well—this time, then,' she answered, looking wistfully at the barrel. 'But what is the man's calling, and where is he one of, that he should come in and join us like this?'

'I don't know. I'll ask him again.'

The catastrophe of having the mug drained dry at one pull by the stranger in cinder-grey was effectually guarded against this time by Mrs Fennel. She poured out his allowance in a small cup, keeping the large one at a discreet distance from him. When he had tossed off his portion the shepherd renewed his inquiry about the stranger's occupation.

The latter did not immediately reply, and the man in the chimney-corner, with sudden demonstrativeness, said, 'Anybody may know my trade—I'm a wheelwright.'

'A very good trade for these parts,' said the shepherd.

'And anybody may know mine—if they've the sense to find it out,' said the stranger in cinder-grey.

'You may generally tell what a man is by his claws,' observed the hedge-carpenter, looking at his own hands, 'My fingers be as full of thorns as an old pin-cushion is of pins.'

The hands of the man in the chimney-corner instinctively sought the shade, and he gazed into the fire as he resumed his pipe. The man at the table took up the hedge-carpenter's remark, and added smartly, 'True; but the oddity of my trade is that, instead of setting a mark upon me, it sets a mark upon my customers.'

No observation being offered by anybody in elucidation of this enigma the shepherd's wife once more called for a song. The same obstacles presented themselves as at the former time—one had no voice, another had forgotten the first verse. The stranger at the table, whose soul had now risen to a good working temperature, relieved the difficulty by exclaiming that, to start the company, he would sing himself. Thrusting one thumb into the arm-hole of his waistcoat, he waved the other hand in the air, and, with an extemporizing gaze at the shining sheep-crooks above the mantelpiece, began:

'O my trade it is the rarest one,
Simple shepherds all—
My trade is a sight to see;
For my customers I tie, and take them up on high,
And waft 'em to a far countree!'

The room was silent when he had finished the verse—with one exception, that of the man in the chimney-corner, who, at the singer's

The singer went on with the stanza as requested.

word, 'Chorus!' joined him in a deep bass voice of musical relish—

'And waft 'em to a far countree!'

Oliver Giles, John Pitcher the dairyman, the parish-clerk, the engaged man of fifty, the row of young women against the wall, seemed lost in thought not of the gayest kind. The shepherd looked meditatively on the ground, the shepherdess gazed keenly at the singer, and with some suspicion; she was doubting whether this stranger were merely singing an old song from recollection, or was composing one there and then for the occasion. All were as perplexed at the obscure revelation as the guests at Belshazzar's Feast, except the man in the chimney-corner, who quietly said, 'Second verse, stranger,' and smoked on.

The singer thoroughly moistened himself from his lips inwards, and went on with the next stanza as requested:—

'My tools are but common ones,
Simple shepherds all—
A little hempen string, and a post whereon to swing,
Are implements enough for me!'

Shepherd Fennel glanced round. There was no longer any doubt that the stranger was answering his question rhythmically. The guests one and all started back with suppressed exclamations. The young woman engaged to the man of fifty fainted half-way, and would have proceeded, but finding him wanting in alacrity for catching her she sat down trembling.

'O, he's the—!' whispered the people in the background, mentioning the name of an ominous public officer. 'He's come to do it! 'Tis to be at Casterbridge jail tomorrow—the man for sheep-stealing—the poor clock-maker we heard of, who used to live away at Shottsford and had no work to do—Timothy Summers, whose family were a-starving, and so he went out of Shottsford by the high-road, and took a sheep in open daylight, defying the farmer and the farmer's wife and the farmer's lad, and every man jack among 'em. He' (and they nodded towards the stranger of the deadly trade) 'is come from up the country to do it because there's not enough to do in his own county-town, and he's got the place here now our own county man's dead; he's going to live in the same cottage under the prison wall.'

The stranger in cinder-grey took no notice of this whispered string of observations, but again wetted his lips. Seeing that his friend in the chimney-corner was the only one who reciprocated his joviality in any way, he held out his cup towards that appreciative comrade, who also held out his own. They clinked together, the eyes of the rest of the room hanging upon the singer's actions. He parted his lips for the third verse; but at that moment another knock was audible upon the door. This time the knock was faint and hesitating.

The company seemed scared; the shepherd looked with consternation towards the entrance, and it was with some effort that he resisted his alarmed wife's deprecatory glance, and uttered for the third time the welcoming words, 'Walk in!'

The door was gently opened, and another man stood upon the mat. He, like those who had preceded him, was a stranger. This time it was a short, small personage, of fair complexion, and dressed in a decent suit of dark clothes.

'Can you tell me the way to—?' he began: when, gazing round the room to observe the nature of the company amongst whom he had fallen, his eyes lighted on the stranger in the cinder-grey. It was just at the instant when the latter, who had thrown his mind into his song with such a will that he scarcely heeded the interruption, silenced all whispers and inquiries by bursting into his third verse:

'Tomorrow is my working day,
Simple shepherds all—
Tomorrow is a working day for me:
For the farmer's sheep is slain, and the lad who did it ta'en,
And on his soul may God ha' merc-y!'

The stranger in the chimney-corner, waving cups with the singer so heartily that his mead splashed over on the hearth, repeated in his bass voice as before:

'And on his soul may God ha' merc-y!'

All this time the third stranger had been standing in the doorway. Finding now that he did not come forward or go on speaking, the guests particularly regarded him. They noticed to their surprise that he stood before them the picture of abject terror—his knees trembling, his hand shaking so violently that the door-latch by which he supported himself rattled audibly: his white lips were parted, and his eyes fixed on the merry officer of justice in the middle of the room. A moment more and he had turned, closed the door, and fled.

'What a man can it be?' said the shepherd.

The rest, between the awfulness of their late discovery and the odd conduct of this third visitor, looked as if they knew not what to think, and said nothing. Instinctively they withdrew further and further from the grim gentleman in their midst, whom some of them seemed to take for the Prince of Darkness himself, till they formed a remote circle, an empty space of floor being left between them and him—

'. . . circulus, cujus centrum diabolus.'

The room was so silent—though there were more than twenty people in it—that nothing could be heard but the patter of the rain against the window-shutters, accompanied by the occasional hiss of a stray drop that fell down the chimney into the fire, and the steady puffing of the man in the corner, who had now resumed his pipe of long clay.

The stillness was unexpectedly broken. The distant sound of a gun reverberated through the air—apparently from the direction of the county-town.

'Be jiggered!' cried the stranger who had sung the song, jumping up.

'What does that mean?' asked several.

'A prisoner escaped from the jail—that's what it means.'

All listened. The sound was repeated, and none of them spoke but the man in the chimney-corner, who said quietly, 'I've often been told that in this county they fire a gun at such times; but I never heard it till now.'

'I wonder if it is *my* man?' murmured the personage in cinder-grey.

'Surely it is!' said the shepherd involuntarily. 'And surely we've zeed him! That little man who looked in at the door by now, and quivered like a leaf when he zeed ye and heard your song!'

'His teeth chattered, and the breath went out of his body,' said the dairyman.

'And his heart seemed to sink within him like a stone,' said Oliver Giles.

'And he bolted as if he'd been shot at,' said the hedge-carpenter.

'True—his teeth chattered, and his heart seemed to sink; and he bolted as if he'd been shot at,' slowly summed up the man in the chimney-corner.

'I didn't notice it,' remarked the hangman.

'We were all a-wondering what made him run off in such a fright,' faltered one of the women against the wall, 'and now 'tis explained!'

The firing of the alarm-gun went on at intervals, low and sullenly, and their suspicions became a certainty. The sinister gentleman in cinder-grey roused himself. 'Is there a constable here?' he asked, in thick tones. 'If so, let him step forward.'

The engaged man of fifty stepped quavering out from the wall, his betrothed beginning to sob on the back of the chair.

'You are a sworn constable?'

'I be, sir.'

'Then pursue the criminal at once, with assistance, and bring him back here. He can't have gone far.'

'I will, sir, I will—when I've got my staff. I'll go home and get it, and come sharp here, and start in a body.'

'Staff!—never mind your staff; the man'll be gone!'

'But I can't do nothing without my staff—can I, William, and John, and Charles Jake? No; for there's the king's royal crown a painted on en in yaller and gold, and the lion and the unicorn, so as when I raise en up and hit my prisoner, 'tis made a lawful blow thereby. I wouldn't 'tempt to take up a man without my staff—no, not I. If I hadn't the law to gie me courage, why, instead o' my taking up him he might take up me!'

'Now, I'm a king's man myself, and can give you authority enough for this,' said the formidable officer in grey. 'Now then, all of ye, be ready. Have ye any lanterns?'

'Yes—have ye any lanterns?—I demand it!' said the constable.

'And the rest of you able-bodied—'

'Able-bodied men—yes—the rest of ye!' said the constable.

'Have you some good stout staves and pitchforks—'

'Staves and pitchforks—in the name o' the law! And take 'em in yer hands and go in quest, and do as we in authority tell ye!'

Thus aroused, the men prepared to give chase. The evidence was, indeed, though circumstantial, so convincing, that but little argument was needed to show the shepherd's guests that after what they had seen it would look very much like connivance if they did not instantly pursue the unhappy third stranger, who could not as yet have gone more than a few hundred yards over such uneven country.

A shepherd is always well provided with lanterns; and, lighting these hastily, and with hurdle-staves in their hands, they poured out of the door, taking a direction along the crest of the hill, away from the town, the rain having fortunately a little abated.

Disturbed by the noise, or possibly by unpleasant dreams of her baptism, the child who had been christened began to cry heart-brokenly in the room overhead. These notes of grief came down through the chinks of the floor to the ears of the women below, who jumped up one by one, and seemed glad of the excuse to ascend and comfort the baby, for the incidents of the last half-hour greatly oppressed them. Thus in the space of two or three minutes the room on the ground-floor was deserted quite.

But it was not for long. Hardly had the sound of footsteps died away when a man returned round the corner of the house from the direction the pursuers had taken. Peeping in at the door, and seeing nobody there, he entered leisurely. It was the stranger of the chimney-corner, who had gone out with the rest. The motive of his return was shown by his helping himself to a cut piece of skimmer-cake that lay on a ledge beside where he had sat, and which he had apparently forgotten to take with him. He also poured out half a cup more mead from the quantity that remained, ravenously eating and drinking these as he stood. He had not finished when another figure came in just as quietly—his friend in cinder-grey.

'O—you here?' said the latter, smiling. 'I thought you had gone to help in the capture.' And this speaker also revealed the object of his return by looking solicitously round for the fascinating mug of old mead.

'And I thought you had gone,' said the other, continuing his skimmer-cake with some effort.

'Well, on second thoughts, I felt there were enough without me,' said the first confidentially, 'and such a night as it is, too. Besides, 'tis the business o' the Government to take care of its criminals—not mine.'

'True; so it is. And I felt as you did, that there were enough without me.'

'I don't want to break my limbs running over the humps and hollows of this wild country.'

'Nor I neither, between you and me.'

'These shepherd-people are used to it—simple-minded souls, you know, stirred up to anything in a moment. They'll have him ready for me before the morning, and no trouble to me at all.'

'They'll have him, and we shall have saved ourselves all labour in the matter.'

'True, true. Well, my way is to Casterbridge; and 'tis as much as my legs will do to take me that far. Going the same way?'

'No, I am sorry to say! I have to get home over there' (he nodded indefinitely to the right), 'and I feel as you do, that it is quite enough for my legs to do before bedtime.'

The other had by this time finished the mead in the mug, after which, shaking hands heartily at the door, and wishing each other well, they went their several ways.

In the meantime the company of pursuers had reached the end of the hog's-back elevation which dominated this part of the down. They had decided on no particular plan of action; and, finding that the man of the baleful trade was no longer in their company, they seemed quite unable to form any such plan now. They descended in all directions down the hill, and straightway several of the party fell into the snare set by Nature for all misguided midnight ramblers over this part of the cretaceous formation. The 'lanchets', or flint slopes, which belted the escarpment at intervals of a dozen yards, took the less cautious ones unawares, and losing their footing on the rubbly steep they slid sharply downwards, the lanterns rolling from their hands to the bottom, and there lying on their sides till the horn was scorched through.

When they had again gathered themselves together the shepherd, as the man who knew the country best, took the lead, and guided them round these treacherous inclines. The lanterns, which seemed rather to dazzle their eyes and warn the fugitive than to assist them in the exploration, were extinguished, due silence was observed; and in this more rational order they plunged into the vale. It was a grassy, briery, moist defile, affording some shelter to any person who had sought it; but the party perambulated it in vain, and ascended on the other side. Here they wandered apart, and after an interval closed together again to report progress. At the second time of closing in they found themselves near a lonely ash, the single tree on this part of the coomb, probably sown there by a passing bird some fifty years before. And here, standing a little to one side of the trunk, as motionless as the trunk itself, appeared the man they were in quest of, his outline being well defined against the sky beyond. The band noiselessly drew up and faced him.

'Your money or your life!' said the constable sternly to the still figure.

'No, no,' whispered John Pitcher. ''Tisn't our side ought to say that. That's the doctrine of vagabonds like him, and we be on the side of the law.'

'Well, well,' replied the constable impatiently; 'I must say something, mustn't I? and if you had all the weight o' this undertaking upon your mind, perhaps you'd say the wrong thing too!—Prisoner at the bar, surrender, in the name of the Father—the Crown, I mean!'

The man under the tree seemed now to notice them for the first time, and, giving them no opportunity whatever for exhibiting their courage, he strolled slowly towards them. He was indeed, the little man, the third stranger; but his trepidation had in a great measure gone.

'Well, travellers,' he said, 'did I hear ye speak to me?'

'You did: you've got to come and be our prisoner at once!' said the constable. 'We arrest 'ee on the charge of not biding in Casterbridge jail in a decent proper manner to be hung to-morrow morning. Neighbours, do your duty, and seize the culpet!'

On hearing the charge the man seemed enlightened, and, saying not another word, resigned himself with preternatural civility to the search-party, who, with their staves in their hands, surrounded him on all sides, and marched him back towards the shepherd's cottage.

It was eleven o'clock by the time they arrived. The light shining from the open door, a sound of men's voices within, proclaimed to them as they approached the house that some new events had arisen in their absence. On entering they discovered the shepherd's living room to be invaded by two officers from Casterbridge jail, and a well-known magistrate who lived at the nearest country-seat, intelligence of the escape having become generally circulated.

'Gentlemen,' said the constable, 'I have brought back your man—not without risk and danger; but every one must do his duty! He is inside this circle of able-bodied persons, who have lent me useful aid, considering their ignorance of Crown work. Men, bring forward your prisoner!' And the third stranger was led to the light.

'Who is this?' said one of the officials.

'The man,' said the constable.

'Certainly not,' said the turnkey; and the first corroborated his statement.

'But how can it be otherwise?' asked the constable. 'Or why was he so terrified at sight o' the singing instrument of the law who sat there?' Here he related the strange behaviour of the third stranger on entering the house during the hangman's song.

'Can't understand it,' said the officer coolly. 'All I know is that it is not the condemned man. He's quite a different character from this one; a gauntish fellow, with dark hair and eyes, rather good-looking, and with a musical bass voice that if you heard it once you'd never mistake as long as you lived.'

'Why, souls—'twas the man in the chimney-corner!'

'Hey—what?' said the magistrate, coming forward after inquiring particulars from the shepherd in the background. 'Haven't you got the man after all!'

'Well, sir,' said the constable, 'he's the man we were in search of, that's true; and yet he's not the man we were in search of. For the man we were in search of was not the man we wanted, sir, if you understand my every-day way; for 'twas the man in the chimney-corner!'

'A pretty kettle of fish altogether!' said the magistrate. 'You had better start for the other man at once.'

The prisoner now spoke for the first time. The mention of the man in the chimney-corner seemed to have moved him as nothing else could do. 'Sir,' he said, stepping forward to the magistrate, 'take no more trouble about me. The time is come when I may as well speak. I have done nothing; my crime is that the condemned man is my brother. Early this afternoon I left home at Shottsford to tramp it all the way to Casterbridge jail to bid him farewell. I was benighted, and called here to rest and ask the way. When I opened the door I saw before me the very man, my brother, that I thought to see in the condemned cell at Casterbridge. He was in this chimney-corner; and jammed close to him, so that he could not have got out if he had tried, was the executioner who'd come to take his life, singing a song about it and not knowing that it was his victim who was close by, joining in to save appearances. My brother threw a glance of agony at me, and I knew he meant, "Don't reveal what you see; my life depends on it." I was so terror-struck that I could hardly stand, and, not knowing what I did, I turned and hurried away.'

The narrator's manner and tone had the stamp of truth, and his story made a great impression on all around. 'And do you know where your brother is at the present time?' asked the magistrate.

'I do not. I have never seen him since I closed this door.'

'I can testify to that, for we've been between ye ever since,' said the constable.

'Where does he think to fly to?—what is his occupation?'

'He's a watch-and-clock-maker, sir.

''A said 'a was a wheelwright—a wicked rogue,' said the constable.

'The wheels of clocks and watches he meant, no doubt,' said Shepherd Fennel. 'I thought his hands were palish for's trade.'

'Well, it appears to me that nothing can be gained by retaining this poor man in custody,' said the magistrate; 'your business lies with the other, unquestionably.'

And so the little man was released off-hand; but he looked nothing the less sad on that account, it being beyond the power of magistrate or constable to raze out the written troubles in his brain, for they concerned another whom he regarded with more solicitude than himself. When this was done, and the man had gone his way, the night was found to be so far advanced that it was deemed useless to renew the search before the next morning.

Next day, accordingly, the quest for the clever sheep-stealer became general and keen, to all appearances at least. But the intended punishment was cruelly disproportioned to the transgression, and the sympathy of a great many country-folk in that district was strongly on the side of the fugitive. Moreover, his marvellous coolness and daring in hob-and-nobbing with the hangman under the unprecedented circumstances of the shepherd's party, won their admiration. So that it may be questioned if all those who ostensibly made themselves so busy in exploring woods and fields and lanes were quite so thorough when it came to the private examination of their own lofts and out-houses. Stories were afloat of a mysterious figure being occasionally seen in some old overgrown trackway or other, remote from turnpike roads; but when a search was instituted in any of these suspected quarters nobody was found. Thus the days and weeks passed without tidings.

In brief, the bass-voiced man of the chimney-corner was never recaptured. Some said that he went across the sea, others that he did not, but buried himself in the depths of a populous city. At any rate, the gentleman in cinder-grey never did his morning's work at Casterbridge, nor met anywhere at all, for business purposes, the genial comrade with whom he had passed an hour of relaxation in the lonely house on the slope of the coomb.

The grass has long been green on the graves of Shepherd Fennel and his frugal wife; the guests who made up the christening party have mainly followed their entertainers to the tomb; the baby in whose honour they all had met is a matron in the sere and yellow leaf. But the arrival of the three strangers at the shepherd's that night, and the details connected therewith, is a story as well known as ever in the country about Higher Crowstairs.

A PLACE IN THE SUN

Charles H. Russell

Des Gould brought him in. He'd tied the boy's shoulder up in his own bloody shirt, with as much care as his anger would allow, and slung him, unconscious, across Jade's withers. Then he had ridden straight back to the Sansoms' house.

'Mescaleros,' he shouted, first, to Fay Sansom, who happened to be on the stoop. 'Burnt the Kennedy place, Mrs Sansom. Got the boy here.'

His voice cracked like a twig in the heat. A tiny shadow danced on the dust at Jade's hooves, so small that Des could not have seen it without leaning out of the saddle. And of course he stayed upright under the weight of the sun.

He brought the boy inside, tenderly, like a father, and laid him where Fay Sansom said. From somewhere, the Sansoms' daughter, Leonora, appeared. Then he went outside, leaving behind the voices of the women, Mrs Sansom's orderliness, and the rushing of the Mexican girls. Des was drifting on the edge of middle age; he was old for a ranch hand. Nearly twenty years before he had ridden into Missouri on the first drive after the war, before the trails were opened up. He had developed a way of talking to himself, working around the corral, or sauntering off alone on a horse, to check fences or look for strays. But he said nothing now, staring out at the horizon, at the head of the porch steps.

'Des.'

He stopped on the second stair, and turned slowly, looking up at the man's face.

'Mr Sansom.'

'That Uncle Sam's boy you brought in?'

'Sir.'

'Well?'

Des looked slightly shocked at this directness. He said slowly: 'Your wife's a gentle lady, Mr Sansom. He'll see the dawn. Mescaleros on their place, I reckon. Half burnt to the ground. I looked around, Mr Sansom. I'd say Uncle Sam's in the burnt parts someplace. An' that greaser kid worked the place, he was lyin' in the sun, hole in his head. Boy was under a beam that fell.'

Des stood, fingering his flat-topped plainsman's hat, unconsciously rubbing the dust there into patterns. He was a lean man still: his hard body seemed a part with his taciturnity. He looked out now toward the yellow plain, crushed by sunlight, beyond the house and its owner.

'Okay, Des,' said Sansom, who was a heavy, troubled man. 'But don't ask me what Mescaleros are doing raiding, this far out. There isn't an Indian for a hundred miles. Now—'

'Those redskin bastards—'

'—And you don't need to tell me.' Sansom had hardly raised his voice, but stood his ground, in his discomfort. 'What about those Jarviss boys? What would they know about this?' When Des did not answer, but only stared, he said: 'We'll see what the boy says.'

Des was going down the steps again, and raising his battered hat. 'I'm going back to those fences,' he said, with a lean dignity.

'Okay.' It was a final, flickering word.

'Nobody but me seein' to the corral work so much now,' Des continued steadily, though his expression remained self effacing.

Sansom creased one eye.

'Thought I'd say.' Des clamped his ancient and beloved hat on his head, and took a shuffle towards his horse.

'Des.' Des stopped. 'I'll talk to the boy just as soon as he understands what it is he's saying.' Sansom was smiling with his eyes.

'Uncle Sam had some money laid by. So they say,' Des remarked flatly. 'Young Clay, there, now, could take off by himself. Could afford to.'

'Old enough to know his own mind.'

'*You* need a hand around the corral,' Des answered righteously, as if it had been Sansom's idea all along. Then he added: 'Could be he's best off with a quiet life.'

Sansom nodded slowly. 'Do what I can, Des.'

'Yes, sir.'

He stepped away unhurriedly, his back straight, without looking back or offering another word to Sansom. He picked up the dropped reins of his horse, who snuffed once, and stood waiting for him to mount, with a patient eye.

* * * *

It turned out, on the morning that James Sansom parked his heavy body next to the Kennedy boy's bed, that it wasn't Mescalero Apaches who had killed Uncle Sam.

'White men?' Sansom's slow face blossomed into alertness.

Clay Kennedy, lying in bed, gave a wry laugh.

'Black,' he said. 'Black masks. Every one of 'em. They could have been any colour. But not red.'

'Oh, God damn,' breathed Sansom, staring at the floor, as if it might suddenly turn soft, and his boots sink in. 'You know anything about this, boy?'

Clay wriggled slightly. 'I think Uncle Sam owed 'em something sir. I think they just came to collect.' Then he shrugged, and looked down at his own length, under the covers.

'Looks like you'd best stay here, son. Or run.' Sansom fell silent.

'Uncle Sam is dead and gone, Mr Sansom,' said Clay slowly. 'His ways weren't mine. I don't think they'll be back after me. Even if they knew I was alive. I don't think they're angry with me.'

Sansom brooded on this, until the boy startled him once more.

'Your wife's been real kind to me, Mr Sansom. And Leonora. And so've you too. It'd be a real pleasure to work for you, sir.'

'Ain't no debt you got to pay, son,' Sansom said, sharply. Then recovered his balance, or his good manners, and added: 'Not that any man with land and money needs to work for anyone.'

Clay Kennedy looked sidelong at the older man for some moments. 'I'll tell you the truth, Mr Sansom. There are things that you get tired of. That's why I'd like to stay. But only if there's a place for me, mind.' He stared away. 'Only thing Uncle Sam was interested in was a dollar. I don't know where he got it from. But I know I'm not poor now. Surely wasn't the farm. Cause if the thieves don't get you, the businessmen will. That land couldn't have paid another year. It's only small. An' you know what it's like. Fences everywhere. This ain't the same country I came to, only six, seven years ago. I *want* to sell up. It's too much for me to deal with.' He looked up at Sansom. 'Too much for me.'

'You go and see Henry, soon as Mrs Sansom says you're fit to start work, son,' James Sansom said finally, and kindly. 'Des went over to your place again, I shoulda said. We buried Uncle Sam, and the kid, I told you that. Des brought back your guns, saddles, what was left.' His mouth worked a little. 'Now you rest up, son. And meanwhile we'll keep an eye on Uncle Sam's place.'

Clay Kennedy smiled. 'Thank you, sir.'

'That's all right now.'

Sansom got himself upright, and lumbered out. If he remained troubled, it was not simply because he had realized that the Kennedy boy knew more than he was going to say. In this open, wind-plagued, sun-cursed country, too huge for the mind to grasp without bursting open into its endless spaces, he knew men would reach for the privilege of silence in order to maintain their right to sanity. So he respected Clay Kennedy's wish to say no more. But he fumbled, was confused, on the matter of justice. For he believed he knew who had killed Uncle Sam, and why; and yet he also wanted to believe that the whole business was over, just as Clay had said. With an uneasy fatalism, then, Sansom shrank from protecting the Kennedy boy in the easiest possible way—by offering to take over his farm. And at the same time he feared the consequences of his inaction. His eyes creased suddenly, as he stepped out into the natural power of the sunlight.

* * * *

Somewhere along the wire, Clay knew, he would come across Des, as he rode up the wire from the opposite direction. Probably they would meet where the Alcaso looped across the Sansom land, on its way to join the Hondo and the Pecos. Peacemaker sensed the water long before Clay; he found himself leaning back in the saddle, holding the horse to a sedate walk. But once in sight of the water, he let her gallop the last few furlongs. Avoiding the mineral-laden, alkaline river, they drank at a tiny spring nearby.

There was no point in going on to greet Des, since he too would probably be making thirstily for the same water. Turning away from the stream's chorus, Clay made for a cove of rocks, a few hundred yards from the fence. Some trees were growing in the semi-circle of rock, amid a patch of grass. He dropped Peacemaker's reins on the ground, and the horse began to munch. From the roll tied behind the saddle he pulled a crumpled hat. It was an ancient four-sided Montana peak that had somhow survived the raid at Uncle Sam's; it had been among the things Des had salvaged.

Clay stalked slowly towards the trees, feeling the ever-present wind on his whole body now that he was on foot. The arms of rock began to reach around him. In the corner of his eye he saw a single dead tree emerging into view amid a cluster of saplings. As if on impulse, he snatched up a small rock and hurled it as high as he could into the air. He stood tensed, his heart thumping, his right arm strained slightly from the throw, as he'd hoped. The stone clattered on the ground.

He was whirling, fingers desperate at the wooden butt, hauling the uncontrollable weight of the pistol from the scabbard, fumbling at the hammer, staring wildly at the foresight. Then the picture gelled, fell into place, in the second before the blast, when the hefty gun was weightless, riding up in his hand. This was always a blank moment. He came out of it hearing the echo of the shot crash about among the hillsides, as if recklessly seeking release from the walls of rock.

He dragged at the hammer again. This time it seemed that the gun slipped naturally into place, that the shock wave from the report flowed easily over him. Holstering the pistol, he dropped the old Montana hat squarely on a spiky bush nearby, and went to inspect the dead tree, some twenty paces away. The trunk was perhaps a foot in diameter; one shot had gone into it at chest height. The other had scraped the white dry wood, like a scar on a man's flank. Thoughtfully,

Clay turned back to look at the dumpy hat, stuck on its bush. He knew it was more than speed that counted. His pistol was, comparatively speaking, ancient: it had been a whimsical purchase of his late father, a .36 calibre Navy Colt from the early 1850s. For the light bullet to be at all effective, Clay had to shoot with extreme accuracy. Besides, its ball-and-cap ammunition was laborious to load, unlike the all-metal cartridges that newer, more powerful Colts took. For this reason too, every shot would have to count. He would have no time to spend in reloading. Clay recognized these facts abstractly, merely as something to be dealt with. In the same way he had realized that Jim Sansom was not going to take over the farm, and therefore, sooner or later, he would need to defend himself. It was no more than logical that he should practise with his weapons. It was more dignified than pleading with the man he now worked for. And why should he do that, when he was scarcely certain that he really wanted to sell?

The hat leapt off the bush. The echoes rambled madly, among the rocks. The hat skipped in the dust and the bullet screamed away into the hillside, lost among the stampeding echoes. Prudently, he left the last two rounds in the cylinder as he poked out the scorched paper cases, pressed in fresh ones, and renewed the percussion caps. He was suddenly aware of being quite alone, on the very edges of Sansom's land.

★ ★ ★ ★

To begin with they followed the river on their way towards town. Next day they would place orders for the ranch, and ride back along yet another section of the wire. But the sound of the water was soothing, for the moment, in the drum-hard sunlight. Des reined in suddenly, to lean and peer into the scarlet depths of a cactus flower. He would squint down his nose at anything, as long as it didn't speak. Except with Clay, he was pointedly shy; and Clay still felt like a stranger, when it came down to it. So they let each other be, though each could always say what he had to. Between themselves, they dissolved into the landscape. Without warning, Des said: 'Them girls at Betsy Stowe's, why, there ain't a decent girl in town.'

Clay smiled. 'I hear Miss Leonora's coming into town tomorrow.'

'And ridin' back again too.' Des spurred Jade gently. 'People out here ought to keep together. Build up links. Decent people.' Des spat.

'Decent people are the ones that get caught in the crossfire. Because decent folk always just mind their own business.'

'You talk a lot, don't you?'

'Des, where I come from, we say what we mean straight. Because we don't always reckon that the other man got somethin' to hide.'

Des was painfully silent. Only the creak of leather, the odd jingle of spurs, spoke against the chatter of water.

'Can't put no blame on a lifetime o' caution,' he finally said between bitter teeth. He shot a look at Clay, and sniffed. 'I been in this country a long time.' He poked suddenly at the horse. 'Bah, old man's thoughts. I don't know what's happenin' to this country. Used to be so wide, so high an' wild. Now it's closing in like a fist. People going crazy. State o' things done that. All this that people worked for, and they're leavin'. West, East, Texas, up to Wyoming some say, leavin' all they done behind. Or the ruin of it. Oh, we're lucky here. This is a quiet corner. And I spend my days mendin' fences, and keepin' animals in a cage. And I seen you and Leonora together. And then I thought o' them Jarvisses, and I don't know what to think.'

Clay listened to his own voice saying: 'You think the Jarvisses killed Uncle Sam, don't you?'

'God damn,' muttered Des. 'Yes, course I do. They need the water that end of their range. You know that. And that valley lets 'em straight out onto the trail in the springtime.'

'Then they're going to have to kill me. Aren't they?'

'Except that somebody put it about that you sold up to Mr Sansom.'

'Aw, hell, Des.'

'At least you're still alive. So far.'

'You know he won't buy? Won't even mention it.'

'And you won't sell anyway. But then Jarviss brothers don't know that.'

'I don't know. Something holds me there. Keeps me hangin' on to that land. Can't stay. Can't leave.' Clay stared at the landscape, which quivered in the heat. 'And another thing Des. Leonora is my friend, I guess. Just my friend. We both know there's a distance to keep. Lord knows what'll become of a girl like that. Country like this.'

The town was a pattern of black and blue when Des and Clay clattered down Roswell's street; a set of shadows flung jagged against the deepening enormity of sky. Amid the gloom hung occasional lights, like Chinese lanterns. Only when they were within a few yards of the sole saloon was it apparent that the citizenry were not entirely at home in their beds.

They rode past, to the livery stable. There, they left Jade and Peacemaker in the care of a melancholic Mexican, who said nothing, but nodded a great deal while keeping his eyes to one side.

The dust on the street seemed still hot, despite the evening cool. Clay's whole body was tired from being in the saddle all day: each part of it quietly pleaded for relief. As if light words would ease the burden, he said: 'Have some company this evening, any rate.'

'Never know who's there,' replied the ever-circumspect Des.

A brief curiosity spread through the dozen or so customers as they entered the saloon, like a mild breath of wind across a meadow.

'Mr Gould,' nodded the barman, a weathered-looking, muscular character called Sturgess. His eyes flicked lizard-like across Clay Kennedy. 'Young Clay.'

'Mr Sturgess.' Clay tipped his hat.

'Surprised you seen need to come into Roswell today. Beer, is it?'

'Thank you, Reuben.' Des's eyes were already searching the spotty mirror above the shelves of bottles and glasses. Clay turned gingerly to lean sideways against the bar. 'Folks is always what you might call neighbourly,' added Des philosophically, gazing straight into Sturgess's flat, pale eyes. 'Have one yourself?'

Clay had his back lodged against the bar now.

'Long as they don't crowd each other,' remarked Sturgess. 'Thank you, don't mind if I do. Folks do go bargin' in.' He slid the full glasses forward. 'Now make y'selves at home, boys.'

Clay glanced gratefully back at the impassive man behind the counter, among his glass and polished wood. Enough had been said for him to register only a deepening sense of that resignation, like a closing in of clouds, which had filled him since the farm had been burnt. So it seemed only reasonable to pick up his beer in his left hand this time.

'Fella at the stables say much?' asked Sturgess.

'Couldn't say he did,' said Clay over his shoulder.

'Talks to some, not to others.'

Des grunted. And Clay was not surprised when the doors soon swung open and three men ambled in. They came straight to the bar, looking and speaking to no one. But Clay told them off: Paul Jarviss, his bulky brother Puss, and their lean foreman, Reg Middlemass. Sturgess, wordlessly, poured them whisky, and left them the bottle. They drank quietly.

Then Puss was turning and smiling, or gloating.

'Heard about your Uncle Sam.' He raised his glass. 'There was no one like Uncle Sam.'

Clay nodded. He was aware that Des, beside him, was moving away to set his glass on a nearby table. It was merely prudence. 'Thank you, Mr Jarviss,' he said.

Paul, turning to stand a little in front of his brother, spoke up. 'Playin' at cowboys now, young fella.'

'Just riding the line.' He sounded fatuous to himself, a trailing voice.

'Not too far from home, though, eh? Not losin' no comforts. Hard life for a fella on the range.'

'Everyone has to start somewhere,' Reg Middlemass spoke kindly to him. 'Wrangler once, m'self.'

'This one's ridin' the line. Cowboy already. No wranglin' for him. Used to be a landowner, see,' smirked Paul Jarviss. 'Always adding a little to his spread, is Mr Sansom.'

Clay looked into their faces. Only Middlemass's sadness was not inscrutable.

'Cowboy got a new gun,' Paul enlarged the subject.

Clay found words again, and clutched at speech. 'No. It was my father's. Nearly thirty years old.'

Paul laughed loudly. 'So y' did *have* a father!'

'Lord save us,' said Middlemass under his breath. 'This is just talk, you know, son.'

Clay nodded. He was watching Puss Jarviss.

'Show us y'gun, boy,' Paul chirped on. 'Old anti-kew gun, eh? Show y' mine. New Colt, forty-four. Show us y' gun.'

'Just one thing,' Clay's lips worked. 'So it's all clear, and it's been said, and it's in the open. You ought to know. Uncle Sam's place is

They came straight to the bar, looking and speaking to no one.

still mine.' He was sliding into the vortex now. But there had never been any way out of this. 'You ought to know that.' He felt out of breath.

'Oh, I wouldn't know nothin' about that, Clay,' soothed Paul. 'Though I figure you won't want to be keepin' the place on, now, will you? Not with the wages I hear old Sansom's payin' you.' He grinned. 'I hear he don't pay you no money, though. I hear he just lets you have that Leonora of his.'

So that's when it happened, it was almost easy, really. Paul was unimportant. It was Puss who was ready to pounce. He looked more distracted than hurt, lurching back with blood welling from his shattered breastbone, his shiny new Colt still only half-drawn. Perhaps it clattered among the table legs as he buckled to the floor, but Clay could hardly hear.

Whereas Paul Jarviss was plunging forward. And into the stench of gunsmoke, and the sound of his own screams. Jarviss's head was streaming from Sturgess's shotgun blast. Flung sideways, he hit Des's table, and disappeared in broken wood.

'No, no. No, no.' Reg Middlemass had one hand flung out, trembling, warding off Des's pistol and the other barrel of Sturgess's pointed gun. Not to mention the staring eyes of Clay Kennedy. The voice was faint amid the singing in his ears from the explosions: or from encroaching nausea.

'Get 'em out, Reg,' said Des coldly.

'Oh, sweet Mary,' moaned Reg Middlemass.

'Just clear it up,' suggested Reuben Sturgess. 'It's best you should take care o' this, Reg. I figure it wasn't your quarrel. It's your whisky in that bottle. You'll be back on your place by dawn.'

Clay slid his gun away, still staring at the bodies. Already the townsfolk were coming forward to see for themselves. A substantial citizen pushed in front of him to get a closer look.

'Evenin', Mr Davison,' Des greeted him briskly. 'List o' goods for you here.' He shoved a creased paper into the unresisting hand of the amazed spectator. 'Mr Sansom's orders. You'll be sendin' 'em out same as usual. Woulda stopped by in the morning for some things for myself. But me and the boy's most likely leavin' tonight.' He glanced at Sturgess. 'Guess you know what happened here as well as anybody, Reuben.'

Sturgess nodded. 'It'll be told right. You go along now, son,' he added, to Clay.

*   *   *   *

He was exhausted. But his aching body was bliss compared with Sansom's voice, Des's complaining, and the vision, constantly returning, of Puss Jarviss's blood spreading from the hole Clay himself had made.

Sansom lumbering about the parlour and shouting: 'God damn it all boy, there'll be a war. Already there's been Dolan and Murphy and that Chisum crowd murdering all over the county. And God knows what else besides. Regulators everywhere. Let alone the Indians. Now this. Don't you know I've got men out riding the line, just doing their job, who they'll be shooting down. Middlemass may be a gelded idiot. But there's still old man Jarviss and that trash he keeps in liquor and horses. I've kept this place going in the face of every damned desperado the devil made and now you bring it home to me. And nothing for law but that prim Governor with his nose in a book. And nice as you please, you're riding out. Not even clearing up your own filth!'

And as Sansom stood with his back to the light, breathing hard, Des's voice was murmuring out of the criss-cross and sun and shadow in the big room: 'You can't leave. You can't leave now. Out here we stick together. Ain't worth a piss in a boot if y' don't. God knows what's coming out of this business but we got to see it through. People's lives here to think of. Lifetimes spent on the land here. That's what we all stand for. It's a way of life. Only goddamn way. I helped build this country up. Uncle Sam was a friend of mine. We done a lot together, we shared the same strife. Now you're giving all that away.'

And Clay was turning between them, hardly able to speak, though the bewildered words heaved themselves out. 'Then why didn't you take the farm? How could I do anything but tell the truth? Didn't you hear what they said about Leonora, Mr Sansom? What's going to happen to her while you carry on trying to mind your own business? Or while Des is trying to defend you all? What are you leaving for her when you go? Do nothing, while they kill Uncle Sam. God knows, he hardly understood right from wrong or what the law meant, but you've let it all go on so long it's going to suck you down with it. But you just let 'em know. You tell them when they come that I wasn't defending *you*. I wasn't being good-neighbourly. It was either them or me. And they can come and get me if they want. But not here. I'm leaving here. Going.'

'And where the hell to?' Sansom snarled.

'The law ain't going to touch you,' suggested Des. 'Or wouldn't, if there was any.'

'Out in the fresh air. That's where. Till I'm let alone. To fight my own fights.'

'I call that running away, boy,' Sansom warned.

'Well, I call it freedom.'

He turned on his heel. His saddlebags were already filled. He fetched Peacemaker, and loaded the quiet horse. He was aware that neither Leonora nor Fay Sansom were anywhere to be seen. But what use were token words? He had no ready explanations. He slung on a cartridge belt, checked the Winchester again, and gave a last few tugs at the cinch. Then he swung himself into the saddle. He trotted out into the afternoon sun, leaving a dancing shadow behind him, and headed south, to where clouds were gathering on the horizon.

By dusk he was riding just below the crest of a ridge, watching the trail a hundred and fifty feet below him. The occasional flash of lightning ahead was like an illusion, or a momentary fracture in existence. Behind him the wind was beginning to provoke. Peacemaker snorted, tossed her head. There was a noise that sounded like a wild cat. Some other rhythm was intruding, besides the gathering wind.

He reined in to listen. Then, shifting the horse around, he could just make them out: perhaps a mile behind, two riders were approaching, their hoofbeats sounding dully through the earth. He eased Peacemaker down a few feet to an outcrop of rocks, and slipped from the saddle. He nestled among the boulders, making himself comfortable with the Winchester. He jacked a round into the chamber. His patience might have been endless. The wind began to howl.

BEWARE OF THE DOG

Roald Dahl

In wartime, an escape often marks not the end but the beginning of an adventure —particularly for a fighter pilot whose mission takes him over German-occupied Europe. . . .

Down below there was only a vast white undulating sea of cloud. Above there was the sun, and the sun was white like the clouds, because it is never yellow when one looks at it from high in the air.

He was still flying the Spitfire. His right hand was on the stick and he was working the rudder-bar with his left leg alone. It was quite easy. The machine was flying well. He knew what he was doing.

Everything is fine, he thought. I'm doing all right. I'm doing nicely. I know my way home. I'll be there in half an hour. When I land I shall taxi in and switch off my engine and I shall say, help me to get out, will you. I shall make my voice sound ordinary and natural and none of them will take any notice. Then I shall say, someone help me to get out. I can't do it alone because I've lost one of my legs. They'll all laugh and think that I'm joking and I shall say, all right, come and have a look, you unbelieving bastards. Then Yorky will climb up onto the wing and look inside. He'll probably be sick because of all the blood and the mess. I shall laugh and say, for God's sake, help me get out.

He glanced down again at his right leg. There was not much of it left. The cannon-shell had taken him on the thigh, just above the knee, and now there was nothing but a great mess and a lot of blood. But there was no pain. When he looked down, he felt as though he were seeing something that did not belong to him. It had nothing to do with him. It was just a mess which happened to be there in the cockpit; something strange and unusual and rather interesting. It was like finding a dead cat on the sofa.

He really felt fine, and because he still felt fine, he felt excited and unafraid.

I won't even bother to call up on the radio for the blood-wagon, he thought. It isn't necessary. And when I land I'll sit there quite normally and say, some of you fellows come and help me out, will you, because I've lost one of my legs. That will be funny. I'll laugh a little while I'm saying it; I'll say it calmly and slowly, and they'll think I'm joking. When Yorky comes up onto the wing and gets sick, I'll say, Yorky you old son of a bitch, have you fixed my car yet. Then when I get out I'll make my report. Later I'll go up to London. I'll take that half bottle of whisky with me and I'll give it to Bluey. We'll sit in her room and drink it. I'll get the water out of the bathroom tap. I won't say much until it's time to go to bed, then I'll say, Bluey I've got a surprise for you. I lost a leg today. But I don't mind so long as you don't. It doesn't even hurt. We'll go everywhere in cars. I always hated walking except when I walked down the street of the coppersmiths in Baghdad, but I could go in a rickshaw. I could go home and chop wood, but the head always flies off the axe. Hot water, that's what it needs; put it in the bath and make the handle swell. I chopped lots of wood last time I went home and I put the axe in the bath. . . .

Then he saw the sun shining on the engine cowling of his machine. He saw the sun shining on the rivets in the metal, and he remembered the aeroplane and he remembered where he was. He realized that he was no longer feeling good; that he was sick and giddy. His head kept falling forward onto his chest because his neck seemed no longer to have any strength. But he knew that he was flying the Spitfire. He could feel the handle of the stick between the fingers of his right hand.

I'm going to pass out, he thought. Any moment now I'm going to pass out.

He looked at his altimeter. Twenty-one thousand. To test himself he tried to read the hundreds as well as the thousands. Twenty-one thousand

and what? As he looked the dial became blurred and he could not even see the needle. He knew then that he must bale out; that there was not a second to lose, otherwise he would become unconscious. Quickly, frantically, he tried to slide back the hood with his left hand, but he had not the strength. For a second he took his right hand off the stick and with both hands he managed to push the hood back. The rush of cold air on his face seemed to help. He had a moment of great clearness. His actions became orderly and precise. That is what happens with a good pilot. He took some quick deep breaths from his oxygen mask, and as he did so, he looked out over the side of the cockpit. Down below there was only a vast white sea of cloud and he realized that he did not know where he was.

It'll be the Channel, he thought. I'm sure to fall in the drink.

He throttled back, pulled off his helmet, undid his straps and pushed the stick hard over to the left. The Spitfire dipped its port wing and turned smoothly over onto its back. The pilot fell out.

As he fell, he opened his eyes, because he knew that he must not pass out before he had pulled the cord. On one side he saw the sun; on the other he saw the whiteness of the clouds, and as he fell, as he somersaulted in the air, the white clouds chased the sun and the sun chased the clouds. They chased each other in a small circle; they ran faster and faster and there was the sun and the clouds and the clouds and the sun, and the clouds came nearer until suddenly there was no longer any sun but only a great whiteness. The whole world was white and there was nothing in it. It was so white that sometimes it looked black, and after a time it was either white or black, but mostly it was white. He watched it as it turned from white to black, then back to white again, and the white stayed for a long time, but the black lasted only for a few seconds. He got into the habit of going to sleep during the white periods, of waking up just in time to see the world when it was black. The black was very quick. Sometimes it was only a flash, a flash of black lightning. The white was slow and in the slowness of it, he always dozed off.

One day, when it was white, he put out a hand and he touched something. He took it between his fingers and crumpled it. For a time he lay there, idly letting the tips of his fingers play with the thing which they had touched. Then slowly he opened his eyes, looked down at his hand and saw that he was holding something which was white. It was the edge of a sheet. He knew it was a sheet because he could see the texture of the material and the stitchings on the hem. He screwed up his eyes and opened them again quickly. This time he saw the room. He saw the bed in which he was lying: he saw the grey walls and the door and the green curtains over the window. There were some roses on the table by his bed.

Then he saw the basin on the table near the roses. It was a white enamel basin and beside it there was a small medicine glass.

This is a hospital, he thought. I am in a hospital. But he could remember nothing. He lay back on his pillow, looking at the ceiling and wondering what had happened. He was gazing at the smooth greyness of the ceiling which was so clean and grey, and then suddenly he saw a fly walking upon it. The sight of this fly, the suddenness of seeing this amall black speck on a sea of grey, brushed the surface of his brain, and quickly, in that second, he remembered everything. He remembered the Spitfire and he remembered the altimeter showing twenty-one thousand feet. He remembered the pushing back of the hood with both hands and he remembered the baling out. He remembered his leg.

It seemed all right now. He looked down at the end of the bed, but he could not tell. He put one hand underneath the bedclothes and felt for his knees. He found one of them, but when he felt for the other, his hand touched something which was soft and covered in bandages.

Just then the door opened and a nurse came in.

'Hello,' she said. 'So you've waked up at last.'

She was not good-looking, but she was large and clean. She was between thirty and forty and she had fair hair. More than that he did not notice.

'Where am I?'

'You're a lucky fellow. You landed in a wood near the beach. You're in Brighton. They brought you in two days ago, and now you're all fixed up. You look fine.'

'I've lost a leg,' he said.

'That's nothing. We'll get you another one. Now you must go to sleep. The doctor will be coming to see you in about an hour.' She picked up the basin and the medicine glass and went out.

Just then the door opened and a nurse came in.

But he did not sleep. He wanted to keep his eyes open because he was frightened that if he shut them again everything would go away. He lay looking at the ceiling. The fly was still there. It was very energetic. It would run forward very fast for a few inches, then it would stop. Then it would run forward again, stop, run forward, and every now and then it would take off and buzz around viciously in small circles. It always landed back in the same place on the ceiling and started running and stopping all over again. He watched it for so long that after a while it was no longer a fly, but only a black speck upon a sea of grey, and he was still watching it when the nurse opened the door, and stood aside while the doctor came in. He was an Army doctor, a major, and he had some last war ribbons on his chest. He was bald and small, but he had a cheerful face and kind eyes.

'Well, well,' he said. 'So you've decided to wake up at last. How are you feeling?'

'I feel all right.'

'That's the stuff. You'll be up and about in no time.'

The doctor took his wrist to feel his pulse.

'By the way,' he said, 'some of the lads from your squadron were ringing up and asking about you. They wanted to come along and see you, but I said that they'd better wait a day or two. Told them you were all right and that they could come and see you a little later on. Just lie quiet and take it easy for a bit. Got something to read?' He glanced at the table with the roses. 'No. Well, nurse will look after you. She'll get you anything you want.' With that he waved his hand and went out, followed by the large clean nurse.

When they had gone, he lay back and looked at the ceiling again. The fly was still there and as he lay watching it he heard the noise of an aeroplane in the distance. He lay listening to the sound of its engines. It was a long way away. I wonder what it is, he thought. Let me see if I can place it. Suddenly he jerked his head sharply to one side. Anyone who has been bombed can tell the noise of a Junkers 88. They can tell most other German bombers for that matter, but especially a Junkers 88. The engines seem to sing a duet. There is a deep vibrating bass voice and with it there is a high pitched tenor. It is the singing of the tenor which makes the sound of a Ju-88 something which one cannot mistake.

He lay listening to the noise and he felt quite certain about what it was. But where were the sirens and where the guns? That German pilot certainly had a nerve coming near Brighton alone in daylight.

The aircraft was always far away and soon the noise faded away in the distance. Later on there was another. This one, too, was far away, but there was the same deep undulating bass and the high swinging tenor and there was no mistaking it. He had heard that noise every day during the Battle.

He was puzzled. There was a bell on the table by the bed. He reached out his hand and rang it. He heard the noise of footsteps down the corridor. The nurse came in.

'Nurse, what were those aeroplanes?'

'I'm sure I don't know. I didn't hear them. Probably fighters or bombers. I expect they were returning from France. Why, what's the matter?'

'They were Ju-88s. I'm sure they were Ju-88s. I know the sound of the engines. There were two of them. What were they doing over here?'

The nurse came up to the side of his bed and began to straighten out the sheets and tuck them in under the mattress.

'Gracious me, what things you imagine. You mustn't worry about a thing like that. Would you like me to get you something to read?'

'No, thank you.'

She patted his pillow and brushed back the hair from his forehead with her hand.

'They never come over in daylight any longer. You know that. They were probably Lancasters or Flying Fortresses.'

'Nurse.'

'Yes.'

'Could I have a cigarette?'

'Why certainly you can.'

She went out and came back almost at once with a packet of Players and some matches. She handed one to him and when he had put it in his mouth, she struck a match and lit it.

'If you want me again,' she said, 'just ring the bell,' and she went out.

Once towards evening he heard the noise of another aircraft. It was far away, but even so he knew that it was a single-engined machine. It was going fast; he could tell that. He could not place it. It wasn't a Spit, and it wasn't a Hurricane. It did not sound like an American engine either. They make more noise. He did not know what it was, and it worried him greatly. Perhaps I am very ill, he thought. Perhaps I am imagining things. Perhaps I am a little delirious. I simply do not know what to think.

That evening the nurse came in with a basin of hot water and began to wash him.

'Well,' she said, 'I hope you don't think that we're being bombed.'

She had taken off his pyjama top and was soaping his right arm with a flannel. He did not answer.

She rinsed the flannel in the water, rubbed more soap on it, and began to wash his chest.

'You're looking fine this evening,' she said. 'They operated on you as soon as you came in. They did a marvellous job. You'll be all right. I've got a brother in the RAF,' she added. 'Flying bombers.'

He said, 'I went to school in Brighton.'

She looked up quickly. 'Well, that's fine,' she said. 'I expect you'll know some people in the town.'

'Yes,' he said. 'I know quite a few.'

She had finished washing his chest and arms. Now she turned back the bedclothes so that his left leg was uncovered. She did it in such a way that his bandaged stump remained under the sheets. She undid the cord of his pyjama trousers and took them off. There was no trouble because they had cut off the right trouser leg so that it could not interfere with the bandages. She began to wash his left leg and the rest of his body. This was the first time he had had a bed-bath and he was embarrassed. She laid a towel under his leg and began washing his foot with the flannel. She said, 'This wretched soap won't lather at all. It's the water. It's as hard as nails.'

He said, 'None of the soap is very good now and, of course, with hard water it's hopeless.' As he said it he remembered something. He remembered the baths which he used to take at school in Brighton, in the long stone-floored bathroom which had four baths in a row. He remembered how the water was so soft that you had to take a shower afterwards to get all the soap off your body, and he remembered how the foam used to float on the surface of the water, so that you could not see your legs underneath. He remembered that sometimes they were given calcium tablets because the school doctor used to say that soft water was bad for the teeth.

'In Brighton,' he said, 'the water isn't . . .'

He did not finish the sentence. Something had occurred to him; something so fantastic and absurd that for a moment he felt like telling the nurse about it and having a good laugh.

She looked up. 'The water isn't what?' she said.

'Nothing,' he answered, 'I was dreaming.'

She rinsed the flannel in the basin, wiped the soap off his leg and dried him with a towel.

'It's nice to be washed,' he said. 'I feel better.' He was feeling his face with his hand. 'I need a shave.'

'We'll do that tomorrow,' she said. 'Perhaps you can do it yourself then.'

That night he could not sleep. He lay awake thinking of the Junkers 88s and of the hardness of the water. He could think of nothing else. They were Ju-88s, he said to himself. I know they were. And yet it is not possible, because they would not be flying around so low over here in broad daylight. I know that it is true and yet I know that it is impossible. Perhaps I am ill. Perhaps I am behaving like a fool and do not know what I am doing or saying. Perhaps I am delirious. For a long time he lay awake thinking these things, and once he sat up in bed and said aloud, 'I will prove that I am not crazy. I will make a little speech about something complicated and intellectual. I will talk about what to do with Germany after the war.' But before he had time to begin, he was asleep.

He woke just as the first light of day was showing through the slit in the curtains over the window. The room was still dark, but he could tell that it was already beginning to get light outside. He lay looking at the grey light which was showing through the slit in the curtain and as he lay there he remembered the day before. He remembered the Junkers 88s and the hardness of the water; he remembered the large pleasant nurse and the kind doctor, and now a small grain of doubt took root in his mind and it began to grow.

He looked around the room. The nurse had taken the roses out the night before. There was nothing except the table with a packet of cigarettes, a box of matches and an ashtray. The room was bare. It was no longer warm or friendly. It was not even comfortable. It was cold and empty and very quiet.

Slowly the grain of doubt grew, and with it came fear, a light, dancing fear that warned but did not frighten; the kind of fear that one gets not because one is afraid, but because one feels that there is something wrong. Quickly the doubt and the fear grew so that he became restless and angry, and when he touched his forehead with his hand, he found that it was damp with sweat. He knew then that he must do something; that he must find some way of proving to himself that he was either right or wrong, and he looked up and saw again the window and the green curtains. From where he lay, that window was right in front of him, but it was fully ten yards away. Somehow he must reach it and look out. The idea became an obsession with him and soon he could think of nothing except the window. But what about his leg? He put his hand underneath the bedclothes and felt the thick bandaged stump which was all that was left on the right hand side. It seemed all right. It didn't hurt. But it would not be easy.

He sat up. Then he pushed the bedclothes aside and put his left leg on the floor. Slowly, carefully, he swung his body over until he had both hands on the floor as well; then he was out of bed, kneeling on the carpet. He looked at the stump. It was very short and thick, covered with bandages. It was beginning to hurt and he could feel it throbbing. He wanted to collapse, lie down on the carpet and do nothing, but he knew that he must go on.

With two arms and one leg, he crawled over towards the window. He would reach forward as far as he could with his arms, then he could give a little jump and slide his left leg along after them. Each time he did it, it jarred his wound so that he gave a soft grunt of pain, but he continued to crawl across the floor on two hands and one knee. When he got to the window he reached up, and one at a time he placed both hands on the sill. Slowly he raised himself up until he was standing on his left leg. Then quickly he pushed aside the curtains and looked out.

He saw a small house with a grey tiled roof standing alone beside a narrow lane, and immediately behind it there was a ploughed field. In front of the house there was an untidy garden, and there was a green hedge separating the garden from the lane. He was looking at the hedge when he saw the sign. It was just a piece of board nailed to the top of a short pole, and because the hedge had not been trimmed for a long time, the branches had grown out around the sign so that it seemed almost as though it had been placed in the middle of the hedge. There was something written on the board with white paint. He pressed his head against the glass of the window, trying to read what it said. The first letter was a G, he could see that. The second was an A, and the third was an R. One after another he managed to see what the letters were. There were three words, and slowly he spelled the letters out aloud to himself as he managed to read them. G-A-R-D-E A-U-C-H-I-E-N, *Garde au chien*. That is what it said.

He stood there balancing on one leg and holding tightly to the edges of the window sill with his hands, staring at the sign and at the white-washed lettering of the words. For a moment he could think of nothing at all. He stood there looking at the sign, repeating the words over and over to himself. Slowly he began to realize the full meaning of the thing. He looked up at the cottage and at the ploughed field. He looked at the small orchard on the left of the cottage and he looked at the green countryside beyond. 'So this is France,' he said. 'I am in France.'

Now the throbbing in his right thigh was very great. It felt as though someone was pounding the end of his stump with a hammer and suddenly the pain became so intense that it affected his head. For a moment he thought he was going to fall. Quickly he knelt down again, crawled back to the bed and hoisted himself in. He pulled the bedclothes over himself and lay back on the pillow, exhausted. He could still think of nothing at all except the small sign by the hedge and the ploughed field and the orchard. It was the words on the sign that he could not forget.

* * * *

It was some time before the nurse came in. She came carrying a basin of hot water and she said, 'Good morning, how are you today?'

He said, 'Good morning, nurse.'

The pain was still under the bandages, but he did not wish to tell this woman anything. He looked at her as she busied herself with getting the washing things ready. He looked at her more carefully now. Her hair was very fair. She was tall and big-boned and her face seemed pleasant. But there was something a little uneasy about her eyes. They were never still. They never looked at anything for more than a moment and they moved too quickly from one place to another in the room. There was something about her movements also. They were too sharp and nervous to go well with the casual manner in which she spoke.

She set down the basin, took off his pyjama top and began to wash him.

'Did you sleep well?'

'Yes.'

'Good,' she said. She was washing his arms and his chest.

'I believe there's someone coming down to see you from the Air Ministry after breakfast,' she went on. 'They want a report or something. I expect you know all about it. How you got shot down and all that. I won't let him stay long, so don't worry.'

He did not answer. She finished washing him and gave him a toothbrush and some toothpowder. He brushed his teeth, rinsed his mouth and spat the water out into the basin.

Later she brought him his breakfast on a tray, but he did not want to eat. He was still feeling weak and sick and he wished only to lie still and think about what had happened. And there was a sentence running through his head. It was a sentence which Johnny, the Intelligence Officer of his squadron, always repeated to the pilots every day before they went out. He could see Johnny now, leaning against the wall of the dispersal hut with his pipe in his hand, saying, 'And if they get you, don't forget, just your name, rank and number. Nothing else. For God's sake, say nothing else.'

'There you are,' she said as she put the tray on his lap. 'I've got you an egg. Can you manage all right?'

'Yes.'

She stood beside the bed. 'Are you feeling all right?'

'Yes.'

'Good. If you want another egg I might be able to get you one.'

'This is all right.'

'Well, just ring the bell if you want any more.' And she went out.

He had just finished eating, when the nurse came in again.

She said, 'Wing Commander Roberts is here. I've told him that he can only stay for a few minutes.'

She beckoned with her hand and the Wing Commander came in.

'Sorry to bother you like this,' he said.

He was an ordinary RAF officer, dressed in a uniform which was a little shabby. He wore wings and a DFC. He was fairly tall and thin with plenty of black hair. His teeth, which were irregular and widely spaced, stuck out a little even when he closed his mouth. As he spoke he took a printed form and a pencil from his pocket and he pulled up a chair and sat down.

'How are you feeling?'

There was no answer.

'Tough luck about your leg. I know how you feel. I hear you put up a fine show before they got you.'

The man in the bed was lying quite still, watching the man in the chair.

The man in the chair said, 'Well, let's get this stuff over. I'm afraid you'll have to answer a few questions so that I can fill in this combat report. Let me see now, first of all, what was your squadron?'

The man in the bed did not move. He looked straight at the Wing Commander and he said, 'My name is Peter Williamson, My rank is Squadron Leader and my number is nine seven two four five seven.'

THE BELL

William Maginn

In my younger days bell ringing was much more in fashion among the young men of —— than it is now. Nobody, I believe, practises it there at present except the servants of the church, and the melody has been much injured in consequence. Some fifty years ago, about twenty of us who dwelt in the vicinity of the cathedral formed a club, which used to ring every peal that was called for; and, from continual practice and a rivalry which arose between us and a club attached to another steeple, and which tended considerably to sharpen our zeal, we became very Mozarts on our favourite instruments. But my bell-ringing practice was shortened by a singular accident, which not only stopped my performance, but made even the sound of a bell terrible to my ears.

One Sunday I went with another into the belfry to ring for noon prayers, but the second stroke we had pulled showed us that the clapper of the bell we were at was muffled. Someone had been buried that morning, and it had been prepared, of course, to ring a mournful note. We did not know this, but the remedy was easy. 'Jack,' said one of my companion, 'step up to the loft, and cut off the hat,' for the way we had of muffling was by tying a piece of old hat, or of cloth (the former was preferred) to one side of the clapper, which deadened every second toll. I complied and, mounting into the belfry, crept as usual into the bell, where I began to cut away. The hat had been tied on in some more complicated manner than usual, and I was perhaps three or four minutes in getting it off; during which time my companion below was hastily called away, by a message from his sweetheart, I believe; but that is not material to my story. The person who called him was a brother of the club, who, knowing that the time had come for ringing for service, and not thinking that anyone was above, began to pull. At this moment I was just getting out, when I felt the bell moving; I guessed the reason at once—it was a moment of terror; but by a hasty, and almost convulsive, effort I succeeded in jumping down, and throwing myself on the flat of my back under the bell.

The room in which it was, was little more than sufficient to contain it, the bottom of the bell coming within a couple of feet of the floor of lath. At that time I certainly was not so bulky as I am now, but as I lay it was within an inch of my face. I had not laid myself down a second when the ringing began. It was a dreadful situation. Over me swung an immense mass of metal, one touch of which would have crushed me to pieces; the floor under me was principally composed of crazy laths; and if they gave way, I was precipitated to the distance of about fifty feet upon a loft, which would, in all probability, have sunk under the impulse of my fall, and sent me to be dashed to atoms upon the marble floor of the chancel, a hundred feet below. I remembered, for fear is quick in recollection, how a common clockwright, about a month before, had fallen and, bursting through the floors of the steeple, driven in the ceilings of the porch, and even broken into the marble tombstone of a bishop who slept beneath. This was my first terror, but the ringing had not continued a minute before a more awful and immediate dread came on me. The deafening sound of the bell smote into my ears with a thunder which made me fear their drums would crack. There was not a fibre of my body it did not thrill through: it entered my very soul; thought and reflection were almost utterly banished; I only retained the sensation of agonizing terror. Every moment I saw the bell sweep within an inch of my face; and my eyes—I could not close them, though to look at the object was bitter as death—followed it instinctively in its oscillating progress

I had not laid myself down a second when the ringing began.

until it came back again. It was in vain I said to myself that it could come no nearer at any future swing than it did at first; every time it descended, I endeavoured to shrink into the very floor to avoid being buried under the down-sweeping mass; and then, reflecting on the danger of pressing too weightily on my frail support, would cower up again as far as I dared.

At first my fears were mere matter of fact. I was afraid the pulleys above would give way, and let the bell plunge on me. At another time, the possibility of the clapper being shot out in some sweep, and dashing through my body, as I had seen a ramrod glide through a door, flitted across my mind. The dread also, as I have already mentioned, of the crazy floor tormented me; but these soon gave way to fears not more unfounded, but more visionary, and of course more tremendous. The roaring of the bell confused my intellect, and my fancy soon began to teem with all sorts of strange and terrifying ideas. The bell pealing above, and opening its jaws with a hideous clamour, seemed to me at one time a ravening monster, raging to devour me; at another, a whirlpool ready to suck me into its bellowing abyss. As I gazed on it, it assumed all shapes; it was a flying eagle, or rather a roc of the Arabian story-tellers, clapping its wings and screaming over me. As I looked upward into it, it would appear sometimes to lengthen into indefinite extent, or to be twisted at the end into the spiral folds of the tail of a flying dragon. Nor was the flaming breath or fiery glance of that fabled animal wanting to complete the picture. My eyes, inflamed, bloodshot, and glaring, invested the supposed monster with a full proportion of unholy light.

It would be endless were I to merely hint at all the fancies that possessed my mind. Every object that was hideous and roaring presented itself to my imagination. I often thought that I was in a hurricane at sea, and that the vessel in which I was embarked tossed under me with the most furious vehemence. The air, set in motion by the swinging of the bell, blew over me nearly with the violence and more than the thunder of a tempest; and the floor seemed to reel under me as under a drunken man. But the most awful of all the ideas that seized on me were drawn from the supernatural. In the vast cavern of the bell hideous faces appeared, and glared down on me with terrifying frowns, or with grinning mockery, still more appalling. At last the

Devil himself, accoutered, as in the common description of the evil spirits, with hoof, horn, and tail, and eyes of infernal luster, made his appearance, and called on me to curse God and worship him, who was powerful to save me. This dread suggestion he uttered with the full-toned clangour of the bell. I had him within an inch of me, and I thought on the fate of the Santon Barsisa. Strenuously and desperately I defied him, and bade him be gone. Reason, then, for a moment resumed her sway, but it was only to fill me with fresh terror, just as the lightning dispels the gloom that surrounds the benighted mariner, but to show him that his vessel is driving on a rock, where she must inevitably be dashed to pieces. I found I was becoming delirious, and trembled lest reason should utterly desert me. This is at all times an agonizing thought, but it smote me then with tenfold agony. I feared lest, when utterly deprived of my senses, I should rise; to do which I was every moment tempted by that strange feeling which calls on a man, whose head is dizzy from standing on the battlement of a lofty castle, to precipitate himself from it; and then death would be instant and tremendous. When I thought of this I became desperate;—I caught the floor with a grasp which drove the blood from my nails; and I yelled with the cry of despair. I called for help, I prayed, I shouted: but all the efforts of my voice were, of course, drowned in the bell. As it passed over my mouth, it occasionally echoed my cries, which mixed not with its own sound, but preserved their distinct character. Perhaps this was but fancy. To me, I know, they then sounded as if they were the shouting, howling, or laughing of the fiends with which my imagination had peopled the gloomy cave which swung over me.

You may accuse me of exaggerating my feelings; but I am not. Many a scene of dread have I passed through, but they are nothing to the self-inflicted terrors of this half-hour. The ancients have doomed one of the damned, in their Tartarus, to lie under a rock which every moment seems to be descending to annihilate him; and an awful punishment it would be. But if to this you add a clamour as loud as if ten thousand Furies were hovering about you, a deafening uproar banishing reason and driving you to madness, you must allow that the bitterness of the pang was rendered more terrible. There is no man, firm as his nerves may be, who could retain his courage in this situation.

In twenty minutes the ringing was done. Half of that time passed over me without power of computation, the other half appeared an age. When it ceased, I became gradually more quiet; but a new fear retained me. I knew that five minutes would elapse without ringing; but at the end of that short time the bell would be rung a second time for five minutes more. I could not calculate time. A minute and an hour were of equal duration. I feared to rise, lest the five minutes should have elapsed, and the ringing be again commenced; in which case I should be crushed, before I could escape, against the walls or framework of the bell. I therefore still continued to lie down, cautiously shifting myself, however, with a careful gliding, so that my eye no longer looked into the hollow. This was of itself a considerable relief. The cessation of the noise had, in a great measure, the effect of stupefying me, for my attention, being no longer occupied by the chimeras I had conjured up, began to flag. All that now distressed me was the constant expectation of the second ringing, for which, however, I settled myself with a kind of stupid resolution. I closed my eyes, and clenched my teeth as firmly as if they were screwed in a vice. At last the dreaded moment came, and the first swing of the bell extorted a groan from me, as they say the most resolute victim screams at the sight of the rack, to which he is for a second time destined. After this, however, I lay silent and lethargic, without a thought. Wrapt in the defensive armour of stupidity, I defied the bell and its intonations. When it ceased, I was roused a little by the hope of escape. I did not, however, decide on this step hastily; but, putting up my hand with the utmost caution, I touched the rim. Though the ringing had ceased, it still was tremulous from the sound, and shook under my hand, which instantly recoiled as from an electric jar. A quarter of an hour probably elapsed as from an electric jar. A quarter of an hour probably elapsed before I again dared to make the experiment, and then I found it at rest. I determined to lose no time, fearing that I might have lain then already too long, and that the bell for evening service would catch me. This dread stimulated me, and I slipped out with the utmost rapidity, and arose. I stood, I suppose, for a minute, looking with silly wonder on the place of my imprisonment, penetrated with joy at escaping, but then rushed down the stony and irregular stair with the velocity of lightning, and arrived in the bell ringer's room. This was the last act I had power to accomplish. I leant against the wall, motionless and deprived of thought, in which posture my companions found me when, in the course of a couple of hours, they returned to their occupation.

They were shocked, as well they might be, at the figure before them. The wind of the bell had excoriated my face, and my dim and stupefied eyes were fixed with a lackluster gaze in my raw eyelids. My hands were torn and bleeding, my hair dishevelled, and my clothes tattered. They spoke to me, but I gave no answer. They shook me, but I remained insensible. They then became alarmed, and hastened to remove me. He who had first gone up with me in the forenoon met them as they carried me through the churchyard, and through him, who was shocked at having, in some measure, occasioned the accident, the cause of my misfortune was discovered. I was put to bed at home, and remained for three days delirious, but gradually recovered my senses. You may be sure the bell formed a prominent topic of my ravings; and, if I heard a peal, they were instantly increased to the utmost violence. Even when the delirium abated, my sleep was continually disturbed by imagined ringings, and my dreams were haunted by the fancies which almost maddened me while in the steeple. My friends removed me to a house in the country, which was sufficiently distant from any place of worship to save me from the apprehensions of hearing the church-going bell; for what Alexander Selkirk, in Cowper's poem, complained of as a misfortune, was then to me as a blessing. Here I recovered; but even long after recovery, if a gale wafted the notes of a peal towards me, I startled with nervous apprehension. I felt a Mahometan hatred to all the bell tribe, and envied the subjects of the Commander of the Faithful the sonorous voice of their Muezzin. Time cured this, as it cures the most of our follies; but even at the present day, if by chance my nerves be unstrung, some particular tones of the cathedral bell have power to surprise me into a momentary start.

A QUESTION OF PASSPORTS

Baroness Orczy

Bibot was very sure of himself. There never was, never had been, there never would be again another such patriotic citizen of the Republic as was citizen Bibot of the Town Guard.

And because his patriotism was so well known among the members of the Committee of Public Safety, and his uncompromising hatred of the aristocrats so highly appreciated, citizen Bibot had been given the most important military post within the city of Paris.

He was in command of the Porte Montmartre, which goes to prove how highly he was esteemed, for, believe me, more treachery had been going on inside and out of the Porte Montmartre than in any other quarter of Paris. The last commandant there, citizen Ferney, was guillotined for having allowed a whole batch of aristocrats—traitors to the Republic, all of them—to slip through the Porte Montmartre and to safety outside the walls of Paris. Ferney pleaded in his defence that these traitors had been spirited away from under his very nose by the devil's agency, for surely that meddlesome Englishman who spent his time in rescuing aristocrats—traitors, all of them—from the clutches of Madame la Guillotine must be either the devil himself or at any rate one of his most powerful agents.

'*Nom de Dieu!* Just think of his name! The Scarlet Pimpernel t call him! No one knows him by any other name! and he is preternaturally tall and strong and superhumanly cunning! And the power which he has of being transmuted into various personalities—rendering himself quite unrecognizable to the eyes of the most sharp-seeing patriot of France must of a surety be a gift of Satan!'

But the Committee of Public Safety refused to listen to Ferney's explanations. The Scarlet Pimpernel was only an ordinary mortal—an exceedingly cunning and meddlesome personage it is true, and endowed with a superfluity of wealth which enabled him to break the thin crust of patriotism that overlay the natural cupidity of many Captains of the Town Guard—but still an ordinary man for all that, and no true lover of the Republic should allow either superstitious terror or greed to interfere with the discharge of his duties which at the Porte Montmartre consisted in detaining any and every person—aristocrat, foreigner, or otherwise traitor to the Republic—who could not give a satisfactory reason for desiring to leave Paris. Having detained such persons, the patriot's next duty was to hand them over to the Committee of Public Safety, who would then decide whether Madame la Guillotine would have the last word over them or not.

And the guillotine did nearly always have the last word to say, unless the Scarlet Pimpernel interfered.

The trouble was, that that same accursed Englishman interfered at times in a manner which was positively terrifying. His impudence, certes, passed all belief. Stories of his daring and of his impudence were abroad which literally made the lank and greasy hair of every patriot curl with wonder. 'Twas even whispered—not too loudly, forsooth—that certain members of the Committee of Public Safety had measured their skill and valour against that of the Englishman and emerged from the conflict beaten and humiliated, vowing vengeance which, of a truth, was still slow in coming.

Citizen Chauvelin, one of the most implacable and unyielding members of the Committee, was known to have suffered overwhelming shame at the hands of that daring gang, of whom the so-called Scarlet Pimpernel was the accredited chief. Some there were who said that citizen Chauvelin had for ever forfeited his prestige, d even endangered his head by measuring his well-known teness against that mysterious League of Spies.

But then Bibot was different!

He feared neither the devil nor any Englishman. Had the latter the strength of giants and the protection of every power of evil, Bibot was ready for him. Nay! he was aching for a tussle, and haunted the purlieus of the Committees to obtain some post which would enable him to come to grips with the Scarlet Pimpernel and his League.

Bibot's zeal and perseverance were duly rewarded, and anon he was appointed to the command of the guard at the Porte Montmartre.

A post of vast importance as aforesaid; so much so, in fact, that no less a person than citizen Jean Paul Marat himself came to speak with Bibot on that third day of Nivôse in the year I of the Republic, with a view to impressing upon him the necessity of keeping his eyes open, and of suspecting every man, woman and child indiscriminately until they had proved themselves to be true patriots.

'Let no one slip through your fingers, citizen Bibot,' Marat admonished with grim earnestness. 'That accursed Englishman is cunning and resourceful, and his impudence surpasses that of the devil himself.'

'He'd better try some of his impudence on me!' commented Bibot with a sneer, 'he'll soon find out that he no longer has a Ferney to deal with. Take it from me, citizen Marat, that if a batch of aristocrats escape out of Paris within the next few days, under the guidance of the d—d Englishman, they will have to find some other way than the Porte Montmartre.'

'Well said, citizen!' commented Marat. 'But be watchful tonight . . . tonight especially. The Scarlet Pimpernel is rampant in Paris just now.'

'How so?'

'The *ci-devant* Duc and Duchesse de Montreux and the whole of their brood—sisters, brothers, two or three children, a priest and several servants—a round dozen in all, have been condemned to death. The guillotine for them tomorrow at daybreak! Would it could have been tonight,' added Marat, whilst a demoniacal leer contorted his face which already exuded lust for blood from every pore. 'Would it could have been tonight. But the guillotine has been busy; over four hundred executions today . . . and the tumbrils are full—the seats are bespoken in advance—and still they come. . . . But tomorrow morning at daybreak Madame la Guillotine will have a word to say to the whole of the Montreux crowd!'

'But they are in the Conciergerie prison surely, citizen! out of the reach of that accursed Englishman?'

'They are on their way, and I mistake not, to the prison at this moment. I came straight on here after the condemnation, to which I listened with true joy. Ah, citizen Bibot! the blood of these hated aristocrats is good to behold when it drips from the blade of the guillotine. Have a care, citizen Bibot, do not let the Montreux crowd escape!'

'Have no fear, citizen Marat! But surely there is no danger! They have been tried and condemned! They are, as you say, even now on their way—well guarded, I presume—to the Conciergerie prison! —tomorrow at daybreak, the guillotine! What is there to fear?

'Well! well!' said Marat, with a slight tone of hesitation, 'it is best, citizen Bibot, to be over-careful these times.'

Even whilst Marat spoke his face, usually so cunning and vengeful, had suddenly lost its look of devilish cruelty which was almost superhuman in the excess of its infamy, and a greyish hue—suggestive of terror—had spread over the sunken cheeks. He clutched Bibot's arm, and leaning over the table he whispered in his ear:

'The Public Prosecutor had scarce finished his speech today, judgment was being pronounced, the spectators were expectant and still, only the Montreux woman and some of the females and children were blubbering and moaning, when suddenly, it seemed from nowhere, a small piece of paper fluttered from out the assembly and alighted on the desk in front of the Public Prosecutor. He took the paper up and glanced at its contents. I saw that his cheeks had paled, and that his hand trembled as he handed the paper over to me.'

'And what did that paper contain, citizen Marat?' asked Bibot, also speaking in a whisper, for an access of superstitious terror was gripping him by the throat.

'Just the well-known accursed device, citizen, the small scarlet flower, drawn in red ink, and the few words: "Tonight the innocent men and women now condemned by this infamous tribunal will be beyond your reach!"'

'And no sign of a messenger?'

'None.'

'And when, did—'

'Hush!' said Marat peremptorily, 'no more of that now. To your post, citizen, and remember—all are suspect! let none escape!'

The two men had been sitting outside a small tavern, opposite the Porte Montmartre, with a bottle of wine between them, their elbows resting on the grimy top of a rough wooden table. They had talked in whispers, for even the walls of the tumble-down cabaret might have had ears.

Opposite them the city wall—broken here by the great gate of Montmartre—loomed threateningly in the fast-gathering dusk of this winter's afternoon. Men in ragged red shirts, their unkempt heads crowned with Phrygian caps adorned with a tricolour cockade, lounged against the wall, or sat in groups on the top of piles of refuse that littered the street, with a rough deal plank between them and a greasy pack of cards in their grimy fingers. Guns and bayonets were propped against the wall. The gate itself had three means of egress; each of these was guarded by two men with fixed bayonets at their shoulders, but otherwise dressed like the others, in rags—with bare legs that looked blue and numb in the cold—the *sans-culottes* of revolutionary Paris.

Bibot rose from his seat, nodding to Marat, and joined his men.

From afar, but gradually drawing nearer, came the sound of a ribald song, with chorus accompaniment sung by throats obviously surfeited with liquor.

For a moment—as the sound approached—Bibot turned back once more to the Friend of the People.

'Am I to understand, citizen,' he said, 'that my orders are not to let anyone pass through these gates tonight?'

'No, no, citizen,' replied Marat, 'we dare not do that. There are a number of good patriots in the city still. We cannot interfere with their liberty or—'

And the look of fear of the demagogue—himself afraid of the human whirlpool which he had let loose—stole into Marat's cruel, piercing eyes.

'No, no,' he reiterated more emphatically, 'we cannot disregard the passports issued by the Committee of Public Safety. But examine each passport carefully, citizen Bibot! If you have any reasonable ground for suspicion, detain the holder, and if you have not—'

The sound of singing was quite near now. With another wink and a final leer, Marat drew back under the shadow of the *cabaret* and Bibot swaggered up to the main entrance of the gate.

'*Qui va là*?' he thundered in stentorian tones as a group of some half-dozen people lurched towards him out of the gloom, still shouting hoarsely their ribald drinking song.

The foremost man in the group passed opposite citizen Bibot, and with arms akimbo, and legs planted well apart, tried to assume a rigidity of attitude which apparently was somewhat foreign to him at this moment.

'Good patriots, citizen,' he said in a thick voice which he vainly tried to render steady.

'What do you want?' queried Bibot.

'To be allowed to go on our way unmolested.'

'What is your way?'

'Through the Porte Montmartre to the village of Barency.'

'What is your business there?'

This query, delivered in Bibot's most pompous manner, seemed vastly to amuse the rowdy crowd. He who was the spokesman turned to his friends and shouted hilariously:

'Hark at him, citizens! He asks me what is our business. Ohé, citizen Bibot, since when have you become blind? A dolt you've always been, else you had not asked the question.'

But Bibot, undeterred by the man's drunken insolence, retorted gruffly:

'Your business, I want to know.'

'Bibot! my little Bibot!' cooed the bibulous orator, now in dulcet tones, 'dost not know us, my good Bibot? Yet we all know thee, citizen—Captain Bibot of the Town Guard, eh, citizens! Three cheers for the citizen captain!'

When the noisy shouts and cheers from half a dozen hoarse throats had died down, Bibot, without more ado, turned to his own men at the gate.

'Drive those drunken louts away!' he commanded; 'no one is allowed to loiter here.'

Loud protest on the part of the hilarious crowd followed, then a slight scuffle with the bayonets of the Town Guard. Finally the spokesman, somewhat sobered, once more appealed to Bibot.

'Citizen Bibot! you must be blind not to know me and my mates! And let me tell you that you are doing yourself a deal of harm by interfering with the citizens of the Republic in the proper discharge of their duties, and by disregarding their rights of egress through this gate, a right confirmed by passports signed by two members of the Committee of Public Safety.'

He had spoken now fairly clearly and very pompously. Bibot, somewhat impressed and remembering Marat's admonitions, said very civilly:

'Tell me your business, then, citizen, and show me your passports. If everything is in order you may go your way.'

'But you know me, citizen Bibot?' queried the other.

'Yes, I know you—unofficially—citizen Durand.'

'You know that I and the citizens here are the carriers for citizen Legrand, the market gardener of Barency?'

'Yes, I know that,' said Bibot guardedly, 'unofficially.'

'Then, unofficially, let me tell you, citizen, that unless we get to Barency this evening, Paris will have to do without cabbages and potatoes tomorrow. So now you know that you are acting at your own risk and peril, citizen, by detaining us.'

'Your passports, all of you,' commanded Bibot.

He had just caught sight of Marat still sitting outside the tavern opposite, and was glad enough, in this instance, to shelve his responsibility on the shoulders of the popular 'Friend of the People.' There was general searching in ragged pockets for grimy papers with official seals thereon, and whilst Bibot ordered one of his men to take the six passports across the road to citizen Marat for his inspection, he himself, by the last rays of the setting winter sun, made close examination of the six men who desired to pass through the Porte Montmartre.

As the spokesman had averred, he—Bibot—knew every one of these men. They were the carriers to citizen Legrand, the Barency market gardener. Bibot knew every face. They passed with a load of fruit and vegetables in and out of Paris every day. There was really and absolutely no cause for suspicion, and when citizen Marat returned the six passports, pronouncing them to be genuine, and recognizing his own signature at the bottom of each, Bibot was at last satisfied, and the six bibulous carriers were allowed to pass through the gate, which they did, arm in arm, singing a wild *carmagnole,* and vociferously cheering as they emerged out into the open.

But Bibot passed an unsteady hand over his brow. It was cold, yet he was in a perspiration. That sort of thing tells on a man's nerves. He rejoined Marat, at the table outside the drinking-booth, and ordered a fresh bottle of wine.

The sun had set now, and with the gathering dusk a damp mist descended on Montmartre. From the wall opposite, where the men sat playing cards, came occasional volleys of blasphemous oaths. Bibot was feeling much more like himself. He had half forgotten the incident of the six carriers, which had occurred nearly half an hour ago.

Two or three other people had, in the meanwhile, tried to pass through the gates, but Bibot had been suspicious and had detained them all.

Marat, having commended him for his zeal, took final leave of him. Just as the demagogue's slouchy, grimy figure was disappearing down a side street there was the loud clatter of hoofs from that same direction, and the next moment a detachment of the mounted Town Guard, headed by an officer in uniform, galloped down the ill-paved street.

Even before the troopers had drawn rein the officer had hailed Bibot.

'Citizen,' he shouted, and his voice was breathless, for he had evidently ridden hard and fast, 'this message to you from the citizen Chief Commissary of the Section. Six men are wanted by the Committee of Public Safety. They are disguised as carriers in the employ of a market gardener, and have passports for Barency! . . . The passports are stolen: the men are traitors—escaped aristocrats—and their spokesman is that d—d Englishman, the Scarlet Pimpernel.'

Bibot tried to speak; he tugged at the collar of his ragged shirt; an awful curse escaped him.

'Ten thousand devils!' he roared.

'On no account allow these people to go through,' continued the officer. 'Keep their passports. Detain them! . . . Understand?'

The six bibulous carriers were allowed to pass through the gate.

Bibot was still gasping for breath even whilst the officer, ordering a quick 'Turn!' reeled his horse round, ready to gallop away as far as he had come.

'I am for the St Denis Gate—Grosjean is on guard there!' he shouted. 'Same orders all round the city. No one to leave the gates! . . . Understand?'

His troopers fell in. The next moment he would be gone, and these cursed aristocrats well in safety's way.

'Citizen Captain!'

The hoarse shout at last contrived to escape Bibot's parched throat. As if involuntarily, the officer drew rein once more.

'What is it? Quick!—I've no time. That confounded Englishman may be at the St Denis Gate even now!'

'Citizen Captain,' gasped Bibot, his breath coming and going like that of a man fighting for his life. 'Here! . . . at this gate! . . . not half an hour ago . . . six men . . . carriers . . . market gardeners . . . I seemed to know their faces. . . .'

'Yes! yes! market gardener's carriers,' exclaimed the officer gleefully, 'aristocrats all of them . . . and that d—d Scarlet Pimpernel. You've got them? You've detained them? . . . Where are they? . . . Speak, man, in the name of hell! . . .'

'Gone!' gasped Bibot. His legs would no longer bear him. He fell backwards onto a heap of street *débris* and refuse, from which lowly vantage ground he contrived to give away the whole miserable tale.

'Gone! half an hour ago! Their passports were in order! . . . I seemed to know their faces! Citizen Marat was here. . . . He, too—'

In a moment the officer had once more swung his horse round, so that the animal reared, with wild forefeet pawing the air, with champing of bit, and white foam scattered around.

'A thousand million curses!' he exclaimed. 'Citizen Bibot, your head will pay for this treachery. Which way did they go?'

A dozen hands were ready to point in the direction where the merry party of carriers had disappeared half an hour ago; a dozen tongues gave rapid, confused explanations.

'Into it, my men!' shouted the officer; 'they were on foot! They can't have gone far. Remember the Republic has offered ten thousand francs for the capture of the Scarlet Pimpernel.'

Already the heavy gates had been swung open, and the officer's voice once more rang out clear through a perfect thunder-clap of fast galloping hoofs:

'*Ventre à terre!* Remember!—ten thousand francs to him who first sights the Scarlet Pimpernel!'

The thunder-clap died away in the distance, the dust of four score hoofs was merged in the fog and in the darkness; the voice of the captain was raised again through the mist-laden air. One shout . . . a shout of triumph . . . then silence once again.

Bibot had fainted on the heap of *débris.*

His comrades brought him wine to drink. He gradually revived. Hope came back to his heart; his nerves soon steadied themselves as the heavy beverage filtrated through into his blood.

'Bah!' he ejaculated as he pulled himself together, 'the troopers were well-mounted . . . the officer was enthusiastic; those carriers could not have walked very far. And, in any case, I am free from blame. Citoyen Marat himself was here and let them pass!'

A shudder of superstitious terror ran through him as he recollected the whole scene: for surely he knew all the faces of the six men who had gone through the gate. The devil indeed must have given the mysterious Englishman power to transmute himself and his gang wholly into the bodies of other people.

More than an hour went by. Bibot was quite himself again, bullying, commanding, detaining everybody now.

At that time there appeared to be a slight altercation going on on the farther side of the gate. Bibot thought it his duty to go and see what the noise was about. Someone wanting to get into Paris instead of out of it at this hour of the night was a strange occurrence.

Bibot heard his name spoken by a raucous voice. Accompanied by two of his men he crossed the wide gates in order to see what was happening. One of the men held a lanthorn, which he was swinging high above his head. Bibot saw standing there before him, arguing with the guard by the gate, the bibulous spokesman of the band of carriers.

He was explaining to the sentry that he had a message to deliver to the citizen commanding at the Porte Montmartre.

'It is a note,' he said, 'which an officer of the mounted guard gave me. He and twenty troopers were galloping down the great North Road not far from Barency. When they overtook the six of us they drew rein, and the officer gave me this note for citizen Bibot and fifty francs if I would deliver it tonight.'

'Give me the note!' said Bibot calmly.

But his hand shook as he took the paper; his face was livid with fear and rage.

The paper had no writing on it, only the outline of a small scarlet flower done in red—the device of the cursed Englishman, the Scarlet Pimpernel.

'Which way did the officer and the twenty troopers go?' he stammered, 'after they gave you this note?'

'On the way to Calais,' replied the other; 'but they had magnificent horses, and didn't spare them either. They are a league and more away by now!'

All the blood in Bibot's body seemed to rush up to his head, a wild buzzing was in his ears. . . .

And that was how the Duc and Duchesse de Montreux, with their servants and family, escaped from Paris on that third day of Nivôse in the year I of the Republic.

A DESCENT INTO THE MAELSTRÖM

Edgar Allan Poe

We had now reached the summit of the loftiest crag. For some minutes the old man seemed too much exhausted to speak.

'Not long ago,' said he at length, 'and I could have guided you on this route as well as the youngest of my sons; but, about three years past, there happened to me an event such as never happened before to mortal man—or at least such as no man ever survived to tell of—and the six hours of deadly terror which I then endured have broken me up body and soul. You suppose me a *very* old man—but I am not. It took less than a single day to change these hairs from a jetty black to white, to weaken my limbs, and to unstring my nerves, so that I tremble at the least exertion, and am frightened at a shadow. Do you know I can scarcely look over this little cliff without getting giddy?'

The 'little cliff', upon whose edge he had so carelessly thrown himself down to rest that the weightier portion of his body hung over it, while he was only kept from falling by the tenure of his elbow on its extreme and slippery edge—this 'little cliff' arose, a sheer unobstructed precipice of black shining rock, some fifteen or sixteen hundred feet from the world of crags beneath us. Nothing would have tempted me to within half a dozen yards of its brink. In truth so deeply was I excited by the perilous position of my companion, that I fell at full length upon the ground, clung to the shrubs around me, and dared not even glance upward at the sky—while I struggled in vain to divest myself of the idea that the very foundations of the mountain were in danger from the fury of the winds. It was long before I could reason myself into sufficient courage to sit up and look out into the distance.

'You must get over these fancies,' said the guide, 'for I have brought you here that you might have the best possible view of the scene of that event I mentioned—and to tell you the whole story with the spot just under your eye.'

'We are now,' he continued, in that particularizing manner which distinguished him—'we are now close upon the Norwegian coast—in the sixty-eighth degree of latitude—in the great province of Nordland—and in the dreary district of Lofoden. The mountain upon whose top we sit is Helseggen, the Cloudy. Now raise yourself up a little higher—hold onto the grass if you feel giddy—so—and look out beyond the belt of vapour beneath us, into the sea.'

I looked dizzily, and beheld a panorama more deplorably desolate no human imagination can conceive. To the right and left, as far as the eye could reach, there lay outstretched, like ramparts of the world, lines of horridly black and beetling cliff, whose character of gloom was but the more forcibly illustrated by the surf which reared high up against it its white and ghastly crest, howling and shrieking for ever. Just opposite the promontory upon whose apex we were placed, and at a distance of some five or six miles out at sea, there was visible a small, bleak-looking island; or, more properly, its position was discernible through the wilderness of surge in which it was enveloped. About two miles nearer the land, arose another of smaller size, hideously craggy and barren, and encompassed at various intervals by a cluster of dark rocks.

The appearance of the ocean, in the space between the more distant island and the shore, had something very unusual about it. Although, at the time, so strong a gale was blowing landward that a brig in the remote offing lay to under a double-reefed trysail, and constantly plunged her whole hull out of sight, still there was here nothing like a regular swell, but only a short, quick, angry cross dashing of water in every direction—as well in the teeth of the wind as otherwise.

Of foam there was little except in the immediate vicinity of the rocks.

'The island in the distance,' resumed the old man, 'is called by the Norwegians Vurrgh. The one midway is Moskoe. That a mile to the northward is Ambaaren. Yonder are Iflesen, Hoeyholm, Kieldholm, Suarven, and Buckholm. Farther off—between Moskoe and Vurrgh—are Otterholm, Flimen, Sandflesen, and Skarholm. These are the true names of the places—but why it has been thought necessary to name them at all, is more than either you or I can understand. Do you hear anything? Do you see any change in the water?'

We had now been about ten minutes upon the top of Helseggen, to which we had ascended from the interior of Lofoden, so that we had caught no glimpse of the sea until it had burst upon us from the summit. As the old man spoke, I became aware of a loud and gradually increasing sound, like the moaning of a vast herd of buffaloes upon an American prairie; and at the same moment I perceived that what seamen term the *chopping* character of the ocean beneath us, was rapidly changing into a current which set to the eastward. Even while I gazed, this current acquired a monstrous velocity. Each moment added to its speed—to its headlong impetuosity. In five minutes the whole sea, as far as Vurrgh, was lashed into ungovernable fury; but it was between Moskoe and the coast that the main uproar held its sway. Here the vast bed of the waters, seamed and scarred into a thousand conflicting channels, burst suddenly into frenzied convulsion—heaving, boiling, hissing—gyrating in gigantic and innumerable vortices, and all whirling and plunging on to the eastward with a rapidity which water never elsewhere assumes except in precipitous descents.

In a few minutes more, there came over the scene another radical alteration. The general surface grew somewhat more smooth, and the whirlpools, one by one, disappeared, while prodigious streaks of foam became apparent where none had been seen before. These streaks, at length, spreading out to a great distance, and entering into combination, took unto themselves the gyratory motion of the subsided vortices, and seemed to form the germ of another more vast. Suddenly—very suddenly—this assumed a distinct and definite existence, in a circle of more than half a mile in diameter. The edge of the whirl was represented by a broad belt of gleaming spray; but no particle of this slipped into the mouth of the terrific funnel, whose interior, as far as the eye could fathom it, was a smooth, shining, and jet-black wall of water, inclined to the horizon at an angle of some forty-five degrees, speeding dizzily round and round with a swaying and sweltering motion, and sending forth to the winds an appalling voice, half shriek, half roar, such as not even the mighty cataract of Niagara ever lifts up in its agony to Heaven.

The mountain trembled to its very base, and the rock rocked. I threw myself upon my face, and clung to the scant herbage in an excess of nervous agitation.

'This,' said I at length, to the old man—'this *can* be nothing else than the great whirlpool of the Maelström.'

'So it is sometimes termed,' said he. 'We Norwegians call it the Moskoe-ström, from the island of Moskoe in the midway.'

The ordinary accounts of this vortex had by no means prepared me for what I saw. That of Jonas Ramus, which is perhaps the most circumstantial of any, cannot impart the faintest conception either of the magnificence, or of the horror of the scene—or of the wild bewildering sense of *the novel* which confounds the beholder. I am not sure from what point of view the writer in question surveyed it, nor at what time; but it could neither have been from the summit of Helseggen, nor during a storm. There are some passages of his description, nevertheless, which may be quoted for their details, although their effect is exceedingly feeble in conveying an impression of the spectacle.

'Between Lofoden and Moskoe,' he says, 'the depth of the water is between thirty-six and forty fathoms; but on the other side, towards Ver (Vurrgh) this depth decreases so as not to afford a convenient passage for a vessel, without the risk of splitting on the rocks, which happens even in the calmest weather. When it is flood, the stream runs up the country between Lofoden and Moskoe with a boisterous rapidity; but the roar of its impetuous ebb to the sea is scarce equalled by the loudest and most dreadful cataracts; the noise being heard several leagues off, and the vortices or pits are of such an extent and depth, that if a ship comes within its attraction, it is inevitably absorbed and carried down to the bottom, and there beat to pieces against the rocks; and when the water relaxes, the fragments thereof are thrown up again. But these intervals of tranquility are only at the turn of the ebb and flood, and in calm weather, and last but a quarter of an hour, its violence gradually returning. When the stream is most boisterous, and its fury heightened by a storm, it is dangerous to come within a Norway mile of it. Boats, yachts, and ships have been carried away by not guarding against it before they were within its reach. It likewise happens frequently, that whales come too near the stream, and are overpowered by its violence; and then it is impossible to describe their howlings and bellowings in their fruitless struggles to disengage themselves. A bear once, attempting to swim from Lofoden to Moskoe, was caught by the stream and borne down, while he roared terribly, so as to be heard on shore. Large stocks of firs and pine trees, after being absorbed by the current, rise again broken and torn to such a degree as if bristles grew upon them. This plainly shows the bottom to consist of craggy rocks, among which they are whirled to and fro. This stream is regulated by the flux and reflux of the sea—it being constantly high and low water every six hours. In the year 1645, early in the morning of Sexagesima Sunday, it raged with such noise and impetuosity that the very stones of the houses on the coast fell to the ground.'

In regard to the depth of the water, I could not see how this could have been ascertained at all in the immediate vicinity of the vortex. The 'forty fathoms' must have reference only to portions of the channel close upon the shore either of Moskoe or Lofoden. The depth in the centre of the Moskoe-ström must be immeasurably greater; and no better proof of this fact is necessary than can be obtained from even the side-long glance into the abyss of the whirl which may be had from the highest crag of Helseggen. Looking down from this pinnacle upon the howling Phlegethon below, I could not help smiling at the simplicity with which the honest Jonas Ramus records, as a matter difficult of belief, the anecdotes of the whales and the bears; for it appeared to me, in fact, a self-evident thing, that the largest ships of the line in existence, coming within the influence of that deadly attraction, could resist it as little as a feather the hurricane, and must disappear bodily and at once.

The attempts to account for the phenomenon—some of which, I remember, seemed to me sufficiently plausible in perusal—now wore a very different and unsatisfactory aspect. The idea generally received is that this, as well as three smaller vortices among the Faeroe islands, 'have no other cause than the collision of waves rising and falling, at flux and reflux, against a ridge of rocks and shelves, which confines the water so that it precipitates itself like a cataract; and thus the higher the flood rises, the deeper must the fall be, and the natural result of all is a whirlpool or vortex, the prodigious suction of which is sufficiently known by lesser experiments'.—These are the words of the *Encyclopaedia Britannica*. Kircher and others imagine that in the centre of the channel of the Maelström is an abyss penetrating the globe, and issuing in some very remote part—the Gulf of Bothnia being somewhat decidedly named in one instance. This opinion, idle in itself, was the one to which, as I gazed, my imagination most readily assented; and, mentioning it to the guide, I was rather surprised to hear him say that, although it was the view almost universally entertained of the subject by the Norwegians, it nevertheless was not his own. As to the former notion he confessed his inability to comprehend it; and here I agreed with him—for, however conclusive on paper, it becomes altogether unintelligible, and even absurd, amid the thunder of the abyss.

'You have had a good look at the whirl now,' said the old man, 'and if you will creep round this crag, so as to get in its lee, and deaden the roar of the water, I will tell you a story that will convince you I ought to know something of the Moskoe-ström.'

I placed myself as desired, and he proceeded.

'Myself and my two brothers once owned a schooner-rigged smack of about seventy tons burthen, with which we were in the habit of fishing among the islands beyond Moskoe, nearly to Vurrgh. In all violent eddies at sea there is good fishing, at proper opportunities, if one has only the courage to attempt it; but among the whole of the Lofoden coastmen, we three were the only ones who made a regular business of going out to the islands, as I tell you. The usual grounds are a great way lower down to the southward. There fish can be got at all hours, without much risk, and therefore these places are preferred. The choice spots over here among the rocks, however, not only yield the finest variety, but in far greater abundance; so that we often got in a single day, what the more timid of the craft could not scrape together in a week. In fact, we made it a matter of desperate speculation—the risk of life standing instead of labour, and courage answering for capital.

'We kept the smack in a cove about five miles higher up the coast than this; and it was our practice, in fine weather, to take advantage of the fifteen minutes' slack to push across the main channel of the Moskoe-ström, far above the pool, and then drop down upon anchorage somewhere near Otterholm, or Sandflesen, when the eddies are not so violent as elsewhere. Here we used to remain until nearly time for slack-water again, when we weighed and made for home. We never set out upon this expedition without a steady side wind for going and coming—one that we felt sure would not fail us before our return—and we seldom made a mis-calculation upon this point. Twice, during six years, we were forced to stay all night at anchor on account of a dead calm, which is a rare thing indeed just about here; and once we had to remain on the grounds nearly a week, starving to death, owing to a gale which blew up sharply after our arrival, and made the channel too boisterous to be thought of. Upon this occasion we should have been driven out to sea in spite of everything (for the whirlpools threw us round and round so violently, that, at length, we fouled our anchor and dragged it) if it had not been that we drifted into one of the innumerable cross currents—here today and gone tomorrow—which drove us under the lee of Flimen, where, by good luck, we brought up.

'I could not tell you the twentieth part of the difficulties we encountered "on the ground"—it is a bad spot to be in, even in good weather—but we made shift always to run the gauntlet of the Moskoe-ström itself without accident; although at times my heart has been in my mouth when we happened to be a minute or so behind or before the slack. The wind sometimes was not as strong as we thought it at starting, and then we made rather less way than we could wish, while the current rendered the smack unmanageable. My eldest brother had a son eighteen years old, and I had two stout boys of my own. These would have been of great assistance at such times, in using the sweeps, as well as afterwards in fishing—but, somehow, although we ran the risk ourselves, we had not the heart to let the young ones get into danger—for, after all said and done, it *was* a horrible danger.

'It is now within a few days of three years since what I am going to tell you occurred. It was on the tenth of July, 18—, a day which the people of this part of the world will never forget—for it was one in which blew the most terrible hurricane that ever came out of the heavens. And yet all the morning, and indeed until late in the afternoon, there was a gentle and steady breeze from the south-west, while the sun shone brightly, so that the oldest seaman among us could not have foreseen what was to follow.

'The three of us—my two brothers and myself—had crossed over to the islands about two o'clock PM, and soon nearly loaded the smack with fine fish, which, we all remarked, were more plenty that day than we had ever known them. It was just seven, *by my watch*, when we weighed and started for home, so as to make the worst of the Ström at slack water, which we knew would be at eight.

'We set out with a fresh wind on our starboard quarter, and for some time spanked along at a great rate, never dreaming of danger, for indeed we saw not the slightest reason to apprehend it. All at once we were taken aback by a breeze from over Helseggen. This was most unusual—something that had never happened to us before—and I began to feel a little uneasy, without exactly knowing why. We put the boat on the wind, but could make no headway at all for the eddies, and I was upon the point of proposing to return to the anchorage, when, looking astern, we saw the whole horizon covered with a singular copper-coloured cloud that rose with the most amazing velocity.

'In the meantime the breeze that had headed us off fell away, and we were dead becalmed, drifting about in every direction. This state of things, however, did not last long enough to give us time to think about it. In less than a minute the storm was upon us—in less than two the sky was entirely overcast—and what with this and the driving spray, it became suddenly so dark that we could not see each other.

'Such a hurricane as then blew it is folly to attempt describing. The oldest seaman in Norway never experienced anything like it. We had let our sails go by the run before it cleverly took us; but, at the first puff, both our masts went by the board as if they had been sawed off—the mainmast taking with it my youngest brother, who had lashed himself to it for safety.

'Our boat was the lightest feather of a thing that ever sat upon water. It had a complete flush deck, with only a small hatch near the bow, and this hatch it had always been our custom to batten down when about to cross the Ström, by way of precaution against the chopping seas. But for this circumstance we should have foundered at once—for we lay entirely buried for some moments. How my elder brother escaped destruction I cannot say, for I never had an opportunity of ascertaining. For my part, as soon as I had let the foresail run, I threw myself flat on deck, with my feet against the narrow gunwale of the bow and with my hands grasping a ring-bolt near the foot of the foremast. It was mere instinct that prompted me to do this—which was undoubtedly the very best thing I could have done—for I was too much flurried to think.

'For some moments we were completely deluged, as I say, and all this time I held my breath, and clung to the bolt. When I could stand it no longer I raised myself upon my knees, still keeping hold with my hands, and thus got my head clear. Presently our little boat gave herself a shake, just as a dog does in coming out of the water, and thus rid herself, in some measure, of the seas. I was now trying to get the better of the stupor that had come over me, and to collect my senses so as to see what was to be done, when I felt somebody grasp my arm. It was my elder brother, and my heart leaped for joy, for I had made sure that he was overboard—but the next moment all this joy was turned into horror—for he put his mouth close to my ear, and screamed out the word *"Moskoe-ström!"*

'No one ever will know what my feelings were at that moment. I shook from head to foot as if I had had the most violent fit of the ague. I knew what he meant by that one word well enough—I knew what he wished to make me understand. With the wind that now drove us on, we were bound for the whirl of the Ström, and nothing could save us!

'You perceive that in crossing the Ström *channel*, we always went a long way up above the whirl, even in the calmest weather, and then had to wait and watch carefully for the slack—but now we were driving right upon the pool itself, and in such a hurricane as this! "To be sure," I thought, "we shall get there just about the slack—there is some little hope in that"—but in the next moment I cursed myself for being so great a fool as to dream of hope at all. I knew very well that we were doomed, had we been ten times a ninety-gun ship.

'By this time the first fury of the tempest had spent itself, or perhaps we did not feel it so much, as we scudded before it, but at all events the seas, which at first had been kept down by the wind, and lay flat and frothing, now got up into absolute mountains. A singular change, too, had come over the heavens. Around in every direction it was still as black as pitch, but nearly overhead there burst out, all at once, a circular rift of clear sky—as clear as I ever saw—and of a deep bright blue—and through it there blazed forth the full moon with a lustre that I never before knew her to wear. She lit up everything about us with the greatest distinctness—but, oh God, what a scene it was to light up!

'I now made one or two attempts to speak to my brother—but in some manner which I could not understand, the din had so increased that I could not make him hear a single word, although I screamed at the top of my voice in his ear. Presently he shook his head, looking as pale as death, and held up one of his fingers, as if to say "*listen!*"

'At first I could not make out what he meant—but soon a hideous thought flashed upon me. I dragged my watch from its fob. It was not going. I glanced at its face by the moonlight, and then burst into tears as I flung it far away into the ocean. *It had run down at seven o'clock! We were behind the time of the slack, and the whirl of the Ström was in full fury!*

'When a boat is well built, properly trimmed, and not deep laden, the waves in a strong gale, when she is going large, seem always to slip from beneath her—which appears very strange to a landsman—and this is what is called *riding*, in sea phrase.

'Well, so far we had ridden the swells very cleverly; but presently a gigantic sea happened to take us right under the counter and bore us with it as it rose—up—up—as if into the sky. I would not have believed that any wave could rise so high. And then down we came with a sweep, a slide, and a plunge, that made me feel sick and dizzy, as if I was falling from some lofty mountain-top in a dream. But while we were up I had thrown a quick glance around—and that one glance was all sufficient. I saw our exact position in an instant. The Moskoe-ström whirlpool was about a quarter of a mile dead ahead—but no more like the every-day Moskoe-ström, than the whirl as you now see it, is like a mill-race. If I had not known where we were, and what we had to expect, I should not have recognized the place at all. As it was, I involuntarily closed my eyes in horror. The lids clenched themselves together as if in a spasm.

'It could not have been more than two minutes afterwards until we suddenly felt the waves subside, and were enveloped in foam. The boat made a sharp half turn to larboard, and then shot off in its new direction like a thunderbolt. At the same moment the roaring noise of the water was completely drowned in a kind of shrill shriek—such a sound as you might imagine given out by the water-pipes of many thousand steam-vessels, letting off their steam all together. We were now in the belt of surf that always surrounds the whirl; and I thought, of course, that another moment would plunge us into the abyss—down which we could only see indistinctly on account of the amazing velocity with which we were borne along. The boat did not seem to sink into the water at all, but to skim like an air-bubble upon the surface of the surge. Her starboard side was next the whirl, and on the larboard arose the world of ocean we had left. It stood like a huge writhing wall between us and the horizon.

'It may appear strange, but now, when we were in the very jaws of the gulf, I felt more composed than when we were only approaching it. Having made up my mind to hope no more, I got rid of a great deal of that terror which unmanned me at first. I suppose it was despair that strung my nerves.

'It may look like boasting—but what I tell you is truth—I began to reflect how magnificent a thing it was to die in such a manner, and how foolish it was in me to think of so paltry a consideration as my own individual life, in view of so wonderful a manifestation of God's power. I do believe that I blushed with shame when this idea crossed my mind. After a little while I became possessed with the keenest, curiosity about the whirl itself. I positively felt a *wish* to explore its depths, even at the sacrifice I was going to make; and my principal grief was that I should never be able to tell my old companions on shore about the mysteries I should see. These, no doubt, were singular fancies to occupy a man's mind in such extremity—and I have often thought since, that the revolutions of the boat around the pool might have rendered me a little light-headed.

'There was another circumstance which tended to restore my self-possession; and this was the cessation of the wind, which could not reach us in our present situation—for, as you saw yourself, the belt of surf is considerably lower than the general bed of the ocean, and this latter now towered above us, a high, black, mountainous ridge. If you have never been at sea in a heavy gale, you can form no idea of the confusion of mind occasioned by the wind and spray together. They blind, deafen and strangle you, and take away all power of action or reflection. But we were now, in a great measure, rid of these annoyances—just as death-condemned felons in prison are allowed petty indulgences, forbidden them while their doom is yet uncertain.

'How often we made the circuit of the belt it is impossible to say. We careered round and round for perhaps an hour, flying rather than floating, getting gradually more and more into the middle of the surge, and then nearer and nearer to its horrible inner edge. All this time I had never let go of the ring-bolt. My brother was at the stern, holding onto a large empty water-cask which had been securely lashed under the coop of the counter, and was the only thing on deck that had not been swept overboard when the gale first took us. As we approached the brink of the pit he let go his hold upon this, and made for the ring, from which, in the agony of his terror, he endeavoured to force my hands, as it was not large enough to afford us both a secure grasp. I never felt deeper grief than when I saw him attempt this act—although I knew he was a madman when he did it—a raving maniac through sheer fright. I did not care, however, to contest the point with him. I thought it could make no difference whether either of us held on at all; so I let him have the bolt, and went astern to the cask. This there was no great difficulty in doing; for the smack flew round steadily enough, and upon an even keel—only swaying to and fro, with the immense sweeps and swelters of the whirl. Scarcely had I secured myself in my new position, when we gave a wild lurch to starboard, and rushed headlong into the abyss. I muttered a hurried prayer to God, and thought all was over.

'As I felt the sickening sweep of the descent, I had instinctively tightened my hold upon the barrel, and closed my eyes. For some seconds I dared not open them—while I expected instant destruction, and wondered that I was not already in my death-struggles with the water. But moment after moment elapsed. I still lived. The sense of falling had ceased; and the motion of the vessel seemed much as it had been before while in the belt of foam, with the exception that she now lay more along. I took courage and looked once again upon the scene.

'Never shall I forget the sensations of awe, horror, and admiration with which I gazed about me. The boat appeared to be hanging, as if by magic, midway down, upon the interior surface of a funnel vast in circumference, prodigious in depth, and whose perfectly smooth sides might have been mistaken for ebony, but for the bewildering rapidity with which they spun around, and for the gleaming and ghastly radiance they shot forth, as the rays of the full moon, from that circular rift amid the clouds which I have already described, streamed in a flood of golden glory along the black walls, and far away down into the inmost recesses of the abyss.

'At first I was too much confused to observe anything accurately. The general burst of terrific grandeur was all that I beheld. When I recovered myself a little, however, my gaze fell instinctively downward. In this direction I was able to obtain an unobstructed view, from the manner in which the smack hung on the inclined surface of the pool. She was quite upon an even keel—that is to say, her deck lay in a plane parallel with that of the water—but this latter sloped at an angle of more than forty-five degrees, so that we seemed to be lying upon our beam-ends. I could not help observing, nevertheless, that I had scarcely more difficulty in maintaining my hold and footing in this situation, than if we had been upon a deal level; and this, I suppose, was owing to the speed at which we revolved.

'The rays of the moon seemed to search the very bottom of the profound gulf; but still I could make out nothing distinctly, on account of a thick mist in which everything there was enveloped, and over which there hung a magnificent rainbow, like that narrow and tottering bridge which Mussulmen say is the only pathway between Time and Eternity. This mist, or spray, was no doubt occasioned by the clashing of the great walls of the funnel, as they all met together at the bottom—but the yell that went up to the Heavens from out of that mist, I dare not attempt to describe.

I muttered a hurried prayer to God, and thought all was over.

'Our first slide into the abyss itself, from the belt of foam above, had carried us to a great distance down the slope; but our farther descent was by no means proportionate. Round and round we swept —not with any uniform movement—but in dizzying swings and jerks, that sent us sometimes only a few hundred feet—sometimes nearly the complete circuit of the whirl. Our progress downward, at each revolution, was slow, but very perceptible.

'Looking about me upon the wide waste of liquid ebony on which we were thus borne, I perceived that our boat was not the only object in the embrace of the whirl. Both above and below us were visible fragments of vessels, large masses of building timber and trunks of trees, with many smaller articles, such as pieces of house furniture, broken boxes, barrels and staves. I have already described the unnatural curiosity which had taken the place of my original terrors. It appeared to grow upon me as I drew nearer and nearer to my dreadful doom. I now began to watch, with a strange interest, the numerous things that floated in our company. I *must* have been delirious— for I even sought *amusement* in speculating upon the relative velocities of their several descents towards the foam below. "This fir tree," I found myself at one time saying, "will certainly be the next thing that takes the awful plunge and disappears,"—and then I was disappointed to find that the wreck of a Dutch merchant ship overtook it and went down before. At length, after making several guesses of this nature, and being deceived in all—this fact—the fact of my invariable miscalculation, set me upon a train of reflection that made my limbs again tremble, and my heart beat heavily once more.

'It was not a new terror that thus affected me, but the dawn of a more exciting *hope*. This hope arose partly from memory, and partly from present observation. I called to mind the great variety of buoyant matter that strewed the coast of Lofoden, having been absorbed and then thrown forth by the Moskoe-ström. By the far greater number of the articles were shattered in the most extraordinary way—so chafed and roughened as to have the appearance of being stuck full of splinters—but then I distinctly recollected that there were *some* of them which were not disfigured at all. Now I could not account for this difference except by supposing that the roughened fragments were the only ones which had been *completely absorbed*—that the others had entered the whirl at so late a period of the tide, or, from some reason, had descended so slowly after entering, that they did not reach the bottom before the turn of the flood came, or of the ebb, as the case might be. I conceived it possible, in either instance, that they might thus be whirled up again to the level of the ocean, without undergoing the fate of those which had been drawn in more early or absorbed more rapidly. I made, also, three important observations. The first was, that as a general rule, the larger the bodies were, the more rapid their descent;—the second, that, between two masses of equal extent, the one spherical, and the other *of any other shape*, the superiority in speed of descent was with the sphere;—the third, that, between two masses of equal size, the one cylindrical, and the other of any other shape, the cylinder was absorbed the more slowly.

'Since my escape, I have had several conversations on this subject with an old school-master of the district; and it was from him that I learned the use of the words "cylinder" and "sphere". He explained to me—although I have forgotten the explanation—how what I observed was, in fact, the natural consequence of the forms of the floating fragments—and showed me how it happened that a cylinder, swimming in a vortex, offered more resistance to its suction, and was drawn in with greater difficulty than an equally bulky body, of any form whatever.

'There was one startling circumstance which went a great way in enforcing these observations, and rendering me anxious to turn them to account, and this was that, at every revolution, we passed something like a barrel, or else the broken yard or the mast of a vessel, while many of these things, which had been on our level when I first opened my eyes upon the wonders of the whirlpool, were now high up above us, and had moved but little from their original station.

'I no longer hesitated what to do. I resolved to lash myself securely to the water cask upon which I now held, to cut it loose from the counter, and to throw myself with it into the water. I attracted my brother's attention by signs, pointed to the floating barrels that came near us, and did everything in my power to make him understand what I was about to do. I thought at length that he comprehended my design—but, whether this was the case or not, he shook his head despairingly, and refused to move from his station by the ring-bolt. It was impossible to force him; the emergency admitted no delay; and so, with a bitter struggle, I resigned him to his fate, fastened myself to the cask by means of the lashings which secured it to the counter, and threw myself with it into the sea, without a moment's hesitation.

'The result was precisely what I had hoped it might be. As it is myself who now tell you this tale—as you see that I *did* escape—and as you are already in possession of the mode in which this escape was effected, and must therefore anticipate all that I have farther to say —I will bring my story quickly to conclusion. It might have been an hour, or thereabout, after my quitting the smack, when, having descended to a vast distance beneath me, it made three or four wild gyrations in rapid succession, and, bearing my loved brother with it, plunged headlong, at once and forever, into the chaos of foam below. The barrel to which I was attached sunk very little farther than half the distance between the bottom of the gulf and the spot at which I leaped overboard, before a great change took place in the character of the whirlpool. The slope of the sides of the vast funnel became, momently less and less steep. The gyrations of the whirl grew, gradually, less and less violent. By degrees, the froth and the rainbow disappeared, and the bottom of the gulf seemed slowly to uprise. The sky was clear, the winds had gone down, and the full moon was setting radiantly in the west, when I found myself on the surface of the ocean, in full view of the shores of Lofoden, and above the spot where the pool of the Mosko-ström *had been*. It was the hour of the slack—but the sea still heaved in mountanous waves from the effects of the hurricane. I was borne violently into the channel of the Ström, and in a few minutes, was hurried down the coast into the "grounds" of the fishermen. A boat picked me up—exhausted from fatigue—and (now that the danger was removed) speechless from the memory of its horror. Those who drew me on board were my old mates and daily companions—but they knew me no more than they would have known a traveller from the spirit-land. My hair, which had been raven-black the day before, was as white as you see it now. They say too that the whole expression of my countenance had changed. I told them my story—they did not believe it. I now tell it to *you* —and I can scarcely expect you to put more faith in it than did the merry fishermen of Lofoden.'

Acknowledgments

The publishers would like to extend their grateful thanks to the following authors, publishers and others for kindly granting them permission to reproduce the copyrighted extracts and stories included in this anthology.

FREE MEN from *Escape from Montluc* by André Devigny. Reprinted by kind permission of Dennis Dobson Publishers and W. W. Norton.

SPRINGING THE TRAP from *The Prisoner of Zenda* by Anthony Hope. Reprinted by kind permission of the Estate of the late Anthony Hope.

CEREMONIES OF THE HORSEMEN by P. L. Frankson. © 1980 Peter Brookesmith.

LORD NITHDALE'S ESCAPE from *A Book of Escapes and Hurried Journeys* by John Buchan. Reprinted by kind permission of Thomas Nelson & Sons Limited.

AN AWKWARD SORTIE from *Flight to Arras* by Antoine de Saint-Exupéry. Reprinted by kind permission of William Heinemann Ltd.

CUTIE PIE by Nicholas Fisk. © 1980 Nicholas Fisk.

FACING THE STORM from *Typhoon* by Joseph Conrad. Reprinted by kind permission of Doubleday & Co.

THE PERFECT RENDEZVOUS from *White Eagles over Serbia* by Laurence Durrell. Reprinted by kind permission of Faber & Faber Limited and Curtis Brown Ltd.

WAR GAMES by Keith Miles. © 1980 Keith Miles.

JEEVES AND THE IMPENDING DOOM from *Very Good, Jeeves* by P. G. Wodehouse. Reprinted by kind permission of the Estate of P. G. Wodehouse, Barrie & Jenkins Limited and Doubleday & Co.

THE THREE STRANGERS by Thomas Hardy. Reprinted by kind permission of St. Martin's Press.

A PLACE IN THE SUN by Charles H. Russell. © 1980 Peter Brookesmith.

BEWARE OF THE DOG by Roald Dahl. Reprinted by kind permission of Murray Pollinger and Alfred A. Knopf, Inc.

A QUESTION OF PASSPORTS from *The League of the Scarlet Pimpernel* by Baroness Orczy. Reprinted by kind permission of the Estate of Baroness Orczy.

Every effort has been made to clear copyrights and the publishers trust that their apologies will be accepted for any errors or omissions.

278 279